The Wrong Sister

The Wrongs Series, Book 1

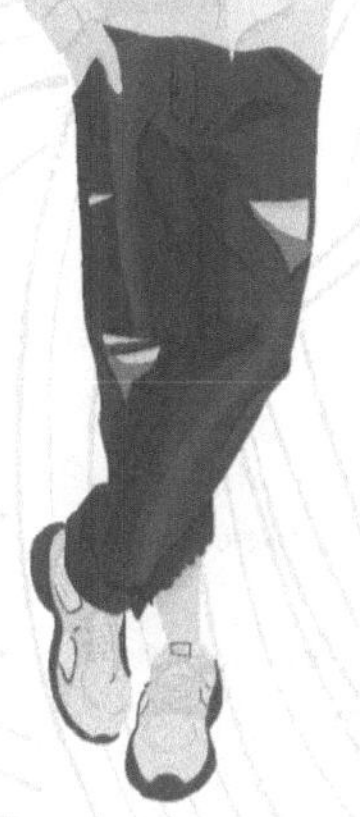

ARIANA CANE

Editor: Lauren Alexander

Proofreader: Lauren Alexander, Amy Briggs

Cover design: Books & Moods

ISBN: 978-1-7338321-3-7

www.arianacane.com

When the right people
meet at the wrong time.

*To my drama-loving queens
who want to have a grumpy billionaire with a long dick for themselves.
I've made one for you.*

PROLOGUE

M aeve

My wedding dress is on fire. Literally going down in flames —while I'm still wearing it. My husband-to-be is trying to put the flames out with no luck because this monstrosity has a trizillion layers glued together for dear life. The diamonds on my corset are heavy. It's laced too tight. The air is sparse.

When my unfortunate groom sees he can't do anything to help me, he grabs me by my waist and throws me into the ocean.

A second ago, I was a torch. And now, I'm a float. With a fluff of flaming tulle layers over my ass.

Yep, that's me.

You're probably wondering how I ended up in this place? *Well,* let's see.

Maeve

"Watch out!" my coworker Ben cries out, smacking into me right when I'm rounding the corner with a venti iced coffee. Without a lid on. The whole thing topples backward. Right onto my chest, to be precise.

"Mae!" Ben groans, stepping aside and trying to save his white shoes from the puddle on the floor. "Be careful."

"You ran into me. Literally ran, Ben." I'm nearly growling from the unfairness of the situation.

"I need to grab oat milk. Sorry." He rushes to the pantry at the back, leaving me soaked with the brown liquid. It was an iced latte with whole milk. In an hour, I'll start smelling like a rotten fridge, and the shift just started.

"Mae!" my boss, Jerome, yells from the front. "Hurry up!"

It's seven thirty in the morning, and the line of customers has already extended out the door. It's only Ben and I here today. Well, plus our boss. Our very useless boss. He's not really helping other than yelling at us to hurry up. This crowd on business days is usually served by at least six people. Being located on the ground floor of a giant office building, our early mornings are hectic to say the least. So I don't know how we ended up here with just the two of us and Jerome.

I grab a towel from the counter and start trying to dry myself the best I can under the circumstances.

"Mae!"

Cool your horses, I nearly yell back with an eye roll, walking up to the counter. "Here."

"What happened to you?" My boss's eyes drop to my drenched used-to-be-white shirt that I embroidered myself only last week and then go up to my hair, which is dyed a soft pink and pinned up tightly.

I have a job interview at twelve, so I don't want my hair looking a mess when I burst into one of the offices of this very same building. I'm tired of being yelled at, so I'm ready to move on. Or *up* as one might say. I am that one.

"You can't serve people like that," Jerome announces in a squeak. "Get an apron and cover that mess."

I *gently* push him away from the register because he's just standing here without actually doing anything. You'd think he could take orders at least to make things move faster, but no. It's not like it's his business or something.

"Tough morning?" a smiling man with the most stylish outfit I've ever seen asks. He's been here every morning, picking up two coffees, since the moment I started working here. He's always been friendly. Not overly chatty, but also not a rude office rat like the majority of people here in the mornings.

"You could say that," I sigh back, side-eyeing Jerome who's now going after Ben. "What can I get for you?"

"I'll take two black coffees and—" He pauses and tilts his

head to the side, giggling a little. "You know what." He snaps his fingers as if he just came up with a brilliant idea. "Today, I'll take just one black coffee with two creams. Thank you, dear."

I ring up his order and run to get his coffee. Under the watchful eye of our boss, of course. He's here to make sure we don't slack off.

The stylish man takes his coffee and whisks away, wishing me 'Good luck.'

Fifteen minutes later, the line is not shorter. Not even by a person. My shirt is even wetter from running around like I've been bee-stung in my ass. A few strands of my sweaty hair have popped out from my strategically pinned updo, so I'm sure I won't be looking good during my interview. Jerome is yelling even louder without offering any help. Ben is about to have a mental breakdown after fetching ten boxes of oat milk in the span of five minutes. The crowd grows aggravated. My hands shake more and more. Ben starts sniffling. Jerome yells louder. My eye starts twitching.

I'm moving on autopilot, taking orders, making coffee, trying to smile. Soon, my smile doesn't dissolve because my facial muscles just get stuck in this position, and I'm sure I look like part of the cast of a horror movie.

"Coffee. Black." Comes a low voice, gruff and raspy. It's not loud per se but loud enough to drown the whole cacophony of sounds in the room. "Now," he adds when I don't react fast enough and jump to fulfill his order.

Here comes the asshole of the morning. There's always one. This time, it's someone new, someone I haven't seen here before. And nearly everyone here is a regular at this point. People stop by to grab their morning coffees before a long day at work, and then they come back to refuel during lunch.

I bring my eyes to a usual level where I'd expect to see a person's face. But I'm met with a chest. A very wide chest dressed in a white shirt and rather expensive gray suit. One that probably costs more than both my kidneys combined.

I lift my eyes a little and nearly whistle. I mean, c'mon, I've been living in New York for the past five years. Attractive guys are a dime a dozen here. And yet, I want to whistle. His face is so symmetrical, it's annoying.

His dark hair is cut short on the sides and a little longer on the top. Not a strand out of place. A normal human activity like walking or breathing would turn my hair wild. Not him though. It just sits on his head in the perfect shape he probably was born with, the damn symmetrical asshole. His face is disgustingly perfect, with a straight, big nose and somewhat plump lips which should never belong to a stuck-up guy like that because those lips are not meant for barking orders.

His pale skin looks like it has never seen the sun, and he might as well be a vampire. Under the bright lights of the coffee shop, he looks almost translucent.

The obvious lack of vitamin D makes his eyes look dull and bored. Like the look on the face of someone who's seen it all and tried it all and now he's bored to tears but he's too bored to even cry, so he just looks like a mannequin from a mall. A very attractive mannequin with very dark circles under his very hard eyes.

"If you're done staring, can I finally get my fucking coffee?" he says. His voice is low and rumbly. So rumbly, I nearly clamp my thighs shut because I feel his voice right between them, vibrating all the right places.

"I'm not."

"What?" he asks in a quiet voice.

"Not done staring." I lift my chin.

He narrows his eyes while they dart toward my eyebrow piercing, and I immediately get the sense he's making judgments. So I squint my eyes even more in return. His nostrils flare. But I don't miss the moment his eyes dip to my front this time where the wet used-to-be-white shirt is still clinging to my chest, probably revealing the purple bra underneath. With no padding—it's too hot for that.

I quirk my pierced brow, letting him know I've noticed, and his well-defined jaw clamps shut. So hard the muscles pop.

"Of course Mae will get your order, Mr. King," Jerome interrupts the beginning of what could have been a fun story of a barista sticking a fork into one man's eyes. "It's such a pleasure to see you here. Very unexpected too."

Even his last name is pompous. Mr. King my ass. I've never met a King in my life but heard of plenty. None of them sound like decent folks.

I plant a smile and go to make his coffee, because I can't afford to lose this job now. Doesn't mean I can't have some fun with his coffee.

2

———————

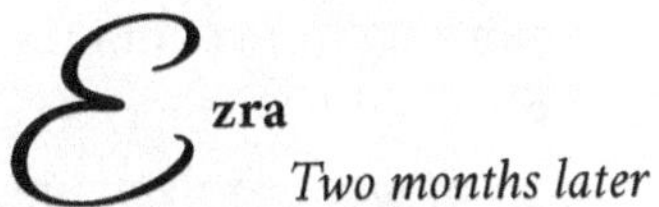

Two months later

"Fuck!" I jump backward as the scorching hot coffee splashes all over my gray wool pants for the second time this week.

"Sorry!" the pink-haired disaster cries out as she circles the counter at the speed of light and starts dabbing a towel over my burnt cock. "I'm really sorry," she mumbles, trying to push harder to get more liquid out but only making more mess. "I don't know how that happened."

Sure as hell you don't.

The towel drops to the floor, but it doesn't stop her from continuing the task she's been doing. Instead of a towel, she starts using her palm, trying to spread the coffee all over me. I push her hand away, but she's reluctant to be rid of my pants apparently, and in the process, she keeps brushing my cock with her hand. Once. Twice. I step backward, and she follows with her damn hand on my genital area.

"Sorry, I really don't know what happened. One second it

was there," a brush over my thigh, "and the next, it's flying." Another one.

I swat her hand away, and she stays away this time, looking sheepish for a change. I know how it happened, but I'm too fucking mad to say something. This...*creature* has been fucking up my coffee order for the past two months since I've started coming here.

How can one fuck up a cup of black coffee? one might wonder. Ask her, she knows. She burns the beans half the time, and the other half she either 'accidentally' drops sugar in it or a splash of whole milk. I don't tolerate lactose. So I found out about the damn milk when I took a sip. A single sip is one sip too much.

I haven't had a decent cup in the morning in two months. Ever since Martin, my assistant, announced he won't have time to pick up coffee in the mornings because he's dropping off his dog at doggy daycare. And when I don't get my coffee before I open my laptop, the day goes downhill before it even starts.

We had a routine. He used to pick up my coffee and wait for me at the revolving doors by the entrance on the first floor. I got my cup, and we were good to discuss the agenda for the day. And now, 'our schedules don't align,' according to him. What the fuck am I paying him for?

Ever since, by the time I reach my floor, I'm ready to spill blood. And she is the reason for that. She's been messing up my mornings on purpose, I'm certain of it. Since the first moment I saw her. She was wearing a wet shirt. Obviously, it wasn't intentional considering it was most likely coffee all over her chest. But she also wore a very thin bra underneath. Light purple. I close my eyes and still fucking remember how her nipples stretched the lacey material. They drew me in like damn lighthouses. I don't think I noticed anything else that day.

Needless to say, that day I came to work with a half-mast and shitty mood, feeling like a creep.

It hasn't gotten better since. Every time I see her, she has something peeking out: The strap of her bra—she likes bright colors. Her arm tattoo—I never thought I was attracted to them. Or even her damn tongue when she lets it out to lick her lower lip which is sometimes painted red. Sometimes, it's natural. And I don't know which one I hate the most.

Today, she apparently decided to up her game. When she placed the cup of freshly brewed, probably poisoned with sugar coffee in front of me, I was ready to bolt before she came with the milk. Then my credit card fell from her hands onto the counter. She went to get it and knocked down the display cups in the process, which knocked down the wooden stand with candy, which knocked down my coffee. Right on my lap. And it didn't have milk, I can tell that much judging by the temperature—scorching hot.

"Oh, Mr. King, I'm sorry!" Jerome comes out from the back. "I don't know what happened."

"It seems to be the motto around here," I say, staring at the girl whose name tag reads *Mae*. I've heard them calling her that. *What type of name is that?* She sends me a quick glare before dropping her eyes down like she's the innocent party here.

"Mae will pay for the dry cleaning," Jerome announces loudly, getting a nasty look from her.

"Why will I pay for it?" Her already big eyes bulge out even more.

"You spilled it, you can pay for it. And Mr. King's coffee is on you today. Go make some more for him."

Her little nostrils flare; her hands ball into fists. "Entitled pricks," she mumbles under her breath.

"What did you say?" I ask quietly, well aware that Jerome didn't hear her. But she doesn't know that. Let her be scared.

Clamping her mouth shut so hard I can hear the sound of her clacking teeth, she marches behind the counter and starts making a new cup. I edge closer to her so I can see if she adds a pump of her spit to it. I wouldn't be surprised. I can tell she wants to because she keeps sending me a side-eye with every move she makes.

"I apologize again, Mr. King. Mae is new, she's still learning."

I've been coming here for two months. How long does a person need to learn how to make a cup of coffee?

Something drops rather loudly—again—and we both look at her. With a toothy smile, she picks up part of the grinder that had fallen out and pushes it back. She looks positively like a shark, ready to attack. Shameful to admit, but I'm scared to drink my coffee now, and I probably won't.

"It's her last warning," Jerome chimes in. "She'll be fired after that."

Another clack. Louder this time. The girl's movements turn jerky. Firing her wasn't my intentio, just to rile her up in return. Like she riles me up.

A few moments later, she comes back and places a cup on the counter between us.

"Here you go." Her cheerfulness is forced. So is her shark smile. "Sir."

The coffee must have burned all the common sense out of my dick because it jerks in my wet pants. Silently grabbing the coffee, I walk out, ignoring Jerome's continued apologies behind my back. I wish I could say I feel bad for her being possibly fired, but I don't. There're a lot of people in this city looking for jobs who are willing to actually work. She'll be fired by the end of today—I'm sure she'll fuck up somehow.

The coffee shop is on the ground level of my building,

and it usually takes me half a minute to reach the doors and then the elevator. But today, I pause. For some reason, I stop outside when I notice a musician by the light pole. He's here nearly every single day, right in front of my building. I don't know what he's expecting because no one in this building sure as fuck has the time to stop and enjoy the music.

I do today though. To my utter surprise, I stop and enjoy the music. Something I haven't done in who knows how long.

He's playing the sax. Very masterfully. And the crowd around us agrees. Is this crowd here every day? I look around, watching people's faces. They're fascinated. They're *in* the music. I used to love jazz, and the saxophone was my favorite instrument to listen to. It's soulful, with room for perfectly flawed mistakes.

That was before though, before I was turned into this damn emotionless machine thanks to my father.

I shove my hands into my pockets, searching for cash, but find nothing. I don't remember the last time I had cash on me; it's all done with cards or by Martin. He usually takes care of everything.

I turn around and walk back to the coffee shop. When the girl sees me, her face turns positively scared. She sure did something to my coffee—she probably thinks I came back for revenge.

"Mr. King? Is everything okay?" Jerome asks, rushing around the counter to me.

"Give me a hundred cash."

"W-what?" He blinks.

"I need a hundred. Cash." I open my palm, expecting him to obey. People usually do.

"Sure." He spurs into action. "Mae, get me the cash."

The girl reaches into the drawer and produces a hundred-dollar bill. Jerome grabs it from her hand and pushes it into mine.

"Here you go, Mr. King."

I take it and turn around without saying a word. The man is an annoying prick who treats his employees like trash. The line isn't any shorter than when I was getting my coffee, and he clearly isn't offering any help. Having only two or three people for an establishment with such a demand during rush hour goes against any humane laws.

Avoiding the narrow-eyed stare from the girl, I turn around and walk outside—right to the man playing on the street. I drop the cash into the open sax case and head to the door of my building. A security guard meets me right when I'm about to walk in.

"I'll take care of him, sir," he says with a nod. But I grab his shoulder, stopping him.

"Don't," I say with a small shake of my head. "Leave him there."

The guard glances between me and the musician with a confused look but retreats back to the building with a short nod.

I walk into the elevator a few seconds later, and people scatter out right away like scared roaches. The cloud of anger following me probably has something to do with it. I press the button for the top floor and mechanically take a sip of my coffee, forgetting about my own warning to not drink it, and spit it out right away. The little shit managed to put salt in it even under my watchful eyes.

When the doors open, they know. The whole floor does because there are no sounds other than a keyboard clicking. Someone from downstairs warned them I was coming. Jessica, the receptionist at the front desk, is standing by the elevator, a leather folder in her hands. Who the fuck knows why she does that every single morning because she doesn't report to me. She's just a pretty face to greet people and make them comfortable. Noah picked her.

"Good morning, Mr. King." Her pretentious, cheerful voice is annoying. "Would you like a cup of coffee?" Her eyes dip to my wet lap. She's clearly curious what type of liquid is on me, and in ten minutes the whole building will know. Unless someone from downstairs missed a giant wet puddle on my black pants.

I pointedly glance at the cup in my hands, and her cheeks turn bright red. "Right. Have a good day then!"

I could use a cup of coffee because this one is spoiled, but for the love of everything, couldn't she see I already have one in my hands?

Marching toward my office, I glance around. People scatter everywhere as I go, burying their heads deeper into their computers and trying to avoid my gaze. I don't hand-pick people for the office tasks; I leave it to my brother and HR. I simply don't have the time for that. So I don't know half their names and don't care to. I pay them good money to stay on top of their game, and it doesn't require me to smile at them.

"Mr. King," Martin greets me with a raised eyebrow just as his eyes land on my dick area. "Good morning?" He's the only one around here, besides my brother, who can get away with sarcasm addressed at me. *And* with refusing to align our morning schedules.

My heavy glare makes him chuckle as I pass him. He follows me hot on my heels.

"You have a meeting at eight fifteen and then another at ten. I moved your dental appointment to midday and your lunch to one."

I pause walking toward a bathroom in my office to stare at him.

"Oral hygiene is important. You'll thank me later."

I nearly roll my eyes but let it slide because I don't think I can function without Martin. Out of the whole floor, he's getting the highest paycheck. And for good reason. I probably should lower it because I stopped getting my morning dose of caffeine, and it was literally part of his job description.

Through the bathroom door, I hear him continue. "You have a call at three and then a board meeting at four."

"Board meeting?" I ask, pulling new pants on. "I wasn't aware of that, and it's my fucking company."

"Yes." He pauses. "I received the email this morning with the request for the meeting and approved it. I thought it would be best or they'll think something is wrong."

I open the door to eye him. "Who requested that?"

"Lebovski." Martin's voice drops, and I know why.

Leonard Lebovski has always been a very eager member of the board. He's the one who never agrees with my decisions and questions them during the meetings, trying to make me look incompetent. His family came into money by marrying into old families with power. Who the hell knows why those families agree to these matches, because other than the pretty face, they bring nothing to the table. I've heard his brother works as some clerk for the city while his wife organizes galas and monthly balls for the rich in her own circle.

I walk to my chair at my desk. "What does he want this time?"

"The rumors fly among us simple folks that there might be an idea of pushing the vote sooner than we predicted." He waves his hand in the air theatrically.

"Is it his idea?"

"Yes." Martin's tone turns serious. "But almost all of them agree. Only Wrong is neutral right now. He's on vacation with his family somewhere, as usual." Martin chuckles because I don't think we've seen Wrong more than once since he joined the board—his family is always 'vacationing.' "So, he doesn't care who will be in the chair."

I level him with a stare. "I *am* still on the chair."

"They keep forgetting that," he chuckles. "But honestly, the feeling on the floor is like they're getting ready to strike. It's too quiet, you know. Too nice."

I mull over his words. I've had this feeling for quite some time now, and Noah agrees. The board is getting ready for something big. They've been throwing little stones here and there since they were brought on by my father right before he retired, but nothing major yet. Nothing that might threaten we'd lose the company.

"Alright." I interlock my hands on the table in front of me. "Keep your ears open."

"Will do. Today's schedule is in your mailbox." He points at my laptop on the edge of the table, then at the coffee cup I placed in front of me. Who the hell knows why I'm still carrying it. "What did she do today? Besides the obvious," he giggles, as if he's enjoying my misery.

"Salt," I sigh.

"Well." He sounds almost...admiring while heading to the bathroom. "I'll get your pants dry-cleaned."

I grunt in response, hoping Martin will take it as a thank you. "Can you send a hundred cash to the coffee shop?" I ask suddenly, making him pause mid step. It's almost theatrical.

He slowly turns his body toward me. "Why would we need to do that? Wanna leave a nice tip for someone?" His face brightens like he's just heard the best news. *What is happening?*

Glaring at him with a silent reminder that I'm the boss here, so my actions are not to be questioned, I say, "Just send a hundred bucks to Jerome."

"That sleazebag." Martin winces. "What did you do?" He looks at me like I'm a misbehaving toddler.

"Cash to Jerome, Martin," I growl, ignoring his further smirks.

"Yes, sir!" He salutes and rushes off.

Glancing out the panoramic windows, I sigh, feeling a ping of jealousy toward my brother who doesn't have to fight silent wars and sit in stuffy boardrooms performing staring contests. He is an architect, and a damn good one, so the majority of his time is spent anywhere he wants, which is usually at the next project.

I miss the time when I could do the same, when I was a free kid at our grandmother's farm who liked building treehouses and running around barefoot.

Pushing intrusive thoughts to the back of my head, I open my laptop and dig into my emails. It's going to be a long day.

zra

That was a long fucking day.

It's past midnight. I'm wrapping a towel around my hips when my phone rings. An unknown number.

"Yes," I bark.

"Is this Mr. King?" an ageless male voice asks.

"Who's asking?"

"It's NYPD. There's been an accident."

My blood freezes. Awful scenarios of my brother getting into a car crash flash through my mind.

I'm able to speak only on the second try. "What accident?"

"There was a fire in your building."

Fucking hell. "How bad?"

"It's the ground floor."

Which can mean anything. If the damage is big, the whole building could be leveled by now.

"Is anyone injured?"

"You'd better come here."

"Be there in a few."

They didn't tell me, so someone must have been hurt. My mind starts spiraling, but I force it to stop. I take a few deep breaths before launching into action. I don't have time to call George, my driver, so I quickly get dressed and run to the garage. I have a couple of cars there just for fun, so I jump into the quickest one. The drive from my place to the office building usually takes ten minutes. I make it in five, breaking a few rules on the way.

When I pull up to the building, it's still there. Standing. The front road is totally covered by fire trucks and police cars. There're a lot of gawking people on the streets for such a late hour.

I head straight to the building when one of the cops stops me. "You can't go in there."

I'm about to explain why I am going to get to that building no matter what he thinks, when another cop comes up to us, the chief, even though he wasn't the one who called me. We know each other from a few dinners and galas. When you grow up in a so-called elite society, you come to know people who have some sort of power around town. I like the guy—he's never bent to my father's threats from what I remember.

"I got it." He smacks the man lightly on the shoulder. "I'm sorry about that, Mr. King. Follow me."

"Is anyone hurt?"

He avoids my question. "This way."

"Is anyone hurt?"

He sends me a funny look before glancing around. "Let's talk in private."

This is suspicious as fuck, and I instantly get a bad feeling about it. Well, another type of bad feeling.

The fire has stopped, and the firefighters walk around, checking everything. The place is a mess.

"This way." The cop shows inside the coffee shop, which apparently took the majority of the hit.

We go inside, past a few firefighters, into the sitting area or what used to be it. Now, it's covered in foam and drenched in water.

But there's something else drenched in water and covered in soot. Someone else. Under all this mess, I see a few strands of pink hair popping out. A female paramedic is standing next to her, trying to press a mask to her face, but she weakly pushes it away.

"What the fuck?" I blink, not believing my eyes. "Is she okay?" I ask the cop, quickly turning to him. The fist around my gut tightens, waiting for the answer.

"Yes," the chief sighs tiredly. "Paramedics checked her. She's fine."

"Why is she here?" I ask him while staring at her.

"This's a good question. Very good indeed. She was here when the fire started."

"Here?" I parrot stupidly.

"Yes." He glances toward the kitchen flooded with foam. "Sleeping in the kitchen."

"Why the fuck would she be sleeping in the kitchen?"

He points his finger at me like I've just won the lottery. "Another good question. And this is why you are here. I think she lives here." He looks around. "Or used to live here anyway."

I blink at him, not understanding what he's saying. Because he's sure as fuck not saying that this chick has been living in the kitchen of the coffee shop which rents a *commercial* space in my fucking building.

I take another look at her and discover, under all the soot, she's wearing yellow *pajamas*. Fucking pajamas.

"How did the fire start?" I grit out the question I'm already suspecting an answer to.

"We think she fell asleep while something was in the oven. We don't know the details yet, but the fire started there. She called 911 when she couldn't stop it herself."

"Okay, thank you." I nod.

The chief looks around before lowering his voice. "We needed you here to know if you wanted to press charges. Maybe it will help with your insurance claim if you have someone to blame."

I watch how this bane of my existence for the past couple of months places her hands on the table in front of her. Her shoulders are slumped forward. She's a picture of pure misery. In fact, so colorful I even consider dropping it. The insurance will pay either way.

Until she lifts her eyes and discovers me in the same vicinity. Her whole demeanor instantly changes. Her eyes turn defiant as she clamps her jaw shut. I bet if she could throw me into the fire right now, she would.

Pressing charges it is.

aeve

The asshole is here. What the hell is *he* doing here?

Is he a building inspector or something? I mean, I know he's been coming here for the past two months, but so do a lot of people. And yes, Jerome kisses his ass more than others, but I thought it's because *Mr. King* is rich. But Jerome tends to kiss a lot of rich asses, so I never paid much attention to how special Mr. King might be. Except, his ass. It's very special, but since it belongs to such a jerk, I stopped admiring it at some point.

Oh, fuck. Is he a cop? I quickly disregard this thought. His suit is too expensive to be anything other than some dude working on one of the top floors here.

His eyes narrow at me, and I squint mine right back. He nods to something a cop is saying and then moves toward me. To my table. To where I'm actually sitting, trying to catch my breath after what has happened.

I didn't mean to fall asleep, I really didn't. I just wanted to close my eyes for a second because I had a double shift today. Or was it triple? I'm just trying to make enough so I can rent a room or a couch or something. My coworker kicked me out of her place three days ago because her boyfriend moved in with her, and he was looking at me 'funny.' Quite frankly, not paying the rent might have been the reason too—I've been out of luck for the past month. Or six.

Needless to say, I didn't get the job I was interviewing for two months ago. Neither did I get any other office jobs I've tried for in the past few months. All my interviews ended up with a note that they were looking for someone with a more 'typical appearance' and that they'd consider me if I was willing to 'change the hair color and remove my brow piercing and reconsider my clothing choices.' So, pretty much, they were asking me to change back into the person I escaped years ago. And this is precisely why, currently, I'm homeless and likely jobless after this fiasco.

Besides being out of luck with interviews, I was also robbed. Twice. All of my money—gone. The room in a cheap apartment I was renting—flooded a month ago. Not by me, surprisingly. My laptop and phone and everything else I owned—ruined. I found a flip phone for twenty bucks, and that's what gets me by these days.

And this job was getting me by too.

All I wanted was a break. A tiny break.

I guess I'll be getting it very soon, I think to myself as I glance around. The place is a mess, and I'm definitely out of a job. And out of a place to sleep too. I can't even imagine how the fire caught in the first place. I mean, I didn't put anything extra in the oven like paper or something, and the alarm hadn't even gone off when I woke up from the heat on my face and something itchy in my nose. I even have a few burnt hairs on my head.

And on top of that, I had to pay for this asshole's coffee out of my pocket. Nine bucks for this overpriced shit. The coffee isn't even that good. The beans are always over-roasted, the syrups always too sweet or tangy. And I had to pay nine dollars for it. I hope the douchebag enjoyed the extra spices I put in this morning specially for him.

He is currently standing next to me with arms crossed over his cashmere sweater. It's past midnight, and he still looks like he just stepped out of a billboard. Life is unfair.

The cop is right next to him, and they both are staring at me with stern faces.

"Yes?" I mumble.

"Mr. King here," the cop points his notepad at *Mr. King,* "has decided to press charges against you."

"What?" I jump in my seat, instantly feeling energized. "Why?"

"Someone has to answer for the damage," the billboard dude grits out. "Someone responsible for it."

"I called the fire department and saved everyone," I cry out. "And I didn't start the fire."

"If you weren't here *sleeping,*" the asshole accentuates, "the fire wouldn't have happened."

"How do you know?" I squint my eyes. "And why are you even here?"

His hard eyes are focused on my face while the 'nice' cop explains, "Mr. King owns the building." He points his index finger on the top, cueing me on the name of the building. King Enterprise. Of freaking course. I nearly roll my eyes.

"I didn't start the fire," I repeat stubbornly.

The cop clears his throat and opens his notepad. "On the call, you said that the oven was burning." He keeps relaying what I said while I glance between the two of them. The jerk looks to be dead set on pressing charges. Which could be a good thing so at least I can spend the night somewhere. Then I remember the movies I've seen about jails and what sort of people can be in there. I don't think I'll survive in there with my big mouth.

Think quickly, Maeve.

The female paramedic who was treating me before and offering oxygen I kept refusing, is getting her bag together to leave. Her curious eyes roam between our unfortunate trio.

Here we go.

"I can't breathe!" I cough, clutching my chest. "Breathe," I sigh, dramatically losing ability to keep my eyes open.

The paramedic pauses and looks at me with a raised brow. I make my eyes as pathetic as possible, trying to silently communicate my cry for help. Her quick assessment of the situation makes me believe in humanity again because she barrels toward me with her bag in her hand.

"Move away," she orders to the coffee douche. "I need to get to the patient."

"She was fine a second ago," he grits out, crossing his arms over his chest.

She regards him with squinted eyes. "It's a delayed response. Happens with trauma patients all the time."

"Let's move away and let her work," the cop urges the douche, who obeys while shooting daggers my way.

When they both are out of earshot, the paramedic presses the oxygen mask to my face.

"Do you know him?"

I nod.

"Is he abusing you?" Her face turns hard.

"No!" I cry out—quietly—right into the mask and then pull away. "No, he's not my boyfriend or anything," I explain quieter. "Just a rude customer who comes here to get his coffee. Very rude," I add with a trembling lip.

The paramedic quickly glances at him. "He looks angry."

I sigh. "It's his building apparently. And now it's burnt, but it's not my fault."

"Yeah, they'll shut it down for sure for now." Her dark, watchful eyes move to mine. "Are you afraid of him?"

"No," I sigh again, thinking if I should explain to her what's really going on. "He wants to press charges. For the fire." I sniffle. "And I can't pay for a lawyer now. Or even a phone call to one to get out of jail." I look at her. "Will they put me in jail now?" I quickly grab the mask from her hands and start breathing into it, feeling all air being sucked away from my lungs. "I can't go to jail."

I start breathing rapidly, my fingers digging into the mask. My heart rate accelerates, trying to break my ribcage from the inside.

"Relax," she starts with a calm tone. "I don't think the fire was your fault. I heard the guys talk, and they think it's a wiring problem. You just happened to be at the wrong place at the wrong time."

I pause. "Really?"

"Yeah." She nods.

"But they won't know that now, right? So I go to jail either way." I side-eye the douche who's watching me without blinking.

"No, they won't," she confirms. "There will be an investigation."

I feel it's the second time for the past hour that my soul is about to leave my body. I am going to jail.

"Do you want to be admitted to the hospital?" she suddenly asks, bringing hope back into my life.

"No," I reply weakly. "I don't have insurance."

"I think you should be admitted to the hospital." Her firm voice makes me look at her eyes. "You have elevated blood pressure, and you might have suffered from too much smoke inhalation."

If she isn't giving me a break right here, I don't know what it is.

"Yes!" I nod rapidly, coughing loudly on the way. "I think I'm having palpitations."

"That you are." She smiles.

$\mathcal{E}$zra

"Where are you taking her?" I ask the same paramedic who shouldered me out of the way. She's moving the pink-haired arsonist on a gurney toward the exit.

"She needs to be admitted," the lady replies without even glancing at me.

"What were you doing in the building at night?" I ask the arsonist over the paramedic's shoulders.

"All questions can be asked after we help her." She pushes me out of the way with her shoulder. "She just inhaled a lot of smoke. In *your* building."

For a second, I feel guilt. The woman, Mae, has been hurt, and all I'm thinking about is punishing her. I'll check on her in the hospital and make sure she's taken care of. We can talk about anything else later.

When the paramedic rolls her out the door, mine and Mae's eyes meet across the room. She subtly lifts her hand

and shows me her middle finger with a giant smirk on her evil face.

That little shit!

I'm tempted to run after them and fight her away from the paramedics just so I can have her for myself to punish. Not sure how, but I'm tempted.

"We can follow them to the hospital and see what we can do tonight about getting her statement?" the chief offers.

I look around at the disarray of the place. Everything is covered in soot. The air is hard to breathe, and they've already put out the flames. She's been here, all by herself. Probably scared out of her mind. Maybe really physically hurt.

The statement can wait until tomorrow.

When tomorrow comes, she's out of the hospital. I know because I'm standing right here, at the reception desk, asking to see her. When they refuse, shoving the privacy policy into my face, I call for a favor and ask the police chief to come by. When he flashes his badge, the nurses turn more helpful but still not very willing.

Sending me an evil stare, they click the keyboard on their computer and print out the paper with the information they have on her.

Which is nothing. She didn't leave her real phone number. Or an address. Or even a real name. And the hospital went along with it.

I contacted Jerome to see if her employer was more useful, but there, too, her number and address had changed—she was sleeping in my building after all.

The name he had is apparently a fake one too. It matches the one she used on her hospital papers. A quick search told me it's a name of a game character or a deer. But I already knew that before I even typed 'Mae Doe' into the search bar.

Which brings me to the question of how Jerome employed her in the first place. Looks like the man was more incompetent than I had imagined.

I'm pissed. I want to find her. I have questions.

The coffee shop obviously has to close down, along with the whole building, until further notice. This is what the city tells me when three inspectors arrive the next morning.

I call builders to come and check the place. Per their reports, there's no damage to the structure at all. The kitchen of the coffee shop was the only place that suffered from the actual fire, and the rest of the area mildly flooded due to the attempts to stop the fire from spreading. At first look, I thought I'd have to gut the whole thing. At closer inspection, it needs a good cleaning and the kitchen remodeled. Plus, some floor damage from the water. That's about it.

It takes me only two days to revamp the whole thing and get it ready for reopening. The builder signs off on it, deeming it safe.

But the city has other plans. They shut me even further down during the following inspections. On day three, a whole artillery of five inspectors comes in and finds multiple nonexistent violations that wouldn't shut down a whole building in fucking Manhattan otherwise.

But I know these are no ordinary inspectors. Their pockets are being filled by the board of my company. The company my brother and I should have inherited. I wonder if Lebovski has something to do with this and make a mental note to check which department exactly his brother works at.

Every passing day costs me hundreds of thousands of dollars. Which makes the board happy because it becomes easier and easier to take my company from me. Being a CEO of a real estate developing company and having one of my buildings 'deemed unsafe' taints the whole reputation. I already have a few people pulling away from deals and some companies requesting to break their leases early.

And she was there to start it all. The pink-haired woman I still know nothing about. Mae. I've been too focused on rebuilding the place to look for her. But I'll change my focus after the building is back on track.

After knocking on a few doors with no results and bribing people with no luck, I'm left with the last resort. The thing I didn't want to do the most. It's time to make the fucking deal.

I pick up the phone and call Martin.

"Yes, Mr. King?" he replies on the first ring as usual.

"Patch me to Wrong on the phone."

A pause. *"Are you sure?"*

"Yes," I grit out.

Another pause. *"Would you like to hold on a second or for me to call you back?"*

"I'll hold."

Beeping on the line. Then a few clicks. Then Martin's voice again.

"Mr. King? Mr. Wrong is on the line."

"Well, well, well," Wrong's voice comes through. *"The mighty has fallen after all. Are you willing to talk about the deal now?"* His gleeful voice grates on my nerves. *"I've heard you're in a bit of a pickle, and Lebovski got you after all."*

Without knowing, he just confirmed my suspicion.

"Yes." I hate myself for doing this, but I have no choice.

"Good. Good," he cackles. *"The requirements are still the same."*

"I figured."

"We're vacationing in French Polynesia, as you're aware, I'm sure. Come here."

I count to five, so I don't explode before speaking. "I can't go on *a vacation*. I have a company to save."

"If you want the shares, you'll come. Have your secretary reach out to mine for the details."

With that, he hangs up.

"Do you want your secretary to reach out to his?" Martin asks through the phone quietly. I knew he was listening. Martin and my brother are the only ones aware of this stupid situation to the full extent.

"Yes," I sigh. "And book me the jet."

"Right away."

Next, I dial my brother. "I'm going through with it," I say as soon as I hear him pick up the phone.

A pause. *"Are you sure?"*

"We don't have a choice. You're coming too."

"Okay."

I hang up, too mad to talk about anything else.

Martin calls a few minutes later. *"The jet is in Chicago."*

"In Chicago?"

"Yes." Martin's tone turns careful. *"Leonard Lebovski took it for his trip."*

"Why the fuck did he take my jet for his trip?" I yell, knowing it's not Martin's fault.

"I'm trying to figure this out, but currently the jet is not here. Do you want me to book you a commercial flight?"

"I don't have a choice now, do I?" I growl.

"One second, stay on the line. I had a feeling you'd want at least something, so I've got the earliest flights ready to go." After a few clicks, he speaks. *"Noah's leaving tonight. You'll be leaving tomorrow."*

"Why not together?" We sure could use this time to discuss the situation.

"You have two meetings today, and one is with the city. We don't want to reschedule that one."

"Right." I pinch the bridge of my nose with my fingers, trying to stop the oncoming headache. "Thank you, Martin."

I don't say it often enough. Or ever. But I'm feeling generous. And desperate.

"My pleasure, Mr. King. I'll be monitoring everything as usual."

"Yeah." I've run out of my thanks.

"Oh, I've forwarded you the inspection report from the fire department. It's in your mailbox."

"What's in there?"

"The cause of the fire has been determined." A pause. *"You might want to look into that."*

And I do. I look into that.

Fuck.

aeve

It's been four days since the fire. Three days since I was released from the hospital and snuck out of there without leaving my contact information. Also, it's been three days since I've been living back on my friend's couch.

"She has to fuckin' go," my friend's boyfriend implores—just quiet enough he thinks I can't overhear—in another room.

"She has nowhere to go," Lulu tries fighting back on my behalf.

"It's me or her. She's been walking around with her bare ass here, trying to seduce me. If I cheat on you, it will be because of her!" the asshole keeps *quietly* yelling at my friend.

Ew. I need to instantly vomit. I don't have many clothes left, only the ones that were still stashed here in my beat-up suitcase. And I own nothing that would show a naked ass. All my underwear is that of a grandma, and I always wear oversized clothing when I'm here. The idea of me showing him my ass is ridiculous. Besides that, he's gross.

My soon-to-be-not-friend Lulu comes out of the only bedroom in the apartment with a stern look on her face with arms crossed over her chest.

"It's time for you to go, Maeve."

"I got it." I rise to my feet with a sigh. "But I haven't been seducing your boyfriend. Just so you know."

She looks to the side. "Just go, Maeve."

Nodding, I grab my suitcase with a broken wheel and walk out of the apartment.

I have no money. No place to stay. A local rich boy is out for my blood. The cops will probably be looking for me soon if he presses charges. I don't even have the money to buy any food for tonight.

Which brings me to not having any choice and doing what I said I never would: call my parents.

"Yes?" my mom replies with a slight surprise when I call her private phone from an unknown number.

"Mom?" My voice breaks hearing her.

"Maeve!" she squeaks.

"That's me," I chuckle like a dumbass. "Hi."

"Are you coming home?"

"Yes," I say, not sounding as enthusiastic as I should when I'm about to ask for help.

"Are you ready to embrace your family?" Mom asks with very present glee.

"Not exactly," I reply vaguely.

A silence on the other side of the line tells me she's not happy to hear that.

"Okay. We can discuss it when you come to us. We're in Maupiti, at our favorite spot."

Aha, the favorite spot I can't afford to come to.

"Mom, can you—" I clear my throat. And again. "Can you please buy me a ticket?"

"Yes, Maeve. Of course," she says, sounding rather happy. *"I'll send you a confirmation soon."*

"Thank you, Mom."

"Sure, Maeve." She pauses while I hear her walking somewhere. *"But honey, please think about what we talked about. It's a part of who we are. It's what we do. Your father won't agree to help you if you don't agree to help him."*

"Okay, Mom," I agree easily because I don't see a fault in promising 'to think.' "I will."

"Good. That's very good. See you soon, honey."

"See you, Mom."

When we hang up, I lean back on the wall of the bus stop next to Lulu's place. I don't have anywhere to go. The coffee shop burned down. But I'm desperate, so naturally I was thinking about going there and just camping, but they replaced the locks the next morning. I checked. My warm jacket got burned, and I'm left with only the thin cardigan I'm wearing now. It used to have a hole on one elbow, so I cut two pieces of material from my old jeans and strategically placed them on both elbows in an attempt at making the whole thing look stylish. It turned out pretty well, if I do say so myself, but it's not exactly warm.

Shivering from the October cold, I wipe my running nose.

"Well, you look miserable." Comes Jeffrey's voice. Another person down on his luck.

"And you look stunning, Jeff."

Chuckling, he limps his way toward me. A big, black plastic bag is stashed in his shopping cart he's pushing in front of him. The saxophone case is hidden inside—I recognize the shape.

"What are you doing here, kid?"

I look at the dark sky and notice low clouds hovering over the city. It's probably going to rain. That'd just top my cake.

"I got kicked out."

He clicks his tongue as he sits next to me on the bench. "The douchebag said that you're trying to get into his pants again?"

"Yep." I bang the back of my head on the wall behind me. "Again. Why is this happening?"

"It just happens, kid." He shrugs his shoulders. "Some people get bad luck. Some people get everything. Life's a bitch."

"Yeah," I agree sadly.

"Are you hungry?"

I glance at the sandwich he's opening on his lap and swallow. "No, thank you though."

I haven't eaten since… morning? Or when did I eat?

He carefully divides the sandwich in two and offers one half wrapped in paper to me.

"No, Jeff. I can't take your food," I say, trying not to look at his sandwich like a starved animal.

He pushes the half to me. "Take it. You've given me plenty before. It's my turn to share."

I look at the sandwich in his hands and say in a weak voice, "But you won't have enough for yourself."

"You didn't have enough for yourself the last time you bought me this jacket." He pats his chest. "But you did it anyway." He waves his hand in the air. "Just take the damn thing, kid."

I accept it with a laugh. "Thank you." After the first bite, I moan. "Damn, Jeff. That's the best sandwich on the whole planet."

"That," he lifts his index finger in the air, "is the taste of freedom when you have nothing else to lose and can enjoy a simple thing like a warm meal. Not everyone can experience that."

"I think you're onto something there, Jeff," I say, taking a hefty bite and savoring it this time.

I've known Jeff for a while now. Something like two years. He helped me when I was about to get mugged or worse. He stood up for me, scaring the guy away, and since then we've become sort of friends. He lives around the corner—literally. He said he's been on the streets for many years now, but he used to be a jazz singer at a popular New Orleans club I actually visited when I was a kid.

Sometimes I bring Jeff food or clothes, and he brings his company. When I moved to New York from Rhode Island, it felt like it was a city of possibilities. No one warned me that the city comes with a side of total loneliness in a crowd. So I enjoy my time with Jeff when he decides to gift me with his presence.

"What are you going to do now?"

"Going back to my parents with my tail between my legs," I explain, finishing my food. I shouldn't have been rushing and should have savored it longer.

"It can't be that bad."

"Oh, it can. Years ago, I left in the middle of the night like a thief. It took me a whole year to call them for the first time. So yeah, I don't think the forgiving will be simple."

He winces. "Probably not. But what's the worst thing that can happen? They'll just brood a bit and get over it."

I chuckle sadly. "I'm afraid it's not that simple."

"Why?"

"The condition for me getting any money from them is marrying a man of their choice."

He rears back and starts laughing. "That's like some ancient stuff from a different century."

"Yep," I sigh. "So is my family."

My phone pings with a message.

> Couldn't send you a picture of the booking. Something's wrong with your phone. Your flight leaves at 8:20 p.m. from JFK. You have a 5 hour layover in Cali and then you need to take a boat from Bora Bora. Don't be late. Father has an announcement to make.
> See you.

Boat from Bora Bora. Not paid upfront. A boat.

"Jeff?" I turn to him. "Where can I get some cash?"

"Sell your feet online," he replies with a shrug.

"Good idea. I should have thought about that before," I mumble to myself. "But what if I need it tonight? Where can I get it?"

"I can give it to you."

I blink. "You can?"

"Yeah."

He digs under his jacket, then under his other jacket. And finally, under his shirt and produces a plastic bag with cash. Then he finds a one-hundred-dollar bill and gives it to me. I hesitate to accept it, so he shakes the money in the air.

"Take it, kid. Some rich dude gave it to me a few days ago, and I didn't know what to do with that. He's been rushing past me every single day, and then he just suddenly decided to pause and enjoy life. Who knows with these rich folks." He shrugs, pushing the money toward me again. "If it's not faith, I don't know what that is."

I carefully take the money, feeling my voice breaking. "Thank you. I will return it to you."

"Yeah." He waves me off. "Go get your life back."

I check the time—it's thirty past four. It might take me forever to get to the airport from here, hopping from bus to bus.

Jumping to my feet, I give Jeff a quick hug. "Thank you, Jeff." My voice breaks. "Thank you. Please don't leave the area so I can find you when I'm back."

He chuckles and pats me on my back. "Go get 'em, kid."

 aeve

"You've been upgraded to first class!" The woman behind the counter smiles, the white gardenia in her hair bouncing as she gestures to me cheerfully.

The first leg from New York to Los Angeles was cramped, and I was in the middle seat. Of course. I had a very smelly gentleman on my right who very much likes eating onions before flights, and on my left, I had a lady with a runny nose who was blowing it every minute. Charming neighbors.

"I have?" I blink a few times. Through the marathon of bad decisions and sad events that have made up my life recently, I can't remember a time where something has worked out in my favor.

"Yes, Ms. Wrong!" Her smile practically touches her ears. "Here's your boarding pass. We'll be boarding first class shortly." She points toward the line for pre-boarding.

Of course, my mother would never buy me a first-class

ticket and all the perks that come with it, so I didn't even count on being comfortable. I haven't flown on my own since that evening I escaped from my childhood home. I simply couldn't afford buying any plane ticket or going on vacation farther than Brooklyn.

"Thank you! Thank you so very much!" I quickly grab the pass in case she checks her computer and finds out there was some sort of cosmic mistake. Bouncing on my feet, I ride the high of knowing I'll be spending my many hours in the air in first class and not cramped between two strangers. I can already taste the mimosas I'll be drinking and all the food I'll be eating under a cozy blanket, sprawled out as I wait for the hours to tick by.

I make my way to the waiting area and plant my ass on a seat, grabbing a *National Geographic* magazine someone has left on a chair and adjusting my beanie that's keeping my unkempt hair at bay. I don't have to wait long; the announcement blares through the speaker, letting me know that first class is boarding. A surge of excitement pounds through me as I quickly collect my things, jump to my feet, and run to the front of the line. I don't get very far before my bag falls from my shoulder, everything spilling out onto the floor.

"Crap," I mumble as I drop to my knees to collect it all. I'm reaching for the last tampon from my stash for a bloody day when the tip of a shiny, expensive shoe hits it almost out of my hands, sending it flying twenty feet ahead.

I expect the person to stop and apologize, but of course he does no such thing. I lift my head to give him a piece of my mind, but I'm met with a wall of a man in a suit with the widest shoulders I've ever seen. Only jerks and true assholes fly wearing suits. They're uncomfortable. Doesn't matter if you need to be in the air for one hour or ten. I wouldn't be caught wearing anything but sweats or leggings. I bet his ass would look good in leggings. Or gray sweats.

Kill me now—I haven't even started my mimosas.

The man proceeds angrily talking on his phone without paying me an ounce of attention while I scramble to gather all my things.

For a moment, I get a feeling of déjà vu. I've seen that ass. And those shoulders. I've heard that voice. But I quickly push it to the back of my head because everything about this trip gives me a bad feeling. While I'm drilling a hole in the douche's back, he barks something at the lady at the gates and heads inside the jet bridge toward the plane with an angry stride.

Verbal reprimanding wouldn't do anything. Men like him think they shit glitter, and it would be just a waste of time and breath. Instead, I flip him off (which does make me feel slightly better) and go back to collecting my belongings.

By the time I get everything back in my bag, the last person from the first-class line is boarding the plane, and I run to the gate, trying to get inside with my group. I'm planning on getting drunk and full before the plane takes off, and I can't do that if I'm not seated.

Once successfully boarded, I hobble to my seat, hoping there's some nice old lady to chitchat with. She could tell me about her interesting life, and we could spend the trip drinking and gossiping about other passengers.

I'm about to stretch my neck and glance at my neighbor when, right in front of my face, an enormous hand pulls up a divider between my seat and theirs, so I can't even see the person.

But I have a pretty good hunch of who it might be. Huge fingers and the sleeve of a gray suit. There goes my fantasy of a nice flight and gossip.

"Do you need any help, madam?" a smiling flight attendant asks me. She has the same white gardenia in her hair as the other woman who told me I had been upgraded.

Deciding not to give the jerk in the next seat any power over my mood, I push the dark clouds away and smile back. "A mimosa would be lovely. Thank you."

"Of course, madam." She nods with a smile and walks to the front of the plane, hopefully to get me a drink.

Making myself comfortable, I finally take my beanie off since I've lost the fear of showing my greasy hair and get ready for the next eight and a half hours of *me* time. I have my newfound magazine, my thoughts, and three seasons of the *Survivor* show I found on the screen. My oversized sweatpants and worn-out T-shirt are my best companions right now. I have a skirt for me to change into when I get to the Bora Bora airport because God forbid my mom sees me looking like I do right now. I'm planning on tucking my T-shirt into the skirt and hoping that it looks like I just stepped out of church, because this is pretty much my only surviving outfit after all the disasters that have been following me around lately.

As for the jerk in the next seat, I don't see him or his face after he pulled the divider between us and stopped hissing to an unfortunate person on the other end of the line.

zra

I hate clumsy people—they make life more complicated for everyone. And more than that, I hate people who think that the world needs to bend for them, and everyone around needs to adjust to their needs because they like to pretend how unfortunate and 'cute' (I nearly vomit at the word) they are.

So, when the beanie-wearing klutz drops her shit in front of the boarding line, making the old dude behind her nearly fall over her, naturally, it irritates me. *Who the fuck wears a beanie in the airport when it's warm outside? Idiots, that's who.* I grab the old man's arm in time to steady him and rush past, annoyed that she's on the same flight. I hope she's on the very opposite side of it, so we don't have to meet again. Ever.

"I don't know if you should do this, Ezra," my brother whines for the twentieth time for the past hour. *"It's a weird vibe out here."*

"I don't have a choice," I hiss back, taking my seat and pulling on my tie, trying to loosen it a little. The plane is too hot for it.

"Yes, you do. We can figure something else out."

"We can't." I turn to the side, trying to fit my bag under the seat while he sighs into my ear so loudly, I have to pull the phone away.

When I'm ready to yell at my brother to stop trying to convince me not to go forward with the deal, someone falls into the seat next to me. I'm in no mood for a chat, so I pull the divider up. I don't want to see anyone. I don't want to talk to anyone. I want a glass of whiskey and to go to fucking sleep.

"Ezra," my brother starts again, but I stop him.

"I'm on the plane and need to shut off the phone."

Without waiting for his reply, I hang up and bang the back of my head on the seat. How did my life turn into such a mess?

"Hello, sir," a soft voice meant to entice says, bringing me out of my dark place. "Can I offer you a drink?"

I raise my gaze to find a beautiful, young flight attendant looking at me. Her white shirt has a few loose buttons on top, revealing her black bra, and her red-painted lips are curved with a suggestive smile. How do I know? I get tons of them. They just don't know they're wasted on me.

"Bourbon. Neat."

"We don't have bourbon," she replies, sounding nervous. "I can offer you whiskey. We have a good one that might fit your taste?"

A loud snort makes me glance toward the sound with narrowed eyes, but the divider between us prevents me from killing whoever is there with mental daggers.

"Whiskey then." I hope the disapproval is obvious in my

voice—people pay well to be seated here. At least they deserve a good drink.

"Of course, sir. Be right back." She hurries away with a slight nod, leaving me with another snort through the barrier between us.

I'm very tempted to press the button and slide the damn thing down just so I can see who the fuck is there with such a loud opinion. But I pride myself on my ability to keep cool. So I take a long, controlled breath and return to my phone to check on emails.

I have a few from Martin with more information about the board. I get another denial from the city about reinstating the building. Again. And tons of angry emails I'm not going to even open. I'll let Martin sort it out.

I reply to his emails and ask him to file another permit request with the city while drinking the whiskey the flight attendant brought. Silently. Her smile disappears after she sees my face. *Good.* I'm not here for pleasure; I'm here for a business deal. The faster and smoother it goes, the faster we all can move on with our lives.

After the food and another round of whiskey, I put my earpods in and play music. This is one of the very few things that still works for me as relaxation.

Soon, I get a pleasant buzz and fall asleep…

Only to be awakened by a loud clatter and a body falling onto me.

"Shit," the person hisses as they are trying to stand up. Pressing their hand into my groin in the process.

I groan and try to remove the person from me.

"Sorry!" A female voice.

The female voice I know. The one that has been bugging me for the last few months.

Mae.

Here. On the same plane. On my lap.

My eyes instantly fly open, free of any residual sleep.

"You," I say as I pull her closer.

"Oh." Her eyes go round.

How the hell didn't I notice her before? I mean, she's hard to miss with her pink hair. How? Oh, wait. She was wearing that stupid beanie on her head and giant clothes ten-sizes too big. The little shit who escaped the hospital before I could talk to her. Before she knew the fire wasn't her fault.

I felt relaxed and content with my fate before I fell asleep. But she's just awoken another wave of rage at the board, my father, and her.

She's frozen on top of me while the plane shakes once again, and her body plasters over mine.

"Crap," she mumbles, trying to push herself away. It's useless, and she ends up kneeing me in the balls.

I groan again.

"Oh, man." She covers her face with her hands, loses balance, and her head falls forward with her stubborn forehead smashing into my nose. She quickly pushes back and looks at me with her dangerously widened eyes. If she opens them a little more, they'll fall out of her skull. "I'm sorry," she whispers, biting her lip.

I squeeze the bridge of my nose between my fingers, trying to stop tears from forming. The plane shakes again, and she tries to pull herself away from me. Only to end up with her knee dangerously close to the same part it's already touched.

I grab her shoulders with both my hands and order, "Don't fucking move."

Another rattle of the plane makes her eyes go wide, and she surges forward, burying her face on my chest.

"We're going to die," she cries out, her voice muffled.

"We're not going to die. But *you* will because I will kill you if you don't remove your knee from my dick."

"Oh!" she cries out, trying to scatter away.

At this point, I know it's useless. We've entered some serious turbulence, and the whole plane is rattling so violently even I get an unexpected ping of fear. The dividers between the seats go down with a loud thud throughout the whole area.

"Where's your seat?"

She points at the next seat while her face is still pressed into me. She's been next to me this whole time, and I didn't even know. I assess the situation and see if I can move her somehow to her spot, but I'm buckled up in a horizontal position.

The plane keeps shaking; people are getting anxious and scared. The girl keeps clinging onto me, and I can't just throw her away to her seat while she's scared out of her mind. Her fingers are digging into my shoulders while her thighs move to my sides and squeeze me. Hard. Very hard. I didn't know she had so much power in that body of hers.

"We're going to die," she starts mumbling without even realizing it, I think. "And I'll never adopt a dog. Or a cat." She sniffles and starts crying. "I'll never try pineapple-ham pizza. I'll never get to say sorry to my sister." She presses her nose into my chest. "I'll never even know what a not-self-induced orgasm is. Or how the Wi-Fi really works." Her words nearly disappear into the crying.

That's some list over there. I would laugh at it if not for the self-induced orgasm part. *How old is she?* I try to actually look at her, but she's firmly pressed into me while mumbling the things she'll never be able to do. The things she wants to try. The places to see. While my mind is fixed on the damn orgasms. *Not even once?*

In the meantime, the captain is making an announcement

about some 'possible rough air.' No shit. The air is rough. Things are flying around. People are crying. The girl keeps clutching to me.

And during all this fucking chaos, the only thing I can think about is her nonexistent orgasms.

aeve

"Hey," a gruff voice calls out. "Hey, it's fine now."

I pull my head away from the white shirt and look up. The shaking has subsided, and order seems to be restored. Flight attendants are quickly moving around, asking if everyone is okay.

I am not okay. Pretty shaken after the worst turbulence I've experienced in my entire life—and I've flown a lot with my parents before—and I can't find any energy to stand up. Or more like crawl away from the douchebag who turned out to be *all right* in a moment of crisis.

I am also not okay because I know I mumble when nervous. It happens like a blackout where I don't remember what I was talking about afterward. And this is always scary. Which family secrets did I spill this time?

"Mae?" he calls again, his voice sounding a bit worried.

I'm sure he said 'hey,' but my mind has probably changed it to 'Mae,' because he sure doesn't know my name.

I hide my face into his chest because I'm already here. "Mmm?"

"Are you alive?" He's calm. Even. Not even slightly bothered by the scare we all just went through.

"I am," I muffle into his shirt, touched by his considerate question. Why does he have to smell so good?

"Then you need to get off." His voice comes out gruff. Pained.

"What?" I raise my torso off him far enough to see his face. "You don't have to be so rude."

"Get the fuck away, Mae," he hisses through gritted teeth.

I open my mouth to tell him off when I feel something under my butt cheeks. Or between my thighs to be precise. Something very hard and very large. I start moving away, trying not to aggravate the situation even more.

Of course, when I'm almost up and away from him, the plane gives another shake. Not as violent as before, but scary enough for me to try to get a hold of anything I might find around deemed to be grabbable. Which ends up being the armrest for one hand and his manhood for the other.

"Fuck!" the man cries out, trying to pull away from my firm grip.

"Sorry!" I jump to my feet, headed straight toward my seat over the divider. In some planes, they fall down to the armrest level, in some—like here—about a foot higher than that.

I should have gone around, just the same way I ended up here. But I'm too stunned, so my brain isn't focusing on the most logical decision.

As I'm climbing over the divider, the plane shakes again. Of course.

"Folks," the captain's voice comes through the speaker, *"looks like we're still riding the same wave. Please stay seated until we say otherwise. The crew will help you with everything you need when we're in clear skies. So hold onto the ones you have next to you, it's going to be a bit bumpy."*

"No shit, Sherlock," I hiss, trying to hold my balance while also trying to throw my body over the fence.

I almost made it. Almost.

Until gravity wins the battle, and my ass falls backward. A muffled groan behind suggests that I might have landed on his face. I quickly wiggle my way off of it, causing continuous grunts from the poor bloke who's trying to help me lift my ass off his face. In other circumstances and with someone else, it would have been hot. But this is the coffee douchebag, and this is me.

Miraculously, the plane stops shaking, and I somehow manage to throw myself over the divider and land on my seat to my utter surprise. I totally expected to land face forward. The moment I'm in place, I start buckling up with shaking hands. I'm not leaving this seat even if I have to pee.

The man's face appears a few moments later. He looks guarded. No wonder—I've assaulted him in multiple ways in the past minutes. Or was it hours?

"You okay?" he rasps after clearing his throat.

"Yeah," I reply, biting my lips. "Thanks for the help. And sorry. For your," I wave my hand at my lap, "you know."

He nods and withdraws back to hide from me. Only to pop back up a moment later.

"How the hell did you end up on my side from there?" He points at my lap too.

Hmm, a very good question indeed. We're seated in the middle of the plane with two-two-two seat configuration, and my row has a lavatory too.

"The bathroom on my side was busy. For a long time." I

wince. "I couldn't wait any longer. So I went around." I point at the walk path behind me. Three rows behind us, first class is separated from the next one by a small space and curtains where people are usually greeted when they enter a plane.

"And ended up with your ass on my face," he confirms with a nod. A corner of his lip twinkles as he shakes his head. "Fucking hell, something like that can happen only with you around."

I narrow my eyes. "What is that supposed to mean? You don't even know me."

He levels me with a stare. "And I prefer not to. You do something to mess up my life on every occasion we unfortunately meet."

I press my lips tighter, listening to his vile but somewhat truthful words. Ever since we met each other about two months ago, something always happens. Usually to him. And to his dick. The poor attachment has suffered enough from my hands.

"You ruined my coffee. Every single time you made it." His voice turns hard. "You spilled the scorching hot liquid on me." Even harder now. "You burned my building."

"Just one kitchen!" I lift my index finger in the air. Should have gone with the middle one.

"Building," he states firmly. "The city shut it down after you left to go to the hospital." He regards me with an accusing stare. "Because you were so hurt, right?"

I swallow but keep my mouth shut. Even though I want to rage. Not very rightfully so. I did lie in the hospital. Not because I was scared of him, but because I didn't have insurance. So I said I was homeless and didn't have an ID. Which was true. Somewhat. I forgot my driver's license in Lulu's apartment when I asked her to keep my suitcase with what I had left for a few days until I made some arrangements.

Having luggage parked in the coffee shop pantry would look suspicious.

So when the hospital staff asked for my ID, I didn't have it on me. It was like a sign from above to not bother and just go with a lie. I didn't mean to escape the law (I think).

"And when I actually went to the hospital, you weren't there," he continues. "And the information Jerome had on you was no good. So I couldn't file a report or press charges."

I feel my cheeks heating up with embarrassment because he's not wrong.

"So, what does that make you? A fugitive?"

"I didn't mean to cause a fire," I try explaining calmly. "I didn't even know the building belonged to you."

He leans forward so his face is on my side now. "You didn't, huh? You know what your fire cost me?"

I shake my head.

"Everything," he spits. His nostrils flare, and the angry man from the coffee shop comes back to life. "And I'll come for the payment."

"Alright, folks," the captain starts an announcement. *"Looks like we're in the clear. Our flight attendants will go and check to see if any of you need medical assistance. Or a strong drink."*

A few chuckles lighten up the atmosphere in the cabin, but they sure can't do anything with my mood which has now plummeted.

Retreating deeper into my seat, I wait for him to get bored and lose interest in a very ordinary me. He doesn't for a few seconds, staring me down with his intense brown eyes. I've never gotten more attention the whole time I've known him than right now.

Then he pulls the divider up, and it feels like the end of the conversation. Which I'm very happy about because I don't know how much more reprimanding I can take.

Why did I ruin his coffee every time? Why? I know he

was rude. The first time I spiked his coffee with too much sugar was because he cut the line and barked his order at me like I wasn't even human. And accused me of staring at him while he was doing the same. Just in a little more subtle fashion.

The second time he barked without even acknowledging my presence. Like I was just a coffee machine and not a person. And then I just couldn't stop because he kept barking like a rabid dog every time he came in, which provoked a fight reaction from me.

Causing the fire in the building was a pure accident. I really didn't even know he owned the whole place. I still don't know what happened because even in the haste of the fire, the smoke wasn't coming from the *inside* of the electric oven. At least, not at first. When I couldn't stop it because it started spreading too far, I called the fire department. Until their arrival, I was trying to stop the flames with towels. It's a miracle I hadn't been burned. I got some smoke inhalation, so it was a good idea to stay at the hospital overnight. Plus, I didn't have anywhere to go at that moment. It was the hospital or the streets until I begged Lulu to take me back to her couch.

And I didn't know they shut down the building. Would I have come forward if I'd known? *Hmm, probably not.*

The rest of the flight is uneventful. Thank goodness. I don't think I could survive more turbulence—after today, I'm done flying. I'll row a boat if I have to, but I'm done with the skies.

The man doesn't pay me any attention, not until we land. Nor later. He rushes out of the plane before everyone else, not giving me even one glance.

I don't know why I feel guilty, but I do. I wish he yelled more at me, so I could yell back. This way, I'd be angry at him and not *sympathetic.*

In the airport, after the baggage claim, I pull out the white skirt from the suitcase and put it on instead of my comfy pants. I don't want to appear too worn-out in front of my family, and the skirt just might make it a little better.

Only a tiny bit, if I'm honest—the turbulence and the last few months of my life have certainly done a number on me.

aeve

"What do you mean there are no more ferries to the island?" I ask the cute clerk, whose level of cuteness is rapidly decreasing as he denies me a path to the family wallet and my salvation. The whole purpose of this trip was to get to them *on time*. On time before I run out of the hundred Jeff lent me. Which is not enough to rent a room, get food, and *then* buy a ferry ticket.

I knew the upgrade was too good to be true and that fate would throw some New York-sized curveball my way for that. Besides the other balls it has already thrown. Being left on the streets of Bora Bora would just top the cake. I mean, it could be worse, but still.

"Miss," he sighs tiredly, as if I've been standing here and begging him for fifteen minutes. Standing—yes, begging— no. Begging started about five minutes ago. The next step will be threats. And then crying. I'll reserve that for later. My last resort. "I repeat—there are no more ferries today." He says every word louder as if I can't hear him. I can. I just refuse to *listen* to him. "The next one is leaving tomorrow at seven a.m."

"I can't afford to stay here overnight!" I shriek, making the clerk raise his brow with obvious disgust.

He scratches his nose, trying to hide a smile behind his hand. "Maybe you should have thought about that before you came to *Bora Bora*," he mumbles, clicking something on his keyboard.

Judgmental much. I shoot him a death stare Darth Vader would be proud of but refrain from commenting since he still might be of use. I spent the last three hours trying to find my luggage with the very few pieces of clothing I have left— the ones Lulu had in her closet because she 'borrowed' them. Well, I borrowed them right back when I had nothing left. When I was finally reunited with my luggage, it was missing another wheel. Now, with two wheels down, I have to practically drag it behind me. The screeching sound it was making as the worker dragged it across the room wasn't pleasant.

"O-okay, are there any other options available?" I try asking nicely. One tends to catch more flies with honey. But I'm running out of the sweet stuff by now.

He sighs again—louder this time. *I heard it the first five times, alright. Drama queen much?*

"You can rent a boat," he says, rolling his eyes like it's such obvious information to the general public, and I'm just wasting his breath here.

"Okay. Great!" It's not really. How can I afford a boat for a hundred bucks? "How can I do that?"

"You need to go on the dock's website and see what they have available," he says.

"Can you do that for me?" I conjure a smile as big as I can possibly muster.

It's wasted on him. "No, because they're a private company."

"O-okay." I'm still trying to smile, but my facial muscles can't hold on much longer. "Can you, maybe, check their website for me?" I add a few quick blinks, hoping it will help. I've always been bad at flirting, but I'm desperate at this point.

He drops his pen on the table with a huff, his head lolling to the side as he rolls his eyes before they settle on me. So much action into one move—the man has lost his calling in dramatic acting for sure. "Lady, do it from your phone!" he says before shutting the window in my face.

My phone. My twenty-buck burner flip phone. This thing can call and accept texts, but I can't even write one of my own because it has only so many buttons. And by the time I'm done with a second word, I want to throw the thing into the wall. So the phone is out of the question.

Wiping the sweat away from my face, I look around and notice a small pier a bit ahead of the ferry station.

Grabbing my suitcase, I head toward a few boats anchored along the wooden walkway.

I don't know what I was expecting but not eight boats total with zero people and zero buildings. Not even a tiny tent where I can talk to someone about renting anything. Where is everyone?

Making my way down the dock, I duck to look into the boats, hoping someone might happen to be inside. This is when I hear an engine starting. It seems to be coming from the very last boat on the left.

I take off in a sprint, dragging my two-wheeled suitcase behind me. It sounds like it's dying a rapid and painful death, exhaling its last violent breath. I mentally order it to survive one last trip and then I promise to bury it with honor.

When I reach the boat, I'm out of breath, I don't have any

energy left, and it's past dinnertime. I should have asked for extra food on the plane, considering it was free. But the jerk next to me and the awful turbulence killed the mood—I even skipped those much-desired mimosas.

My suitcase slows down my already unsteady run, and my face has melted into my décolleté. I feel like a gross, popped balloon.

The small fishing boat is about to take off, so I don't have time to think. I grab my suitcase and throw it on board. Then I throw myself with a half jump half fall, hitting the railing and landing face-first with my foot hooked on the ledge of the boat, the hem of my skirt covering my head, and my ass hanging midair. I must be a sight to behold. I hope my suitcase landed better, otherwise it'll be down another wheel.

Suddenly, the engine stops, and a loud voice booms somewhere from behind me, quieting all other sounds around. "What the fuck?"

It's familiar. The rasp and angriness in it are familiar. The disgust too. And the slight growl.

I don't think he's talking about my underwear with a yellow duck saying 'Don't quack with me' on the back, even though it's the view he's currently seeing.

"What the fuck is this?" The voice turns menacing. And even though I'm beyond any fear at this point, I get a shiver. I have some self-preservation left.

Trying to unhook my foot from the railing, I only make it worse. When the owner of the deep voice gets tired of seeing me struggle, he grabs me by my waist and lifts me in the air.

"Oof," I breathe out, trying to cover my bum. But he's already placing me on my feet, and gravity helps my skirt hide the duck.

"Oh, c'mon," he cries out dramatically. "It can't be true." He lifts his face to the sky with the king of all groans.

"Oh, stop it." I fix my skirt around my thighs because I need to make my hands busy.

I can see by the way his chest expands that he's preparing himself for a big speech, when another voice comes out of nowhere.

"Hey, hey, young lady. What are you doing aboard my ship?" A shorter man appears in my peripheral vision, but I can't bring myself to break eye contact. When I don't answer, the man comes around to stand next to *Mr. King*, whom I give one last withering look to before directing my attention to the newcomer.

The new man looks like he's from the islands, and I instantly feel better, dropping my attitude only a notch. The local people are always very welcoming, and I feel a spark of hope that I actually might have hit the jackpot. I don't care what this grumpy loser has to say—the boat belongs to this man.

"I need to get to Maupiti Island." I shoot him a sincere smile.

"Huh!" He claps his hands. "Look at that, we're going that way already, so you've come to the right place."

My nemesis whips his head toward the man, breaking his heavy stare. I consider it a win—anything to make him sour.

"I already paid you to get *me* there," he says, his voice low and threatening.

"That's okay." He waves him off. "This young lady needs help. We can't leave that nice lady here."

"Yes, we can," the jerk grunts through gritted teeth.

I raise my voice. "No, you can't."

He turns to me with a murderous look on his face. "Yes, we can."

I come up to him and press my finger between his pecs. "No, you can't. Is it your boat?"

"That's my ship, Miss, and I'm the captain," the shorter

man chimes in, and I turn to him with a sweet smile on my face.

"Of course it is, Captain," I reply in a sugary voice.

The man beams, and I know I won this round. You know how else I know? The man beside him is clenching his jaw so hard, he may crack a tooth. I wonder if his asshole is clenched just as tight. It probably is.

I look him right in the eyes. "You're going there anyway. What's your problem?"

His body grows even more rigid as he scoffs in disgust before storming inside.

The captain looks around worriedly. "The water is getting rough, Miss, you might want to head inside with him." He makes a move to pick up my suitcase, but I stop him with a wave.

"Don't worry, it'll be easier to drag when we arrive. How long will it take by the way?"

"About an hour." He looks at the horizon, a crease forming between his brows as he looks back at me. "Go inside, Miss."

I look through the glass at the sulking giant and then back to the water in front of me. The waves are small at the moment, shimmering in the low sun, but obviously the captain knows more about what to expect than I do. The choice is obvious. "Don't worry. I'll go inside in a minute; I just want to get some fresh air."

"Sure, Miss," the man says as he makes a move to the door. But before he can disappear, he turns back to me one more time, a stern look in his eye. "Be careful though. Once it gets too rough, I want you inside. That's an order."

"Aye-aye, Captain!" I salute my hand to my temple, making him smirk.

When he disappears behind the door, I pull my black shorts out of my bag and pull them on. I slide the skirt off over them, fold it neatly, and place it back in my suitcase. I wanted to make a good impression when I showed up today, but with the way I'm looking right now and the time I'll be arriving, that ship has clearly sailed. Pun intended.

"Why are you here?" a voice asks, startling me. *How long has he been here?*

I roll my eyes because of course he'd come to ask that. I'm actually very curious about why he's here too.

"I'm trying to get to another island." I nod at his direction. "The same as you are."

He crosses his arms over his enormous chest. "Are you stalking me?"

My brows jump up. "Stalking *you*? Are you stalking *me*?"

He's holding my stare until he grunts and disappears back inside the tiny cabin.

He's right though—what are the odds of us being next to each other on the same plane, and then together on the same boat heading toward the same island?

Shrugging off the weirdness of the situation, I take a seat on the floor and lean against the railing. It's the first time I let myself really look around me and take in what's happening. The wind has gotten stronger since I had my less than friendly conversation with the rude clerk at the ferry station, and sitting here now, I can feel it whip against my already sunburned face. I can't tell if it's cooling the sting a bit or making it hurt more.

I close my eyes, allowing myself to feel it all.

But what I don't notice is that my eyes are closed for far more than a minute. And that the wind gets stronger. Quite a bit stronger. Or that the boat starts shaking. No. Instead it just feels like some kind of lullaby.

I sleep through it all.

aeve

The pressure on my chest is painful.

It's rhythmic. Repeating a few times before stopping. Then again. There's a second of nothing before I feel my lungs being forcefully expanded. It's excruciating.

Another cycle starts.

Why can't I breathe?

When the pressure on my chest returns, I feel the sting of water coming back up my throat before I gasp. It shoots from my mouth. Over and over. I gasp for air and cough, spitting water everywhere. My nemesis is sitting by my side on his knees. His breathing is labored. His eyes trained on my face with, well, I'm not sure what. Dare I say it looks like worry?

With a cough comes more water, and I keep retching, grasping at my throat as the never-ending supply of salty water burns it. I can feel his warm hand on my back as he helps me sit up.

Once I can breathe normally on my own without trying to vomit the ocean, I look around. We're on a beach, and it's dark. The moon is bright in the sky, but not bright enough to grasp reality fully.

My clothes are soaked through; I can feel granules of sand all over me, and I don't have my sandals on. Squinting in the moonlight, I don't seem to have my two-wheeled suitcase or half of my sanity either.

I glance around and don't see anything else. I mean *anything* else at all.

"What happened?" I croak.

King appears to be scanning my body, only responding when he's satisfied with his assessment. "We hit a storm."

"And it hit us back?" I ask. My voice is still raspy from retching, but apparently my brain is still attached inside my skull if I can manage to crack a joke.

In the moonlight, I think I see a ghost of a smile play on his lips, but it's gone as quickly as it appears. "Seems that way."

My head whips around. "Where is the captain?"

The man stares at the direction of the ocean. "I couldn't find him. I saw your hair in the water, and that's how I was able to find you. The moon," he points at the sky, "came out just for a second. You got lucky."

"Oh." My spirit instantly dies.

Taking a deep breath to prepare myself, I attempt to stand but quickly fail. The moment I'm up, my feet stumble, and I go down like a house of cards. He catches me right before my limbs get tangled underneath me, risking a broken bone. Something that would make this unknown situation way more complicated.

"You were out for a long time." His voice is still husky,

even though he's been talking for some time. "Give your body a break."

"Okay," I agree easily. He's obviously right. My shoulders slump in defeat, my legs folded in front of me.

"Do you know where we are?" I ask after looking around one more time.

He stands up, turning away from me and watching something in the distance. "Have no fucking idea. We didn't make it even halfway when we got hit by a massive wave, so I'm sure we're not at our final destination."

"That's weird," I hum under my breath.

"What is?" He turns his face to me for a moment.

"Local waters are usually calm and not known for waves or storms." My forehead wrinkles with confusion. This is the first time I'm hearing of anything of the sorts around here.

"One found us." He sounds sarcastic. I think. I don't know him well enough, but from what I've seen, he might not possess any sense of humor to actually deal with sarcasm. "Must be the rogue one they make shows about."

The rogue waves that take big ships out. Ours didn't stand a chance.

"True. Let's wait then," I say, pulling my knees to my chest.

"Wait for what?" He tilts his head, looking at me with open curiosity.

"Rescue," I snap, stating the obvious.

He's quiet for a moment before speaking. "I don't know when they're coming."

"What?" I ask again because, surely, I'm mistaken, and he's not saying what I think he's saying.

"I don't think he had a chance to send a distress signal." The explanation seems logical, but I refuse to accept it.

"The captain?"

"Yes."

The mention of the nice captain willing to lend me a hand sends ice down my spine. I really hope he's okay.

"Well," I start, "they'll notice we went missing and come find us."

"Are you planning on sitting here the whole time you wait?" He folds his arms over his giant chest.

"You told me I need to give my body a rest." I quirk a brow.

"You swallowed half the ocean and vomited even more. You'll be dehydrated soon. You need water."

"Rescue will have water," I counter stubbornly, and stare at the ocean, expecting a rescue boat to arrive any minute.

But there are no helicopters or motorboats. The high waves, beating the sand in front of us, are the only sound. There are no whistles or cries of people looking for us. But I'll wait. It's the twenty-first century, and we don't leave people stranded on islands. Besides that, someone might actually come from the depth of the island itself. The chances of us landing on an uninhabited island are slim.

"Suit yourself." With that, he completely turns away, leaving me to myself and my misery.

"Where are you going?" I cry out, suddenly not liking the idea of being here alone.

"To check the island," he replies without turning back.

I make a move to stand up but don't follow through. "But what if someone comes for us?"

"Tell them I'm around."

"Nope. You snooze, you lose." That should bring him back, right?

Wrong.

"Works too. I'd rather be stuck on this fucking island."

The wind picks up as he says those last words, and I'm not quite sure I hear them correctly. If I got it right, that'd be a really odd thing to say. No one wants to stay stranded. Right?

Looking at his figure disappearing in the dark, the idea of staying here alone in the storm with no one around doesn't seem so good anymore, but what if someone comes looking for us, and no one is here? I chew on my lip, contemplating on what to do. But as I'm thinking, he keeps walking, indeed leaving me here alone.

I don't have a choice. I put my big girl shorts on and walk to the nearest tree. It doesn't provide much coverage from the elements should they decide to rain on me, but it gives good support for my aching back. I slide down, leaning on the palm, and wait for the rescue to come and save us.

aeve

When I open my eyes, rescue is still not here. Neither is the storm. The sky is bright blue; the crystal-clear ocean is a picture of peaceful paradise from TV commercials.

I stretch my aching body and stand up.

The island doesn't look so hostile during the day. The sandy part of the shore doesn't take much space, giving in to the life of the land with all its blooming greenness. The grass and palms start growing about fifteen feet away from the water, so I'd suspect this is where the high tide ends. Good thing I chose the tree far from it, or waking up would have looked much different.

And I know we're on an island because we're in the middle of an ocean in French Polynesia, an absolutely beautiful place that consists of numerous islands separated from each other by a massive body of water. And we were headed from Bora Bora to Maupiti Island which was supposed to be an hour and a half away by speedboat, according to what the nice captain said. So we could end up anywhere, including any number of habitable islands. It's time to stretch my legs and go find some people. My unfortunate neighbor has probably found humans and left me here, alone and thirsty.

The more I walk, the thirstier I become. And the more desperate. It pains me to say it, but King was right—rescue hasn't come yet, and I'm probably dehydrated. My head hurts, my skin hurts, my tongue is like a cotton ball in my mouth made of cotton disks. I don't know if he ended up in some nice house and already called for help, but all I want right now is some water.

I keep walking I don't know how long, until an already familiar voice calls out to me from somewhere.

"Hey, stop. Hey." Louder this time when I don't react right away because my brain simply can't make my body move fast enough. "Hey, stop."

I stop, my back stiff as a board as I look around. But I don't see anyone. Disregarding the voice as part of my dehydrated imagination, I keep walking.

"Wait!"

I stop once again, my shoulders slumping as I turn around and find the stuck-up giant moving my way. I squint into the morning sun, trying to see him as my eyes adjust to the brightness shone in my face.

"Is it you?" I shield my eyes from the sun with my hand, my eyes burning. My tongue is swollen, and I can barely speak.

The closer he comes, the larger he looks. I let my eyes get used to the halo behind him, trying to figure out if he's real or just part of my feverish imagination which tends to run wild from time to time.

How long can people survive without water before going crazy? Am I past that point? If not yet, then I'm quickly approaching it, because there's no way it's the same stuffy man I've seen. King is an office rat with a stick so high up his ass, it was probably scratching his tonsils. This guy, who ditched the jacket and rolled his sleeves up, looks like a natural, relaxed part of the local fauna. Who seems entirely too comfortable to be without a keyboard and a sharp Parker pen in his hand. And shoes. His giant feet are bare. The closer he comes, the more they look like skis.

Yep, dehydrated.

"It's me," he grumbles in an annoyed manner. "I found water, but I don't have anything to bring it in. Let's go."

He turns away, gesturing for me to follow him. My default setting is to fight with someone who orders me around. But that's on a good day, and this is a bad day. A very bad day. So I silently follow him, hoping he won't murder me in the nearest bushes. Even though I know he probably dreams of doing so.

It's when my eyes land on his back that I falter, nearly tripping. Sure, I know he's big. He's always looked imposing in that suit of his. But after our first encounter I stopped seeing him as a man and started seeing him rather like an annoying creature sending me angry glares every chance we meet.

But now... I feel like a veil has been taken off my eyes, and I'm seeing him in a new light. His shoulders are the broadest I've ever seen, stretching the dirty, white material of his shirt to the fullest extent. If he were any bigger, I'm positive it would rip. *Wait*, there *is* a rip. Right down the right side of his back. His pale skin peeks through, nearly blinding my poor eyes.

With every move, his muscles ripple beneath his shirt, hypnotizing me. On first look, I'd never think he had so many of them, and definitely not so prominent. *Was he hiding all of that under that suit all this time?* I press my fists into my eye sockets, wiggling them and trying to bring my old vision back because I'm clearly tripping.

When I stumble again, I roll my eyes at myself for being too *thirsty* and shift my attention from his back to my surroundings.

We walk in silence for a few minutes—ten? Or is it twenty?—through tall and short palms of different kinds. There're no paths, no people, just chirping birds and a few chickens here and there. *How did chickens get here? If there're domesticated animals, there should be people, correct?*

Soon, I hear the sound of splashing water. It's not loud, but it's there. Unless it's my imagination, but I don't think so this time. The more we walk, the louder the sound becomes.

King pushes green, hanging branches to the side, revealing a small waterfall of the purest color I've seen only on laptop backgrounds. Until this moment, I didn't know something could look so pure. I rush toward the falling water and cup my hands under the stream, filling them with the icy goodness. And drink it.

I drink it until I can't take anymore and only then do I sit my ass down on the plushy grass and look at my nemesis who delivered me to this wonderful source of life.

Now, when my thirst is satisfied, I can appreciate the view. And by the view, I mean my surroundings, not the fine ass in front of my face.

We're in a small opening between the palm trees. Some are overgrown and some are not. And even though the place seems like a human hand hasn't touched it yet, it looks in order. Like nature is taking care of itself without our interference, and it couldn't have looked better.

The waterfall forms a small pond that doesn't go anywhere. Most likely, there's some sort of underground river or cave leading water away from here.

"It's a small island." King's words take me out of my observation.

"What?" I look up at him, and yet again, he's standing against the sun, and I still don't see his face so I can't read his expression.

"The place is an island, and there're no people," he explains, slower this time, like I couldn't hear him before.

My head whips around. "No people? Are we on a deserted island?"

"Uninhabited. To assume it was deserted would mean that someone used to live here. But I found nothing. The place is empty." He scratches his cheek. "Do you have a phone on you? Mine sank with the boat."

Sank. With the boat. All the minute pleasure of enjoying the moment instantly plummets down when I remember the human life that might have been lost.

"Phone," he reminds me in a slightly irritated voice. "Do you have it?"

"I think so." I start patting the pockets of my shorts and, to my surprise, find my phone still inside. "I got it!" I cry, pulling it out.

King stretches his open hand, silently ordering me to hand him my phone. It's not like I can do anything with it now, so I pass it to him. Maybe he can breathe some magic battery life into it, I don't know.

He carefully takes it with two fingers from my hand like it's used underwear and brings it up to eye level.

"What the fuck is that?"

"It's a phone," I explain slowly. "People use it to call other people."

"This is a piece of shit." He opens it and starts pressing buttons. "Of course," he groans. "Nothing works on this fucking dinosaur."

"Hey!" I stand up and pry my phone away from his big,

dirty hands. "It's all I can afford now after you got me fired without the last paycheck. Leave it alone." I push it into the back pocket of my shorts.

"*I* got you fired?" he asks, raising *both* of his brows. I meet him with a death stare, hoping he'll get a clue to drop this subject.

"What are you going to do with it anyway?" He clearly gets the hint.

"I'll put it in rice when I'm back to the land where they, well," I shrug, "have rice."

He snorts. "Unbelievable. How old are you if you still believe in this crap?"

"None of your business." I purse my lips and crawl back to the lake to drink. When I make a boat with my hands to get some water, another hand suddenly swats mine, making me drop all the water. "What's your problem?" I yell into his face.

"We don't know how clean the water is here," he replies gruffly.

"We just both drank the same water over there," I point at the waterfall, "just fine. I didn't see you slamming your face in the stone."

"Yes, the running water." He points at the waterfall and then at the pond at the bottom. "We don't know how long this has been here. Might have grown bacteria in it, and I don't fancy dragging your half-conscious ass around."

I jump to my feet and place my hands on my waist. "I wasn't asking you to drag my ass anywhere."

The pose I'm striking would be very intimidating if my face wasn't staring at his chest. I lift my head up to face him, but the damn sun is behind him like a halo.

I take a step back just so I can see it, and lo and behold, this man is fine. And I mean *this* man. The man who appears in front of me is changed. All angular and rough, like unpolished canvas with raw strokes of masculinity. He was annoyingly pretty back in real life, with his perfectly styled hair and unblemished skin.

Today, he looks different. There's something wild on his face I haven't noticed before. Maybe it's his slightly pink cheeks from the blistering sun. Or his disarrayed hair. Or his rolled to the elbows sleeves. No matter what it is, I can't stop staring.

Dark, straight brows sit low on his brown eyes, making him look like a hawk on a hunt. Thick lashes leave shadows on his already dark under eyes. Looks like the man hasn't slept in years. The pink covering his milky cheeks—a clear indication that he's an office rat and hasn't seen sun in about the same number of years he hasn't slept.

He undid two buttons on his shirt, baring his thick, corded neck before me. Free of restraints and free for me to ogle. I've never been known to be a neck person, but I'm slowly being converted as we speak.

He places his hands on his hips, mimicking my pose, and somehow, he looks more intimidating than me. Maybe it's his well over six-foot height talking, or maybe it's his linebacker shoulders. Might also be his sharp eyes that are currently making me super uncomfortable.

"I dragged your ass from the ocean yesterday," he reminds me.

"And I thank you for that," I reply sincerely in a gentle voice, shoving my attitude deep inside for a moment. "Now, I shall set you free. Bye." With that, I turn away and start walking.

"Where are you going?" he yells to my back.

"To take full advantage of no people around," I yell in response without turning back.

I'm grateful to him for saving my life, but I'm ready to embrace my Robinson Crusoe life. I'm broke and could use a few extra days before I have to crawl back to my family, kissing their ass and asking for help. As I see the situation now, it's free land, free food—if I find it—and free swimming sessions whenever I want. It's not ideal, but it's much better than what I had in New York for the most part.

First, I need to explore the island to be sure it's really uninhabited. He might have been lying. He didn't look too willing to wait for rescue to arrive. My only issue is that I can't venture too far from the water source since I don't have a bottle or anything to carry it with.

I glance around and notice tons of coconuts on the trees but no means to open them. When I was a kid and we used to travel to tropical places, I once saw how a local boy was opening a coconut. But I don't think I can replicate it. He did it with a machete, and all I got are nails and teeth. I guess after a long starvation, I might have to figure out how to use them. But I'm not there yet, so the coconuts move aside for now.

Carefully looking around, I start exploring the island, memorizing the path back to the water. To my horror, it doesn't take long to make a full walk around—the island is truly small and not inhabited. All I saw were chickens and a bunch of other small animals, too fast for me to even recognize them.

As I'm nearing the waterfall, a loud cracking sound makes me pause. I tilt my head, trying to find the source of it, and follow it. On the beach, King is snapping thin palm trees and putting logs together, creating a shelter. With his bare hands. And I mean bare. He ditched his shirt, and now he's wearing his white undershirt that clings to his body more than a white T-shirt in a wet T-shirt contest.

Every time he rips into a log to pull it aside, his whole body strains, making the muscles pop. It's like watching Captain America pull the logs apart.

While I'm gaping, he's smashing those long trees as if they were tiny twigs. Then he carries them to one place to build a perfect little home for himself.

Oh, that smart bastard! He wants to sleep nice and dry. The wet season is upon us, and I bet it won't be fun to get wet every day. I remember how rainy the tropics get from traveling with my family.

I march past him and look for a place for myself. I don't need anyone's help, especially his. Plus, I don't think he'll be willing to offer it after all our interactions.

About a hundred feet or so away from his already decent-looking shelter, I find the perfect place for mine. Three palm trees already bent together, creating the structure for what I have in mind. All I need now is to stick them together for good and build the rest.

Easy-peasy. The water source is nearby. The beach is in front of me in case rescue comes while I'm sleeping. The place is perfect. If not for the grunting giant to my left and his perfect-looking shelter. I can do better!

As I start pulling the palm branches, the sun goes up, and my skin starts burning. I could use some sunscreen, but I have none. Natural sunscreen will have to do. So I dig my fingers into the soil, deep inside where the moisture gathers, pull the dirt out, and spread it all over my cheeks, forehead, neck, and arms. The burnt skin instantly chills, and I let out a loud moan of relief.

The cracking and rustling stops. I look at my neighbor—he's standing up and holding a huge log in his hands.

I lift up my middle finger at him and go back to cutting the branches. Cutting is a very fancy word for what I'm doing to them actually. Trying to rip a branch off a palm is not an easy task since it feels like they all are glued together. King doesn't seem to have a problem though, because his shelter is looking like an actual livable shed, almost professionally built. While mine looks like it's one breath away from falling apart since my branches are all messed up and not bushy at all. Even though I know all the tips and tricks which are still very fresh in my head due to bingeing *Survivor* on the way here, it's not as easy as the show makes it seem. I thought I was small but mighty, but turns out, the latter doesn't apply to me.

I probably could have asked for help—just a little bit—if he was someone else. Anyone else.

Glancing at my creation, I admit to myself that I probably would never be picked for the show, or my season would end ten minutes in.

I send an evil glance his way and continue with my task, making frequent trips to the waterfall. Despite the high humidity, my body seems to evaporate its liquid into thin air with the speed of light. Having a bottle would be very helpful right now.

Soon, the sun begins setting, and my house looks like a ready-to-fall-apart shithole. I have no food, since I've been so focused on building this disaster, and no real shelter. If it rains at night, I'll be sitting under the sky, tired and hungry, drenched down to my bones.

A loud male moan draws my attention, and I stick my nose out from my shelter to see what's happening. King has half a coconut in his enormous hands and takes a sip out of it. He's sitting on a big log with his hand perched on his bent knees.

My mouth instantly starts salivating, and I swallow, suddenly aware of how hungry I am. And thirsty. And angry. And my blood sugar is probably so low I'm a second away from passing out.

In the meantime, he takes another sip and glances my way. I purse my lips and turn away.

Another moan follows, and I can't help myself and look. *Who the hell moans so loudly?*

Now, right on the sand next to my beachside nemesis is the other half of the coconut. The man meets my eyes with a short nod at it. I swallow again and purse my lips, refusing to give in to temptation. A ghost of a smile makes a brief appearance on his lips, and then it's instantly gone as if I imagined it. He nods again—without a smile this time—and pushes the coconut my way.

I sigh loudly, finally giving up my independence. I'm about to sell my dignity for food—story as old as life.

Dragging my feet toward him with my head hanging lower than my self-esteem, my stomach churns. I swear I can taste the coconut in the air.

Feeling less guilty the closer I get to the delicious goodness, I decide I can be all strong and independent later. Today I'm too hungry for that.

zra

I knew she was going to come out eventually. She's been building that atrocious thing the whole day without bothering to think about food. When I found ripe coconuts, I knew I should get a few extra and bring them to her hideout. Once the sun sets, hunger will get to her. Somehow, I feel responsible for the woman since I found her body floating in the water facedown.

Or maybe I'm lying. Maybe it happened when I saw her sitting in her pajamas in the coffee shop in my building. Covered in soot and desperation.

I don't like caring for other living things. The only things I'm responsible for are my company, my mom and brother, and the rest of the legacy we've been trying to save. People come and go, but legacy stays.

I don't do social things. I don't do people. I like sex just like any other guy does, but sex takes a lot of effort. You need to take a woman out and to chat the whole evening before sex happens. That's what my brother does, and he's good at it.

I understand and don't mind spending any amount of money on a woman. But I do mind spending my valuable time and chatting with someone. Chatting is a total waste of time, and I don't understand why people put so much meaning into that.

Which brings me to my current problem.

I'm stuck on an island with a woman who always chats. All the time.

When I saw her land on the deck with her ass up in the air, I nearly choked on saliva, thinking there's no way *she* would be here, far from the airport and on the same boat. Because of everyone I've known in my life, only she would be unlucky enough to make that type of landing.

But when I was done staring at the duck on her ass, I finally was able to shift my attention to her hair. Which is always hard not to notice. The pink of her hair is not exactly pink. It has a light shimmer to it, almost like glitter. The woman is a fucking unicorn.

The next thing that threw me off was my stupid eyes shifting back to the duck. It was hard not to notice it, as it stared at me right from the middle. Did *this* duck sit on my face?

And when she started jiggling it, trying to get on her feet instead of her face, I couldn't help my pants growing tighter. My body remembered how those jiggles felt on my lap. And my face.

I groan inwardly, cursing her along with her duck and the damn boat wreck.

With that being mentioned, it's safe to say I'll not be having fun stranded on this island for an unknown number of days. I can't fucking lust after someone I totally hate. She's been the bane of my existence for the past couple months, and now she's followed me here. The place where I could actually enjoy some solitude with lavish nature, coconuts, and my hand.

Sighing to the sky and hoping I won't go insane, I check on my neighbor in a ripped shirt and duck hiding under her black shorts. She is also inexplicably covered in mud now.

All afternoon she's been struggling to move those branches as if they weigh a ton. Every time she lifts one, she grunts and puffs like she's moving a mountain. She made a few frequent trips to the waterfall, but I imagine she got thirsty the moment she was back. I've been timing her walks, and they couldn't last more than a few minutes. She's been rushing back and forth, wasting more energy than she was getting from consuming water. She's probably exhausted by now. And hungry. Definitely hungry.

As she slowly approaches me—scratch that, not me but the coconuts I've placed on the sand by my side—she's looking more and more sure and dare I say bloodthirsty? Her eyes are trained on the coconuts—*those on the sand, sadly*—and her little hands are squeezed into funny fists the size of a ladybug. If I didn't know any better, I'd say she would fight me for these coconuts.

I get a little too excited since my sweaty pants are getting a little too tight. Who knew traveling in a dress suit wasn't the best idea. But in my defense, I never travel for pleasure, only business. To think of it, I don't even remember vacationing since I've become an adult. If ever.

I'm spreading my legs wider, giving some room for my clearly insane dick if it's getting aroused by the sight of that disaster I've come to loathe, and make myself busy with a coconut in my hands.

"May I?" she asks, pointing at the closed ones by my side.

I nod and push one toward her. She takes it in her hands

and retreats back to her monstrous shelter that will blow away with the first sign of wind. Once she disappears behind the bushes, the sound of something smashing into something reaches my ears. I could have offered to crack the coconuts, but I want to see her ask. Beg me to. She can do that, I know she can.

She *owes* me that. If she wasn't there to use the damn oven, the fire might not have started. But she was. She burned my building, costing millions of dollars by now, a few lost future projects, and possibly the CEO position in my own company. She escaped from the hospital to avoid charges. She landed on my face during the turbulence. She nearly broke my cock in two when she grabbed it like a door handle. I dragged her body from the ocean and breathed life back into her. She was turning blue when I carried her to shore. I didn't know how long I'd been doing CPR when she came back to life. I was sure I cracked some ribs, but she seems fine. I saved her life. The least she could do is be more grateful. There're good ways to show gratitude. Some really good ways.

Fuck that. I spread my thighs even wider because apparently something is wrong with me if imagining this woman begging me to crack the coconuts makes me hard as said fuckin' coconut itself.

I swear to God if I keep thinking the word coconut one more time, I'm going to go insane.

A few minutes later, she comes back out. Her face is red, and her shoulders rise and fall with an alarming speed. She's like a little raging bull with pink hair and matching cheeks.

The bull marches toward me while I'm drinking the coco… the water from the nut and stops a few steps away with one hand on her hip and the nut in the other.

"How did you open it?" She sounds like she's forcefully squeezing words through her tightly shut lips.

I look up at her with a raised brow, expecting her to do better. I know she can.

She rolls her eyes and starts tapping her foot on the sand. "How did you crack the coconut?"

I keep looking at her, taking slow sips from my... nut.

She sighs and forces a Cheshire cat smile on her face. "Could you please share with me how you opened the coconut so I can try and do the same?"

I swallow the juice and point at the palm tree next to us. Her eyes follow my finger and then return to me. "What are you saying?"

I lift a corner of my lips, enjoying the sight of her angry face. I never knew it could be so entertaining to anger another human being, but I like seeing her getting the side of the coin she's been giving me.

She groans loudly, turns around, and walks toward the same bushes she just came from. More banging sounds and a few minutes later, she emerges with the full co... the uncracked nut in her hands and marches toward me with an even more determined look on her face. Her jaw is clamped tight, the muscles in her cheeks moving under her tanned skin, her hips swaying.

Once she reaches me, she drops the coconut on the ground and takes the same pose.

"How did you crack the damn thing?"

I nod toward the palm tree, letting her figure out the rest on her own or learn how to be more polite.

"I tried that. I beat it on the tree, but it doesn't crack." Her nostrils flare. She looks funny, like a little angry doll.

"And what do you want from me?" My voice comes out even rougher than usual. It's rough when I'm in the office, trying to talk to people, but it's worse when I'm quiet for some time.

"I want you to tell me how to do it." Her tightly pressed

lips remind me of one of the outlets at the back of a computer.

"I just did."

"No, you didn't." She blows the hair out of her face. "You just nodded your big head in the air."

Inwardly smiling, I ask, "I can open it for you." Then add thoughtfully, "If you want, of course."

I don't know why I can't just tell her what to do, but somehow, I want her to depend on me for this since she pretends to be so independent otherwise.

"Yes!" she exclaims enthusiastically, and then she adds in a quieter voice, "Please."

I take two coconuts from the sand and walk into the trees. She follows me. *Unfortunately.* I'd prefer to keep my little secret for now and hold this information over her head.

"Why are you going over here?" she asks from behind me. "Do you have tools hidden somewhere?"

I send her a murderous look. She should be scared by it like everybody else is. But she's clearly not everybody else, because she quirks a brow with a silent question I don't have an answer to. So I secure the first coconut between the roots with the pointy side up, grab a giant stone I found before, and start smashing it on the top to soften the husk. Once it's thoroughly smashed, I take the coconut and start pulling the husk away.

"Seriously? You gotta do that?" She sits on her knees and watches my movements.

Every single one of them. I show her how to clean coconuts from the husk while she keeps glancing at her fingers which look too delicate to be able to pull a coconut apart. How to find the perfect spot on it to crack it open and smash it on the same rock I used before.

Hearing her swallow, I glance at her and notice her eyes

trained not on the food in my hands but at something on my arms. Or is it shoulders?

I look at them, trying to figure out if there's a huge black widow on them or something, but find nothing. When I look back at her, she's flushed beneath mud-covered cheeks, and I fear she might have a fever.

Placing one cracked coconut at my feet, I pull the other one apart, trying to preserve as much water as I can. Offering both to her, I wait for her to take them. But she doesn't. Instead, her big, blue eyes look up at me.

"Are you sure?"

And suddenly, I feel like the biggest ass in the universe. A very rare occurrence for me.

"Yes," I reply gruffly. "Just take it. I'll open another one."

"Okay," she says in a small voice and takes the halves from my hands. Lifting one of them to her lips, she starts drinking.

I should be cracking another nut, but I'm too busy gawking at her neck swallowing the water she's drinking. I've clearly spent too much time in the sun since this behavior is unusual for me.

Her shoulders are covered in dry mud, there are splotches of the same substance on her face, and yet, I can't stop staring.

When she's done, she tries to scoop out the meat with her fingers. A useless task since her fingers are too delicate, so I take it from her and crack it into more pieces. Then I give it back to her, and she accepts it with an even quieter 'thanks.' I nod in return and give her another coconut to drink.

She takes it carefully and places it beside her feet. "I'll save it for later. I don't know how to open them."

I sigh, cursing myself. "Just drink it." My tone is anything but welcoming, but I can't help it. "I'll open more for you."

"Thank you," she says, drinking one half and saving the other one.

I nod and start walking back to the shelter I've made for her, but she calls out.

"Hey. Are you sure you don't want this one?" She stretches her arm holding a coconut toward me. "You're bigger. You probably need more energy."

My eyes move from her hand to her face before I forcefully shake my head and go over to the waterfall. Taking a dip in the ocean sounds like a good idea, but there's no fuckin' way I'm going in there at night where weird creatures come out to play.

So I refresh myself in the water, drink as much as I can, and fill two halves of empty coconuts with water for later. By the time I'm back to my shelter, the little thing is sleeping in her newest creation. Her ass is sticking outside since the place is too small for anyone but a child to fit in.

I walk closer to the shore and sit on the sand. No one is around. No one.

But I like it. I like to be alone. I've been running like a hamster in a wheel for years, burning myself into nothing, trying to barrel through people to prove to everyone I'm worthy of the company. To prove that father was wrong for not trusting me. I was being so loud that I forgot how to hear myself or anyone else.

I don't know how long I've been sitting here, just listening to the sounds of the island. To the whistling of the wind. Crackling of the leaves. Odd, unexpected noises local animals make. Numerous chickens clucking. Why the fuck are they bickering at night? Aren't they supposed to be sleeping?

The more I listen, the more I understand that the unfamiliar sounds or the lack of the car honks and sirens on busy streets don't bother me. Throughout the day, I found myself checking my empty pocket for my phone. It's an old habit, considering I have access to my company with its help, and when I don't have it, I feel out of control.

I love control. I thrive on it. I love predictability and order. But I don't remember the last time I let myself just sit and enjoy the present without thinking how to get control over our company back. And by the end of the day, I nearly forgot that I was supposed to have the gadget with me.

I don't know if anyone will find us. If someone will ever show up. This may be long term. When the storm started, we thought it'd pass, and we'd make it through. But the huge wave came out of nowhere and flipped the tiny boat. The guy could call it a 'ship' all he wanted to, but a fact is still a fact—that thing was a small motored boat and wasn't built for a storm like that. I didn't even know the area was prone to all this crazy weather.

But the ocean became quiet just as fast as it became violent. When I emerged from the water and finally got enough air to think coherently, there was no boat or anyone else. The fact that I noticed the woman in the water was a miracle itself. Thank fuck for her bright hair and the moon shining right upon it like a theater spotlight. And the next miracle happened when she started breathing again—I don't even know how long she'd been without oxygen at that point.

Shuddering at the thought that I might have been here alone which suddenly doesn't sound so appealing, I rise and walk back to my shelter. I built it big enough for the two of us to fit in, but she started making her own, so I didn't offer for her to join. Big deal.

Glancing her way, I notice that her ass hasn't moved an inch. She's probably exhausted. Satisfied that she's alive—somewhat—I crawl to my shelter and quickly fall asleep.

14

Maeve

The coconuts take over my body a couple of hours later. I wake up with an urge to pee. Like right now.

I peek my head outside of my shelter to check for any bystanders—meaning to see if my neighbor is taking a leisurely stroll under the stars. A useless task, really, since my 'house' doesn't have decent walls. Or a roof. I pretty much sleep outside. Which wouldn't be bad considering we're in a warm tropical place, but it's the beginning of the rainy season, and it's only a matter of time until I'll be soaked to the bones.

The darkness is pitch black—I can't even see my feet. Where the hell is the moon? Oh, right, it's covered by the clouds, so I see nothing. Absolutely nothing.

I could pee right here, but he might hear me. What's more embarrassing than that? So I decide to walk a little bit farther, hoping I can find my way back.

The roots of numerous plants are painful on my bare feet, and I jump, trying to avoid the edges poking out of the ground, only to end up landing on something so sharp, that I fall on my knees, crying out in pain.

"Ouch!" I shift my body so I'm sitting on my butt instead of praying to the rainy gods on my knees. Feeling my knees with my fingers, I find one of them busted open. It's cut and bleeding and already stings. I wipe the dirt off it, feeling warm blood seeping under my fingertips.

"Fuckity fuck," I mumble, angry at my own clumsiness and the stupid darkness and the damn moon which has checked out on me when I could actually use her help.

When the pain subsides a bit, I crawl on my battered knees to the nearest palm and hold on to it for dear life while I try to pull myself together. When I'm almost up, my foot lands on something sharp, and I go down again.

"C'mon!" I yell into the universe just as the first raindrop falls on my face. Then another. It's not long before my face is drowning in the tropical downpour. The water is warm, but it's not so gentle beating on my face.

I give up on the idea of ever getting up and lean my back on the palm. How long can people survive under the heavy rain?

As I stare into the darkness ahead of me, I feel the darkness staring back. Like the shambles my life is in, it mocks me with its inevitable destruction. Because once we get rescued, my family will tear me into pieces. For running away in the first place. And then for running back.

My parents are not bad people per se. They just live in a different reality than the majority of people. I was born into the same reality and thought it was the only one for a long time. When my views didn't align with theirs, I was forced to find another reality and leave.

Suddenly, something gigantic and steely hits me on the

shoulder. "Fuck!" I yell as I jump to the side, grabbing my shoulder. "What was that?"

I try rotating my shoulder but can't figure out if it's broken or just bruised because it feels like it's going to fall off all together.

"What the fuck happened?" King's voice echoes from the darkness around me.

"My luck happened," I mumble, not caring if he hears me or not. "If you don't want to get hit by lightning, I recommend you move as far away from me as possible because this," I point my index finger at the sky, "is the last thing that's left for me to make my life totally miserable."

His sigh is so loud, I can hear it through the heavy rain. A big body places itself next to me, I can feel its presence to my right. It's demanding and hard to miss.

"What happened?" he repeats his question calmer as if sensing my last nerve dissolving into nothing.

I sniffle. "I think a coconut fell on my shoulder."

"Damn." This is the first genuinely *emotional* emotion I've heard in his voice. "Are you okay?"

I try rotating my shoulder again and wince. "Hurts like a son of a bitch."

"Is it broken?" The sudden concern in his voice makes me feel sorry for myself, and my lips start trembling.

"I don't think so." I try moving it a little but instantly stop when it starts hurting. "I don't know. Most likely bruised."

"Let me see."

I snicker. "Good luck with that." I can't even see him and he's sitting right next to me.

"I'll feel it."

A moment later, I feel his careful fingers probing in search of my shoulder. When they finally land on my elbow, he slides his hand up to my shoulder where his fingers start probing carefully. I don't think I've truly comprehended how big the man really is before because the way his palm covers my arm makes me shiver.

"Tell me if it hurts."

When his hand moves to one particular spot on the top of my shoulder, I cry out. He retreats from the painful spot but keeps moving toward the back. Then his other hand joins in, and he tries moving my shoulder a bit.

"Oh," I exhale in pain, and he instantly retreats.

"I don't think it's broken, but definitely very bruised. It'll hurt more tomorrow."

I chuckle darkly. "Love your optimism."

"I'm a realist," he deadpans.

I look at him—well, toward his direction—but don't see his face very well obviously. What life has he had that made him so jaded? "Shocking."

It takes me a second of sitting in the rain before I'm quickly reminded of why I came out here in the first place.

"What were you doing here anyway?" he asks as if reading my mind.

"I came out here to pee."

A pause. "Here? Why here?"

"Because it's far enough from the camp to be decent."

Another pause. "Why can't you pee there?" He sounds so puzzled, it's almost hilarious.

"Where?"

"Next to your place."

"Because I sleep there!" I exclaim in horror.

"The rain will wash it away before it even hits the ground," he contradicts in that robotic tone of a machine answering service I totally hate.

"Okay, fine." I roll my eyes to the sky—a big mistake since it gets flooded with the forceful rainy stream. I don't know if my retinas will survive it. "Because you sleep there."

"Me?"

"You can hear me peeing."

He chuckles at first. Then some more. Then it grows into a quiet laugh—a very tasteful one. In fact, it's so nice and soothing that for a second there I forget that I need to go. Why is his laugh so beautiful? It was already unfair that a grouch like him was given the body and face of a fallen angel, and now he also has a nice laugh. *C'mon, Universe, don't put all your eggs in one basket.*

"Have you?"

"What?" I ask, too lost in my own thoughts to follow his.

"Peed." He laughs again and mumbles under his breath. "Can't believe I'm talking about this."

I lift my chin up even though he can't see. "No, I haven't. The roots and then the coconut attacked me before I could get to business."

Something like a snort makes me narrow my eyes and stare in the darkness, trying to see his face. "Go, I'll wait."

"Go where?"

"Pee."

"Not with you here!"

"I won't see or hear anything. Trust me, the rain and the ocean are loud enough to cancel out *any* noises around here."

I sigh but don't move. There's no way I'll be doing my business in his presence.

"Do you need to do it here? I can wait over there." I suspect he indicates a direction, but I can't see him clearly enough to confirm and have to trust he means far from me.

"Okay," I reply grouchily because I really don't have a choice. It's either I pee in my already wet pants—which won't change the situation much—or I do it as a decent human would with pants off. "Can you at least step away a little bit?" I ask with a resigned sigh.

His laugh gets farther away.

Sighing again, I find a tree with my hands and crouch

behind it. It's funny to think I'd be hidden behind a twig like that, but it gives a mental barrier between me and him.

It takes me a while to relax even though a moment ago I was about to pee my pants.

"Can you walk a little farther?" I yell to him.

I swear I hear his grunt from here, but he does as I ask. Now I can go about my business.

When I'm finally done, I come out from behind the palm and head toward him. I don't make it far because my feet get caught between roots, and I fall down again. The whole body forward from all my five-five glory.

"Ouch!" I cry out, trying to scramble back. My knees and palms took the worst of it, and I feel like they're bleeding.

"What happened?" His voice is right next to me.

"Lost my dignity," I mumble and hear a loud snort before I feel big hands wrapping around my shoulders and pulling me up. Once I'm on my feet, one of the hands grabs mine and pulls me with him. A blink later, I'm in his arms bride-style.

"What are you doing?" I squeak, feeling like a total idiot. I've never been carried in someone's arms. Never. My twig-like prom date my parents found for me could lift only a spoon. Guys I've dated in New York weren't into carrying or caring. I'm sure there's a good guy out there who can do all of that—I just haven't found him yet. And I refuse to believe that King can be one of *those*. Because he is not. Nope.

And he just proves it by talking.

"Making sure you won't break a leg. I don't want to cater to your needs tomorrow."

"Right." I roll my eyes. For a moment there, I thought he was actually worried about me. Nope, my wishful thinking was squashed into the ground like an annoying bug. He just doesn't want the only other person on the island to get injured, so he doesn't have to stay here alone. Humans are communal creatures. Even this one.

"I can walk on my own just fine," I say grouchily as I nearly stumble over some overgrowth. He pulls me along with him, saving me from a face-plant.

"Yeah, I saw that," he mumbles back, not raising his voice to a normal tone. When we come out on the clearing of the beach, he heads left, and I pull my hand away from his.

"What?" he asks, sounding annoyed.

"My house is that way." I point at my place, not knowing if he'll see it.

"Your house is a piece of junk about to fall apart. You can stay at my place."

I exhale loudly like a bull before an attack. "My house is just fine, thank you very much." I cross my arms over my drenched chest to keep from going for his eyes with my broken nails. "I appreciate your help. Farewell now."

"Farewell now?" he repeats like he has some problem understanding.

"Yes, meaning goodbye, arrivederci, go away." I accompany my explanation with a dramatic wave of my hand.

A laugh would be a good word to describe this exhale he makes, but he is him, and by now I'm sure he doesn't possess a sense of humor.

"Farewell to you too."

With that, he heads toward his shelter. A very dry shelter, most likely. And cozy. With a good roof.

I'm not jealous. I am not.

15

*E*zra

I felt horror spiking in my blood when I heard her shriek through my deep sleep and the white noise of the ocean and rain. I thought she was getting eaten alive by a giant animal and rushed outside to help. And it wasn't because I didn't want to stay here alone, because quite honestly, I prefer solitude to her chatter. But the idea of her being hurt made *me* hurt. Maybe it's some sort of newfound responsibility because I saved her life—God knows I've never been a knight in shining armor.

Weird thoughts.

Finding her losing a battle with a coconut because she was trying to pee deep in the jungle was funny. Why would she go so far? It's only her, me, and the rain. The sound of it beating on the leaves is so loud, I can barely hear myself think. Who knew that the lack of the city could be just as loud as the big city itself?

I crawl back into my shelter and check the walls. As I expected, it's holding against the elements just fine. We used to build small play structures and treehouses at our grandma's farm, and using mud to glue things together was highly useful. I recall my recent wish about returning back to those times, thinking that I should be more careful about what I wish for since life might grant it. *Do I feel as free as I expected to?*

My brother would be proud of me if he saw me today. He's always said that I'm no fun. Well, I'm plenty fun now. I'm living in the wild, by myself, and I'm not even checking my phone.

Granted it's lost somewhere at the bottom of the ocean, but I actually can survive without one, despite what he might think.

The rain intensifies, but my conscience is clear. I offered Mae a shelter, and she refused. It's on her now.

The morning brings the sun, and the jungle will dry out in an hour. I climb out of my shelter and stretch my body. The first day was a good workout building this shelter, but I can't let my body, or my mind go stiff. Otherwise, I'll go insane. I need to find something to do today.

Once I'm out, I glance at my neighbor's place. It seems to be empty. I look around and don't find her anywhere. I open a coconut and drink it, then go to take a swim in the water. It's warm and very calm. Different sorts of fish are everywhere, curious about who's in the water with them. I freeze, mesmerized by the variety of colors around me.

When was the last time I just stood and watched the world around me? This place is fucking beautiful.

I swim back and forth along the shore, not venturing into the deeper water because I don't fancy one of my precious balls being eaten off by a hungry shark.

When I'm done, I go to the beach and check my neighbor's shelter. Still empty. Where is she? It's not like there are a lot of places to go around here, and if she was on a water run to the waterfall, she should be back by now.

Something pinches in the middle of my chest, like a little, annoying needle. *Worry.* It's fucking worry. How pathetic and desperate am I becoming here?

I grab empty coconut halves and head toward the waterfall. If I don't find her there, I'll start scouting the island. It's truly very small, and I'm sure I'll find her eventually. I just hope a random wild coconut hasn't fallen on her head, killing her before I can. Those suckers are heavy, and with the right speed, they can do some serious damage.

Feeling my steps picking up speed, I almost run into the opening of the waterfall.

She's there. Her pink hair is floating in the water as she floats on her back with no bra. Or anything really. She's splayed like a sea star, gazing into the sky. Her pointy nipples are staring there too, peeking from the water every time she moves.

I feel out of place. Like I've just walked in on someone doing something inappropriate. And naturally, I want to do inappropriate things too. Right away. So does my dick suddenly straining my pants.

I mentally shake my head, trying to figure out what sort of hold this woman has over my body. It's been acting odd when she's around. Every single time.

Not wanting to be caught staring, I turn around. Quickly. But apparently not quickly enough because she yelps and sinks into the water.

"What are you doing here?" she shrieks from the top of her lungs.

"I came to get some water." I go with a half truth. No need for her to think I actually might care about her.

She rolls her eyes as she starts moving toward the shore,

keeping her body under the water. Which doesn't help much because I'm getting quite an eyeful. Of course, she notices this.

"Turn around!" she cries out, sinking deeper into the water.

"Sorry!" I yell back and whip around, feeling embarrassment creeping up my neck. It's not like I've never seen a naked woman's body before, but seeing *hers* makes it somehow different. I've had this body lying on top of me in a moment of crisis. Those hands clutching to my chest. That face pressed into my shirt because she was looking for comfort only I was able to give her.

After some splashing, I hear her moving around and the rustling of clothes.

"You can turn around now."

I slowly come to face her only to find her sending angry glares my way. Her arms are crossed over her midriff, right under her chest. The wet material of her green shirt clings to her body, prolonging my torture. You'd think my dick would get the memo and calm the fuck down, but no. The fucker stands straight and proud. It's hard to hide it in these damn dress pants. And I wonder for the tenth time why I decided that it was a good idea to travel in a suit.

She shifts her pose awkwardly, then shakes her leg and winces. I look down to find her knees scraped from the fall last night.

"You're bleeding," I note the obvious.

Her eyes follow my gaze. "Yeah, there's not much I can do. I'll try to keep it clean and try not to fall again," she replies with a subtle shrug of one shoulder.

She's right, there's nothing we can do about that here. But she surprises me once again with her attitude toward it. The women I've been around would make a big fuss about it.

With a sigh, I say, "C'mere."

"What?"

"Sit here." I point at a spot on a big stone. "I'll check your knee."

"W-why?" She blinks.

"Because we don't want it to get infected. Sit."

Still blinking quite dramatically, she takes a seat and stares at me, waiting for what I'll do next. It's a very good question because I don't know what I'll be doing next myself—I've never tended to anyone's wounds. Or my own to be fair.

Swallowing a sudden lump of shyness in my throat, I kneel in front of her. A small sound escapes her lips. Something like a surprised sigh.

I carefully grab her leg by her shin and place it on my thigh. I have no idea why I'm doing that because I can see the scrape just fine from here. When her small foot lands on me, so close to my cock, I remember why it was not such a good idea.

Trying to focus on the task I'm actually supposed to be doing, I look at the wound. It's a nasty scrape, a long and deep one.

"I think the water cleaned it pretty well," I croak. "But we don't want any dirt to get inside. Wait a second."

I pull the hem of my undershirt and rip a line off the bottom.

"What are you doing?"

"We need a bandage," I explain, refusing to look at her face.

"I'll be fine," she protests weakly. It must really hurt.

I carefully wrap it around her knee. It takes me two tries to make it not fall apart, and when I finally lift my eyes to her face, I find her teeth sunken into her bottom lip. Her eyes are focused on my hands which are currently still placed on her leg. When she catches up to me finishing my task, her eyes dart to mine.

"Thanks!" she squeaks.

"Yeah."

I jump to my feet and walk a few feet away, trying to erase the awkwardness I've created. While she's looking everywhere but at me, all I can do is look at her.

When I'm done staring, I remember that I haven't apologized yet. I don't do it often, but it feels needed now.

"Sorry, I didn't mean to snoop on you." This comes out gruffer than I mean for it to be.

"I know," she sighs. "I just didn't expect you. I guess I'm enjoying this situation a little too much."

"Taking it like a vacation?" It feels like I'm not the only one not eager to return to the land of the living.

She shrugs and adds with a small smile, "I haven't had a vacation outside of New York for a long time. And here is free housing and free food."

"Food? What food?" I ask, barely able to contain my smile.

"We'll find something."

We. She said we.

"We should check the island from both sides. The first day, we were wrecked and might not have noticed something. And now, we know what we will be looking for."

"What?"

"Food." Her smile turns predatory. "Any food. Papaya and bananas should be around here for sure." She points toward the side of the island we haven't explored yet. I went there on the first morning, but I was more concerned with finding out if the island connects to big land rather than looking for a banana.

"Sounds good."

She lifts her arms in the air and does a long, thorough stretch, moaning at the end. Her clothes cling to her wet body. My poor dick gives up and jumps again, and I pray she doesn't look down at my pants.

"Your shoulder better?" I ask in a husky voice, not able to control it. My body acting like a traitor when Mae is around is starting to get to me.

She rotates it lightly. "Yeah. A lot. Maybe the water helped. It was a bit chilly in the morning." She keeps rotating it, making her tits jiggle. And that doesn't help my situation.

"Did it bruise?"

She grabs the hem of the T-shirt neckline and pulls it down, baring her shoulder—her very purple-looking shoulder.

"Hey," I exhale, rushing to her. "Are you okay?"

Her silence makes me bring my eyes to her face. She's watching me carefully with her big, blue eyes.

"I'm fine," she replies in a soft voice. "It's just a bruise. It hurts, but it's not broken. It's all that matters. Plus, there's nothing we can do now. So, complaining won't change much." She shrugs the other shoulder, disregarding the subject. I know people who wouldn't get up from bed if they had something like that.

I let myself look at her. Like really *look* long enough to notice how soulful her eyes truly are. How much more mature than she seemed at first. How interesting she truly appears to be.

"We should split up," I offer quickly, hoping that by the time we reconnect, her shirt will dry out, and my cock will have some relief. And my mind will remember why we didn't like her in the first place.

"Good idea." She closes her eyes and takes a full breath in. "Damn, this feels good."

I lift a brow. "You seemed desperate yesterday."

She looks at me with a smile. "And I'll be desperate again when the rain hits, but now, I'm good. Just have to take everything you can from every day, you know? Let's go. When it starts raining, the jungle will be slippery."

"Were you a Girl Scout or something?"

"Or something." It's all she offers with a mysterious smile and takes off toward one side of the island.

I head to the other one.

She was right, when it's wet, the ground will become slippery. And with all the roots popping out from everywhere, it's a recipe for a broken ankle. She's already proven to be a danger to herself by walking at night like a newborn kitten and scraping her legs and arms.

With my long legs, I try to cover as much ground as I can, so she doesn't have to. I really don't dream about carrying her around when she slips and falls. Even though she'd probably insist on crawling on her own. She seems to have some sort of disaster following her close on her heels. Starting with my building and the fire. Then the boat where she landed face-first on the floor with her ass in the air. I mean, that must have hurt like hell. I wasn't interested in comforting her because she was standing in my way to my final destination to get the damn deal done so we can have our company back. Plus, when I recognized her as *her*, the wave of rage I felt was a bit too much even for me.

Shaking my head to myself, I say a silent prayer to the universe that in my absence, the board won't take any actions. The news about my disappearance must have hit them by now, and my brother would have temporarily taken charge. He's good at playing *Game of Thrones* and can hold off the voting as long as possible, even though he doesn't like it. His passion lies in projecting the unique buildings we plant everywhere. He's the creative of our company.

I wish I could influence things back in New York from here—not having anyone around *and* still moving the company sounds like a dream come true. But reality is different—I'm here, and everything else is there. There's nothing I can do about it.

For a moment, I remember her words and decide that I'll just go with the flow, taking it day by day. If we don't have food, we don't survive. If we don't survive, there won't be any deals happening. Ever. And if I'm completely honest with myself, I don't think I could live my usual life if something happened to the woman I'm stuck here with.

Somehow, due to the constant jokes of fate, we got together here. Again. I saved her life. I literally breathed it into her. And I feel like I owe her something. How fucked up is that?

As I walk around, it's getting a little darker, and I look up at the sky. The clouds have reached us rather fast. So far, I've been able to find two banana palms, and I got a few bunches off one of them, remembering the place where I found them. It's not far—nothing here is far—so we can easily walk here when we run out of this supply.

"Hey, big dude!"

My head whips around, looking for the source of the voice.

"Big dude!"

Is she talking to me? Big dude? I think I can get on board with that.

"Giant man!"

A small body rushes toward me through the trees. Her cheeks are red, her pink, tangled hair flying behind her. She smashes into me full force, her hands landing on my chest in a weak attempt to stop herself. I drop my bananas and catch her instead.

"What happened?" I push her away and quickly rake my eyes over her body, looking for injuries. "Who's chasing you?" Acting on instinct, I push her behind me and narrow my eyes at the jungle, looking for a wild animal chasing her.

"I found papayas!" She sounds excited like she's found a boat to take us out of here.

"What?" I spin toward her.

"I found papayas! We're saved!" Her voice is so happy, I can't even find energy to be mad.

My eyes narrow at her. "And that's why you ran here like crazy?"

"Well, yes. It's going to be raining soon, and you need to climb the palm to get them," she announces, looking sheepish.

"*I* need to climb it?"

"Yeah." She winces. "I tried and couldn't. I just keep sliding down." She glances down at herself, spreading her legs like a little frog. "I even scratched my thighs. Look."

My eyes dip to her thighs, and they're really red and raw. From friction.

Fuck.

I quickly avert my eyes and point at the bananas on the ground. "I found bananas. It should be enough to keep us going until we can get to the papayas."

"Oh," she exhales, looking at the bananas with furrowed brows. "I wanted to return you the favor by finding food for the coconuts you offered before."

"We're not in a competition," I say softly, and she looks at me with sad eyes.

"I just wanted to bring something to the table too, you know?" Then she adds with a sniffle, "After everything I've taken."

"I know," I sigh. Because this is something I really do. I've been trying to prove to our father how useful I am all my life. But it's never been enough. "You're bringing—"

She looks at me with expectation.

"Bringing—" I'm struggling to find something, and her eyes narrow.

"Bringing what?" she asks.

"Entertainment," I reply, rolling my lips inward, trying not to laugh at her angry expression.

She leans down and grabs one banana bunch and heads back the way she came. "Let's go. I've got plenty more of that," she's clearly referring to the entertainment, "where it came from."

"I sure hope you don't," I mumble under my breath, earning a snarky glare.

Taking a deep breath and trying not to laugh is a very difficult task when a tiny cloud of fury is walking in front of me with her head held high, her small free hand curled into a fist, and her steps jumpy. Every time there's an obstacle in the way, she jumps over a root like a little bunny, her hair flying behind her. She's hilarious. I'm sure, in her eyes, she looks vicious with that little fist and the bananas wielded in the air like a weapon. In reality, she looks like a pink Easter bunny.

And I find myself smiling watching her. Odd.

16

We walk for quite some time before she stops and points up, where the tops of tropical trees meet. Upon checking them, I indeed find papayas hanging from them. And they are at the top. Like at the very top of very tall trees, untouched by humanity or hurricanes.

I swallow, imagining myself climbing up there to get the fruits and scratching the shit out of my already bruised dick. Can I maybe put it in my back pocket for safekeeping? What are my options here? I've got a big dick, alright, and I can't just tuck it between my legs. It's always in the way.

"Here they are. All you need to do is climb up there," her index finger points at the top, "and get them. Maybe, like, shake it a little when you're at the top, I don't know." She makes a gesture of shaking something with her hands. "We don't have a knife, so maybe you can get a big, fat stick and beat them with it."

"Beat them with a fat stick?" I blink. All I'm thinking is how I'm going to protect *my* stick. And I'm definitely not planning to beat anything with it. *What is she talking about?* "What do you mean?"

Her brows go up to her hairline. "Big stick." She points at a twig by her feet. "Beat." She makes a motion with her hands of hitting someone with a bat. "Papayas." She draws the shape of the fruit in the air. "Many papayas." She keeps drawing them. "Stick." Her finger goes again to point at the twig. "Beat." Repeating the motion. "Papayas." She points at the trees.

"I got it," I reply, annoyed when I finally understand what she's trying to tell me, my head fuzzy from thinking with my own stick.

"Are you sure?" She sucks her lips in. "I can try and explain it again." Her big, blue eyes blink rapidly, making me even more annoyed.

"I got it," I rasp and walk toward the palm. Grabbing the tree with my hands, I place one foot on the side of it, testing if I can keep my dick from being squashed if I press myself too close. Then I place the other foot and start climbing. Shit, it's easier than I thought.

"You're doing great, Tarzan!" She chimes in from the ground, nearly making me slip. "Oops, sorry!" she yells. "I'll be quiet."

Rolling my eyes, knowing she won't be quiet because she doesn't know how to, I keep climbing up. Thank fuck for my five-in-the-morning gym sessions. I'd feel like I'm not man enough if I couldn't climb this shit and get her the damn papayas.

When I'm at the top, I try to reach for them. They're firmly planted, refusing to be separated from each other and the tree.

"You forgot the stick. To beat them with!" she suggests

helpfully from the ground. "Maybe I can throw it at you. *To you*! I meant *to you*!" she quickly adds much louder.

Without waiting for my reply, she throws the damn stick, and it hits me on the shoulder.

"Oops! I'll try again!" Sounding cheerful, she's already picking up the fallen thing while I yell,

"No!"

But I'm too late, and the sharp side of her stick hits me in the cheek. "Fuck," I growl.

"Oops! Sorry!" She giggles. "I'll try again!"

"No!" I roar, but again, she's not the person to listen. The stick is coming my way. For such a small thing, it packs a pretty decent punch. The only way she'll stop hitting me with the damn thing is if I catch it, so I throw my hand in the air and catch it as its flying straight into my face.

"Damn, you *are* Tarzan. I'll call you Tarzan now."

Rolling my eyes—again—I aim and smack the fruits off the tree. They fall down like a charm from a broken chain.

"Oh!" she yells, running to the side. "A little warning maybe?"

I glance at her, standing on the ground with her hands on her hips, a little to the side from the fallen papayas. She looks all right, that's all that matters. And she'll get her papayas after all.

"Sorry," I say loudly, not sounding sorry in the slightest.

"Yeah, sure you are," she replies, scratching her nose with her middle finger and making me roll my eyes, questioning her maturity.

With that, she sits on the ground to inspect the fruits. "We should eat them faster because they hit the ground pretty bad, so they might rot if we leave them like that."

"Okay. Step to the side, I'll try something."

This time she chooses to listen and gets out of the way in a second.

Holding myself glued to the palm, I somehow manage to take off my T-shirt. Besides my dress shirt, it's the last piece of clothing I can wear around here. The black wool jacket I stashed in my shelter is not the best option for not frying under the sun. I tie the neck of the shirt in a knot, creating a bag.

Then I lift myself even closer to the top, and the tree makes a weird squeaking sound. Not good. I need to hurry up. So I quickly gather a few more papayas and stuff them into the bag.

Balancing myself, papayas, and the damn tree is not an easy task. By the time I'm back to the ground, I don't want to eat the damn things. All I want is a banana and to lie on the beach. Surviving is turning out to be exhausting.

Before I even step foot on the ground, she grabs the shirt-bag from my hands like a kid grabbing candy. Her eyes are shining, and her shoulders are up like she's about to jump in celebration.

"Thank you, Tarzan," she says with a wide smile while her eyes roam over my bare torso. And she seems to be liking it judging by how her eyes are glued to my middle.

She clears her throat when she notices me noticing her and says, "Let's eat."

I glance up at the sky. "It's going to rain soon for sure."

"Yeah." She follows my gaze. "We've got time to get back and enjoy it before it pours."

She pulls one papaya from her shirt and sinks her teeth into the narrow part, peeling the skin away little by little to reveal the fleshy fruit beneath. "Do you want some?"

I shake my head because I don't think I'll ever want to eat it again—I've been traumatized enough.

We walk in silence the whole way while the only sounds are our footsteps and her sinking her teeth into the juicy fruit.

By the time we reach our camp, my shoulders are begging for me to itch them, so I do. Then I scratch some more. And more. I even look to see what's happening when she starts talking.

"You're burning."

"What?"

"Your skin is burning." She takes another bite, pointing her finger at my shoulder. "You had the shirt on, but once you took it off, you got burned."

"No way." My head whips from side to side, trying to see what she's pointing at. "It's too fast. We've been walking for only maybe fifteen minutes."

She snorts. "Dude, you're pretty much a vampire. Your skin has never seen the sun. All you need to get nice and crispy is ten minutes."

"It's seen the sun," I contradict.

"Alright, I'll bite." She smiles widely, showing off her teeth with a piece of papaya stuck in them. "When was the last time you went outside for a walk?"

"I walk plenty," I grit through my teeth.

"From a building to a car, I bet," she mumbles and then adds louder, "And when was the last time you took off your shirt playing something outside? Or even chilling, I don't know." She shrugs. "Grilling meat on your back porch."

"I don't have a porch."

"Of course." Her smile grows wider. "You have a penthouse. My bad."

Her stereotyping, no matter how annoying, is actually spot on. I haven't been on vacation for nearly five years, and even before that I didn't go someplace warm. The last time my full body has seen the sun was... *When was it?* I don't even remember. Maybe in college when I played football? We played in uniforms. Before that? I don't remember. But that's because I don't have time. I'm growing an empire, and emperors don't take days off. Their brothers do, but not the emperors. Never them.

"You need to put some dirt on."

"What?" I blink.

"The dirt." She nods at our feet. "We don't have sunscreen here, unless you want to go and dive in search of nearby shipwrecks and their sunken goodies." Thinking about *sunken goodies* and all the other shit that can be found at the bottom of the ocean quickly makes me choose her option.

"So what do you do with the dirt?" I ask, probably sounding like a moron.

She starts imitating putting sunscreen on herself, and she does it on her chest. "Put it all over, just like that. At least you'll survive until rescue arrives."

That's what she was doing before, probably. Covering herself in natural sunscreen.

"And you need to do it pronto," she notes, eyeing my shoulder. "Or you'll burn to a crisp."

Suddenly, her hand comes up to my waistband on the side of my body and pulls it away maybe an inch. I glance down too. She's right. There's a very definite line between the parts that were covered and exposed.

"The sun is the most treacherous when it's hidden behind the clouds," she continues. "You won't feel it until you have a fever and start vomiting all these precious bananas we've found."

I've never had heat stroke, but I've heard of it being vicious. Growing up, we never had a chance to go to warm places because our father always worked, and our mother didn't want to go anywhere without him. Then I went to a college where I had to work my ass off to prove that I can be the best in the class. I had to be because I knew my father was going to make me a CEO. It was our family company. He inherited it from his father, my grandfather who, in return, got it from another male ancestor.

After that, I was busy trying to find a way to get back the ownership of the company my father *didn't* leave to me and my brother. So yes, I haven't had much time for leisure.

When we reach our camp, my shoulders are in pain. So are my arms and neck.

"Sit," she orders, pointing at the fallen tree. "I'll cover the worst parts so it will be easier for now. Then the rain will wash it away anyway, so you'll have to reapply if it keeps hurting."

I drop the papayas by our feet and plant my ass where she pointed out. She steps deeper into the woods and comes back with a pile of mud on a giant leaf.

"Your skin will feel dry. But it's that or being a piece of smoked meat."

"Do your worst," I say, drawing my shoulders back like before a battle.

"Don't threaten me with a good time," she mumbles under her breath, making me bite my lower lip. Sometimes her expressions make no sense, but at the same time they do. I feel a sudden wave of gratitude that I'm not alone on this island.

She covers my most itchy parts, tracing her fingers over my hot skin. She's careful and precise. Calculated. And while I'm subtly trying to move my legs because I get a little too excited from her touch, her brows are furrowed with concentration. Being able to focus is a very admirable trait in a person.

When she covers the last part on my neck, focusing a little too long at the bottom of my hairline and raking her nails over the sensitive skin, she steps back to admire her work. She's clearly satisfied because she gives a short nod to herself more than to me and goes to the ocean to wash her hands.

The first raindrop falls on my nose when she's back. She sends a sad glance at my used-to-be-white shirt currently being used as a bag for her papayas. "You probably want to put it inside your house, so it stays dry."

"Yeah."

I take the fruit out, grab the shirt, and head toward my house.

The rain stops in a couple of hours, and I climb out of the shelter to look around. My neighbor started fixing her poor excuse of a bungalow. I head toward her to help, grabbing a handful of palm leaves to put on her roof.

She meets me with a glare. I carefully place the leaves on the ground next to her and retreat back to my place to see what else I can fix. I add a few more leaves, spread the gooey mud on a few holes and secure anything that might fly away if the wind hits.

Then I go to get a few more coconuts and bring more water. While keeping an eye on my neighbor. She does the same, but her shelter is not looking good. I think tonight she'll be soaking wet if it rains again. Judging by the sky, it will.

I'm contemplating if I should invite her over, but recalling her glare when I came to help, I don't think she'll be happy with my offer. So I go about my evening, taking a dive in the waterfall, collecting more water on the way back, and retiring for sleep.

When I'm inside my shelter, the first drop of the evening rumbles over the leaves on my roof without getting inside. I feel not exactly happy, but maybe content. I haven't had a desire to check my phone in hours, there's no itch to check my pocket. All I can think about is how to get food, stay dry, and maybe take a peek at my neighbor's ass.

Speaking of food, I don't know how long I can survive on sugary fruits. I need protein. I'm hungry. Tomorrow, I need to see what I can do about that. But for now, sleep. The days end early here, and I don't remember having more restful sleep.

Ezra

I don't know how long I've been sleeping, but it's still dark when I wake up. The sound of heavy rainfall doesn't let me go back to sleep, so I lift myself up on my elbows and look outside. The wall of water is so thick I can barely see anything past a few feet. Yesterday evening, it started as a short-lived rumbling with a promise of quickly going away. Today, it doesn't seem to be stopping at all.

Glancing around, I feel a ping of pride for the quality of shelter I've built. The water's dripping through a tiny hole in one corner, following the pole into the ground. That's about it. I need to cover it tomorrow to make sure everything is dry. Other than that, the place is perfect. I'm glad I decided to build it on a small hill, so the water doesn't collect inside. A thick layer of palm leaves keeps me somewhat cozy. It's better than sleeping on the ground.

I try going back to sleep, I really do. But my mind keeps

drifting to the other human on this island. I should just close my eyes and stop thinking about that since she let me know very clearly that she didn't need my help.

Yesterday felt like a breakthrough where we actually talked like human beings without trying to rip each other's throats out and did some work together. Her constant clumsiness doesn't annoy me as much anymore, so I decided that we can actually tolerate each other enough to survive until the rescue. Once we get to the mainland, we will never see each other again. Ever. I've had enough of our very unfortunate interactions.

But she had other plans about coexisting peacefully when she refused my help with a glare like I was taking her firstborn.

After tossing and turning, I eventually give up. The night is dark, and there's nothing useful I can do until the sun comes up, but staying inside—*alone*—is getting on my nerves.

I peek my head out but can't see much through the darkness and rain. I'm so used to bright streetlights everywhere I go that the beauty of nature seems muted.

Straining my eyes, I try to see what my neighbor's doing. Naturally, I don't see a thing. So I climb outside and run to her 'shelter,' which is currently falling apart. When I reach it, I find her staring ahead, hugging her knees. She's not sleeping, and the closer I look, the less I think that she's slept at all. Her body's not moving, and she's in a trance of sorts. It's creepy.

"Hey," I call out quietly, startling her anyway.

"Holy shit!" she cries out, placing her hand to her chest.

"You're wet." *Fuck, seriously, Ezra?*

"So are you." She lifts a brow, looking a little less miserable than she was a second ago.

"Because I was running here. Come with me." I nod toward my place. "My shelter is dry."

She peeks outside—if there's even an outside for *that*—inspects my shelter as if she can see it from here, and then looks back at me.

"Are you inviting me over?" Her voice sounds coy, like there's a hint of a smile on those pouty lips of hers.

"Are you coming?" I decide to keep my game because I'm starting to feel a thing I haven't felt for a long time—guilt.

She nods and jumps to her feet. I'm soaking wet, standing under the pouring rain. At least it's not cold, otherwise it wouldn't be fun to have pneumonia out here without antibiotics. We both run to my shelter, and I let her get in first. She bends, meeting me with her shorts-clad ass. And I'm stunned for a moment before I gather my wits to follow her inside.

As we pile in, the palm leaves on the ground get wet too. *Fuck.* So much for a dry place.

With two people, it suddenly seems small. Very small. She's sitting on her knees, mimicking my pose, and we're almost touching.

I notice she's shivering, and I lean to the side of her toward the corner where I folded my suit blazer I use as a blanket. It's ripped in a few places but still works as intended. I expect her to pull away because there's not enough space here. She doesn't. Instead, she stays in the same position while I accidentally brush her arm while retrieving the blazer.

"Take it." I push it toward her, trying to avoid any further skin contact.

"What?"

"You've been sitting there, wet, for who knows how long. We don't need you to get sick. Change into that."

"Oh," she mumbles, looking down at herself. "Right. Can you—"

"Yeah, sure." It's too dark to see much more than her

outline, but I quickly turn around anyway and listen to the sound of sticky clothes being peeled off a wet body.

"I'm done."

I turn back and find her sitting in the same position I found her—hugging her knees. My blazer is so big on her, she's able to almost wrap its front around her legs. The wet shirt and shorts lie in a pile by the entrance.

This is the moment when I understand that she has almost nothing under my jacket. Only her skin and the duck on her ass. The silky material of the inside is clinging to her skin just like it was to mine, and I suddenly feel the intimacy of the moment. It's not the close quarters, even though it doesn't help the situation, but sharing the only piece of clothing we have left. It's touched both of our bodies. Our skin.

"Thank you," she says quietly, bringing me back to the reality of our situation.

All the previous fight has clearly left her voice, and I don't like it. So I just nod, not knowing how to react to her simple gratitude a moment after I imagined us being one united thing. So fucked up.

"What about you?"

"What about me?" I parrot like an idiot. All my wits are lost.

"You're wet too. You can get sick, and I took your only dry clothes."

"I have another shirt." I look at the ripped mess of a white dress shirt I stashed in the corner because it has more holes in it than put-together material. "It's fine." I shrug one shoulder.

"Take it off at least, so you're not sleeping in wet stuff, you know. Maybe by the time we wake up, it will be sunny, and our clothes will be good to go. It's usually like that here.

Rain, rain, and then boom," she weakly snaps her fingers, "the hot sun out of nowhere."

"You've been here a lot?"

"When I was a kid." Her voice sounds sad. "Not so much anymore."

I nod, once again not knowing what to say. Talking was never one of my strongest traits. That's why I have my brother. He talks enough for the both of us.

The longer we sit, the worse my wet shirt feels on my skin, so I decide to follow her advice, take it off, and put it by the entrance to dry in case the rain stops while we sleep. But once I rid myself of the clingy material, my pants feel what I'd assume wet diapers stuck to the whole lower part of my body would feel like. Not cool.

"Do you mind if I take these wet pants off?" I ask her.

She shakes her head and goes back to staring out of the shelter.

I quickly pull my pants off and place them next to the shirt. Silky boxers don't feel so good when soaking wet, but it's better than if I'd been wearing tighty-whities.

"I'm gonna sleep. I don't know if they'll find us tomorrow, but we need to look for more food. We need protein for energy. I can't keep running on sugar." I shake my head with disgust.

"Yeah." Her voice is absent, as if she hasn't heard me.

For a moment, she felt like someone I knew. A person from my life. Despite how fucked up our connection really is. The feeling was faulty. Not helpful.

It's better *this* way. Separated mentally. We can get by as total strangers forced into circumstances without really knowing each other. If she does get to know me, she might not like what she discovers. And I might like it too much.

I'm her only hope here. As she is mine. If I learn things about her, it might make me *want* things I can't have. And I can't think about anything other than the deal I was going toward. I need it to happen, so all the years I've spent going toward my goals won't go to waste.

I glance at her miserable posture once again, and, with a sigh, I grab the shredded dress shirt from the corner. Slightly twisting my body, I spread it over her bare legs, and turn away from her.

She doesn't make a sound.

Maeve

I've been waiting for him to finally fall asleep for so long my eyes almost fell out of their sockets—that's how hard I've been trying to make them look anywhere but at him.

I knew he's a large man since he's so tall and that jacket of his is big, but man oh man, I didn't expect him to be so freaking ripped *and* lie next to me nearly naked. In a very touchable distance. And he's like a sculpture ripped. Insanely ripped. How did I not suspect any of this when I saw him in the coffee shop all those times? It may be dark, but I haven't forgotten his coiled body or how it felt under my touch as I applied mud to it earlier. And now he's practically naked right next to me.

My initial thought of him being an office rat due to the pale color of his skin that has never seen the light of day still stands. I swear his skin is almost transparent.

But it sure as hell has seen the luminescent light of a gym.

Looks like many hours at that. Besides those mega pronounced delta and wing muscles or whatever they're called, he has these little muscles connecting those big ones. Those muscles have their own muscles, and I could see them all.

When he grabbed that tree and lifted himself up, I swallowed. Hard. When he was up there and took his undershirt off and I got an eyeful of his arms and pecs, I nearly whistled. Because this man has a very impressive physique. Lifting himself up that palm like a giant monkey was not what I envisioned when I called him. To be honest, I had zero expectations that he actually would climb the tree. What I wanted was for him to help me get papayas down by maybe throwing coconuts at it or something. I didn't expect him to actually get up there. But he surprised me. He does that a lot actually.

I wanted so badly to be the first one to find food and bring it to him as a thank you for not letting me starve the first night, but he managed to find bananas first. Good thing I at least was able to help him with the sunburn. To my utter surprise, I find that I don't want him to suffer. Yes, my initial hatred toward him was justified. *Somewhat.* But we're not there anymore. Plus, he has his own reasons to dislike me. And yes, I labeled him 'an asshole'—deservingly so—but we're thrown together into this situation, and he's proven to have a different side to his assholishness.

To think of it, it all makes sense. The more assholey the assholes are, the better they look, and this one seems to be a descendant of a Greek god. Like maybe Ares or someone equally powerful with a dark cloud of anger and pheromones over his head. Because I don't know what's happening, but I can't stop staring at his back. Maybe it's the heat talking or near-death experience—who knows. Anyhow, I can't wait to get all the control over my body back.

His insanely sweet gesture of covering my legs with his last shirt took away the final bit of resentment and anger I had for him. It was so unexpected and thoughtful, my eyes turned itchy. I wanted to thank him but couldn't in fear I'd start bawling. So I just stayed silent.

I'm not sure how long I've been sitting here, but the rain has slowed down and the darkness isn't quite so thick anymore. Sighing, I try to get rid of his pretty image from my head. Only to move my eyes lower and land them— *accidentally, of course*—on his butt. I swallow when I see his thighs. Muscular thighs. His suit pants must have been custom tailored to comfortably contain those thick columns.

And where did he get something like that? I eye *all* the big things again. I mean, he's clearly an office rat and must spend a lot of his time in a chair. I wonder how much he can squat. Can he squat with me in his arms? That'd be awesome.

I wouldn't mind sinking my teeth into those muscular thighs.

Startled, I sit up straighter. *What the hell am I even thinking?* It's probably hunger talking, nothing else, but his thighs do look delicious.

Feeling guilty for being caught even when no one saw me, I quickly lie down and stretch my body as far as possible from the man. Which is not far considering we're sharing a handmade bungalow, and one of the 'sharing' people is very large.

I end up tossing and turning without any hope of sleep. So I turn to his back and start watching his muscles expand with every breath. With every inhale, it grows bigger, sucking all the air out of my own lungs. With every exhale, he breathes it back in.

It's weird. It's calming.

I don't notice when I fall asleep.

I wake up dry and warm. And very hungry. Snuggling my face into the dry warmth, I moan with pleasure. It feels so good.

Someone clears their throat and rasps, "We need food."

I jump up and to the side, nearly breaking the wall of the freshly built bungalow. The man rises up and sits on his butt, turning away from me.

"Yeah!" I cry out when I didn't need to and run outside.

Only when I'm outside do I remember that I'm still wearing his blazer, duck undies, and a mismatched bra without padding. In horror, I turn toward him. Only to find him turning *away* from me.

Do I really look so bad? Tough shit, he'd better get used to it because I'm not jumping back into my ripped shorts and T-shirt. We're on the island, and he can pretend I'm wearing a bikini. I'm not sure why I'm so embarrassed being seen in my undergarments.

I drop his blazer and straighten my back with pride.

"We need to look for food," I remind him about his own words.

"Yeah," he rasps. "Give me a second."

"What are you doing there?" I start walking toward him.

"Nothing." He quickly grabs his pants and pulls them over his lap. "I just need to get dressed."

I raise my brow. "There's no dress code here, you know. You can pretend your boxers are swimming shorts. I won't tell anyone." I smirk.

"I know." He waves his hand dismissively. "Just for mosquitoes and stuff."

I snort. "All mosquitoes are fried. They'll come out at night, so you should be good till then."

"Yeah, sure." He disregards me, turns completely away,

and starts pulling his pants on. I didn't know he's such a prude, but to each their own. I walk to the ocean and splash some water over my face and even gargle some. There is no better disinfectant and mouthwash than natural, salty water. Works for wounds too which I feel right away. All of them. On the soles of my feet and little cuts all over my legs and arms. And my poor bruised knees.

Welcome back to nature, Maeve.

"You ready?" He walks up to me.

"Sure. Let's go."

He quickly washes his face too, and we head toward the trees. At the waterfall, we drink. A lot. And once again I regret not having a bottle with me because we don't know how long we'll be roaming around, and we might get thirsty. Halves of coconuts don't hold much, but it's the best we've got.

On cue, my stomach lets out a loud growl of a wounded animal, and I regret eating the last banana yesterday evening and thinking that I should have saved it for energy in the morning.

"With so many chickens, we should be able to find some eggs," he suggests, and my belly growls even louder. He looks at me with an amused face. "Let's go."

I follow him deeper into the woods. "How are you not hungry?"

"I am."

"Then why doesn't your body let out these god-awful sounds like mine?"

"Discipline. Ever heard of that?" he asks mockingly.

I let out a growl. Like an actual growl of anger. Which makes him snicker. Which makes me even angrier, and him snicker even more.

Suddenly he presses his finger to his lips. "Sh-sh," he

hisses, pointing toward a pile of medium-sized rocks not far from us. "There."

I follow his hand and find a few chickens walking by. Two of them are lying under one of the rock formations, making funny sounds.

"We wait."

"For what?"

"They're sitting on the eggs. Or maybe laying them. Eventually, they'll get up. Maybe," he adds with a lopsided smile, looking boyish.

I glance at him with wonder. "How do you know?"

"I just do."

After giving him a curious look, I stare back at the chickens. And stare. And stare. Turns out, laying eggs takes time, so I find a palm and sit, leaning my back on it while the giant keeps watching the chickens.

"What's your name?" I ask.

He turns his face to me, looking confused, so I press my hand to my chest, and his eyes follow it.

"We've slept together." I start counting on my fingers. "And you've already bought me dinner. I burned your building."

His head turns toward me with whiplash at the last words, I'm sure. I choose to ignore his glare and continue.

"I've sat on your face." Another finger.

He starts coughing.

"I've touched your, you know, equipment." I wave my hand in the area of his groin, and he takes a quick step back. "And I don't know your name. Just that Jerome called you King. It's weird. We should be on a first-name basis by now." I shrug. "I'm Maeve. What about you?"

He swallows like he's nervous to share his name after he shared the literal shirt off his back and returns his eyes to me. "Ezra."

"Wow. Such a cool name. I don't think I know anyone with that name."

He doesn't reciprocate the compliment and goes back to watching the chickens. It's not like I expected him to. But it's not everyday you walk around meeting Maeves, you know?

"I knew your name," he says in a quiet voice. It almost feels like he shouldn't be saying it. "Well, at least a part of it. Mae. I just didn't know it was a real one." He swallows. "Considering your prison break, I figured it was bogus," he adds with a slight note of humor in his tone.

"Mae?" I ask, confused, ignoring the prison part. I thought we were past that point.

"Yeah, that's what they called you in New York?"

"How do you know?" I feel my brows drawing together. "I thought the hospital didn't give you the name." I recall telling them the first name that came to my mind—Mae. I didn't even think about pretending to be someone else. When the nurse asked me about my last name, I threw out "Doe" like they use for unnamed people; that's what I told Jerome when he hired me on under the table at the coffee shop, and he didn't ask questions.

"I just did." He turns away, showing that the conversation is over. I watch the back of his head, hoping he'd turn back and explain how he actually *remembers* anything about me. Other than the fact I might have accidentally caused a fire in his building. I mean, I didn't even know his first name, and I might have had a couple of weird dreams—*accidentally*—starring him. And some of them were pretty violent with me stabbing forks in different places.

If he knew my name—a part of it—all this time, maybe he really said it on the plane, and I didn't imagine it. The turbulence situation suddenly takes on a new level of intimacy, making me feel shy.

"What do you do for a living, Ezra?" I ask, trying to divert attention from the sudden weirdness between us. "I mean other than bounty-hunting my ass to press charges."

The man owns a whole building in a very expensive district in New York. He's probably doing something interesting with his life.

He turns to me. His expression changed. "We don't need to know anything about each other. We wait for rescue to arrive and then we go our separate ways. I'm not interested in you, and you're not interested in me. I don't want to know anything." His heavy stare drills holes in my eyes. They're like hot lasers trying to put this information into my brain. "And trust me, *you* don't want to know anything about me either."

What in the ever-loving hell has happened between a few minutes ago and just now?

Trying to save face, I dramatically roll my eyes. "I wasn't propositioning you. Just wanted to have small talk. We're stuck here, anyway."

"Small talk is a waste of time," he says, turning around, and I flip off his back. My initial assessment of the man being a dick was not wrong. Unfortunately. Fate could be nicer and stick me with a cool person here. But no, I've got him, the king of all dickheads, who's dead set on giving me whiplash with his mood swings.

I eyeball him with furrowed brows, trying to figure out what kind of sand flea bit his ass at night and drank away the blood of the decent guy who covered my legs with his shirt.

He was harsh, but I suppose he wouldn't change overnight. Maybe it was a fluke before, and today the pumpkin has replaced the fancy carriage after all. Spending a night in his shelter was just a part of surviving. He was an asshole when I met him; he's the very same one as I'm learning more about him. Even though he fed me and invited me to his dry bungalow. I appreciate it though. No matter how much he reverts to that person from the coffee shop, I will always be grateful for all the good things he's already done for me. So I let this one slide.

Still, I keep my mouth shut, not wanting to be told off again like an unwanted insect.

A few moments later, commotion in the chicken community makes me stand up with excitement. I stretch my neck like a giraffe, trying to see what's happening, and find a rooster jumping on one of the chickens.

"Oh, someone's getting luck—" The rooster jumps off three seconds later, before I can even finish the sentence. "Shit, that was fast. I'm sorry, lady. I feel for you," I mumble quietly. But Ezra hears it because a weak smile tugs on his lips.

"Had a bad experience?" *Was it a joke he just cracked?*

"What happened to 'not asking questions'?" I counter with a smug smile, making air quotes.

After sending me an evil stare, he heads toward the stones. A rooster spreads his wings and makes a move to attack Ezra but doesn't actually go with it. He just jumps around, flapping his wings and making loud clucking noises. Ezra pushes a hand *under* the still-sitting chicken and pulls an egg. And then another.

"Whoa! Where did you learn how to do that?" I ask, creeping closer since the rooster is now eyeing me.

"What happened to not asking questions?" he repeats my phrase, barely able to contain his smug laughter.

"Touché," I admit, feeling like we might have broken the ice a little bit.

He checks two more spots and brings more eggs. Total of four. They are not big but way better than nothing.

"We don't have fire, obviously. So it might not be to your taste."

"Stop profiling people around here," I say, shooting a glare his way, dropping the fact that I've been doing the same to him since the moment we met. "Eat them," I say as I stare at the eggs in his hands.

"Maeve?" His voice cracks with a note of humor.

"Mhm?" I keep staring.

With a loud sigh, he stretches his arm toward me. "Take some."

"Okay." I carefully pick one egg from his open palms, noticing how large they are that they can fit all the eggs at once. "Thank you."

"Take more," he offers gently.

I shake my head. "Nah. I'm good. You build stuff and find everything and all that. You need energy. I'm good, really." Reinforcing my statement with a smile, I grab a small stone from the ground and carefully tap on the top of the egg, trying not to crack the whole thing and lose its precious elixir. When the top is soft, I carefully peel it away, revealing a tiny hole, and bring it to my lips. Once it reaches my tongue, I moan and finish everything in two, maybe three seconds flat. And I don't even like eggs. But I guess hunger can make you change perspectives.

"Take more." He pushes the eggs toward me, ordering this time.

I shake my head.

"Take it." His tone is firm. "I don't want to carry you around when you pass out from muscle atrophy. You look like you're two breaths away from it."

How is he saying such a shitty thing with such a good intention?

"I'm good," I reply stubbornly, even though my stomach

lets out an embarrassing cry. Ezra pushes another egg into my hands, curling my fingers over it. So I'm pretty much forced to eat it too and suddenly feel much better. A cup of coffee would top the cake and make for the perfect morning in paradise. But we have only water, so we go back to the waterfall.

Once we're there, Ezra goes for a dip. He spends a few minutes in the water before walking to the waterfall and standing under it like a shower.

I lean back on my elbows and enjoy the show. *I mean, what else is there to do, right?*

Once he's done with a thorough cleaning of himself, he comes out of the water and plants his butt next to me.

"We gotta talk, Maeve," he says, sounding grim.

"What about?"

He sighs. "About what we're going to do."

I push my elbows off the ground and sit straighter next to him. "Do you really think rescue isn't coming?"

He chews on his lips before replying. "I don't know. When the wave hit, the guy didn't have a chance to report Mayday. It was in a matter of seconds, honestly. And out of nowhere. So I don't know if they even know where to look. We've been here for what? Two days? And no one's here yet. We need to look for options while the rescue's looking for us. It might take them some time."

I roll my lips in. "They should have some GPS equipment on those boats, right?"

"Maybe," he agrees skeptically. "But have you actually seen the boat? It's from two centuries ago." Then he adds with a smirk, "Maybe even older than your phone. Though I doubt it."

I punch his shoulder with my fist as if we're two longtime friends. "Don't insult my technology."

"I haven't seen any," he says, squinting, and I punch him

again. He suddenly turns serious. "We need to figure out what we will do until they find us."

"Do you think they will?" I ask, because finally the reality is setting in.

"Eventually." He nods. "It's the twenty-first century, and people don't just disappear in shipwrecks. Besides that, I'm sure your family will find you missing soon. Parents? Husband?"

Did that sound a bit like a question?

"Parents, yes. Probably. I don't have a husband though." I decide to put all my cards on the table.

"Boyfriend maybe." Then he rushes to add, "He'll report you missing, you know."

I chuckle, rather sadly. "Yep, I don't have one of those either."

"Good."

"Good?" I ask with a quirked brow.

"I mean," he clears his throat, "good that your parents will report you. That's what I meant."

Sure, that's what he meant. "What about your wife? Do you think she already reported you missing?"

He snorts. "I don't have a wife yet. And with my luck, I won't."

Well, that sounded awfully vague. What's up with his luck? He could be feeding fish on the bottom of the ocean. Or he could have ended up stuck here with someone way less pleasant because let's face it, I'm a catch.

Then I eye him again. *Fi-i-ine*, he's a catch too. He's built us—*himself*—a house. Found water. Whisked me away from the depths of the ocean.

I suddenly sit up straight, pressing my palms into the ground.

"Holy fucking shit!"

"What happened?" He grabs my shoulder.

I slowly turn my face toward his.

"Are you okay?" His eyes roam over my face. When I don't respond and just keep staring at him, he says, looking worried, "Maeve?"

Without wasting another precious minute of valuable time, the weight of the situation settles over me, and I launch myself at him. I straddle him, wrapping my arms around his shoulders and hug him with all my might. My thighs squeeze him for dear life.

His body is awfully stiff underneath me. His arms are two cold, overcooked noodles by his sides.

I don't care. I'm trying to express all my gratitude through my body because I think it will show it better than my words would. So I push all the warmth I have in me to him.

"Thank you," I whisper into the crook of his neck. "Thank you so much."

"For what?" He sounds genuinely confused. Clearly, my warmth isn't working.

"For saving me. And for feeding me." I sniffle. "And for not letting me die of cold at night." I think I'm smudging my snot all over his shoulder.

His arms tentatively come around my back. Carefully, he puts a little power into his hug.

"It's okay," he whispers back gruffly.

I sniffle. Hiccup. And then start crying. Out of nowhere, I start crying. My body's quaking with each sob, and his arms wrap around me tighter.

"It's okay, Maeve," he says in a soothing voice, which only makes me even more upset. It's like a dam has been broken, and now this waterfall just can't stop.

While his hand draws soothing circles over my back, his other is firmly placed on my lower back, keeping me attached to him. It feels safe. It feels good. He feels good. Big and strong and capable.

I don't know how long he's been holding me like that, but when my cries finally subside, I weakly push away from him. I don't want to detach from him, but he's right, we need food to help our situation.

I climb off him and go back to my previous spot.

"Thank you, Ezra. Really." I wipe my nose with my slightly burned forearm. "I came off as a very ungrateful person at first. I know that." He opens his mouth to say something, but I raise my finger, silencing him. "But I think I was just in shock. I'm usually okay, you know. But for some reason, it took me a minute to catch up. I'm sorry and thank you."

"Don't apologize." His voice sounds very rough even though I know he doesn't mean for it to be that way. Ezra happens to be a decent guy. Deep inside.

I shake my head. "I have to. I'm just so used to living on my own that it's hard to accept any help."

"Because it always comes with a price?" he asks carefully, and my head whips to him.

"Yes." I watch his face more carefully, thinking there might be some hidden, dark secrets under his Adonis appearance.

"I understand."

"You do," I confirm, believing him too easily because I know he really does.

"Maeve?"

"Hm?"

"My help comes free. Okay?"

I swallow a dry lump before replying. "Okay."

The corner of his lips quirks up in a half smile, making a stiff man suddenly look like a playful guy. "I wouldn't mind you giving me a helping hand carrying coconuts to our house."

"Not for free?" I ask dramatically.

"Of course not." He smiles.

"Phew," I exhale. "Got me scared there for a second. I thought for a moment you were being *nice*. Don't go all soft on me now, Tarzan."

19

Ezra

As we walk back to the shelter, I keep thinking about her words. And how her body trembled in my arms. Even though she was right atop my dick, it didn't feel sexual. Even though I have to admit it felt very good.

What I did feel is her breaking apart. It broke me too. I don't know how to comfort anyone, let alone a woman. Yet it felt natural to wrap my arms around her and just hold her while she let it all out. I held her until her body stopped shaking and her breathing became normal again.

I wanted to hold her longer, but she pushed away. Gently, yes, but it was a sign to let go. At least one of us has a working head on their shoulders.

Somehow, in this span of a few days, she's shifted from being the menace of my existence to someone connected to me for the time being. No matter how long or short it might be. And I must take care of her until then.

"How do you know about chickens?" She walks ahead of me, so she has to keep glancing back at me when she talks.

It's nice to see someone paying attention to me when they talk and not being stuck in their own business. *Is that how people around me usually feel?* I've been focused on my work for so long, my phone has become an extension of myself, so my attention to anyone is never one hundred percent.

"We spent summers with my grandma on a farm in Arkansas," I say, feeling a sudden ball of warmth in my chest. Those were the times when my brother and I were *seen*. When our father noticed that we were like any other normal kids every time we came back to New York, he quickly stopped our visits, saying that we were becoming too soft for what he had in mind for us.

"Really?" She squints like she's searching for something on my face. "I didn't take you for a country guy."

"I'm not," I snort.

She throws me a funny look. "I beg to differ. You seemed very knowledgeable when you dove right under those birdies." She demonstrates how I picked up the eggs, looking way more dramatic than I was. "And you knew they had more eggs there and all that. I mean, wow. You're Superman in my eyes."

"Have I been upgraded from Tarzan to Superman?" I smile back. Am I... flirting? *What the fuck?* A week ago, I wanted to strangle her, and now I'm turning into some mushy shit ready to talk nonsense just to see her smile. *Who the hell are you, Ezra King?*

"Is it Friday today?" She suddenly pauses mid step. "Or is it Sunday? We should celebrate it."

"Celebrate Friday?" I ask with a raised brow.

"Yes," she replies in a *duh* tone. "Or Sunday."

I want to ask her to elaborate on the celebration of a day of the week, but she's already moved on.

"If we don't get rescued by then, of course." She snorts at herself like the idea of staying here for an extra two days sounds too absurd.

"We might," I suggest hopefully.

"Or we might not." Her enthusiasm is quickly dying. "You know, the last time I checked, I think forty-six out of one hundred and twenty or so islands in French Polynesia are uninhabited." She glances at me, waiting for an answer. When I shake my head, she continues. "And we landed ourselves on one of those." The way she says it doesn't sound very sad.

"Are you that type of person with a half-full glass?" I can't help but ask. Because since the moment we met, she's been one big bubble of joy. A very annoying one sometimes.

"And you," she taps her finger on her chin, "let me guess, no water in the glass at all?"

"I'm a realist," I repeat, in case she's forgotten.

"Okay, *realist*," she says mockingly. "Tell me your ideas."

"I don't have any," I deadpan. "Just stay alive until rescue arrives, that's it."

"Sounds good to me. We need food. And water. We already have shelter, but we might need to reinforce it. Well," she giggles, "*you* might need to reinforce since I'm pretty much useless in this department."

"You seem very knowledgeable in other ways." I'm not even trying to stroke her ego as I say it. I've never been to these islands and know nothing about them. "Is there anything poisonous here?"

"No-o-o," she says a bit defensively, like I've personally offended her. "These islands are a true paradise. Nothing is poisonous. Nothing is big enough to eat us either. No big sharks, only little reef guys and sting rays. Totally harmless. They're like cute pets. Wanna pet them?" Her eyes light up. "We can."

I wince, not agreeing with any type of shark being cute, but she continues, not noticing my face.

"I'm sure there's a lot of other stuff we can eat. I've seen chickens on the big islands but didn't know they live here too. I have no idea how they even got here." She points toward the ocean. "We can fish and make sashimi." Turning to me, she smiles sheepishly. "If you know how to fish, because I don't."

I nod with a smile, and she lets out a sigh of relief. "Thank goodness I'm stuck here with you."

My smile grows wider because I'm slowly starting to feel the same about being here with her as a companion. The world must be ending if this is happening.

"We," she clears her throat, and it sounds awfully like she just laughed, "*you* need to reinforce the bungalow. If the rain gets stronger, the water might get through. We got lucky that the sun came out because when the real wet season hits, the humidity will be insane."

"Yes, ma'am." My cheeks are starting to hurt from smiling —I haven't used these muscles for a long time. My brother wouldn't recognize me if he saw me right now.

"That's what I can think of." She shrugs. "They'll find us eventually. It might take some time, as I said. But they will. There're a lot of islands, and some of them are spread far apart. And I definitely will be late to get where I needed to be!"

One might think being late somewhere is not a good thing, but she sounds very happy at the prospect. And I suddenly become curious what sort of an event makes her want to miss it.

Am I imagining it, or is she really happy about that? I sure as fuck am. I'm treating this stranded situation as a vacation. My brother should be able to hold the front for now.

"We can celebrate Friday. Or Sunday." Then I add

hurriedly, trying not to sound *that* enthusiastic, "I mean, if you want."

Her face brightens with the most beautiful smile. "I'd love that very much."

"Deal then." I point toward the bungalow as she called it. "Shall we?"

Maeve bends down to remove a blade of grass from between her toes. Her tits nearly fall out of her bra which covers pretty much nothing. I'm suddenly painfully aware that I don't have a blazer to cover me. Just like I didn't have it back in the shelter when I woke up with her body so close to me. I didn't even have pants, for fuck's sake. All I had was my boxers, and it's not enough to contain what I have in there. I'm six-foot-three, and my dick follows the proportions to a T. Not that I've ever complained about that—or anyone else for that matter—but now it feels very uncomfortable.

aeve

He's flirting. He definitely is.

So much has changed from the man in New York to the man here. Seemingly free from the constraints of his obviously high position. Douchebag turned hero under the power of the sun. *Or clouds*, I think, glancing into the sky. The sun has disappeared, making the oncoming rain palpable in the air.

I noticed the change in Ezra after the hug. I mean, a hug can do that to a person, but I thought I was on the receiving end of it. But looks like the magic power of a hug works both ways.

I can sit and complain all I want about his mood swings and the whiplash I'm getting from them. Or I can sit and ride along with them. There's literally nothing I can do to change him. We're not close friends. We're not friends at all. In fact, we're pretty much enemies if one wants to get technical.

I doubt my reprimanding will do him any good other than making him even angrier. He probably has his reasons for being the way he is. I mean the man hasn't seen the sun in years, maybe it's the lack of vitamin D. The island seems to be healing him from the sicknesses he didn't even know he had. The more D he gets, the better his mood will become.

Speaking of D. I've seen his. I just peeked. *Accidentally, alright!* But it's a very hard thing not to notice. Very *hard.* When he climbed that palm tree? He excited the bejesus out of me. So I just *had* to throw a stick at him. Plus, I had to pay for his dickheadedness in New York. Our score now is even, and I can move on with being nice.

I shake my head, trying to get rid of the *hard* picture from my mind. I felt it too, under my butt cheeks. I felt everything. And how nice it was to be squashed to a body like his. I've never had a large boyfriend. I mean, I've had very fit guys, but Ezra is not just fit. He's huge. Everything about him is giant, including his presence. He's the quietest person I've ever met, and yet I always know where he is. He's that type of a human who naturally takes a large amount of space, and I don't mind it one bit.

"What are you thinking about?" His voice suddenly bursts into the middle of my wild imagination.

"What?" I ask, blinking away the thoughts I'm not planning to share with anyone.

"That thing you do with your face," he says with a smile in his voice.

"What thing?"

"This." He brings his hand to my face, grazing my cheek with the back of his fingers. "When you show all your emotions running through your head." His touch stays on my skin a moment longer than necessary.

"I do that?" I smack my hands on my cheeks in horror, secretly trying to erase the feel of his gentle touch away.

"Yeah," he chuckles. "All the time. I saw it at the coffee shop when you would shoot daggers at me."

I shoot him one right now too. "You deserved it."

"Maybe." He smiles.

"Maybe?" I plant my hands on my hips. "You were a dickhead."

"Maybe." He laughs this time. "You were too."

"I was not!" I cry out outrageously.

"You were." He nods a few times. "You were spiking my coffee with salt."

"One time!" I lift one finger in the air. The middle one. "I did it one time! And you deserved it."

"I did not," he contradicts with a mischievous smile.

"You did too." I stop and squash my index finger into his chest. "You made me pay for your coffee."

"Your boss did." He looks so full of himself. "And to be fair, you spilled a hot-ass coffee on me."

"I was having a bad morning!" I cry out, throwing my hands in the air. "A really bad morning. And you weren't helping with your stupid attitude."

He cackles while moving the palm leaves away from our path. "What happened with your morning?"

Suddenly, I don't feel so chatty. I recall the reprimanding I got from Jerome and the pay cut, when my pay was already small to begin with because I was working for cash, and it instantly dims my brightness. The fight leaves my body as I feel my shoulders sagging down. A moment of silence is heavy in the air.

"We can get those vines as decorations," he says, changing the topic and pointing at the trees ten feet away from us.

I follow his finger and discover dozens of green vines hanging from the trees. "As garlands? Over the entryway?" I exhale in awe, feeling a bit better. "That'd be so cool!"

"I knew you're one of those," he notes smugly.

"One of who?" I can't even find energy to be mad at him for his very questionable tone.

"People who celebrate every holiday and decorate the shit out of their houses, filling the space with junk."

How on earth did he manage to make a good thing sound so bad?

"Well, yes. I am. Life is too short to be prude and stuck-up." I let my brow raise a little with a subtle hint about him being one of 'those.'

"Touché," he laughs. "Let's go get them."

We gather the vines and go back to the camp. I head to my shelter only to be stopped by his voice.

"Maeve." He sounds annoyed. "Let's not do that, okay?"

I whip around and rush to his shelter, rambling all the way. "I just wanted to be sure you're not regretting inviting me to your place because now it might be awkward when you don't want me there anymore, but kind of don't have a choice because I'm already there. And you are there. And you know that when I'm—"

"Stop." He shushes me by pressing his finger to my lips. "You talk too much."

My first reaction is to protest, and he knows it because he presses his finger a little harder.

"Too much, Maeve."

I give him a short nod.

We should be moving on after a nod, but instead, my tongue decides to press for freedom through my lips and peeks outside. His finger is outside. I do a very quick lick, pull away, and rush to gather leaves for the shelter. His quiet and unmoving figure is making me give myself a few mental slaps—why did I decide to make it even more awkward?

When he finally snorts and starts moving, I hear myself producing a very loud exhale. *Way to go, Maeve. Way to go.*

While I'm decorating his bungalow, he brings wet mud

and fixes a few cracks in the walls. He also adds palm leaves to the roof and walls, securing them with the vines we brought. He seems to be really enjoying working with his hands. Because, to me, the place already looks good. But he likes making it better. He likes getting his hands dirty. I swallow, watching him work. His arms move, making veins pop. His skin has gained some color, and he's not nearly as translucent anymore. And it becomes him.

The more Ezra works, the better the place looks. I just wish it was a little bigger so both of us could sleep inside without touching each other. Even though I don't mind him touching me with his legs, thighs, or other parts, it seemed to weird him out. The morning after we spent the night together in here, he refused to look at me all morning.

"I'm going to run to get some water."

He pauses smacking the palm leaves and nods before returning back to work. His body is glistening with sweat, and not the fake kind models use to appear on billboards. This sweat comes from the hard work of making us feel secure. For a moment, I'm reminded why I left my family and decided to venture into my own life. Even though Ezra is clearly not a blue-collar guy, I wouldn't say that right now. So I'm just left enjoying it however long it will last.

I make a few trips back to the shelter to fill out as many half coconuts as I can. Ezra had to replace a few because the old ones didn't look so fresh anymore—the heat was getting to them.

By the time I'm done with the last run, Ezra has built some sort of curtain slash door to cover us from the side rain. I whistle, admiring his handiwork. He glances at me with a lopsided smile.

"What was that about?"

I shrug, suddenly embarrassed by my reaction. I'm always

loud and outspoken, but not to the point where I whistle seeing a dude work with his hands.

"You've made us a door," I say, trying to save face.

"Oh, yeah." He scratches the back of his head. "Figured if the wind hits from this side, we're fucked."

He said 'fucked,' and my brain got just that. Fucked. It's scraped of all coherent thoughts, and now I'm just blinking, trying to remember what I asked. Or he asked. Or he said. All I know is *fucked*.

What is wrong with me? I've never been so horny. Is it the sun? It's the sun. I glance up, finding the traitor peeking from behind a cloud. It knows it's to blame for my hormones. I squint at it with a murderous look on my face.

"You're really weird. You know that?" Ezra asks, not even trying to hide his amusement.

"I own it." I shrug and look around. "It's going to get dark soon. We should go get some food for the evening celebration and the morning after. I don't like walking around on an empty stomach."

"You and me both."

He quickly finishes fixing the bungalow and goes to wash up in the water. I can stay here and admire him from afar, but I prefer a close-up look. So I follow him to the water.

I have only one set of clothes, and constant washing in salty water makes them nearly unmanageable. They've already ripped in a few places and are barely holding, so I pull my shirt and shorts off, staying in only my lilac bra and duck undies.

Ezra has already taken off his undershirt he's still trying to wear and pants, which used to be black but they're not anymore. You'd think something so expensive should hold their form and color a bit better. I glance down at my bra I got at Target for ten bucks. The thing looks better than his ten-million-dollar pants. *I probably should lend it to him.* I giggle to myself and head into the water. What's the point of being stranded on an island if we can't enjoy the calm, warm waters?

"What are you doing?" he asks gruffly.

"Swimming," I reply, submerging into the water up to my neck.

"Naked?" He sounds totally horrified.

"I have clothes on," I correct him, not trying to hide sarcasm.

"Those are not clothes," he says with disgust.

"These cover much more than some bikinis do. And I didn't take you as a prude, Ezra. Have you never seen a woman naked?" I ask with mock horror.

"You know what I mean, Maeve. You can't walk around like that."

"Like what?"

"Like that." He motions toward me with disgust.

I glance down at myself. "What's wrong with that?"

"Your bra is fucking see through." He waves his hand in my direction. "I can see your nipples, Maeve. And your white underwear? When it gets wet, it leaves zero to the imagination. Zero, Maeve," he adds, sounding tortured. "Exactly zero." His voice almost turns into a whisper.

"I have beautiful nipples."

"I know, Maeve. I fuckin' know." He wipes his face with his hand.

"Wait." I stop making slow circles around him and stand up. The water is shallow, so I'm only in the water to my hips. "Are you looking at my nips?"

"It's very hard not to notice them." His neck moves with a swallow as his eyes unapologetically land on my chest.

I glance down at myself just to make sure I'm not covered in ocean algae which would totally ruin the picture I'm going for. When I bring my eyes back up to his face, my gaze slowly trails his body, stopping on his silky boxers. And something underneath them. The material clings for dear life to the largest dick I've ever seen. It's very well proportioned to his body. It's so big I have to swallow. Like I'm eager to taste him, and I'm not usually one to give head. There's nothing wrong with it, but I've just never been into it.

It twitches under my attention, and I swallow again.

"I see that it can be hard." My voice comes out raspy. Swallowing the thirsty saliva didn't help at all.

"Maeve," he calls out huskily.

"Yes," I squeak.

"I can't do that." His voice is that of a tortured soul.

"Do what?"

"I can't get involved with you."

I find his troubled eyes. "I'm not asking you to."

"Fucking you is getting involved," he growls out, clenching his enormous fists. "And I don't see how it will go any other way if we keep doing this."

"Doing what?"

"This." He motions between him and me. "Playing. Flirting. Tempting."

"Tempting?" I parrot. "Do you think I'm tempting you on purpose?"

He looks at the sky with resignation before returning to me. "Not all the time, but you do. And even when you're not trying, you still do. I haven't had anyone for a really fucking long time, and you being you is not helping."

This is where he loses me. "Being me?"

He sighs. "Yes, being all cheery and *agreeable*."

"Agreeable?" I ask with a high-pitched voice. "What have I agreed to so far?"

"Maeve," he exhales my name. "I really can't do that with you."

"Are you married?"

"No." A painful growl.

"Do you have a girlfriend?"

"No."

"Are you gay?"

He very pointedly looks down at his dick, still straining the underwear.

"Not at the moment," I chuckle. "Okay. Cool. I'm not any of those things either. And I'm not asking you to jump into bed with me, you know."

"I know you aren't." He sighs. "But we both know this is where it's going."

My eyes roam along the shore. "I can go to my side of the camp tonight."

"You can't. I'll go there."

"What? No!" I cry out with mortification. "You literally built it, and now you want to give it away to me. You can't do that. You won't even fit. And there's not much to fit in, to be honest."

He follows my eyes and glances between his bungalow and my shit shelter. "We will figure something out. Let's wash up and go get some food for our Christmas."

I eye him from under lowered lashes. I was just talking about celebrating Friday-Sunday, and the grump has upgraded it to Christmas. Who am I to stop him?

"And you won't be a Grinch?"

"I won't. Even though he was very misunderstood."

I freeze and squint my eyes at him. "Did you just crack a joke?"

"Don't get used to it," he says, splashing me with water.

I squeak and splash him back. In doing so, I keep moving myself in the water toward him until I end a couple of feet away. He's splashing me right back, not noticing how close I am.

I do. I notice. I feel his presence deep in my core. Deep in my clenching pussy and suddenly weak thighs.

In one of the splashes, I misstep and fall forward. Right into his arms. His reflexes prove to be absolutely extraordinary, and naturally he catches me. My splayed palms land on his well-developed pecs while his large hands grab my sides right in the underarm area. They're touching my entire side boob, and his big fingers are almost on my nipples.

The splashing stops. His eyes dig into mine. I swallow the anticipation and fear down because despite what he might think, I'm scared of him. More precisely, his rejection. He made it very clear nothing can happen between us, and he made it seem like I'm the overeager one in this duo.

But what I'm seeing right now totally contradicts that. His eyes are burning as they land on my slightly open mouth. My body nearly flush to his feels his very *hard* intentions regarding *us not happening*.

His biceps are strained. Like he's trying to hold himself together. His lips are one, hard line.

His hands are slowly crawling to my back, drawing me deeper into his embrace.

I lick my lips, feeling the saltiness of the ocean on them. His eyes narrow even more, his mouth opens a little. My breathing turns shallow. I'm ready. I'm ready to feel his big body holding mine in a different manner. Closer. Like I'm his.

I am—

A large wave next to us reminds us what we're about to do. He pushes me away, and I almost fall backward but catch myself in time.

"Sorry," he mumbles, turning away. "We need to go."

"Yeah." My own voice is so miserable, I want to give

myself a hug. Why can't we kiss? It's not like I need it so much.

I'm lying, I do need it. In fact, I don't know if I've ever been attracted to someone in such an odd and strong way. I don't know why the idea of kissing me is so repulsive to him, but it makes me feel insecure and small. Is it because he still remembers how we initially met? I'm past that point. Is he?

Cursing the water for being so shallow, I rush as fast as I can toward the shore. If I was swimming, it'd be faster.

"Maeve," he calls out, but weakly. Not really expecting me to turn around. It's almost like a mandatory bark of a not very good guard dog when the dog knows no one will get scared.

"Time to hunt for food!" I yell without turning back. "I'm hungry."

Behind me, I hear his very unenthusiastic splashing. He's moving toward the shore, but slowly. Once I'm on solid ground, I rush to *his* bungalow to grab his jacket so we can use it as a bag.

I'm stashing coconut halves in it when I feel his presence behind my back.

"It's not you, Maeve, it's—"

"Oh, shut it! If you say it's not you, it's me, I'll throw this coconut," I bounce it in my hand, "at your head. And you know I don't miss."

He doesn't need to know why. I've been prepped to become a perfect wife since I was a kid; therefore I attended all possible classes and sports because you never know what your future husband will be into.

When I was a kid, I didn't know any better. But when my brain began working enough to understand that there're ways of living other than only being someone's wife, I learned about other things. And being married to someone per your parents' archaic rules was not the way for everyone.

It might work for some, and in fact, my parents were married like that, and they're very happy together.

But it's not for me. I wanted a different life. I needed that.

All my skills from the previous years of doing different activities seem to be coming in handy now. I can swim away from my embarrassment, run around the jungle searching for big bananas, and throw coconuts at a very annoying face.

"Alright," he sighs heavily, like I'm the one who blatantly rejected him and hurt his feelings. "Let's go look for food."

"Yep. I'll go that way," I point at a random direction, "and you go the opposite way."

"Maeve," he growls my name as if he has a right to do so. Like we're so intimate that he thinks just one slightly changed cadence will make me drop to his feet. "Don't be difficult."

"I'm not," I reply with a forced smile. "This way we will cover more ground. See! Smart." I point a finger at myself.

He watches my face for a few moments before giving me a short nod and departing toward the side of the island where papayas grow.

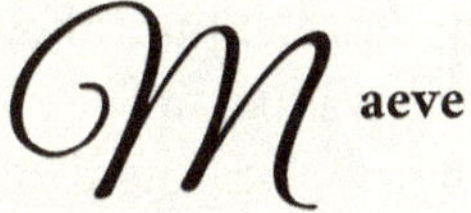 aeve

So much for a cheery time.

This morning, we had grand plans to celebrate Friday-Sunday or whatever day it is, and now, we're sulking in our own heads.

I came back with a bunch of bananas, way more than we need for two days, but I'm getting hungrier by the hour. These fruits and a few eggs are not enough to sustain my body, especially with all the walking we do.

I don't even know how Ezra survives these days. He's giant, and I'm sure his body needs way more calories than I do. We do need food. We can try fishing, but neither of us has tried making a fire. We might need it because this is the only way we'll last till the rescue.

Ezra's chewing on coconut meat while I sip water. It's dark and a bit chilly. It's not usually like that, considering the local climate doesn't allow sudden temperature drops between days and nights, but today, it's chilly. Maybe I got a little more sun than I should have, and now my overheated body is sun sick. It's an actual thing; I learned from spending hours in the sun in my childhood. This is why the sunscreen is crucial. I've been covering myself in mud, but the moment water or sweat hits you, it comes off. It takes time to reapply. So the possibility of my body overheating is very much in the air.

I subtly glance at Ezra. His shoulders are hunched forward while his jaws are slowly moving, chewing the coconut. His eyes are glassy as he's looking ahead in the darkness. The moon graced us with her presence today, and for a change, we can actually see the island at night. It's pretty. It could be someone's honeymoon destination if they had food and means to leave whenever they wanted to.

My gaze slowly moves along the shore. The sound of calm waves carefully caressing the sand leaves a cozy feeling deep in my chest. The fresh scents of the ocean and pure, untouched nature give a hopeful feeling to my fazed mind.

"I'm sorry, Maeve," Ezra suddenly says in that deep voice of his.

"What for?" The nature has been so calming that I've forgotten what I was mad about.

"For acting the way I did. In the water before." He glances at the back of his hands like they hold an answer to everything. "I didn't mean to hurt you. I just… can't get distracted now." His head turns to me, and his tortured eyes find mine. "Do you understand?"

"Yes. You were clear from the beginning when you told me we just need to survive, and we don't need to know anything about each other." I look at the quietly splashing water before returning to him.

The corners of his lips fall down. "Yes, I said that. Didn't I?"

I sigh. "You were right about that though. This, right here," I wave my arm at the general direction around us, "is only for a few days. We don't like each other, and our lives outside of this place definitely don't align."

He snorts. "Why do you say that?"

"P-p-please." I roll my eyes. "Your underwear costs more than the whole contents of my sunken luggage. Including the suitcase. You probably spend fifty-five hours a day in your corner office overlooking the city and eat at restaurants every day where your assistant makes reservations for you."

"That's..." he swallows, "oddly accurate."

"See." I widen my eyes at him. I know. Because I used to be in the same world he lives in. "And I've been surviving on ramen for the past few years." On cue, my stomach growls. I'd give everything for a bowl of ramen right now. I make a mental promise that when I get back to the mainland, I'll never be sad eating ramen—it sure beats eating bananas. "My clothes are from thrift stores, and I work in a coffee shop. In *your* building." Then add with a sigh, grabbing a banana from the ground, "Well, used to work there anyway."

"It's not my building. It belongs to the company I own."

I glare at him with a scrunched nose while angrily peeling the banana. "Does it really matter? We're not going to see each other again, and it's for the best. This, right here, is a fantasy. Once real life hits, your snobby nose will be tipped back up, and I'll turn back into a pumpkin."

"Don't you want to change that?"

"A-a-a-and just like that, your nose is back," I say with a glare.

"No, I didn't mean it like that." He throws his arms in the air. "I'm genuinely curious. You're young. Smart. Why do you stay at the place where your boss treats you like shit?"

"How do you know he does that?"

He gives me a *c'mon* look.

"Do you enjoy it?" he keeps pushing.

"Of course not!" I blow up. "But people have different life circumstances. Plus, I don't have a college degree to get a well-paid job. I've been trying for the past few months, and look where it got me."

"You don't have to have a college degree to get a well-paid job."

My turn to snort. "Right. Say it to the people in HR of every company in the world."

"My company hires a lot of people without a degree."

"To do what? Bring you coffee?"

"That too. But once they prove themselves, they move up in the company. We don't keep good employees just because they have a degree. It's the twenty-first century, Maeve. We're better than that." His tone is sure of the words he speaks. Like he's living in some alternate reality.

"If you believe that, then you're even more delusional than I am." Shoving the peeled banana into my mouth, I start chewing it like a maniac.

He blinks. Then blinks again. And then starts laughing. "You're a bit odd, that's for sure."

I grab another banana from the bunch, rolling my eyes at his unfunny comment.

"But I like it. Turns out I was missing odd," he adds with a soft voice.

"Great. Happy for you," I deadpan.

"We don't have to go our separate ways after this. I can help you with a job. We can be—"

I smack my hand over his mouth, while I'm still holding the banana in it. "If you say that word, I swear I'll shove this banana up your nose."

His shoulders start shaking as he tries to pull away.

"Seriously, Ezra. Don't."

He nods, laughing with a banana smooshed to his face.

When I let him go, a vibrant, rich laughter shakes the whole island. He opens his mouth to say something, but I shut it down with a glare and a shake of the banana peel in my hand. He bites his lip and turns away.

"I'm going to sleep. Merry Christmas or Friday or whatever."

With that, I rise to my feet and head to my shelter. A hand lands on my shoulder, making me stop.

"Take mine. I'll stay in yours."

Without waiting for my reply, he walks to my falling-apart shelter and climbs inside. *Inside* is a strong word for it. He's lying with his back on the ground, his legs are sticking out starting from his hips. So pretty much only his torso is covered. And again, *covered* is a strong word. I built that monstrosity myself and know for a fact it doesn't cover anything. The first raindrop will find its way in the inch-wide holes throughout the whole construction.

I hope there will be no rain.

It's raining.

I'm awoken by the constant sound of heavy drops rustling the trees around me. Blinking the sleep away, I sit and try to peek outside. Yep, looks like it's been raining for a long time, but I'm nice and dry. Sticking my head out even farther, I look in Ezra's direction but can't see anything. The clouds are covering the moon, and that's the only source of light around here.

I take his jacket, my shirt, and my shorts off. These are the only dry clothes we have between us, and I don't want to come back and sit inside completely soaked.

Then I run to Ezra and find him trying to fit in the shelter, without any luck, of course. His knees are propping the top of the shelter—this is how low the ceiling is. The water is running from the inside through the ground like a small river. It's pretty miserable inside, I know from experience.

"Ezra," I call out, and he makes a motion to sit up but hits the ceiling with his head.

"Fucking shit."

"Yeah," I agree, wincing. "Let's go to your place."

He—carefully this time—climbs out of the shelter while I take a step back, freeing the space for him. My bare foot steps on something sharp, and I cry out, shifting my weight and nearly falling over. Ezra's hand shoots ahead, wrapping around my waist, attempting to prevent my fall. We both freeze, until his palm slowly moves down. To my side and then down to my leg, feeling the naked skin under his touch. It pauses on the side of my thigh, right below my underwear, for a second before he jerks back.

Rolling my eyes at him, I say, "I'm not here with that sort of an invitation. I took my clothes off so something remains dry. Let's go. We're both adults and can keep our hands to ourselves."

All my talking falls on deaf ears because I feel his intense stare trying to make out everything below my talking mouth through the darkness.

"Ezra!" I call out, trying to draw his attention.

I can almost *feel* his caressing look on my wet skin. It's like little blows of cold air landing on the path to my face, raising goosebumps all over my skin. He knows I'm nearly naked, and now he can imagine that.

Now *I* can imagine that.

"Ezra," I repeat, losing patience. He was the one to put boundaries between us just to act like they're not for him.

"Yeah." I hear the huskiness of his voice even through the sound of the rain and ocean.

"Let's go." I turn around to head toward the dryness. I

hope he's following, otherwise my dignity will be left out there with him.

Before getting into the bungalow, I squeeze as much water from my hair as possible and get inside. He follows a moment later. Without pants. He ditched them by the entrance. So we are left with pretty much nothing. I pass him his dry jacket, which he takes and puts on himself while I wait for him.

"Can you turn around so I can change?"

"Oh, yeah. Sure." He whips around, leaving me with his wide, rigid back. It's always so tense, I wonder how his bones don't snap at some point.

I quickly replace my wet duck undies with dry shorts and take off the bra and put the dry shirt on.

"I'm good now."

He turns around and shifts a little closer to the exit.

"You can't sleep there. You won't fit," I state the obvious.

"Right." He looks at the space between us like it's an unsolved math equation and carefully moves closer to me. I scoot over to the side too, giving him more space. He needs more than I do.

"Well, good night."

"Yeah. Night."

I turn to my side and push my arm under my head. I really miss pillows. And blankets. And mattresses. And ramen. Damn, do I miss my ramen. It will be the first food I eat when we get off this island.

His large body is moving behind me, trying to settle as far from me as possible. Once he's comfortable, he lets out a loud exhale. I have one to match it, but I refrain from it. One miserable person is more than enough per square footage right now.

"Maeve," comes his gentle voice after a few moments. "If

you had an opportunity to do anything you want in this world, what would you do?"

I don't know what sort of question that is, and if he'll just throw my dreams back into my face for not pursuing them.

"Anything?"

"Anything," he replies without moving.

I'm quiet for a long time before I decide to share my wildest dream. "I'd like to be a fashion designer." Swallowing my embarrassment down, I add, "I'd like it very much."

He doesn't say anything in return. Not a peep. But he also doesn't laugh. It's a win, I guess.

Last night, I fell asleep watching his back rhythmically moving. Tonight, I refuse to do so. Instead, I start counting little droplets that sneak inside the wall. One. Two. Three…

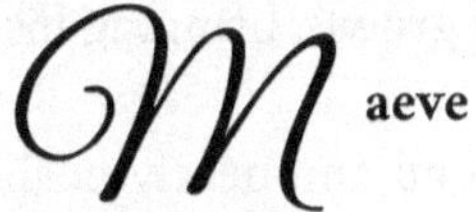aeve

It's cozy. And warm. And I'm slowly moving up and down, up and down, like riding a boat on gentle waves.

A boat on gentle waves?

I startle awake and find myself on a steadily moving chest. Half of my body is draped over Ezra's. My leg is resting on his not-resting cock. My head is on his chest while his arm is snaked under my neck and around my shoulders. My eyes are pained from keeping them so wide.

I carefully detach myself from his body and try to pull away before he wakes up in horror and finds our tangled limbs. But when I try to pull away, the arm under my shoulders tightens and brings me closer to him.

I push on his chest, but he tightens his grip further.

"Calm down," he rasps with closed eyes. "We're 'ready here. Let me enjoy it for a fucking minute." He presses me closer to him, and my leg ends up squashing his cock even more. He lets out a low moan.

I freeze. My eyes wide, my lips pursed with determination.

"Maeve." His voice turns melodic. "Chill the fuck down, would you?"

I push away from him, and he lets me this time. "You're giving me whiplash, asshole! Make up your mind about what you want! One minute you tell me nothing can happen, the next—oh!" I don't finish because he's on me a moment later. Grabbing my waist, he flips me in the air and gently lands me on my back. His large body stops on top of me, not quite touching, but just a hair away.

"You're driving me fucking crazy," he growls, bringing his face to mine.

I lift up my head away from the ground and nearly push my nose to his. "The feeling is mutual."

"I know," he exhales while he pulls away a little and focuses his gaze on my lips. "Everything you do, from the moment we met, drives me insane. All of it." He leans closer. "You've driven me *mad* from the moment you narrowed your eyes at me." Closer. "Remember that? You marked me as your enemy exactly at that moment."

"I didn't," I hiss between my teeth. "You were a douchebag who thought everyone is beneath him."

"Guess what?" His face is almost touching mine. "I still think that."

"That just proves my point." I inhale the scent of his sunkissed skin. It's so close to my nose. His presence is so demanding. "You deserved that salt in your coffee."

"And that scorching hot liquid on my cock?" he half whispers, half hisses.

I lick my lips. "That too."

"And the fire?"

"I wish I was the reason for that." I push my nose to his. "I regret not doing it earlier." I'm pouring all the hatred and desperation and regret from the past few years of my life into these words. "You and your narcissistic brain deserve it."

I want to dig my fingers into his face. Scratch his skin with my nails. He's the center and example of everything I've run away from. Everything I've detested. Everything I used to be.

He groans with so much resignation and desperation that I'm not sure how this situation is a good thing. But I don't have time to think about it because he smacks his mouth on mine.

"You." A kiss. "Drive." A kiss. "Me." A careful nib. "Insane." A bite.

I gasp for air because I wasn't ready for this sensual assault, but he doesn't let me breathe. He deepens the kiss and moves his body a little to the side, so he leans his weight on his left arm while his right one gets free rein of my body.

He slows down for a moment and pulls his head away. His crazed eyes are darting between mine. His chest is touching mine with every inhale. His neck moves with a slow, deliberate swallow like he's giving himself time to think. And me. He's giving me time to think.

My heart is racing, pounding against my chest. Its frantic drumbeat echoes in the silence between us. Or is it his heart?

A bead of sweat forms on his temple and runs down his cheek and onto his nose. His eyes dip to my mouth and he feverishly licks his lips. If I didn't know any better, I'd say he's having a pretty rough time controlling himself. So much for *not getting to know each other*.

I lift my finger to touch his lower lip, and he instantly sucks it into his mouth. My own falls open from the unexpected gesture. He starts swirling his tongue over the tip of my finger, and I feel those movements on my clit. It's like my finger is connected to my private parts with one long, currently super-electrified nerve.

The tension in the air is so thick I practically can grab a handful of it.

I bring my free hand to his hair and gently thread my fingers through it, raking his scalp with my nails. His body shudders on top of mine, sending this electric current into me. I move my hand to the back of his head and pull him toward me.

His hesitation vanishes with my dignity on this island. Releasing my finger from his mouth, he shifts his body completely atop mine and leans on his outstretched arms. His thick, corded forearms end up on either side of my face, and this is the best foreplay I need. I've always been a fan of arm porn, and Ezra looks like he is its daddy. Sometime during the night, he took his jacket off and covered me with it, so now I'm gifted with all his almost-naked glory.

And I'm not going to let it go to waste. My newly freed hand lands on his chest and starts greedily exploring all his pronounced muscles. I can't even control the thirsty hussy I've become because it's moving like a maniac on its own, dipping into every single curve of the little grooves of his body.

Including ones on his stomach area. And then lower. I can't stop at this point. I'm curious and released from the bounds of morality.

Once my fingers graze over the lower part of his body, I feel the muscles jerking under my touch. It makes me brave, so I let my finger gently brush the skin right under the band of his boxers.

His head falls between my shoulder and my head with a rough chuckle.

"You're enjoying it too much." His voice is breathless as he hides his face in my hair.

"So are you."

Another painful cackle while my hand continues drawing careful lines over his skin. The muscles keep jerking. At some point, his whole lower part gives a forward thrust, and now I chuckle.

"Impatient, are we?" I breathe out into his ear.

"Little witch."

In a second, the power shifts. He grabs both my wrists and secures them on top of my head with one of his hands. The other one lands on my throat, and I don't think I've ever felt our size differences more than at this point. His hand totally covers my throat and then some.

I swallow instinctively under his touch, and he feels it. His gaze dips to my throat for a moment before returning to my eyes while he puts a little pressure on it.

"I love control, Maeve," he whispers to me. "Everywhere."

He finds my eyes to make sure I understand. I do. I think. I've never dated a super dominant person, and Ezra seems like he can be a lot. Especially, with how truly large he is.

I'm putting my decision on pause for a second and listen to my body. I have zero doubts that if I refuse anything right now, Ezra will crawl away from me with a painful hard-on and shitty attitude, but I'll be granted my wish of solitude.

I listen and listen. And listen. Any warning signs. Any red flags. Anything that can tip me off. Nothing happens. None of the warnings come alive. Somewhere, at the back of my mind, my consciousness is trying to remind me about our initial meeting and his assholishness, but I shove it back down where it came from.

The situation I'm in probably requires me to be scared. I mean, I'm on an uninhabited island with a giant-ass man with control issues and nowhere to escape. But I don't fear him. At all. In fact, I wasn't scared of him when he was all growly and jerky in the airport, plane, and then the boat. Not even for a little bit. I was annoyed with him, yes. Mad, for sure. But never scared.

"Maeve?" His voice is borderline begging. Maybe it's because he needs an answer, and the unknown is killing him. Or maybe it's because he needs a *positive* answer. Regardless, I know mine.

"I don't mind losing it sometimes," I say.

"What?"

"Control." Licking my lips, I try to smile but can't force it on my face because I see his. It's pained. Confused. Lost. "Did I say something wrong?" I ask, not understanding what's happening. I thought he'd be happy to hear that because this is what he wants, right?

"Maeve." My name is a growl on his lips as he buries his face in the crook in my neck. "Why now?"

"What now?"

He pulls away. "Doesn't matter. I don't give a fuck anymore."

I see the exact moment his decision snaps in place. His pupils dilate even wider if it's even possible, and his nostrils flare. He lands his lips on mine.

Without wasting any further time, his tongue pushes my lips apart and sneaks in. His hands move to my chest, feeling every curve without shame. He went from zero to one hundred in a matter of a literal blink.

His body presses me into the ground with enough force for me not to even think about escaping. It feels good. I know he's holding his weight so as not to crash me, but I want more of him. I feel greedy. I wiggle my legs away and throw them around him, wrapping him in my own hug.

Once my heels land on his ass, he makes a jerking movement, brushing his length over my very heated pussy. Naturally, I dig my heels deeper, making him repeat the gesture.

His roaming hands somehow crawl under my excuse for a shirt and massage my tits. I've never been known for them to be sensitive, but again, maybe I wasn't encouraged by the right man.

The thought that Ezra might be anything but right is ridiculous because of the way my body reacts to his. I think this is the first time in my life I understand the definition of chemistry between two people. Even when I hated him, I wanted him, and I was annoyed at this, and then wanted him more.

And now all of it is in my hands. Which I use to my advantage. He might be a control freak, but I love sneaking my touches here and there while I can. I'm curious to see what he'll do further, but for now, I'm getting my fill.

When my hands graze down his sides to his hips, his stomach muscles spasm. Interesting. So the whole area is his erogenous zone. I manage to squeeze my hands between our bodies to caress his lower stomach, and he lets out a low growl into my ear he's currently licking.

"Maeve," he rasps with a warning tone.

I giggle and work my hands faster, trying to push them under the waistband of his boxers and find his cock. I've felt this thing smashing into me, and now I want to feel the girth of it in my hands. He's not trying to fight me off very hard, so my hands finally land on his dick, and I let out a moan of satisfaction. Before this thing is even in me, I feel it stretching me. I don't think I've ever had someone this size, but I'm willing to try.

I push his shorts down with my hands and feet currently still locked on his ass.

He bites my earlobe with a whisper. "Bad girl."

"What are you going to do about that?" I whisper back with a mischievous smile even though he can't see it.

He dips his tongue inside of my ear and then bites it before pulling away.

"What? No!" I grab his shoulders eagerly, making him laugh.

With a masterful and well-trained touch I don't appreciate very much, he rids me of my shirt, the shorts follow right after. For a moment, my mind races with the idea of all the 'other' times he's done that, detaching me from the pleasant present. But when he lowers himself on top of my body, again just a hair away from touching, and brings his face to mine, I'm reminded that *I am* the one here.

"You're very greedy." His voice is husky and satisfied. "I love that."

"Great. Now, kiss me!"

Laughing, he shakes his head. "Control is mine, Maeve. Remember that."

I cover my face with my hands with a loud groan, making him laugh even harder at my misery. What did I agree too?

He slowly starts moving himself lower, touching my skin here and there in the process. Until his body settles between my widely spread legs and he hooks his arms under my thighs. Digging his fingers on the top of them.

"Control is mine." He suddenly blows on my overheated pussy. "You can come only when I say you can."

"What?" I lift my head to look at him.

Then, he slaps me. Right on my very swollen vagina.

"What?" I cry out.

"Quiet, Maeve. Not a word. All I want to hear is your moans."

With that, he covers my clit with his hot mouth and starts licking. My back arches, and my hips move forward onto his face. His grip on my thighs intensifies as he continues his assault. When I'm definitely fucking his face, his finger joins his tongue, and I'm getting so high I don't think I can come down from here without crashing—

Then he withdraws his finger and his mouth.

"Ezra," I moan his name loudly. "Please."

"Not yet."

"Please." I'm not beyond begging at this point, and he knows it because he brings his body up.

"Control is," a kiss on my lips, "mine."

His hard cock slams into me. "The first time you come," he growls into my ear, "will be around me."

I wrap my arms around his back, trying to bring him closer to me. His size is big. It's stretching me to the point where it might have been painful if I weren't so ready for him. He worked me like a damn strained string.

"Ezra," I cry out. "Please."

My pussy is aching. My thighs are shaking. My hips keep moving forward to meet him.

Our bodies are sweaty. We are sleek as we move together. I didn't know I could feel so much passion having sex before, but Ezra is driving me insane with his fully in control voice and strained body.

I also didn't know I could be ordered like that when I'm about to come. Turns out, I just needed a good ruler.

He moves his face to mine and whispers into my mouth. "You can come now."

He brings his hand between us and presses on my clit. Just fucking once. Once. And I'm flying off the highest cliff into a deep ocean of swirling orgasms. One after another, the waves keep crashing into me. And as I suspected, I don't think I can climb out of it.

He joins me a moment after. I can nearly see him in the same swirling high.

His constant growling into my ear, jerking movements of

his hips, and the hot mess spilling out from the place where our bodies are joined are a clear indication that we are in this together.

When we're both able to breathe, he flips on his side and pulls me on top of him.

"You'll be the end of everything I've built, Maeve," he whispers, pulling my hair away from my sweaty forehead.

zra

"You're very good at being told what to do," I whisper into her hair, knowing she'll get pissed. I love seeing her riled up, she's not shy to share her opinion and call me on my bullshit. It's refreshing.

As expected, I get smacked on my chest with her tiny palm.

"Ouch," she cries out, shaking her hand until I grab it and plant a kiss on its palm. "You're a jerk."

"I know," I reply smugly. "But I have a suspicion that you love it."

She's quiet, but I can feel something unspoken in the air. I've learned by now that she'll say what she has to either way, but letting her do it on her own terms is a sure way to get a few extra points. And extra information—Maeve loves to talk.

"You've changed your mind." She doesn't explain what she's talking about, but I'm pretty sure either way.

"I have."

"Why?" She starts drawing little circles on my chest with her finger.

I exhale slowly, trying to find the right words. "It's hard not to when I was forced into it."

She tries pulling away jerkily, but I pull her back to my side where she belongs.

"Relax, I'm joking. It was destined to happen. It was either we'd fight or fuck." Then I add with a laugh, "We're good at both."

Her snort into my skin is the only answer until the heavy silence fills the space, and I know she wants to say something.

"You said," she whispers, "I'll be the end of everything you've built." *Fucking hell, it was a moment of orgasm-induced weakness. I hoped she didn't notice.* "What did you mean?"

I'm not ready for this conversation. Not yet. Not after everything we both have felt. On my terms, when I'm ready, I'll explain it. Maybe tomorrow. Maybe never. I don't want to destroy this blissful moment I've never felt before.

Today is too good to ruin it with the truth.

"Not now, Maeve. It's… complicated."

She swallows. "Okay."

I feel her withdrawing after that, and this is the last thing I want. Having her in my arms is the best thing I've felt in years, or maybe even my whole life, and her silent detachment hurts more than I expected.

I let her get up and put her clothes back on while silently watching her fast movements. When she's out of the bungalow, I pull my boxers on and follow her. She's walking toward the water, and my eyes zero in on her thighs. Specifically, on the dripping cum on the insides of them. I've never thought of the view being so arousing, but it is.

I fucked up.

Well, maybe not. To think of it.

"Maeve," I call her, coming closer. "I came inside of you."

"I've noticed," she replies without turning back and starts cleaning it with the salty water. For some incomprehensible reason, it drives me mad. Her desire to get rid of the evidence of my presence so fast.

"I will take care of it." I swallow a giant dry lump in my throat. "Of you."

A nasty glare is all I get for me trying to be considerate of her well-being.

"What the hell do you mean?"

"I mean." I clear my throat and straighten my back. "I'll take care of you and a baby if we, you know." I gesture at her midriff.

She rolls her eyes and goes back to cleaning. "I'm on a shot."

"Come again?"

She slowly turns her face to me and raises her brow with an obviously sarcastic question.

"I mean how are you on a shot? Why?"

She blinks like I'm the stupid one here. "Because I'm twenty-three and have a healthy sex life."

I feel my jaw clenching on its own, probably snapping a few teeth in the process. "Healthy sex life?" I repeat her words slowly.

Another deliberately measured blink from her with a clear meaning to drive me nuts.

"It's when people are of age, and they have sex. A healthy, consensual coitus?" She's waiting for my response, but all she's getting are my clenched fists and a tight jaw. So she continues. "Coitus? Like what we just did? When you put your penis into my vagina? Your schlong into my coochie?" she adds when I don't reply.

I'm about to go ballistic when I notice a jerking muscle on her cheek. I've been so focused on her words about her having sex with other people that I totally missed the moment she started having fun with it.

"Your well-proportioned member into my—"

"I got it!" I cry out, not able to take any more of her colorful synonyms.

This is where she can't take it anymore and doubles over with laughter. "You're a very uptight dude." She shakes her head and washes her face with the water.

"Are you really on a shot?" I need to confirm it for peace of mind.

"Yes," she sighs. "Don't worry, you're free, big man."

"I'm not worried, Maeve. I wasn't joking when I said I'd take care of you."

Her laughter is emotionless, and I don't like it. "I heard."

I watch her taking a dip in the water when she gets tired of wiping my cum off her thighs. It's a lot. And I really don't like her wiping it off so vigorously. I've never been into a breeding kink, but she has made me broaden my horizons.

I join her a moment later. The water is insanely hot, and it's only the morning. We can probably get some fish around here. It will be a good test of my masculinity to stand against the fish. I'm sure we can figure out a fire when we have incentive to fry the food.

I sit in the water while she's slowly splashing back and forth in front of me. At some point, I can't wait anymore and ask, "Do you have someone back at home? That's why you need a shot?"

She sends me an odd look. "Why are you so hyper focused on it?"

"I dunno." I shrug nonchalantly, trying not to show how

important her answer is. "Just curious." Just curious to see how many fuckers I need to get rid of when we go back to the reality of our lives.

"I don't have someone back home," she answers with lots of anger she just summoned out of nowhere. "Do you think I'd sleep with you if I had?" Now, she's totally offended, and I can't really blame her. I wish I could say I feel bad, but I don't. Now I know what I need to know.

She can be mine. She *is* mine; she just doesn't know it yet. My problems on the mainland? I'll figure something out. Right now, it feels like we've fallen out of the loop where everyone is moving. Like we were given this opportunity to pause and reassess our lives. At least, *I* was given it for sure.

And this reassessment sure as fuck happened. A few days without my phone, money, and name is all I needed to see that my old life with my old goals was a false idol.

"Sorry," I mumble, not feeling it at all. And she knows it. She already knows me so well because she gives me an evil eye and swims toward the shore.

Of course, I follow her. Like a fucking lost puppy.

And why did it take me so fucking long?

We grab some leftover fruit and water in silence, collect our stuff, and head toward the waterfall to replenish the pantry. There's a dark cloud on the top of her head, indicating that she's mad at me. Very mad. I know a thing which could chase the cloud away, but first, I need to get her in the mood.

"Do you want a papaya?"

She loves them, and we've run out. The last one from yesterday turned out to be rotten, and Maeve's sour face when she opened it gave me an idea how I can get back into her good graces.

"No." Her tone is short.

"Are you sure?"

"Yes."

"Alright then. I want a papaya. Let's make a detour."

I turn to walk in front of her, lean forward, and place my shoulder in her midriff.

"What are you doing?" she squeaks, digging her fingers into my sides as she holds on.

"Going to get a papaya for us."

"I don't want it."

"Tough luck because I want company."

"Even the one who will be the ruin of everything you've built?" she asks, copying my tone mockingly.

I sigh and smack her ass with my palm, making her squeak again. "Not now, Maeve. We're getting damn fruit for you."

She's quiet again. Thinking. Calculating.

"When will you tell me?"

"Tomorrow," I promise. "I will tell you tomorrow."

Would it be enough time for me? Am I asking too much of her?

Maybe. But that's all I've got for now. Tomorrow, it will be another day, and I will be ready for that. Today, I want to enjoy being left out of the loop from real life, here, in this paradise with her.

After a few deep breaths, she relaxes on my shoulder. "Tomorrow then," she agrees.

And I ask myself, how did I get her in my life? And why now? Do I deserve her? No. Will I do anything to keep her now? Yes. Am I a psychopath to make such a life-altering decision based on a few days spent together? Maybe.

I get papayas for my insatiable woman, who's currently singing "I like to move it move it" while I climb the palm. I nearly fall down from laughing because she sounds so off-key, she even scared all the nearby chickens. But she's trying really hard to sing at the top of her lungs, and she's laughing.

She looks so carefree and happy I wonder what type of life she has back in reality. Is she always this happy? Or is the island changing her too?

We eat papayas even though I loathe the taste, but she's trying to convince me that the enzymes in there are good for us. Like we don't get enough fiber eating only fucking bananas and coconuts the entire time we've been here. Which reminds me I should try fishing and go collect more eggs.

So we do just that, after I nearly vomit trying to swallow the awful papaya she's hand-feeding me. The only good thing out of it is me licking the juice off her fingers while she's biting her lower lip. Every time her white teeth sink into the pink flesh, my cock jerks, and I wonder if throwing her on the ground and fucking right now would be too soon?

We get some eggs, a lot more than before, and eat half of them right there. A skinny rooster tries to nip me, and I promise to come after him if it doesn't work out with the fish. The bird surrenders because he takes a step back probably after seeing my determined face. *I'm here to impress a woman, pal. You'll lose every step of the way.*

"Did you just have a standoff with a bird?" Maeve asks, biting her cheek in a weak attempt not to smile.

"Yeah. I'm protecting my territory." It's easy to talk to her. Easy to joke. She gets me, the authentic me.

"You should piss on that tree." She points at one of them. "And that one too," the next tree, "to mark your territory. It seems to be a big one. Big ones are good."

"I just might. Will you watch?"

"Will you swing your schlong?" Her eyes twinkle with mischief.

I shake my head, trying to force her words away from my memory. "Don't say this word anymore."

"Schlong?" she cackles.

"Yeah, that. Don't."

"Why?"

"It traumatizes me."

"But you've got one." She giggles, stepping away to the side.

"Maeve," I warn.

"What?" She smiles, taking another step backward.

I put everything on the ground, making sure the eggs are placed very carefully. "Come here."

"Nope." She bites her lower lip and hides her hands behind her back.

"Now." I lower my voice to that growl that seemed to raise goosebumps on her skin. It works. Her nostrils flare as her pupils dilate with anticipation.

"What if I don't want to listen?" Her tone is challenging.

"Then run."

She takes off a second later. I give her a head start before I run after her. Her giggles allure me from between the trees. I know where she is every step of the way, but I like the chase as it turns out. And she likes being chased. So we play.

Until I catch her by the waterfall, and we do the thing I've wanted to do since the moment I saw her naked. I fuck her from behind. While her cries are muffled by the sound of the falling water and my hand.

Tomorrow, we will talk.

24

Maeve

I wake up to a loud sound that seems too foreign in the natural perfection of this place. Multiple orgasms might have scrubbed my brain clear, and it takes me a good minute to comprehend my surroundings.

Rubbing my eyes, I'm trying to figure out where it's coming from. It's not Ezra's heartbeat that has become all too familiar at this point. It's something else.

He's still sleeping soundly with his hand thrown over his eyes. His chest rises and falls in a steady rhythm. I peek outside—it's still early. The island's just waking up. The sun shines right in my face, and I have to shield my eyes from it in order to see anything.

A boat. A fucking boat!

I rush back inside and shake his shoulder. "Ezra, wake up! There's a boat here!"

"What?" he mumbles as he tries opening his eyes.

"A boat!" I cry out and press my mouth to his in a happy kiss. "They found us!"

It's natural to assume his face would turn happy. But it's not the case. Instead, dark shadows instantly cloud his eyes, and his lips form a thin line. His jaw sets, and I can even see muscles moving under his skin.

He slowly climbs out of the place that has become our home for the past few days.

"Ezra." I touch his hand. "What's wrong?"

But he pulls away from my touch like I'm some sort of fly on his sleeve.

"Ezra?" My voice turns small.

His ice-cold eyes turn to me. "Not now. We'll talk later."

That was vague. And cold. Detached. Not at all like the man who was with me yesterday. Yes, we don't know much about each other, and he promised we'd talk today. But his tone has changed. It's not promising anymore. It's... something else.

I step backward, stumbling over my bare feet. The sand feels too cold, the air too muggy. I'm suddenly aware of my half-naked body, so I hug myself with my goosebump-covered arms.

The boat is coming ashore. Before it's even fully settled, a tall, dark-haired man jumps out of it. He strides toward us. The closer he comes, the faster he walks. When he's on the shore, he rushes toward Ezra and grips him in a tight hug.

"I thought you were dead, brother," he says as Ezra hugs him back.

Well, I expected that. Ezra mentioned him having only his brother, so it's only natural that he'd be the one coming to his rescue.

"Not so fast," Ezra laughs, smacking his brother on the back. His voice is different, carefree. Not like he was a minute ago with me.

When they're done with their hugs, the man turns toward me.

"And who are you, Friday?"

"I am Crusoe, he's Friday." I point at Ezra, making his brother laugh. I expect my beachside companion to laugh with us, but he doesn't. His face remains stoic when he looks at me.

"Nice to meet you, Crusoe." He comes and offers me his hand. I don't notice that I'm still hugging myself, so I drop my hands and grab his for a handshake. "I'm Noah, his," he nods toward Ezra, "brother."

"I'm Maeve," I offer with a smile.

At the mention of my name, his brows shoot up, and he glances at his brother. "Maeve? As in Maeve Wrong?"

"Yes." I squint my eyes at him. "How do you know?"

"Let's go," Ezra says in a voice that demands to be heard. The very same one he used on me during our first meeting. The cold, stuck-up suit uses it, not the Ezra I've come to know.

Noah's eyes narrow even more when his gaze moves between me and Ezra. Then he offers me his elbow while eyeing his brother. "Milady, may I escort you to our transportation?"

"She can walk by herself," comes Ezra's gruff voice along with his gloomy presence.

At his words, I instantly grip Noah's arm. "Thank you, milord."

Noah lowers his elbow so it's easier for me to hang on to since the man is as tall as Ezra and flashes me a wide smile. "My pleasure. Oh, wait a second." He gently loosens my arm and shakes off his T-shirt, staying in nothing but male sweat and ultra-ripped muscles like his brother. Then he passes it to me. "Put it on. I don't have anything with me, and I doubt there is anything decent on the boat. There're two guys in there," he nods toward the boat, "so you probably will be comfier this way."

I accept with a smile, pulling it on. When my head pops out of the collar, my eyes are met with a stone-cold face and thinned lips. Muscles on Ezra's jaw are moving side to side. He's pissed.

Well, fuck you, Ezra.

We walk toward the boat in silence. Noah's support is the only thing that helps me get through the walk of shame. Because this is what it feels like. Like I'm some shameful secret Ezra doesn't want to come out because he hasn't talked to me once.

Not when we ride the boat to the islands. Not when Noah is telling me the story of how my family raised hell in all Polynesia trying to find me. And how the nice captain of the boat appeared on one of the islands. He was washed ashore and was in a coma for a few days. When he finally woke up, he gave the officials the approximate location of the crash, and this is how they were able to find us.

Ezra doesn't talk. Nor does he express any emotions at the news that the captain is alive.

We go to the car to drive us wherever. I have nothing on me, so I just go with the flow, hoping that wherever we end up, they'll let me borrow some money and clothing. Or at least a phone. I can make do in this T-shirt. It's long and covers my thighs like a dress. I was way more exposed on the island.

It's not an island anymore, Maeve. It's back to reality.

And I understand it more and more with every passing second when Noah brings Ezra up to speed with what is happening in their company and an upcoming board meeting. About how they need to act fast if they don't want to lose everything they've built.

Turns out, I was wrong, and Ezra is not out of my

league. He's on a different planet. When he started talking to Noah, he shifted back into that persona from the coffee shop. The ignorant King on his high horse. The untouchable one. The unapproachable. Not my Ezra from the island. Not the man who held me while I was shaking with fear.

When I left my family, I left that world behind me. I was born rich. And I was rich until I ran away from home in Rhode Island to New York. My parents didn't tell me much about where the money was coming from, but I knew they were investors of inherited old money. That's about it. When I was growing up, knowing anything other than how to be presentable in society was not required. Therefore, I knew almost nothing about my father's dealings. And I knew even less after I separated from them. So I don't really know if Ezra is from old or new money. I'd never seen him in my life before he appeared in the coffee shop with a scowl on his face.

Judging by what I'm hearing, they have some giant real estate developing company I know nothing about because I've been living under a rock for the past few years. And the burnt building is not the only property they own. Something this big would be spread all over the internet and the front page of Forbes. But I have a flip phone. I don't spend mindless hours scrolling through social media and news, so I don't know much about what's happening with the cool kids. I watch TV at work, and that's about it. I might be young, but my mind is vintage.

I've never had an urge to Google someone's name as much as I do now. Something is itching at the back of my head. Some understanding. Some idea I might not like. I think he's from the same world I'm trying to get back to. This could be very bad. My parents won't be happy if they get a whiff of me playing survivor games with a rich dude from New York they might know. Someone who can actually be from the same social circle.

Ezra still hasn't said a word to me. He even took the furthest seat away from me. I mean, it's a minivan, there aren't many options available for a fella of his size, but he climbed to the very back seat where he sits like a grasshopper with his knees pretty much in his face.

Every second on the boat, I was aware of him watching me. But he hasn't looked at me since we stepped foot on solid ground. All he does is look out the window while his brother talks. Noah looks at me from time to time, and it's natural considering I'm sitting in the middle row on the seat next to him.

"Can I borrow your phone?" I suddenly ask Noah.

His eyes once again shoot from me to Ezra as he pulls out his phone from his jeans and passes it to me.

I type Mom's phone number and wait. She picks up on the third ring.

"Hey, Noah-honey. Did you find him?"

This is so not good. I glance at Noah, trying to figure out how she knows it's him and why she calls him honey, but I decide to leave the questioning for later. I'm too exhausted and emotionally drained for that.

"Mom?" My voice breaks.

A pause. *"Maeve?"*

"Mom, it's me."

My mom starts crying. *"Maeve, you're alive."* Then she yells to my father. *"George, Noah found Maeve!"* Then back to me. *"Honey, are you okay?"*

"Yes, Mom." My voice turns barely audible.

"Noah will bring you to us, honey. Don't you worry!" She lets out a loud sigh of relief. *"It's so wonderful that he's the one who found you. He's going to be your family soon. I'm so happy he was there for you!"*

He was there for you. Not 'I'm happy you're alive' but 'happy he was there for you.' And family? I eyeball him subtly. How exactly is he going to become my family? My mom clearly having his number saved in her phone and calling him *honey* totally freaked me out. Is he my sister's future husband or something? Can her engagement be the 'big news' they were going to tell the world about? That might add up.

"Okay, Mom. I guess I'll see you soon."

"Yes, dear! Very soon. I'm so excited!" And she hangs up without saying goodbye. It's been her style as long as I can remember, and I see nothing has changed.

I pass the phone back to Noah as I feel two hot stares on my face. I glance between him and Ezra and retreat into my seat, trying to appear small. Well, smaller. I don't have energy to congratulate him now, nor can I say how happy I am for him because I don't feel happy. Not with Ezra's eyes drilling a hole in the back of my skull. He finally decided to pay attention to me, and this is how he chooses to do that.

"Happy to be back in the land of the living?" Noah asks with a warm smile.

"Yay," I reply unenthusiastically, making his smile turn into a sad one. He carefully takes my hand which has been resting on my lap since I don't know what to do with it and gives it a gentle squeeze.

Ezra clears his throat loudly and asks Noah, "When is the board meeting?"

Noah twists his body so he's facing him. "Seriously? Now?" He sounds angry.

"When?" Ezra repeats through gritted teeth.

"Well, I was able to make them hold off on that. We agreed it happens when we find you, so we can attend it." He snaps his fingers and clicks his tongue. "Oh, right. You can't because you'll be busy with your wedding and honeymoon."

My head snaps toward Ezra like someone's just slapped me.

"Noah!" he barks.

"What do you want from me, asshole?" Noah snaps back, losing all the euphoria from finding his brother alive and well.

I try swallowing a giant lump in my throat but can't. It sits in my airway, not letting me breathe.

Wedding? Honeymoon? Becoming family with Noah? Is Noah the wrong brother in my assumption?

"Maeve?" calls out the voice that I thought had become *mine*. "Maeve." A slight note of begging doesn't help me breathe. Nor does his hand on my shoulder that suddenly feels like a brick of lead. I shrug, forcing him not to touch me.

"Maeve?" he calls again.

"Shut up, Ezra," Noah barks back and turns toward me. "Maeve, do you want me to drop him off here and drive you somewhere?"

I shake my head.

"I don't have anywhere to go," I whisper, suddenly feeling tiny.

"The fuck you will!" The asshole chimes in at the same time from the back seat.

Noah slowly turns toward him. "For the love of everything, Ezra." He takes a deep breath and exhales loudly. "Shut the fuck up."

The tension is palpable in the air, and I feel like Ezra is about to go for his brother's jugular. I don't know why though. Did he want to tell me the happy news himself? He had plenty of time to do so before Noah showed up, so quite frankly, I don't want to hear anything now. Was it the thing he said I was going to ruin? Everything he's built. Like his fucking family? With my sister? I am *the other woman* now. To my sister.

I'm about to vomit.

"Can I borrow some money?" I ask Noah quietly. "All I had was a hundred bucks I borrowed from a homeless guy, and now it's on the bottom of the ocean." I sniffle miserably. "I don't want to ask my family for anything."

I don't care if my request seems weird since I prefer asking for a loan from a stranger—hence Jeff—rather than my family, but it's hard to explain our dynamics without seeing us around each other. Granted, I haven't seen my family for years and was hoping something might have changed. But it hasn't. I heard it during the phone call. And nothing will change, that much is already clear.

"I'll give you my card," Ezra says before Noah can utter a word.

Noah keeps quiet, letting me decide if I want to accept the offered help. I slightly shake my head, so he pulls a wallet out of his pocket, takes out a black card, and passes it to me.

"Give her my card." The jerk keeps talking, but we both ignore him.

I take the card with a quiet "Thank you." He just nods with a loud sigh and twists in his seat again to face Ezra.

"I'll drop you off at the hotel and then drive Maeve to wherever she needs."

"She goes to the same hotel," Ezra orders through his teeth, using that commanding voice from the coffee shop.

I jump in my seat and face him. "Stop telling everyone what to do! I don't want to be on the same planet with you, let alone a hotel!" I point my index finger at his face. "I don't want to see you. It was just the island, right? No backstories, no attachment. Just passing time and trying to survive, right?" I start laughing at the end of my speech, and somehow, even my laughter is pathetic.

"Maeve." His breath hitches. "I said I was going to tell you tomorrow, but he showed up before I could say anything."

I sneer at him like a wild animal—I can't believe he's blaming his brother for showing up and preventing him from telling his fucked-up story.

I raise my fist in the air, imagining shoving it into his mouth so he can't say a word. "Shut it." When I turn away from him, I say, "You had plenty of time to tell me everything, and yet you haven't. I have to see my family. I don't have a choice. It was supposed to be *a reunion*. I'm already crawling to them with my tail between my legs. And you just took my tail away!"

Noah swallows. "I heard."

My head whips toward him. "I see. I bet it was a good story."

He winces. "Not particularly."

"What the fuck is going on?" Ezra pushes his face between the seats, but neither of us gives him a response. I'd like for him to know how it feels to be left out of the whole story. Just like I feel right now. And betrayed. I want him to feel very betrayed.

"Are you sure you want to do it now?" Noah's eyes shoot to the back seat for a moment.

I sink back into my seat. "No, but I don't have a choice." I shake his card in the air. "I'm keeping this though. I'll pay you back."

He waves his hand dismissively. "Don't worry about it. We're almost family now."

We both wince at the reminder of it.

The work talk is forgotten, all of us go back to our own thoughts, and the driver turns up the volume of a cheery song higher. It's an old song I used to love, but now it will always be associated with this miserable experience in my life where I just found out that the man I love belongs to my sister.

25

Ezra

My chest aches. I think I'm about to get a heart attack. Why the fuck did my brother open his big mouth and spill what I began suspecting all along? I knew something was wrong. And he knew too. The more he looked at her, the more I knew.

I saw how all the blood drained from her face. I knew this was the moment I lost her. She detached herself from me more effectively than I've been able to detach myself from reality the moment my brother showed up in our little paradise. Spending these days on the island with her was the best thing that has ever happened to me.

Me begging for her to look at me did nothing. And even if she did, what the fuck would I say? Yes, I'm an asshole who slept with you while I knew I was going to get married in a few days. I haven't even seen the bride. Not once. Let alone kiss or fuck her, but it doesn't matter now. It's her sister, and she'll never forgive me. I don't even know if I want her to forgive me. What will it change? A chance of making her my mistress after?

What are the odds of them being related? I must have done something really bad in my previous life if fate has done me this dirty.

I felt so alive. I don't even remember when I've had a similar feeling before, and like an addict, I couldn't say no to it. I knew she'd be the one to get hurt in the end. I knew I'd have to go through with the deal. It's the only way to save our company. Something that has been in our family for four generations. Something I've spent my life rebuilding and prospering. We have almost doubled our profit and employees for the past five years. And yet, my company is about to be ripped away from me.

I should have told Maeve everything yesterday, right after we had sex, and explained that it was an arranged marriage, and I didn't have a say in the matter.

But the day was too good to ruin.

And now, everything is ruined.

I wish I could blame my brother. I wish.

"Maeve," I call her name quietly, but my brother chimes in with a stern look on his face. He looks so righteous, it's fucking sickening. I know about the orgies he participates in, and he'd be the last person to judge me. "Maeve," I repeat louder. "Can we talk?"

She's staring at the window without giving me the slightest indication that she's heard me. Feeling Noah's stare on the side of my face, I turn to him with a silent question. He subtly shakes his head and nods at Maeve.

I want to rage. To grab him by his shirt and throw him out of the car for daring to tell me how to speak with her. But common sense prevails for a moment, and I decide to actually think about what he's suggesting. Giving her time.

Can I do that? I don't have it. I need to talk to her before she goes into that hotel where the whole family—including my *fiancé*—are expecting our triumphant arrival.

I can give her until then.

The rest of the drive is miserable. Maeve's shoulders slightly shake from time to time, and I can almost imagine her big, blue eyes shedding tears. I know she's trying to cry silently and be strong because she *is* strong. She doesn't want me to see that, I'm positive of it. I bet if I was out of the car, and my brother was the only person here, she'd jump on his lap to cry on his shoulder. She needs to be held right now, and the fucker has always had this ability to make any woman pliable. Not me. Never. It's hard for me to connect to anyone, that's one of the reasons I love control. If I rule the process of sex, it's predictable. The connection can't happen because I don't let it.

With Maeve, it was different. The connection came whether I wanted it or not. Before I even buried myself deep inside her. She just blew through all my defenses leaving no prisoners. I bet when I'm back in the hotel and dealing with the aftermath of my decision, he'll swoop in like a damn knight in shining armor.

I've never been jealous of my brother, but I guess there's a first time for everything. He needs to know she's off limits. Especially now when she's so vulnerable.

When the car pulls up to the hotel, I get a little surprise. It's not exactly the kind of hotel I'm used to. The greeting building is a large, one-story bungalow that doesn't look like the grand place I know I'm paying a shit ton of money for. But again, I've never vacationed, so maybe this is what people like.

When the bellman opens the door of the car, Noah jumps out first and stretches his arm toward Maeve to help her when I intercept and jump out before her. His face is marked with irritation, and I wait for his eyes to meet mine. When they do, I talk in a low voice so only he can hear.

"She is off limits, Noah."

He rears back as if I just punched him in the face. "You're so fucking stupid, I don't even know how you survive around people. Hitting on her is the last thing on my mind. Trust me."

With that, he shoves me away and waits for Maeve to climb out. "Do you want to meet your parents now, or I can sneak you into your room?"

She swallows and glances at him like he hangs the moon. "My room, please."

My brother nods and takes her hand. "We'll go this way." He points toward the row of bungalows. "Your parents booked you a room that way."

Right before they're about to leave, a female voice cries out. "Maeve!"

We all turn toward it and find a petite blonde woman in a pink dress running toward us.

"Bea?" Maeve asks weakly, and my heart sinks. I know who she is. I've seen her in the pictures of their occasional family outings. This is my future wife, or at least, as it was initially planned. "Bea." Her voice drops to a guilty whisper.

The blonde runs to Maeve and envelops her in a hug. Her body is shaking. "You're alive, Mae. You're alive," she says through tears, moving her hands along her sister's back like she can't believe Maeve is real.

"Yes, I am," she replies unenthusiastically and hugs her sister back. "I'm sorry."

"What for?" Bea pulls away and starts looking at her. "It's not your fault your boat sank, silly."

"Yeah." Maeve averts her gaze from her sister to quickly glance at me.

Bea wraps her arm around Maeve's shoulders. "Let's go. Mom and Dad can't wait to see you."

"Where are they?"

Bea looks to the side, replying. "They're playing tennis. They were very stressed, you know." *Like playing tennis can reduce the stress while you thought your daughter was dying.*

"I know," Maeve sighs, accepting this answer.

"What the fuck is wrong with them if they don't want to meet their daughter after they thought she was dead?" I'm well aware I'm not containing my anger very well, neither am I trying if I'm honest.

Bea shifts her attention to me. With a slowly raised brow, she says, "And you must be the groom."

I notice the exact millisecond when Maeve flinches and pulls away from her sister, visibly withdrawing into her shell she's created since Noah opened his big mouth. My jaw clenches, seeing her hurt.

"I see your father has made a decision without me."

"Would you be here if you didn't agree with it?" Bea looks like a China doll at first, but now her nostrils flare like she's a wild animal sniffing for blood. Probably mine.

"Maeve, you okay?" I ask in a lowered voice because there're already too many people watching us. I don't give a fuck about that, but she seems to be anxious by all this attention.

She gives a short nod without watching me.

"Let's go. I'll walk you to your room. You need to catch your breath." Noah swoops in, walking toward Maeve and putting his arm around her shoulder in a protective gesture I don't appreciate very much right now.

I watch his movements carefully, not blinking. Scared to miss a tiny indication that the Noah I know is after her. But I find none. He's treating her like a sister. I want to go with them and talk to Maeve before she clamps down even more or worse, like escape this fucking island. But I can't. A heavy stare from my not-happening wife needs my immediate attention.

"I'll come to you in a second," Bea calls out to Maeve and switches her fairy attitude back to glaring at me with her arms crossed over her chest. "So, the groom."

"Hello, Beatrice." I can try being polite even if it's the last thing I'm feeling right now—or ever—because I'm the asshole in this situation.

"You missed all the official announcements for obvious reasons, so now—"

"What?"

She blinks. "What what?"

"The announcements were made?" I feel the blood draining from my body. "Who the fuck made them when I was missing? What if I was fucking dead? Who'd you marry then?"

She rears back at my outburst, but I don't feel sorry. Or ashamed. All I feel is fucking rage.

"How about your board or whatever taking over the company? My father did you a huge favor, and you should be grateful."

I lean back toward her. "Without me fucking agreeing to it."

"Yeah?" She rises on her tippytoes. "Then why are you here?"

I don't know why I'm so mad at her. Because she's right. I knew her father would want to marry off his daughter to me. And this would be the only way I'd get the decision-making voting power. The majority of the shares would be back to me and Noah.

"When was it announced?" And why the fuck hasn't anyone told me about that yet?

"The moment Noah texted my father," she says quietly,

visibly losing all of her anger. "He called the board and said that you were found and now he's happy to announce that you'll be marrying his daughter."

I squeeze my jaw together so tight, my molars grind.

I wanted to talk to Beatrice and put everything on the line, but I need to speak to my brother first.

Without saying another word, I turn away and march to the reception where a smiling lady with a white flower behind her ear greets me while glancing between me and Beatrice. Curiosity on her face tells me that our conversations weren't as quiet as I thought.

"Mr. King, I'll get your room keys," she announces, typing something on her computer. "You have an over-the-water bungalow with all the—"

"The keys," I bark, stopping her unnecessary explanations I don't have patience for.

"Right!" She squints, nearly jumping. "Of course. Room one-oh-ten." After quickly pushing the sleeve with the cards toward me over the counter, she jumps backward and tries to plaster the same friendly smile on her face.

I grunt and grab the keys, leaving the lobby as fast as I can. The instructions with arrows are pretty clear, and I find my bungalow without troubles. It's the largest and furthest from the shore. I press the card to the scanner and go inside. A quick glance around is all I can do before heading to the fridge and grabbing a beer. After chugging it down, I change into clean sweats and a T-shirt I find in the closet and go outside. I don't have time for a shower. I need to speak to her.

When I open the door, I'm met with Noah's lifted fist he was about to knock on the door with.

"Going somewhere?" he asks with a raised brow.

"Yes," I bark, angry at him ruining my life at the moment. "Move away."

"Not yet. Go back. We need to talk."

"Noah," I growl a warning.

He levels me with a stare. "You wanna hear it first."

I take a deep breath, go back, and fall on the couch. "What?"

He slowly walks to a chair and sits in it. "First of all, I'm glad to see you alive. This is not how I imagined our reunion to be."

"No shit." I wipe my face with my hands.

"I was—" He clears his throat before continuing, and this is the first time I focus on anything else other than my pain about possibly losing Maeve.

I look at him. I actually *look* at him. His cheeks are sunken, and there're dark circles around his eyes. He lost weight. Possibly as much as I have, which makes no sense. I was the one on the damn fruit diet for days. His usually perfectly styled hair is a mess. Clothes in disarray.

He takes a deep breath before continuing. "I'm really glad you're okay."

I place my elbows on my knees and lean forward. "I'm sorry, Noah. I—" My turn to pause enough to collect my thoughts. "I don't know what came over me."

"I know." He nods. "I figured that out the moment I saw you watching Maeve on the island and then nearly biting my head off."

"It's such wrong fucking timing." I fall on the back of the couch, covering my face. "Why didn't I meet her before? Before I made this decision and accepted Wrong's offer."

"Then you wouldn't have met her," he says with a sad smile.

I shift my attention to his face and find him mindlessly staring ahead.

"Yeah, I wouldn't have."

Suddenly, he pulls his wide smile back on and slaps his

knees with his open palms. "This is the time for my 'I told you so.'"

I drop my hands. "You could have the decency to look a little remorseful."

"I'm not." His tone is firm. "I told you from the beginning it was a fucked-up idea to marry just so we can have the voting power back."

"Not the voting power, Noah. The company. Our company. The company we've been rebuilding for the past five years."

He leans his elbows on his knees and leans forward. "Is it worth it?"

"What?" I ask, not knowing what exactly he's asking.

"Proving our father wrong. Is it worth it?"

"The company was in our family for generations," I hiss. "Until he fucking decided that he didn't trust us enough to lead it. It's our company, Noah. Our name on the building. Our legacy they want to take away from us."

Our father inherited the company, and he didn't have to fight for the rights for it like he's making us do.

Noah's quiet. Deep in his thoughts. "I don't care that much, Ez. I really don't. I can find another place to work. Look what you've done already. Every company will fire their CEO the moment you resign from King Developers. I can build any place on earth, I don't give a fuck. Let's just leave."

I know he doesn't give a fuck. Because I'm the eldest one. I've always been trying to prove myself worthy of our father's time. I was supposed to lead the company. It had to be me and my brother. But now we have a bunch of assholes breathing down our neck and dragging our company down with their wrong decisions.

"I can't," I say. My words are final. "But I need to talk to Maeve. Explain things."

"Yeah, about that." He averts his eyes. "You might want to do that now then."

"Why, Noah?" His tone makes me clench my fists. "What did you do?"

He throws his hands in the air in a surrendering gesture. "I didn't do anything, but the blonde sister was storming down the path toward Maeve's bungalow when I was leaving. And she looked furious."

"Fuck."

Noah winces. "Yeah. Apparently, the eldest daughter ran away from home about five years ago. She's on a shitlist. No money. No trust fund. And today is the first time she's meeting them since she left."

"What?" I rear back. "And her parents are just playing tennis?"

"Guess so," he says, spreading his arms. "Almost forgot." He speedwalks to the bedroom and comes back with a phone in his hand. "I got this updated for you. Should have all your shit in there."

I take the phone. "Thanks."

He nods and heads toward the balcony. "I had Martin order you some clothes and deliver them here. No one knows your style choices better than him. By the way, your view is better than mine. Plus, we still have shit to discuss. Room three-three-one. It's on the left. Follow the chickens, they have a giant nest next to her bungalow."

"Alright."

I run to the door and out. It doesn't take me long to find her bungalow, but seeing it makes me mad. It's the smallest one on the whole shore. Tiny. Really tiny. Not much bigger than the shelter we had on the island. And not much nicer.

I take a deep breath for bravery before I knock on her door when I hear the raised voice. One raised voice. Beatrice. She's yelling at Maeve who doesn't fight back.

"You left me. I was seventeen!"

Without wasting any time, I knock. Loudly.

The door flies open, and my not-happening wife meets me with furious eyes.

"He's here. I'm done anyway." She storms past, knocking her skinny shoulder into me. I pretend that it hurts and step away. It's wise not to aggravate the situation, despite how much I want to tell her to come back and apologize for yelling at Maeve.

When the door is closed behind me, I look at the woman who has changed my life perspective in the short time I've known her. She looks so small with her arms wrapped around herself.

"Hey," I say quietly.

She doesn't respond.

"Can we talk?"

"You're talking already." Her voice is coarse, as if she's been crying.

"Yeah, I guess I am." I look around, not knowing how to actually start saying what I came here to say. I was in such a rush that I didn't rehearse a speech or even think through what I wanted her to know. "This room is small."

"It's fine." Even her voice is small.

"I'll get you another room."

"I said it's fine. I don't need anything from you." She wipes her nose with her sleeve.

"Right." I nervously look around, feeling like I'm totally fucking it all up. "Are you okay?" I ask when I find my voice again.

"I'm fine." A sniffle.

"Maeve." I take a careful step toward her, and when she doesn't back away, I take it as a good sign and take another one. At that, she looks like a deer caught in headlights, and I instantly stop. "I'm sorry."

"For what exactly?"

Good question. "For everything I guess," I reply, unsure of what would be the right thing to say.

"For lying to me?" Her voice is stern.

"I wasn't lying. We just didn't talk about our lives outside of the island."

"Sure. We didn't talk about anything because you didn't want to." For the first time, her hard eyes focus on mine. "Now I see why."

"It's not that." I feel like the biggest scam on the planet.

Her brow goes up.

"I mean, that's not all of it. I generally don't get close to people. I'm very…" I clear my throat. "How to put it?"

"Emotionally undeveloped?" she suggests helpfully. "Stupidly self-centered? Outrageously dumb?"

"Not exactly," I deadpan. This is so not the way it was supposed to go. "Cautious with people." She still looks guarded, so I continue with my explanation. "I don't get along with anyone, and I prefer not to. This is why I wanted to keep our lives away from the island. All I wanted was to get by and get back to our normal lives. Without forming any attachments. But then you happened."

"Me? How? Was I climbing into your lap or something?"

I smirk. "You actually were. At one point. And on my face."

Her cheeks pinken as she flattens her lips into a very thin line. I know it's probably the wrong thing to say, but her sheepish look is worth it.

She looks around as if someone is listening and speaks in a low voice. "I slept with you while you were engaged to my sister."

"I wasn't engaged."

"But you were, Ezra." The way she says my name has

changed. It's different. Cold. Detached. "You were coming here to announce your engagement."

I move toward her, and she backs away. So I stop again. "Not exactly. I was coming here to discuss the engagement with your father. Well, I didn't know he was your father. It's purely a business deal, nothing else. We've never even seen each other."

"It doesn't matter. The whole world knows now." Her voice waivers at the end. "You have to marry her. She has to marry you." Her voice turns panicky. "And I have to watch it."

She moves to the window. "I am *the other woman*. In my own sister's relationship." She places her hand on her chest. "Today was supposed to be the day when I came back to my family. I knew it would be shameful." She laughs sadly. "I just didn't know how much. You *made* me the other woman, Ezra." She looks up at me. "And now, you'll have to marry your real woman."

26

Maeve

"Maeve." His voice is begging. His eyes are pleading.

And my heart matches it. But it doesn't matter. I can never give it what it wants.

When Beatrice came here, she was very clear about what she wants.

"Maeve, I can't believe you'd do something like that to me." Her eyes are shiny like she's been crying on the way to my room. "And this is after all the shit you've put me through when you ran away."

"I didn't know he was your boyfriend," I try explaining.

"Fiancé," she corrects, accentuating the word with a glare. "He's now my fiancé according to the entire world."

"Fiancé," I agree, because there's nothing else I can do.

"So, you just go and randomly sleep with people on vacation?" She's nasty, and I don't remember her being so nasty before. I guess sleeping with her fiancé brings out the worst in her. And I can't even blame Bea—I don't know how I'd behave in a situation like that.

"It wasn't a vacation." This is the first time I snap back. "We didn't have food or shelter. Or even water at first."

"And what? You had to exchange saliva? Did it bring you close together, and you had to jump each other's bones?"

I stop letting her walk over me for a second and look at her. "Do you love him?"

"What?"

"Do you love him?" I repeat the question quieter.

"The love will come," she replies, turning to the side.

"So it's a no."

"Of course not! I've never even met the guy. He was supposed to be my ticket out." She's breathing rapidly like she's on the verge of a panic attack. "And you? Do you want to tell me that you love him after spending a few days with him?" She rolls her eyes. "He must be really good in bed."

"Bea," I call quietly as I watch her so familiar and yet unrecognizable face. "What happened to you?"

"Me?" She laughs. "You happened, Maeve. You left me with our freaks for parents who tried to pawn me off to the richest dude between eighteen and eighty in the vicinity."

"But you always wanted to get married." It's true. Since I discovered I had a brain, I wanted a different life. But Bea wanted to get married. She wanted to have a family, a kid. A big house with a dog and daisies in the front yard.

"On my terms, yes. Not when I was seventeen and the dude was forty-five."

Sudden fear wraps its poisonous tentacles around my heart and squeezes. "Bea, did they—"

"No. He withdrew the proposal after a few minutes in a room with me. As you can imagine, it didn't go well with our parents." Her laugh is humorless.

"What did they do?"

"Nothing." Her eyes turn cold. "They did nothing."

Just like they did nothing with me.

"Bea," I whisper her name like I used to when she was upset. But that was a long time ago, and she's not the same person anymore. And maybe my voice is not so calming anymore either.

"You left me. I was only seventeen!" She's on the verge of crying. Her nose is turning red. Her eyes watery.

"Bea, it doesn't mean—"

A knock on the door interrupts our conversation.

"This may be your knight in shining armor. I'm going to the bar to get shitfaced before I have to go back to reality."

She knocks into Ezra with her shoulder on the way out, and I follow her with my eyes until she disappears from view. My sister and I are typical cases of children not getting enough love from their parents. We always seek validation and ways to prove that we're worthy of it. It's been like that all our lives.

Our father has always wanted to have boys so they could carry on traditions. But instead, he got us. Surprise. We had almost zero value to him other than being married to someone influential and rich so they can play golf together and keep pretending like the world outside their circles doesn't exist. This is how they saw our future as well.

Right after I left, Father decided to venture into a different sort of business endeavor and invest in one of his old friend's companies and become an active board member. That's what Bea told me when we spoke a year after my escape. Most likely, Father hoped to find a husband for her faster this way. Or maybe he was just bored.

I left because I didn't want to be part of that life and be married off to one of his candidates.

One of whom my sister had apparently inherited from

me after I left. I didn't even suspect back then that my *engagement* would be transferred to her.

He was awful. I was eighteen and he was forty-three when we went to a dinner. Extravagantly rich with power in very high ranks.

I hated every second of it because his leery eyes never raised above my neck. On the ride back home, he groped me, and I punched him in the face. He was yelling profanities when I got out of the car and ran the rest of the way home.

At home, I rushed to talk to my parents who told me to go and apologize because no lady would ever behave this way. And he was a very respectable man. This is when I finally figured out that it would always be my word against someone else's. I'd always be on the losing side of every argument.

I got my suitcase ready the same night. I kissed my sister goodbye when she was sleeping, walked out the door, and never looked back. The first thing I did was dye my hair red and pierce my eyebrow to truly show them how tainted I was, in case they decided to come and try to drag me back to the old pervert.

They never tried.

I called my sister a few months after that, thinking there was a search going on for a missing person—me. No one reported me missing. No one cared enough to make it public. My sister was told that I ran away with my boyfriend and never cared for them. It took me a few calls to convince her otherwise. I guess between those calls she became a reluctant bride with a dowry and was presented as an alternative to the perverted groper because our calls became few and far between, and she never told me much anymore. I wish I could go back and punch him in the nuts. I mentally shudder thinking about what he could have done to her if he was so handsy with me.

I think I understand why Bea said her marriage to Ezra was her ticket out. It's not only so our parents notice her for what she is, a person with dreams and hopes. But for the escape from them that a marriage offers. When this type of emotionally abusive life is all you know, it's hard to believe you deserve anything else. I know. I've been there. If not for that situation in the car, I might have been at the same place she is.

And I can't take this hope away from her. I need to fix that. And the only way I can fix that is by disappearing again. She'll never forgive me and will never forget. If I'm here, in their lives, it will be a constant reminder that *I tried him first but can never have him anymore.* An unspeakable thing between sisters, no matter how estranged they are.

Besides that, I don't think I can survive seeing them happily married together. It sounds like torture. The time we've spent together was short. But not short enough to not catch feelings.

"Maeve," his voice is begging. "What do you want me to say?"

"Nothing." I sniffle. "Nothing you can say will change anything. It's all fucked up. I want you to go and apologize to my sister." I take a deep breath, braving myself for the most difficult thing for me to do. "Then I want you to go and get ready for the wedding."

My insides are trembling as I speak. It feels like a physical punch to the gut. It must be the same for him too because he rears back. His brows are pinched together. His eyes are full of hurt.

"Wedding?" He turns away, shaking his head. "This is what you want to discuss? My wedding to your sister?" His tone is spiteful, and I expect him to say more. To explain himself more. I want that.

But instead, he pulls the doorknob and walks out, leaving

me stunned and alone. I thought he'd fight more. I hoped he would. Feared it as well. But he just walked away.

I take a long, hot shower and pull on the clothes I found in the smallest closet I've ever seen. Picked out by my sister, I'm sure of it. She's always been the girliest girl one could find. The most comfortable thing I find are black lacy shorts and a white silk top without sleeves. I look down at my body and notice how much I've tanned. No amount of mud can truly save my skin from the wild local sun.

I don't have a suitcase or any clothes of my own. Nor do I have any money. I came here to beg for it. I can't ask any of my family for money. The only thing I do have is Noah's card. Without any other choice, I'll have to use it to buy myself a ticket and get back home.

Wait. I pause. *Home? Where's that now?*

I plant myself on one corner of the bed. *Where will I go? I have nothing. Absolutely nothing left.*

Looking around me, I see that even if I had any stuff, I wouldn't have a place to put it. This room reminds me too much of the tiny shoeboxes I've been living in these past five years. It's the farthest room from the main path with no walkway to it. Chickens have made a nest right underneath it, making it impossible to even hear myself think because those feathery creatures are so loud. A queen-sized bed takes up the whole space. With only one nightstand on one side, the other side of the bed is pushed against the wall. I'm not sure who would ever want to spend money on something like this, but I was given this particular room—the farthest from them and possibly tiniest of them all. This is how they've always thought of me.

The ringing stationary phone brings me back to the present and the urgency of escape. I ignore it. But it keeps ringing. At some point, it becomes obvious that it's for me. Hesitantly, I answer it.

"Hello?"

"You're thinking about running away again, aren't you?" my sister's voice booms through the line.

"Bea, I—"

"Yeah, I know. You're good at it." She sniffles loudly. *"But at least you could help me deal with the aftermath of everything."*

"Bea, the wedding is happening."

Her sad laughter is my only answer.

"Stay at least for tonight to talk to our parents." Her voice drops. *"You owe me that much."*

My heart breaks at her pained tone.

"Okay," I whisper back. "I'll stay for tonight."

I'll stay to become the center of the inevitable disaster, but she's right. I owe it to her not to leave her alone.

 aeve

"Oh, dear, what have you done to your hair?"

This is the first thing my mother says to me after five years of not seeing her daughter and a week of thinking I was dead.

"This color looks so cheap," she continues, taking a lock of my hair into her hand instead of enveloping me into a motherly hug. "It makes you look like you've never listened to all those lessons I gave you. Your appearance is your everything, honey."

"I've missed you too," I reply sarcastically, making her squint her botoxed eyes. They almost don't shut anymore. Has she had surgery? To think of it, I don't recognize her much. I've probably been gone too long, and a lot more things have changed. Have I changed so much too?

"Don't get that tone with me." She tries furrowing her eyebrows with no success. "You made us all worry."

"Apologies about that." My voice is dripping with sarcasm. "I shouldn't have gotten stuck on that island."

"You really shouldn't have," my father chimes in, walking toward us with two glasses of amber liquid in his hands. They both look like they are going to a golf course. "We wanted the whole family for the announcement."

"Which announcement?" I ask.

"Bea's engagement, of course," Mom explains with a smile, accepting the glass from my father and lifting it in the air toward Ezra who is standing with his brother by the table. "Your father's associate is going to become a new member of our family."

A sudden arrow to the chest would have been less painful. If I nursed some stupid hope about Bea forgiving me and moving on before, now I know it's just a dream. If the whole world knows now, there's no way this wedding can be stopped. My parents would kill the groom and drag his dead corpse to the altar before calling off the whole thing.

"About that," Ezra starts, his voice menacing. "I thought we were going to discuss the deal when I arrived. Not just announce it to the whole world before we've even spoken."

"What is there to discuss?" Father says. "You want your company back. I want my daughter married. I told you that was the only clause I was interested in. You agreed to come here. We both know what that means."

"I prefer making decisions for myself," Ezra hisses.

"Tough luck, boy," my father continues, clearly not reading the room. "It doesn't always work like that in the business world." He takes a sip of his drink, looking smug with himself. "There's nothing you can do now. Welcome to the family," he laughs smugly.

Ezra glances at me before staring at my father. "The wedding is off."

Father chokes on his drink and starts coughing.

"You can't do that!" Mom cries out, pulling on her pearls around her neck. I watch the poor thing nearly giving in to the power of her anger.

"I can, and I'm doing it." He walks to Bea who still hasn't uttered a word. "I am sorry, Beatrice. You're probably a wonderful woman, but this marriage won't be happening." He sends me a quick glance before returning to Bea who watches him from under her brows. "It was a mistake to ever make this deal with your father."

Bea doesn't say a word, to my surprise, but watches Ezra like a predator watches its prey.

"The whole world knows about this!" my father bellows. "Do you think you'll have your company after that? They'll take it away from you because you can't keep your promise. I will destroy you!"

I can tell he's telling the truth. His pride got hurt. The whole world will know about this rejection. My father won't let it slide.

"Noah." Ezra suddenly turns to his brother. "What was said in the announcement?"

"That the Wrongs and Kings are going to unite in a sacred ceremony," Noah explains quickly like he rehearsed it.

"Were the names given?"

"No."

Ezra, still standing next to Bea, turns toward me. "Then the Wrongs and Kings will unite."

A moment of silence is a welcome gift. I can almost hear the mechanism moving inside my parents' heads trying to figure out how it's still possible. I must admit I'm confused as well.

"How?" Mom asks.

"I will marry a Wrong," he says while looking at me. "Just a different one."

Everyone gasps. I do it louder than them.

"What?" Father looks between me and Ezra. "You will marry her?" He points at me. "Maeve?"

"Yes," Ezra confirms with a nod.

"Are you sure? I mean, you're a public figure, and she doesn't look like a wife you want to show off." Father chuckles with a smug smile on his face. "No one in our world would take you seriously if you married her," he finishes, after giving me a quick onceover.

The next movement is a blur. Ezra grabs the front of my father's shirt and gives him a good shake. "I will forgive you this time. And only this time, because you are her father. But you've just run out of your free passes. From now on, talk with respect when you mention my fiancé or don't talk at all."

My father opens his mouth to say something, but Ezra brings him closer to his face. "Nothing at all."

I can almost feel my father's turmoil about the situation. This humiliation he's experiencing in front of everyone. Threats to his authority. I wish I could say I felt bad, but I don't. He humiliated Bea and me a lot of times throughout our childhood for tiny things, so I don't give a shit. Plus, their size difference makes it a little comical, and I nearly want to chuckle. Seeing how small my father looks next to Ezra, I don't understand how I could ever fear him before. All those times I thought he was larger than our fucked-up life, but now, I see how small he really is. How miserable with his false ideals.

When Ezra lets him go, he walks to me. "Our families made a deal." His jaw is tight, his eyes cold. "You will marry me."

"I don't recall you asking."

He leans closer and whispers so only I can hear. "You owe me. For that fire." He pulls away and announces to everyone louder. "The wedding will take place. The bride will be different."

I step away to look at his face because for a moment there, I forgot who I'm dealing with. The asshole from the airport. The man who's always thinking about the next deal. I've become his next deal.

"No," I hiss into his face.

"Yes," he hisses back, grabbing my arm and dragging me toward one of the closed doors. His grip is strong but doesn't hurt. And this is the only reason why I'm not clawing at his arm. "I need a minute alone with my bride," he announces to the room in a tone that suggests not to argue.

"Mae?" Bea's only word for the day.

"I'm fine." I nod to her, following Ezra to a separate room which looks to be a small restaurant area.

Shutting the door behind us, he turns to me and leans in. "You fucking owe me. You nearly cost me my company because of that fire. And now you'll help to get it back."

I move my jaw from side to side, imagining his jugular between my teeth.

"You *will* marry me," he repeats, using the same commanding voice he saves for bed. "Or I'll turn you over to the authorities back in New York and you will go to jail for arson."

Jail sounds much better right about now than the prospect of marrying him.

"My father told you that you will regret it," I say to him, truly believing my own words. "I am the way I am because I wanted to run away from this life. And now you want me to return to the life I hate?"

His nostrils flare. The muscles on his jaw move under his skin as he leans to my face. "Why are you here?" His voice is an angry whisper.

"What?"

He inches closer. "Why the fuck did you come back to this island? Back to your family and this lifestyle if you despise it so much?"

I clamp my jaw tight, trying not to bite his vile tongue off.

"Why did you come back, Maeve?"

He doesn't need my answer because he already knows it. I've said it before, and he's using it against me.

"You know why," I hiss through gritted teeth.

His eyes dart between mine before he pulls away. "Exactly." With that, he opens the door and walks out, right to the bar where he pours himself a hefty drink, almost to the brim. And then he downs it in one go.

When I'm done shooting daggers into the back of my probably-groom, I walk back into the room too, where my mother rushes toward me. "You will marry him," she announces loudly with a raised head, like she's announcing the queen of England entering the room.

"What is it with you people and your obsession with this archaic tradition?" I say more to myself, knowing well enough I'm losing this battle.

"This is how our world works, Maeve, and whether you like it or not, you're part of it," she says, picking invisible lint from her shirt. "The faster you accept it, the easier it will become."

My blood starts boiling. I've been here for all of two hours, and my parents have already put the weight of their decision-making on my shoulders. They've always done that. Always making life-altering decisions for us, only to inform us when it's a done deal.

I shift my attention to Ezra who's watching me from behind the rim of yet another full glass. His stare is intense. He's not the same person I spent the last week with. He's just another dictator.

If I marry him, I get financial freedom. I think. He's

wealthy, and he'll become even more so after this deal is done—he clearly needs something valuable from my father if he's willing to marry me of all people. Plus, I get to be away from them, my own family, who obviously didn't miss me much.

Half of all marriages end up in divorce, and we for sure will be among them. I'll just have to figure out how to survive until then.

I find my sister who still hasn't uttered a word throughout the whole scene. She's silently watching everyone in the room with arms crossed over her chest. Her stare is heavy. Offended.

She was the one who wanted to marry him. Will she forgive me if I take this unfortunate opportunity as my own way out? Maybe I can help her when I have my freedom.

"Okay," I sigh, making everyone let out the breath the whole room had been holding. All for different reasons.

The only one that surprises me the most is Ezra's. It's not victory I see in his eyes.

It's relief.

aeve

A knock on the door of my tiny bungalow brings me back from the memories of the day. I was about to take a warm bath and fall asleep for the next ten years and possibly miss the wedding. We haven't set the date yet, so I have hope left that it still might not happen at all. Maybe my parents will find some decency and let me off the hook. Maybe even Ezra finds some and stops threatening me with jail.

When I open the door, I find my sister with arms still crossed over her chest and a hip popped to the side. I step aside, letting her in. She walks in, fumes coming out of her ears.

"Hello, Bea," I probe carefully, trying to figure out the level of her anger.

"You can't go through with this wedding," she starts off the bat, turning toward me.

"Why?"

"Because he was mine first." Her chin goes up.

"He wasn't yours, Bea." My voice is careful. Considerate. Suddenly, I don't like her calling him hers. "You've never even met him. Plus, you don't really want him."

"But we were announced as a couple. He was going to go through with it until Dad opened his big mouth," she says, rolling her eyes.

I walk to the couch and sit. "You don't want him, Bea," I repeat. "He's not that much different than Mom and Dad are."

"And you are suddenly okay with that?" She laughs. "You agreed pretty fast for someone who doesn't want to be tied to anyone."

I chew on my lower lip, contemplating if I should tell her the truth. I don't know this person after all. Beatrice has changed a lot since I've seen her last. So have I. But seeing her worried eyes and anxious foot tapping on the floor makes me believe that we both will benefit from me opening up to her.

"We knew each other from before all of this," I start quietly.

"Oh," she exhales surprisingly. "From New York?"

"Yes," I confirm. "I was working in the building he worked at. Well, he owned. Still owns I think. And I might have accidentally started the fire there." I wince at the end, remembering how that night went down. "And then I might have escaped the hospital when he came to press charges against me."

"Ohmigod!" she exclaims, jumping to my side and taking a seat next to me. "Are you okay? What happened?"

Sincere concern in her voice makes my chest ache.

"I fell asleep next to the electric oven. And I guess it went up in flames. I woke up when it had already caught fire."

Her eyes squint. "And the asshole wanted to press charges for that?"

"I mean..." I'm looking for the right words without it seeming like I'm trying to save him in her eyes. Because that would be totally ridiculous. "The city shut down the whole building. Indefinitely, I assume. So yeah." I shrug. "I guess he has it out for me."

Her mouth forms an *o* before she turns her worried face to me. "So he wants to marry you to make your life miserable?"

"Maybe. I don't know." I shrug again. "I don't know much about him."

"Besides the size of his dick apparently," she mumbles under her breath. Just loud enough to ensure I could hear her.

I clear my throat before speaking. "I didn't know he was engaged. You know me."

"Do I?" She looks at me, tilting her head to the side. "It's been five years, Maeve. A lot of things have changed. Plus, I didn't think you would escape in the middle of the night like you did. So I guess I've never really known you."

My heart squeezes in my chest. "That's not fair. You know what they did."

"Yeah, I know." She smiles sadly. "You know why? Because when you left, they kept doing that to me. They treated me like furniture they had to show and marry off to the best candidate."

"And you think Ezra is the best candidate?"

"He's under thirty and doesn't have a saggy butt," she explains, rolling her eyes. "Trust me, better than the last ten dates Mom sent me on. He was supposed to be my ticket out, you know. I thought I could be rid of them."

"But you'd be in a loveless marriage."

She snorts. "I don't believe in love anymore. Marriage is a transaction. And this one was a very clear one."

I tilt my head, watching my very romantic sister speaking pragmatically. A lot has changed, that's for sure.

"What is Ezra getting out of it?"

She walks to the window and peeks outside. "Dad's shares so he can get the voting power back or something. I guess their dad brought in the board when he retired because he didn't trust his eldest son to keep it afloat."

Oh, that might suck. This might be one of the reasons Ezra is the way he is. Cold, calculated, calloused. Daddy issues can do that to anyone.

"So, he really needs this marriage," I think aloud.

"He needs the dowry that comes with it. That'd be a win-win. Dad executes his lifelong dream and marries his daughters into even more money, and King gets control of his company back. Somewhat."

"Huh."

Bea's turn to narrow her eyes and stare at my face, looking for answers. "Why did you agree to marry him so easily? Isn't that why you ran away in the first place?"

"Blackmail," I sigh, telling one part of the truth.

"What?" Her brows jump to her tan hairline.

"He said he'll put me in jail if I don't marry him."

Now her brows draw together in confusion. "Why not marry me then?"

I chew the inside of my cheeks, not knowing what to say. Deep down, I wish the answer would be that he got so connected to me, that he simply didn't want to have another woman by his side. But in reality, I don't think he's that type of person. In reality, he's more like my father than I'd like to admit.

When everyone is sure I am the intended bride, I'm graciously moved into a more spacious room. A bungalow to be precise, sitting over the water. It has an adjoined room and a shared balcony. I can only suspect it's my groom's because this bungalow looks to be the largest one. And those are saved as 'honeymoon suites.'

Needless to say, I'm not complaining about the change, considering the old room didn't even have a decently working air conditioner. This suite is like something you'd expect from a five-star resort. Something I forgot existed.

While I'm admiring the ocean view from the window, a knock comes at the door. I'm not surprised to find my father when I open the door. He pushes past me without waiting for an invite.

"The wedding is tomorrow morning. Your mother secured the official. Be ready."

He literally makes a three-sixty halfway through the room and walks out, leaving me standing with an open mouth and blinking. Shit just got too real, too fast.

29

Ezra

"Are you sure about this?" Noah asks me for the millionth time in the past twelve hours. "I don't give a fuck about the company and even less about our father's approval. You shouldn't either."

"Leave it, Noah. I'm going through with it."

He comes to fix my tie like I'm twelve. Apparently, it's very easy to get a custom-made suit overnight if you're very determined to do so. And Mrs. Wrong was very determined. She secured an official for the ceremony in less than an hour. On a weekend. After ten p.m. The decision about setting the wedding day was done yesterday at eight in the evening. By midnight, we had everything set up.

"If I didn't know you any better—which I do, of course," he says with a smug smile, "I'd say you actually *want* to go through with this marriage."

I snort, pushing his hands away. "Right. I've never wanted

to get married. Much less to someone like her," I say, suddenly hating myself for no obvious reason. I've said and done worse things. So why does the idea of putting this information out there not sit right?

"Someone you like, you mean?" my annoying brother asks with a quirked brow I'd like to punch.

"No," I grit out. "Someone so out of my world."

"But she isn't, is she?" Noah asks carefully. And I know what he's doing. We both do. "She's from your world."

"Is she?" I question his sanity. "She detests everything I work for."

"And yet, here we are," he singsongs, looking happy with himself. "Getting you up and ready for your *just-married* night." He can barely contain his laughter. "Oh wait." He brings his index finger in the air. "You've already done that."

I stare him down. "I don't need to get ready. I'm not fucking eighty."

"You'd be surprised," he mumbles, and then adds louder, "Anyway, you liking her might actually make this situation bearable. I know you've been forced into it, but so has she. Don't forget about that." Then he adds with a dark chuckle, "To think of it, she's got the worst end of this deal. Living with you, brother. For five years?" A shake of his head. "Especially with you behaving like a Neanderthal because you like her and don't know how to treat her 'cause of that. Like pulling pigtails in school."

"I don't like her, Noah." It comes out as a growl. "And the idea of being married to her sounds like torture." I pause, contemplating if I should tell him the whole story. "Do you remember what I mentioned about the chick in the fire?"

His forehead wrinkles with concentration. "Yeah, something about a homeless woman sleeping there. That's about it."

I didn't tell him the whole story. For some incomprehensible reason, I didn't want to share it. Maybe I wanted to keep her indebted to me only. Maybe it was something else.

"The cops thought she caused the fire."

"No fucking way." He falls into the chair with an open mouth. "Can we charge her? Will it help to save the company?"

"It will," I answer vaguely. "But not for the reason you think. Maeve is the woman from the fire. Blackmailing her into marrying me is a good way to ensure we'll get the shares because she'll stay married for all the years it's needed to retain them." I drop the part where I could easily marry the other sister and be done with it—she was very eager to escape her 'fantastic' family and for sure would have stayed for five years written in the contract Wrong presented me. He'd transfer the shares the moment we sign our names, but they go back if the marriage is done before the five-year mark.

"Maeve?" He blinks.

"Maeve." I nod.

"The homeless person sleeping in our building is the daughter of a multimillionaire? The very same one you're about to get married to?" His eyes keep widening with every word as they settle in his mind.

"Yes, it's her. So we've known each other. And man," I wipe my face with my hand, "she's one hell of a disaster. I mean, from the first moment I met her, she's been fucking with me."

"Wait, wait, wait." He stops me with a raised hand. "Is she the same one who kept messing with your coffee in the mornings and made you a fire-breathing dragon before you even stepped foot in the office?"

I nod.

"Oh, shit." He starts laughing. "This is going to be interesting. You definitely should go through with this marriage. It will be entertaining if anything."

I gloom over his words. His enthusiasm and sudden change of his opinion about this scheme make me pause and wonder if I'm actually doing the right thing. If my brother so easily agrees to it, it's probably not.

"She's cool," he continues explaining why I should go with it. "Smart, funny, from what I've gathered so far. And beautiful."

I snort. "And entitled. She can't do anything. I mean, nothing. Everything she touches goes up in flames." Including my skin and mind. When she touches me, I'm a goner. This is why I can't let this deal become more than just a deal.

"You mean literally I suppose," he cackles.

"That too."

Something rattles outside, and Noah rushes to check it. He opens the door to the balcony and lets out a surprised gasp.

"Hi." His voice is one of a squeaking rabbit.

"Hello, Noah."

At Maeve's calm voice, my heart freezes. How long has she been there?

"How are you?" Noah asks, trying to sound cheerful. No Oscars for this guy anytime soon. "What are you doing here?"

"Our rooms are adjoined," she explains calmly, jerking her head at another door. "And we share the balcony."

"Yeah," Noah laughs shakily. "I see that."

"Maeve," I call, coming outside.

Wearing a fluffy, white robe, she's leaning her elbows on the rails, staring at the ocean without acknowledging me.

"Maeve," I repeat. "I—"

What am I going to say? I can't say shit with Noah here. He's my assurance that I won't turn into something I'm not. That I won't change the goals I've been trying to reach all my life. One week on an island wouldn't change that. It shouldn't.

"See you in two hours," she says, turning away and disappearing inside of her room.

"Fuck." I cover my face with my hands and walk back inside.

"Fuck indeed. I like Maeve," Noah starts, earning an angry glare from me. "Not like that," he adds, throwing his hands in the air. "Just like a person. She seems very genuine and caring."

"She is," I sigh. This is something I've learned about her so far. She can be prickly, but she always cares.

"And you like her."

I grunt, not exactly agreeing with him.

"It was just the circumstances. The mainland and real life will change everything."

"Maybe. Maybe not." Then he adds, changing the subject. "When will he transfer the shares?"

"When the marriage is sealed."

"You mean after you fuck?" he asks with amusement.

"No, asshole. When we sign the certificate."

"Works for us. Did you get the ring?"

"Martin ordered it. It's over there." I point at the nightstand. It was delivered this morning.

"You asked your assistant to buy your bride a ring?"

"It's an arrangement." I shrug one shoulder, trying to convince us both of how uncaring I am about all of this. "I don't give a fuck what she wears as long as she does."

A gloomy cloud comes over his head, annoying the hell out of me. He always does that.

"What?"

"I mean, you're getting married anyway. Why not put some effort into it?"

"It's an arrangement," I growl. "I don't give a fuck."

His prolonged silence makes me turn toward him. "What?"

He doesn't respond. Just shakes his head with quiet disappointment.

aeve

"Such a douchebag," Bea fumes when I walk back inside. The flowy skirt of her knee-long pink dress follows her like a veil. This is what she'd wear every day when we were kids.

"You heard?"

"The whole island heard." Her little nostrils flare as she jumps to her feet. "You don't have to go through with that, you know. Fuck him. Let's just run away somewhere together."

"I've tried that," I say with a sad smile. "And look where it landed me."

"It landed you right back to me. Maybe it's destiny." She walks up to me and takes my hand. "He's not getting you." She speed walks to the closet and pulls out the suitcase she brought for me yesterday.

"I thought you wanted him for yourself."

She rolls her eyes. "That was before I learned a few things

about him. You're doing me a favor by taking him off my hands. But really, let's just leave. I have some money stashed away; it will be enough for us for a couple of months. And then we will figure something out."

"I can't," I whisper.

"Why?" Her brows draw together.

"I don't want to go to jail," I explain quietly.

"He won't go through with that." She sounds a little doubtful. "Plus, he knows our parents now. It'd be awkward."

"Parents that hold the voting shares for his company he's about to lose," I remind her. "If he can't get the shares, he'll do it out of spite. I go to jail. They get cast out from the society because of their wayward daughter: me." I point a finger at my chest. "So yeah, I can see all of it happening. And no matter which scenario I go with, I always end up locked up."

That draws her attention and makes her stop moving around my closet.

"He can blackmail *them* with my jail."

"And they'd let him." She resumes her chaotic activity.

"What do you think they'll do to me for that?"

She stops again. "Probably deliver you to jail themselves. If it comes *from them*, it gives them extra points with the society for being good citizens."

"Yep."

"Shit."

"Yep."

A knock on the door interrupts our conversation. Expecting my mom to rush inside and smother me with her threats, I open the door wide. But it's not my mother. In fact, I don't even know who it is because the whole space alongside the doorframe is covered in white tulle. It's everywhere. It's giant. It's sparkly.

"What the—"

Someone on the other side moves this white monstrosity through the frame, getting stuck halfway in. With a few French curses, the person pushes through. A tall Tahitian lady can barely manage what I assume is the wedding dress.

"Where do you want it?" she asks, trying to wipe sweat from her face with her shoulder.

"Here." My sister jumps into action. "On the bed."

The lady drops the dress on the bed—not so gently may I add—and rushes outside without waiting for any signatures or anything really. All we hear is her constant "Merde."

I walk up to the bed. "Is that...?"

"Your dress." Bea points at the white, sparkling monstrosity.

I whip my head toward her. "No fucking way I put this on."

It takes us forty-five minutes to put it on, and it's as hideous as I expected. It's big. Really big. But very tight. In fact, we can barely tighten the corset.

"Breathe out," Bea orders while pushing her knee into my ass. I'm not sure how she's managing to keep balanced and not fall. "Exhale, Maeve. For fuck's sake."

"I can't breathe!" I squeak. "I can't wear this."

"No pain, no gain," she grunts. "This was Mom's dress. You know it's a tradition to be married in that."

"Why the hell does she have this dress with her on vacation?"

Bea puffs, trying to pull my corset closed, nearly breaking my ribs. "She's had it with her since you turned eighteen."

I try to turn my head back to look at her, but she smacks my shoulder to stay still. "How come I've never known that?"

"Because you ran away almost as soon as you turned

eighteen. And then I guess she was saving it for me," she explains nonchalantly. And for the tenth time—today only—I wonder what she's been going through while I was gone. In our century, no one should be expected to get married when the opportunity arises just to satisfy their parents. It's barbaric and not what we've been evolving for.

"I'm sorry, Bea," I mutter, not knowing how to express how truly sorry I am for leaving her. Not them, but her.

"It's fine."

To my surprise, she does sound fine. Too fine. Too happy.

I'm happy that she's happy. But why is she? She was so upset the other day when she figured out she wouldn't be the one marrying Ezra.

"Ouch!" I cry out as her knee digs into my butt while she pulls the strings too hard.

"All done!" she exclaims happily, stepping aside to look at her creation.

I turn to face the mirror and cry out. Literally in horror.

First of all, my mom was like two to three sizes smaller than I am, and this corset barely covers my nipples. I can't breathe because it's too tight, and my boobs are about to push my head off my neck.

Second, the dress itself has a large skirt and underskirt and fifty thousand rings underneath it. It makes me look like Cinderella if her dress was on steroids. And not the good kind. I'll need a double door if I want to fit anywhere. Or triple.

Third, the feathers. The dress has feathers. I never noticed them in Mom's wedding pictures, but here they are. In big quantities. Sprinkled throughout the whole skirt, they make me look like I've just had a fight in a chicken coop and lost.

The corset is sparkling with gemstones and diamonds. I detest them. That's what I was forced to wear once I turned thirteen. And when you wear a shit ton of diamonds, you're automatically excluded from being a normal kid doing normal kid stuff.

"Oh, no."

"You don't have a choice." Bea rushes to me and grabs the front of my corset. Trying to pull it toward her, she says, "Can you, maybe, like push the girls down a bit before they suffocate you?"

"Let me try."

I push on my boobs from the top while she keeps pulling on the corset. But it's stuck to my body as though my own skin has been replaced by lace. Bea did her job very well, trying to attach the damn thing to my body.

"Okay," she says, stepping back with a puff. "You look good just like that."

A wince on her face tells me all I need to know.

"You've always been a bad liar."

I start walking toward the closet, but nearly trip over my own feet getting stuck in the skirt.

"Where are you going?"

"To change into something else. I'm not getting married in *that*." I glance down at myself.

"Yeah, good idea," she agrees easily and joins me in the closet.

The door suddenly bursts open, but I don't remember sharing the keycard with anyone.

"You look amazing!" Mom exclaims as she steps into the closet with us. With the three of us and this damn dress, there's not enough space to even move around. But it doesn't seem to bother her. She steps right to my face and starts fixing my hair around my shoulders with a disapproving glare. "You should have put your hair up. This dress should be worn with an updo," she finishes, clicking her tongue. "I looked so much different. I had to starve myself for two months to fit in it. You certainly could have stayed on that island a little longer. And that atrocious hair color," a dramatic shudder, "cheapens this wonderful dress."

I share a quick glance with Bea but don't say a word. Anything we say will be used against us.

"Anyway, time to go."

"What? It's almost another hour until the wedding."

"We moved the time." She claps her hands. "How exciting is it?"

"No! Why? No!"

"Yes!" Mother's eyes sparkle like the diamonds on my dress. "Let's go." She grabs my arm and pulls me away with her.

"Wait. Mom, wait! I don't even have shoes on."

"You don't need them," she says while pulling me toward the door with her iron grip.

I stumble a few times, but it doesn't seem to stop her. Bea runs after us and tries to grab the hem of the dress in her hands, so I don't fall face-first.

"Why don't I need shoes, Mom?"

"We moved the wedding to the beach. It's better for the pictures." She chuckles. "Imagine the headlines: Wrongs keep the long-lived tradition going by allowing their daughter to get married on the beach."

There's so much wrong with her gleeful words, but I don't have time to get into that because all I'm trying to do is not trip over my dress and keep my nose attached to my face.

Bea mumbles something behind me, clearly mad at Mom's words.

When we get to the opening on the beach, the first thing I notice is the groom standing under a giant arc of white gardenias. Two small round tables on each side of it are covered in white candles and more flowers.

Wearing a black suit with a white shirt and black tie, Ezra

looks anything but like a happy husband-to-be. With his nose deep into his phone, it feels like this wedding is the last place he wants to be. Noah's standing by his side, whispering something to him with a hand on his shoulder. He has a black suit on as well, but no tie.

At some point, Ezra's jaw squeezes shut, and he shakes his head. After that, Noah pulls away and stops talking.

There're a few people I don't know, some of them are photographers who will make sure the world will get a very unrealistic picture of the perfect ceremony. My father's waiting for me at the beginning of the aisle.

When someone notices us, the music starts playing. A live band is performing the classic Wedding March, the music that's supposed to bring excitement to everyone's hearts.

Ezra brings his face up. His brows suddenly draw together, nearly forming one line.

Even this hideous dress can't change how beautiful Maeve is.

I'm not a fashion expert, but the thing she's wearing is atrocious. Besides that, I don't think she can breathe. I know her tits are juicy, but right now I think they're too juicy. I mean, they are right next to her neck. And every single man in the vicinity is salivating over them.

I don't like it. I licked them first. They are mine.

Her father offers her his elbow, and she grabs it, nearly tripping over the dress, which is clearly way too long for her.

They start walking. To be precise, they try walking, but the skirt of that dress is so wide they can't fit together without them both tripping over it. Mr. Wrong takes a couple of steps to the side and stretches his arm to her. She tries to lean on him with no success, and I see the moment she gives up on the whole idea of fighting with the dress. Accepting his elbow with her one hand and trying to grab a part of her giant skirt with another, she ends up pulling feathers off it with every single try. By the time she manages to get a hold of the skirt, her cheeks are pink with anger.

The whole walk toward us is painful to watch. They trip, bicker, and then trip again. By the time they reach us, Maeve's face is totally red. Large beads of sweat roll down her temple and then down her neck. Then they disappear right between two big globes pushed to the top. They are pushed so close together, the drops have to fight their way through.

With a wide, happy smile, her father passes her hand to me. I try taking it, but she stumbles again and rears back, trying to gain her balance. In the process, the dress moves one of the tables on the side. I rush to help her, but surprisingly she quickly finds herself on her own feet and squares her shoulders back as if preparing for the fight of her life.

"Dear guests," the official starts. "We've gathered here—"

A faint smell of smoke suddenly reaches my nose, but I disregard it. It intensifies a moment later.

"Shit!" I jump around Maeve because apparently her dress caught fire from one of the candles when she bumped into the table. "Fire!" In a second, I start throwing sand on the fire while it starts rapidly moving up the skirt of the dress toward her body.

She whips around on instinct, moving the fire far away from my attempts to stop.

"Don't move, Maeve," I order, throwing more sand on her.

"Shit!" Noah rushes in and joins me.

"Hot! Hot! Hot!" Maeve starts swirling around like a hamster on a wheel, and the fire moves even faster. She'll get bad burns in a few seconds, so I need to act fast.

"Stop!" I bark and put my foot on the skirt. She keeps trying to move, but Noah does the same, and we both are able to stop her. I grab the waist of the skirt and try to rip it apart from her body. Little feather fireflies and gemstones or whatever the fuck they are fly away, igniting even more feathers on the way. It takes me a few seconds to try to get her rid of the flaming skirt, and it's a few seconds too long.

Beatrice drops to her knees next to us, joining us in our attempts to throw sand onto the flames.

"Hot, Ezra! It's hot!" Maeve cries out, her voice turning desperate.

My own blood is boiling as I'm ripping into many layers of the dress while Noah's trying to do the same. It's not working. The feathers catch fire too soon, erupting into little volcanic flames, making her squeal. Her scared voice makes me move faster. It's taking too long. Might be too late.

"Move away," I yell to Noah who instantly jumps back.

I grab her by her waist, reach the ocean in three long strides and throw her in the water. It's not deep but she sinks to her waist. I'm next to her in a second, trying to rip the rest of the skirt away.

When it's floating away, and I'm left with her trembling body in my arms, I let my eyes assess the situation.

Her hands are holding onto my shoulders. Her eyes are wide and unfocused. I grab her by her waist again and lift her up from the water, checking her legs for damage. Thank God I find none.

"Back, back! Put me back."

I quickly obey her request, hoping that a slightly chill morning ocean will cool down her skin.

"Where does it hurt?"

"Legs. Just hot. Very hot." Her voice is shaky.

"Let me see." I lift her up again.

"It's fine." She gulps for air like she's about to have a panic attack. "It's not burnt. I don't think so. Just hot. Let me sit in the water."

"Ezra?" comes Noah's voice. "Is she okay?"

"I think so," I reply, without turning to him. Odd that he's the only one interested with her whole family present.

"Maeve?" comes Beatrice's voice. "Are you okay?"

"I'm okay," she whispers and starts chuckling.

"What?"

"The fire?" she giggles. "Seriously? Again?"

I snort, only now comprehending the irony of the situation. The fire has come full circle.

"Are you really okay?" I ask quietly, letting a note of emotion slip into my voice.

"Yes." She nods. "I'm fine."

"Well, everyone is alive. Shall we continue?" comes her mother's voice, nearly making me bark at her to shut the fuck up and read the room.

"Wrongs are a very determined bunch," Maeve whispers with a small smile and rises to her feet.

"Do you want to stay here a little longer?"

"No. Let's go."

I'm helping her to the beach where a few cameras are pointed in our direction. Every single one of them was hired by the Wrongs—I'd prefer to avoid publicity. But whatever comes out of it, we still should have a wedding photo.

I glance down at Maeve. With the worry of the moment gone, I finally notice that she's wearing nothing but white panties, similar to those she wore on the island, and a corset. Nothing else. Nothing. Her wet panties are see through. For everyone. With her tits out like that and now her ass, I'll have to go through many brawls by the end of the ceremony.

"Take it," I say, pulling off my wet suit blazer and fixing it on her shoulders.

"Thank you," she whispers back gratefully, pulling the front of the blazer together. It looks so big on her, only the tips of her fingers come out of the sleeves when she moves. I like her wearing my clothes. I noticed it back on our island. She looks so vulnerable under my suit that it evokes some ancient protective instinct in me.

Noah rushes to us, taking off his blazer. "Do you want to get the dry one? Here."

"No," I state firmly. "She'll have mine."

They both stare at me with wide eyes, and I lower my voice, facing her. "Stay in mine." She blinks at me, a bit lost in the moment. So I add gentler, "Please." Her having mine is crucial. She needs to have my clothes because it will touch her body. I don't want her to wear anyone's jackets ever again. She's mine, and no one can take her.

Suddenly, the weight of the situation comes crashing down on me.

What if we didn't stop that fire? Maeve seems to attract trouble. So being hurt during her own wedding because her ridiculous dress caught fire seems like something she'd do. Not by choice, but it seems to be the story of her life.

She watches me for a few moments before speaking. "Okay."

Spoken in such a soft and compliant voice, she nearly makes me go insane. I didn't know I needed to hear her say it. I didn't know I needed for her to just agree with me without a fight. Just once.

"Okay." I nod in return and help her toward the altar, leaving a smiling Noah behind us.

She stumbles a few times, probably due to adrenaline crashing down, and I catch her. I don't even feel her weight. At all. Like she's air. My muscles are taut, my movements jerky. Crashing with adrenaline is not an issue for me right now. Nor will it be for the next twenty-four hours, I feel—I don't remember being so scared in my life.

"Well!" Her father claps his hands together. "Come, darling, let's get you back to the altar."

I tighten my hold on Maeve's elbow because I feel a sudden murderous desire to throw her father in the ocean and keep him under the water.

"Ezra?" she whispers.

"Sorry." Instantly releasing my grip, I help her to the altar.

Everyone's camera is pointed at us. No matter how much money I give them, one of the greedy bastards will sell the photos. Tomorrow the whole world will see it. This is precisely why I wanted the ceremony to be as small as possible, and the number of guests to be zero.

I don't notice Beatrice until I hear her quiet voice. "Are you really okay?" Glancing toward the voice, I find her touching Maeve's shoulder with her hand. The gesture is careful like she's scared to spook her.

Maeve's hand covers Beatrice's. "Yes. Don't worry."

The blonde sister doesn't sound convinced. "Just say the word, and we will be out."

A weak smile with a quick shake of Maeve's head is her answer. So Beatrice steps back, picks up a flower lying on the sand, and heads to the altar.

I look down at Maeve. She's clutching the front of my blazer at her chest, trying to keep it together. Her wet hair reminds me of the way she was on the island, wild and free. A far cry from the timid creature standing in front of me now.

"Now, let's move on with the ceremony!" Mrs. Wrong announces cheerfully. "What a way to start a marriage! With a bang!"

It's a fucking bang all right.

Shooting her a glare, I'm mentally trying to convince myself not to murder Maeve's family. I thought I was forcing her into this situation, but more and more it looks like I'll be saving her from her insane family. In ours, at least our mom is all right. In hers, they all seem to be out of touch.

Maeve mumbles something.

"This way!" Mrs. Wrong ushers us, pointing at the confused official at the altar. "He's waiting."

Maeve's mumbling grows a little louder.

"Go on," Mrs. Wrong continues her crusade.

Maeve's mumbling turns into an audible whisper with clearer words.

"Maeve, honey, come on. Let's finish this part so we can go and celebrate."

"Stop!" comes a loud cry.

Everyone stops talking at once.

"Just stop," Maeve says quieter, taking a step backward. Then another. "I can't do this. I can't."

Right after, she leaps around in the air and takes off running toward the bungalows.

"Maeve!" Mr. and Mrs. Wrong yell at the same time. "Get back here!"

"Shut up," I bark at them, not thinking how Mr. Wrong's reaction can influence my future. Oddly, I don't give a fuck.

"Excuse me!" The mother rears back as if I've offended her very being.

I don't grant her a response but kick out of my shoes and take off after Maeve. Should have ditched them a long time ago—Maeve would say that only douchebags wear shoes on the beach.

I find her rushing toward our suites.

"Maeve," I call out calmly, making her glance at me quickly and pick up the pace toward her destination. So I repeat, "Maeve. I have a proposition for you."

She laughs with her back still to me. "Yeah, I've heard."

"A different proposition. You might like it."

That makes her pause but still not turn to me. I take it as a good sign and walk up to her rigid statue.

"If we get married, I'll give you power."

She snorts. I keep going.

"Real power. Money. Freedom. You can do as you please with it. Including showing your parents what pieces of shit they are." I walk around to face her and look deep into her eyes, seeing what she really wants. "Fuck, burn down the whole society for all I care."

Her eyes dart to my face. I knew it would catch her interest.

"They think they can control you and your life. But watch what you can do when you have my name and free access to my money."

Her intense, blue eyes watch mine almost without blinking.

"Why would you promise that? We don't even like each other."

"We don't have to like each other. I need my company back, and you need to get away from them. It's a win-win. We can make a contract. In fact," I pull my phone from my pocket, "I already have one. Just read it through and make changes." *But don't spend too much time reading.*

"Just like that?"

"Just like that." I nod. "I want my company back."

"Why?"

"Why what?"

"Why do you want your company so badly that you're ready to sign your life away just like that?"

I feel anger stirring inside, but it's not toward her. She's asking a valid question. The right question.

"I want to prove to my father that he made a mistake."

"By inviting the board?"

I try to mask my surprise that she's figured this out so fast. "Yes. He didn't trust me to keep the company afloat, so he opened it up for investors and gave away the voting power. The majority of it," I sigh. "They were waiting for the right moment to strike to take the rest from us."

"How?"

"They can vote against me. When the fire happened, and the building got shut down, we lost a lot of clients, therefore money. This is a good opportunity for them to show how incompetent I am."

"I'm sorry." Her voice is filled with guilt. "I'm sorry the fire happened."

"I want our company to be back in the family." This is the first time I say it out loud to anyone other than Noah. "Where it belongs. This is why I need the shares."

"And my father has the majority?"

"No," I reply with a shake of my head. "But he has enough to make me a majority owner. Us. Noah and me. We can veto any decision if we have it."

Her white teeth show up for a moment and bite into her lower lip. "And me?"

"Read." I push my phone into her hand. She brings it to her face and starts reading.

"It says we have to stay married for five years," she says, lifting her face to me. "No one told me about that yesterday."

"Yes. It's your father's condition or he pulls the shares back."

She keeps reading, and after a few more moments, she passes the phone back to me with a sigh. "It all looks good for you. You get the shares and the fantastic company for the foreseeable future. And what do I get really?"

"Freedom." I shrug. "In all meanings of the word."

She worries her bottom lip before nodding. "Okay. Let's do it. But we will live our separate lives."

"To an extent," I reply vaguely, fucking happy she didn't read the whole thing apparently.

She looks down at herself. "I don't think I can show up at my own wedding looking like this."

I grab her hand gently. "I think you look ready to take on the world. But if you need armor to stand against it, I'll support you. Do you want to go and put something on?"

Her eyes brighten as she stares at my face. Then she looks down at herself again, letting go of the edges of the blazer she's been holding. "Nope," she finally says. "I'm good."

 aeve

His pupils dilate when I say that. His tongue peeks out to lick his lower lip just as his throat bobs.

"You're good," he says huskily with unfocused eyes. His obvious interest gives me the courage I needed.

Squaring my shoulders back, I fluff my hair, giving it volume and happy that it didn't go down in flames like my dress, and head back to the venue, hoping he'll follow. Otherwise, my return won't be so epic.

He doesn't let me down. Hot on my heels, Ezra's there too. A quiet presence of power. Someone who doesn't bow under my father's pressure because he's got enough of his own. Someone who can teach me to do the same.

The moment we show up, cameras start clicking, and Ezra quickly moves to walk by my side, showing the whole world that I'm not a lonely psycho in grandma's panties and a corset covered in diamonds. Mom hired the paparazzi to show how awesome this ceremony would be. Well, the joke's on her. Now the whole world will see what really happened here. Even though I'm sure she'll be controlling what can be shown from today's disaster.

"And she's back," my father announces the obvious for everyone. "Just like we predicted," he cackles, and I skip a step. Ezra's hand instantly grabs mine, steadying me before anyone notices my misstep.

"The whole world," he whispers.

"The whole world," I say, sending him a grateful look.

Bea's standing by the arch at the bride's side. She has a bouquet of white flowers in her hands and a very concentrated look on her face. When she notices me, she tries drawing my attention with a subtle wave of her hand. When I look at her face, she mouths *I'm sorry.* I give her a quick nod of acknowledgment because she has nothing to be sorry about. But she still looks like I'm about to walk into a death trap. I should have been more honest with her and told her that I'm not opposed to extending our deserted vacation and spending more time with Ezra.

Noah's standing with his hands behind his back, his pants wet from walking into the ocean to offer me his jacket. He drops his hands by his sides when he sees us coming.

The official is wiping down sweat from his forehead. He looks tortured. He probably didn't expect to be in the center of such a pickle when he woke up this morning. When he notices us, he quickly grabs his book from the table and flips through the pages.

I want to run to him and be done with this charade, but Ezra's hand stops me. A squeeze of his hand on mine and his deliberately slow walking urges me to follow his lead. The walk is torture. It's long. It's miserable.

But despite the pitiful looks, with every step I take, my

shoulders seem to grow wider. My head seems to sit straighter. And my smile wider.

By the time we reach the arch, I'm owning every single moment of my situation. Of my awful outfit. Of my rat's nest of hair. Ezra's blazer on my body gives me the confidence I forgot I had. It reminds me that everyone is here because of me. Us. This is my wedding, even if it's fake. And I'll be the one dictating the mood.

I flip my hair back, brush sand from my groom's arm, and finally turn to the official.

"We are ready," I say, proud to be still standing here after everything. If not for Ezra, I'd be hiding with hens somewhere under a bungalow until everyone leaves the island.

The official smiles, looking around, and starts talking.

A small, soft hand grabs mine. Just for a second. And squeezes. A tiny encouraging gesture I didn't know I needed. My sister showing me that she's here.

The official starts his speech, but my father interrupts him in the rudest way possible.

"Yes, we've heard that before. Skip to the good part," he snaps, rotating his wrist in the air with a motion for the official to continue. The poor official starts sweating even more. He takes out a tissue from his pocket, dabs his forehead, and flips a page of his notebook.

"Alright. Okay." He looks lost, trying to focus on me and Ezra. "Ezra King, do you agree to take this woman, Beatrice—"

"It's Maeve," Bea chimes in as a few chuckles erupt through the small crowd.

"What?" the official asks, blinking.

"The bride's name is wrong."

"Yes, that's what it says." The official shakes the book in Bea's face. "Beatrice Wrong."

"Yeah, that part is right," she explains, leaning closer to him. "But the bride is Maeve Wrong, not Beatrice."

"But it said—"

"Just fix the damn name and keep going," she hiss-whispers back to him.

"Okay, alright." His eyes widen as he looks between her and me. "Alright then. Ezra King, do you agree to take this woman, Maeve Wrong as your rightful wife? And cherish her in—"

"Yes," Ezra interrupts the official, who seems to be one breath away from fainting.

"Okay. Good, I guess. Where were we?" He starts riffling between the pages again.

"Ask her now." At Ezra's order, the official's eyes focus on something in his book, and he quickly lifts his head to me.

"And you, Beatrice Wro—"

"It's Maeve!" This time, more voices come in a chorus, making the poor man sweat like a sinner in church. He dabs his handkerchief over his forehead, trying to even his breathing at the same time.

"Yes. Right." He dabs his forehead some more. "Ms. Wrong—"

"Call her by her name," Ezra interrupts him once again. "I want everyone to know that it's the right woman being called my wife."

A loud exhale escapes my mouth at his words as I stare ahead, refusing to look at him. Because if I do, I might end up climbing him like a tree.

"Right. Of course. Ms. Maeve Wrong." He pauses, quizzically looking around in case anyone else has objections. When none come, he nods to himself with satisfaction and continues. "Ms. Maeve Wrong," he repeats, looking at me. "Do you agree to take this man, Ezra King, as your rightful husband? And che—" He stops himself after a quick glance at Ezra. "Do you agree?" he addresses me again.

I look at Ezra's face. At his eyes focused on my face. At his intensely pressed together lips. And for a moment, it feels real. Or maybe I let myself believe that.

His brows slowly draw together, and I realize I still haven't replied.

"Yes."

His nostrils flare as he takes a big breath in.

"You can exchange rings now." The relief in the official's voice is loud and clear. He wants to be anywhere but here. When no rings are produced from Ezra's pocket, the poor man starts sweating again. "Rings? Anyone?"

"Here." Noah rushes in, shoving a black velvet box into his brother's hand. "I've got it."

Ezra grunts something and opens the box. And this is the moment I'm faced with the biggest diamond I've ever seen. It's gigantic. And covered in even more diamonds around it. And pearls. God, there're pearls. There's so much going on my eyes are starting to hurt.

When he picks it up, it even looks heavy. When I offer my hand to him on instinct, he pushes this enormous construction onto my ring finger. Oddly, it fits perfectly, and sadly, it weighs a ton. I swallow, imagining how I'll be moving around New York without someone trying to cut my finger off. I'm sure this thing costs a lot of money. So much good could be done with it. So many items bought for the homeless shelter Jeff goes to sometimes. Money toward repairing the damage from the fire. A new boat for the captain.

I realize everyone's waiting for me. And this is where I came unprepared. I didn't even think about that.

"I don't have a ring for you," I whisper shamefully. "I didn't thi—"

"That's okay," he says back quietly and then adds for the official louder, "Please, move on to the next part."

"Well," the man sighs, "I pronounce you husband and wife. You may kiss the bride."

"Oh," I sigh, making a little *o* with my mouth. His gaze drops to it. "Are we going to do that?"

"We've done this before," he whispers, bringing his hand behind my lower back and pulling me closer to him.

I'm pressed into him so closely, I can feel the beating of his heart in his chest. His uneven breathing resonates with mine.

He lowers his face to me, and his lips give my mouth a quick brush. Very quick. I'm not sure I haven't imagined it. Then he releases me just as quickly and steps backward. Cheers and congratulations erupt around us while my new husband wraps his arm over my shoulders and leads me to the side, away from the photographers.

My parents and Bea join us a moment later.

"Well, my boy, welco—

When my father sees Ezra's face, he loudly clears his throat before continuing.

"King, welcome to the family." Then he turns to me. "You've been good for something after all. Color me surprised."

Ezra regards him with such a hateful stare, my father starts coughing again.

"Anyway. I've made the order to transfer the shares to your name. Remember about the clause though," he adds, laughing. "Don't make me come back from my retirement due to your unwise decisions."

Mother, trying to make the situation better, ends up making it worse. She jumps to me to envelop me in a hug, but quickly pulls away, scrunching her nose. "You smell like smoke and seaweed, honey. You need a shower."

And these are my parents in a nutshell.

Someone's phone rings. Noah. He picks it up, says a few words, and comes back to us.

"Martin said it's all set."

Ezra looks at his brother. "For good?"

Noah nods.

"Good," Ezra says with a crooked smile and turns to my father. Grabbing the front of his jacket, he pulls him toward him. My father lets out a squeak and tries to pry Ezra's fingers away from himself. "Listen here, old man. Nothing will stop me now from punching the ever-loving shit out of you if you ever disrespect my wife again. There's no clause about that in the contract. This is the last warning."

The atmosphere is daring. The air is heavy. While a million butterflies are flying inside of my belly. No one has ever stood up for me like that. No one. And it feels so good.

Or those butterflies are here because he called me his wife? Me and my body are so confused.

"I can take my shares—" my father starts.

"You can't," Ezra hisses in his face.

A gleeful smile spreads across my father's face. "Then I'll take my daughter back."

The smile turns evil. "Try."

With that, he lets go of my father, wraps his arm around my shoulder where it already feels natural, and leads me away.

"Where are you going?" my mother asks.

I turn to her with a sad smile. "Away from here, Mom. Far, far away."

Some people get nice parents. Some people get my parents. Some people might ask why I'm complaining when I had all the luxuries and things I wanted growing up. But they'd be wrong. The only thing I wanted they couldn't give me. Parents being real parents, keeping the needs of their children above other things. I just wanted someone to love me.

"Maeve." Mom's voice breaks strangely at the end. But it's not enough to make me stop. It used to be enough—a small change of cadence when I thought she might have felt something. But I've learned it's not the truth. I don't think my parents are capable of loving anyone but themselves and money, and for the first time in my life, I'm okay with that.

We're slowly walking toward our suites with Noah and Bea hot on our heels.

"I'll take care of the press. Make sure no bad pictures are spreading."

"They'll sell them anyway," I say sadly, knowing how vicious those guys with cameras can be.

"Not when I talk to them." He winks at me, and I smile back. "Plus, you look fabulous. Everyone would be happy to even peek at you."

I lift a brow, glancing down at myself and then back at him. He chuckles when he notices my face.

"Where are you going now? To the honeymoon?" Bea asks, barely able to control her laughter.

"What if they're going to their honeymoon. Are you jealous, little mouse?" Noah chimes in. Arrogance dripping from his voice.

I want to open my mouth and tell him to keep it shut, but Bea beats me to it.

"I wasn't asking you, big knucklehead."

Trying to cover my laughter, I let out an accidental snort, making Ezra chuckle. A quick glance at him tells me that he's trying very hard not to laugh but failing. His teeth are sunk into his lower lip. Little crinkles are around his eyes. He almost looks like the Ezra from the island.

"Oh, you think you're so smart, huh."

"Smarter than you obviously if you think it's normal to call people names when they don't even know each other."

Noah's chuckle is dark. "You'd say so, wouldn't you."

My head whips toward him. His gaze is on Bea while she's staring ahead. Did I miss something? There's too much unspoken between the two. My sister's back is too rigid even for her. Noah's eyes are too intense. I don't know him very well, but he's appeared to be an easy-going person from the start. The fun brother out of the two. And now I'm seeing a completely different one. Do both King brothers have a Hyde side? That would explain a lot.

I shoot a quick glance at my own Mr. Hyde, whose assholishness appears very much nonexistent right now. Quite the opposite—he's my knight in shining armor.

"If I wanted your opinion, guess what?" My sister's voice is very bitchy if I may say so myself. She used to reserve it for special occasions for *very* special people. How Noah has already gotten on that list is beyond my understanding. "I'd ask you."

"Like I would give you the time of day to respond to it," Noah snorts. Sarcasm loud in his tone.

"Noah," Ezra calls out. "What the fuck?"

"That's okay," Bea says, shaking off his insult like geese do the water. "Some people's worlds are so small, they try to bring themselves up by putting other people down."

Noah lets out a low growl mixed with a mumble. It's hilarious and a bit concerning if I'm honest. What the hell did I miss?

"O-kay," Ezra starts after glancing between the two before focusing on Noah. "Are you coming with us?"

"Where?"

"To New York."

"What about your honeymoon?" He jerks his head in my direction.

Bea clears her throat, folding her arms over her chest, and gives Noah a pointed look which he chooses to ignore.

Ezra shakes his head, chuckling. "We're heading to New York."

"Are you ordering the jet?"

"Flying commercial," Ezra replies with a wince.

"Then I'm staying for a day or two. I have things to do here."

"Like the waitress who pushed her boobs in your face when you complimented her shoes?" Bea deadpans, surprising me once again. I don't recognize my sister at all. But quite honestly, I'm loving this new, bold version.

Ezra makes a weird sound, something between a laugh and cry, but instantly tries masking it by coughing into his fist.

"I feel like I'm sensing a pattern of jealousy here," Noah murmurs, leaning closer to Bea who makes a face full of disgust.

"I'm sure this is how you lift yourself up at night."

Noah's nostrils flare, making him look so much like Ezra at the moment.

"Alright!" I jump in between the two, preventing our wedding from ending with a murder. "We need to get ready to go. Noah, can I keep your card until I can figure out my financial situation?"

"No, you can't fucking keep his card," Ezra hissing into my ear. "The only card you'll be using is mine."

"Yeah?" I ask, turning my face to him and finding him too close to me. "So you can have all the power over me?"

His eyes turn stormy. "I already told you that you'll get your financial freedom when we get married. I tend to keep my promises."

"Freedom even from you?"

"Even from me." He leans just a hair closer, but it's

enough for him to be all in my space. Big and imposing. Taking all the air out. "But if someone ever had power over you, it'd be me."

I blink the horny fog away from my eyes. "I thought you didn't care."

"I never said that," he says quietly, for only me to hear.

33

She remembers. Just like I do.

At this moment, I can tell by the look in her eyes. She wants me to possess her. She sure as fuck liked me calling her *wife*. And I sure as fuck liked calling her that even more.

I think she liked that little game we played where she relied on my decision-making, and I relied on her obedience to keep me sane.

Turns out, it was a little more than a game to me, and I started craving it at some point. But not right away, no. I like her defiance before submission. I like her fight.

I like how cloudy her eyes turn when I tell her she can't take shit from anyone else but me.

"Okay, if you're done eye-fucking each other, maybe you can wait until you get to your room to consummate the marriage," Noah suggests playfully, reverting to his usual banter. This little blonde thing brings out something I forgot

Noah has. What the fuck happened between them while we were out on the island?

"Shut up," I say back without anger. It's sort of my mandatory response to his stupid jabs.

"Martin just texted," Noah says, shaking his phone in the air. "Your plane tickets are arranged. The car will be here in two hours."

"That soon?" Maeve asks, her voice surprised.

"Did you want to stay to chat with your folks some more?" he asks with a raised brow.

"No, I just—"

"I'm leaving too," Bea blurts out.

"What?" Maeve whips her head to her while Noah does the same silently.

"Yeah. Tonight." Her throat moves. "I bought a ticket yesterday."

Noah's brows draw together while he keeps his attention solely on her. *Interesting.* Is she the reason he wanted to stay here another day?

"Why?" Maeve asks.

"For the same reason you left. I should have done it a long time ago."

"I—" Maeve looks around helplessly. "I can't help you yet, but once I find a job, I can help you. Maybe you can wait a little bit?"

For some reason, her words make me angry. Why does she need a job? Why can't she take my help? I'm her husband now for fuck's sake.

"No." Bea stops her with a raised hand. "I need to do it on my own."

"Bea," Maeve whispers. "It's not that easy. We—" she clears her throat before continuing, "weren't exactly prepared for this life. And it will take you a minute to adjust."

Beatrice walks up to Maeve and takes her hand. "I know.

But I need this." She lowers her voice. "I need to find me, you know? Like you have."

"I'm still searching," my wife whispers back. "I mean, look at me now." Her voice turns sad. Sad at the prospect of her ending up *right here*, married to me.

Her sister smiles and pulls her into a hug. I swear to God if Noah opens his mouth to throw a jab at Beatrice, I'll punch him in the face. Suddenly, I feel very protective of that girl. Like she's part of my family now. Well, technically she is. But it's more. I think she means more to Maeve than either of them are willing to admit, so I'll make sure Maeve always has her sister in her life. God knows I want to throttle my brother ninety percent of the time, but he's my brother, and he always has my back.

Plus, Beatrice deserves it after letting me off the hook so gracefully. Yes, I heard them fighting, but all siblings do. And I'm sure it's a little harder when one of the sisters takes someone's groom. But they came together, and Beatrice has been standing by Maeve's side since then. It's changed my perspective. Maeve has changed a lot in this short time.

Beatrice whispers something into Maeve's ear, gives her a squeeze, and lets go of her. Then she walks up to me with a determined look of an angry hamster. She stands in front of me, pushing her index finger into my chest.

"You, big guy, better take care of my sister. We've had shit for parents, so we've never known something good growing up. I don't know what your story is, but you'd better not use her as a therapy tool. Otherwise, I'll be coming for you." She rises toward my face on her tippytoes. It doesn't help much because she's short, just like her sister. "Trust me, I've got some skills to make your life miserable if I need to."

I want to laugh, but I don't. So I just nod.

"You think I'm joking?"

Noah snorts.

Beatrice rolls her eyes and continues her threats. "You may laugh all you want, but I can find dirt on anyone." She inches closer. "And I won't be scared to use it."

Fuck me, but at this moment, I believe her. So I nod again, more respectfully this time. She watches me with narrowed eyes for a few long seconds, before nodding back at me and walking away without giving us a spare look.

I glance at Maeve to make sure she's okay. She's smiling, looking proud. Well, that's all I need.

I notice a dark cloud in my periphery: my brother. He looks like he's about to blow, and I don't recognize him once again. I know he can be a mean motherfucker when he wants to. But he's never been like that about a woman—he's usually very suave with women flying toward him like bees to honey.

I don't have any doubts in my mind he's this way because of Beatrice. Something happened between them. Something that made them both this way.

Something that made *us* this way too. Something we can't quite name yet.

I shift my attention back to Maeve who's still smiling. But now her attention is on Noah. She knows it too, and she seems to be okay with that. I guess that means I have to be okay with that too.

"Who's Martin?" she asks suddenly. "I've heard the name a couple of times."

"My assistant."

"And he doesn't want to share him," Noah adds grouchily.

"Because I found him first," I deadpan, annoyed with the same conversation we've been having for a long time. "Find your own."

"I have assistants, they just don't last," my brother complains like he usually does.

"That's because you run them into the ground." I think for a moment and add, "Or fuck them."

"I do not."

"Do too. How many have you had in the past year?"

Noah purses his lips tight because he has nothing to say. He runs through them faster than I did before I found Martin. One might say my brother is even more demanding. Which is saying something.

Dropping this never-ending discussion, I look at Maeve. "Let's go. We need to get ready."

With a short nod, she heads toward our suites. I'm about to follow her when Noah's hand lands on my shoulder. I glance at him with a questioning look.

"You'd better make it real," he says seriously. "I think this is it," he adds vaguely and goes in the opposite direction. I guess I'll see him in New York.

aeve

I'm staring at a giant ring on my finger that was supposed to belong to my sister. When did he buy it? Before he came here or after? Was it meant for her or for me?

I feel like I'm taking the leftovers, and it leaves a bad aftertaste.

My sister. She was supposed to be here, in my place. I wonder where she's going and how she'll do on her own. I think she will manage—she's always had this secret internal strength she was scared to show. I hope she'll be fine. I think she will, especially after seeing her backbone probably for the first time ever.

I haven't really felt like I've had a sister or family for quite some time, but when I saw her, I was quickly reminded of how it feels. Watching Bea stand up for me made me realize that I've always had her despite what we both have gone through.

I was eighteen when I left. I didn't have any skills, so I moved from job to job, getting fired on a regular basis due to literal lack of working capability. I was sleeping in the cheapest motels I could find because I was running out of money. I'd like to say I managed it in the end, but that'd be a lie. I had to borrow money from a homeless guy for fuck's sake. How will my sister, who's lived under our parents' thumb much longer, survive on her own?

I'm staring outside the moving car, refusing to acknowledge Ezra. Because if I do, I'll probably end up on his lap, crying into his neck. And then licking it. Definitely licking. It's very delicious, I remember.

He hasn't said a word to me since we left the hotel thirty minutes ago. There's no animosity in the air from him, just the aura of ignoring poor me. It's like he's reverted to his old self, the one from New York. I could easily slip into a dark place of my own mind because of that, but I've come to learn that Ezra's behavior is erratic, which makes it hard to predict which version of him I'll meet. So I either have to be okay or go mad. I'm unsure why he's this way, but if I had to bet, I'd say it's because he himself doesn't know how to treat this new situation between us. It throws him off balance, and for a person who thrives on having control over every aspect of his life, it might be challenging. Giving him some time to adjust will probably pay off in this long-term scheme we are in.

I'm in pink shorts and an oversized white T-shirt at least three sizes too big that I bought for myself in the hotel gift shop, and he's in a suit. Again with the suit in this fucking heat. If this doesn't tell me that he's back to being the man who rudely demanded coffee at our first meeting, I don't know what does.

The car comes to a stop, and the driver jumps out to open the door for me. I can manage by myself just fine, but it's his job. So I smile politely and go to get my bag with the shit I'll never use—the things I borrowed from Bea. The things she bought for *her* honeymoon.

Ezra reaches the trunk before me. He's pulling his suitcase out, and I lean to take my bag. He grabs it before I can reach it, growling, "No wife of mine will be hauling her own bags."

"I'm not a real wife," I hiss back. I don't know why I'm suddenly edgy, but all of it has started feeling too real, and I'm forgetting that the marriage is arranged.

"We're in public. In public, you are." His hard eyes warn me to drop it.

I want to fight him for the handle of my damn suitcase, and he feels it because his nostrils flare as his eyes focus on my thinned lips. I hate that his stare makes me swallow. I hate the chokehold his presence has on my body's chemistry.

With a deep inhale, I straighten my back and follow him to the boat. A larger one this time. I must admit that I'm having some issues with boats now. This one is new and very shiny, and the crew size is larger, but I can't make myself step foot off the wooden pier. I physically can't make my legs move.

I feel blood draining from my hands from my grip on the rails.

"Miss?" the smiling crew member calls from the boat. "Do you need some help?" He stretches his arm toward me, offering me to take it. But I'm paralyzed with fear and can't move. "Miss?"

"I'm here." His soft voice is next to my ear. Then, big arms come around my waist and back, and I'm being carried through the small, mobile bridge onto the boat. "Grab the luggage, please," Ezra says to someone while moving with me toward the back of the boat.

My fingers dig deep into his shoulders. My breaths are

ragged and uneven. I've never had a panic attack, but I think this is it. I've also never feared boats or water so much, but that was before I'd almost drowned.

He carefully puts me on a bench, but I wrap my arms tighter around his neck, refusing to let go. My action must look desperate, but I'm beyond pride at this point. Ezra instantly shifts our positions, and I end up on his lap. I'm not ashamed to say I need it now. I need him. I don't know anyone on this boat, including myself because this person is not me. He's the only one I'm familiar with, so I'll hold onto him until Mr. Hyde resurfaces.

He leans his back on the bench, pulling me closer to him. With my right side pressed firmly to his strong body and his arm wrapped around me, I finally manage to take a first deep breath and fill my lungs with enough oxygen to think rationally. He leans his chin on the top of my back and inhales deeply too.

We sit like that for some time until the island disappears from view and my breathing calms down. I pull away from his chest and look around. There're small dots of islands here and there, but we're surrounded by water. By a big body of water that can swallow this boat whole and spit us out on yet another uninhabited island to survive by ourselves yet again.

"Would it be so bad though?" Ezra murmurs next to my ear.

"What?" I whip my head to look at him. "How do you—"

"I'm thinking the same thing." His eyes dip to my lips. "I assume."

I'm taken by a moment of weakness and his strong shoulder to cry on. By seeing the same Ezra from the island. I let my eyes trail over his face and land on his lips too.

And then his phone rings. With a sigh, he shifts his body to pick it up, and I take it as a cue to leave. I make a move to rise, but his heavy hand lands on my lap and presses me down.

"King," he replies into the phone, holding my eyes with his. "Yes." I wiggle, trying to stand up again, but he presses me harder. "My place, yes. Everything from the list." A pause. "I said everything." He listens to someone saying something before adding another "Yes."

When the phone is back in his pocket, his hand lands on my lower back.

"Are you okay?" Despite the roughness of his tone, it's filled with concern.

"Yes. Thank you for, you know, helping me through that. I've never had a panic attack before."

"They suck."

"You've seen one before?"

He takes a moment to answer. "I've had them before."

"Really?" I feel my brows disappearing somewhere deep into my hairline without possibility of it returning to my face. I'd never think a man like Ezra would admit that.

Looks like he didn't think he'd admit it too because he carefully moves me away from his lap. His face shuts down instantly as he stands up from the bench.

"I need to make another call."

"Ezra," I call gently, but he's already off the deck and inside the cabin, leaving me alone with the endless ocean.

Ezra

Why the fuck I decided to turn soppy and share some absolutely unnecessary information about having panic attacks is beyond my understanding. I've already learned that Maeve has a tendency to rob me of common sense. This is one more time I'm wondering if I made the right decision. A wife who makes me *feel* is not a good thing in our line of business. I probably should have gone with the original one who stirred exactly zero interest. That way, I wouldn't have had any distractions.

But no, I decided to follow my dick and insist on having Maeve or no one at all. How am I supposed to treat this as a business deal if her scent alone drives me insane?

Seeing her scared to get on the boat made me feel her fear deep in my chest. It fucking ached. And then that dickhead offered her his hand like a damn knight in shining armor, and I snapped. I wanted to throw her over my shoulder and carry her inside the cabin and make sure she's too busy with orgasms to think about her fears of anything. But when I moved closer to her, I felt that fear coming off in waves from her small, rigid silhouette. She wouldn't deal well with roughness. So I found gentleness I didn't know I had deep in me and was rewarded for that. Caring for her, holding her in my arms like her only lifeline made me feel larger than life.

Until I opened my mouth to spit out the truths no one needed.

I ring Noah's phone. He's staying on the island for another day to clean up the rest of the mess, and I'll owe him for that big time.

"Yeah." He sounds like he just climbed out of bed.

"Don't tell me you just slept with someone."

"Why? You jealous? You sure could sleep with that new wife of yours and do us all a favor and stop being a dick."

"I'm not a dick," I grit out.

He snorts. *"Yes, you are. And I'll be taking bets in the office once I'm back."*

"What bets?"

"How long it will take Maeve to realize that and run away from you."

I growl, imagining Noah's neck under my fingers. It only makes him laugh harder.

"Already fucked up and need my advice?"

"Like it'll ever work. I need you to make sure my place is ready for her."

The pause that follows is concerning.

"Why?"

"Because I want Maeve to be comfortable."

Another pause.

"Can you just make sure Martin follows through on all my instructions?"

These fucking pauses begin driving me insane.

"Noah?"

"Yeah. I'm here."

"Will you check on Martin?"

"Ezra, Martin always follows through. Better than I ever would. Why do you suddenly question him?"

"I just need another set of eyes, that's all."

"Ezra," Noah laughs. *"Are you in l—"*

"Just get it fuckin' done," I growl into the phone and disconnect the call. I don't need his stupid assumptions right now. Not when I'm confused as well.

I spend the rest of the ride as far away from Maeve as possible but always keep an eye on her in case she has another attack and needs my help.

But she doesn't.

She also gets off the boat without needing my assistance, and I feel slightly disappointed. I was hoping to be needed by her. In my sick mind, I like her relying on me.

The staff brings the suitcases to the waiting limo, and we get inside the same way as before: silently. I don't know what to say because every single thing that comes out of my mouth turns me into some whiny shit neither of us need. I can't stand that person when I'm around her. That person will not do what I must do. That person would not have the guts.

We get our tickets and walk through security to the gates. The boarding is soon, so we just take a seat and wait. In silence.

When our boarding is announced, Maeve takes off like a rabid dog is after her juicy ass, and I follow shortly after, keeping my eyes on said ass because it's now mine, and I can ogle it any chance I get.

She's in the plane way before me, and when I step inside and walk toward our seats, I'm stopped by a flight attendant with a wide smile and red lipstick.

"Hello, sir. May I help you?" Her voice is full of honey. I don't like honey.

"No," I cut off her further questions. This is me on any day; I don't have time for pleasantries. I have money, and I pay people a good amount of it to do what I need them to without the need to be polite. I don't even need them to be polite with me, just do your fucking job. Silently, preferably.

Her smile drops for a second before it's planted back on. Her eyes dip down with a quick glance over me and return to my face.

"Let me know if you need anything." Her annoying smile goes wider. "Anything."

It wasn't very subtle, so I ignore her, hoping she'll get the hint. I've never been interested in quick hookups, and I'm not about to start now. Especially, when I'm fresh out of vows. Even if they were forced, I made them.

When I walk to my seat, Maeve meets me with an angry glare. Her narrowed eyes shift between me and the attendant who just stopped me in the aisle. Is my new wife jealous?

I stick my carry-on in the overhead bin and plant my ass in the chair which seems too small for me. She puffs and huffs while trying to situate herself like she hasn't already done that. I watch her. She checks the contents of the toiletry bag provided for us by the airline. I watch her. She gives me a side-eye and continues checking everything around her. I watch her. She scratches her cheek. I still watch. She wipes the bead of sweat running down her temple. And I watch it. She becomes agitated and whips toward me with tiny slits for eyes, and I barely can contain my smile.

"What?" She sounds beyond annoyed.

"What?" I parrot, biting the inside of my cheek.

"Done flirting with that lady? Or is she coming back?"

I let a smile graze my lips—I do it more often around her

than I have in the past few years combined. "Are you jealous?"

"I'm not," she snorts, like the idea itself offends her. "But I don't want to be made a fool."

"You think I'd cheat on you?"

Another snort. So loud this time, it attracts the attention of people around us, so she quickly lowers her voice. "You slept with me while being engaged to my sister. Forgive the fuck out of me for being concerned."

My shoulders go rigid. I turn my body toward her and lean my elbow on the divider between us so she can hear me better. "I wasn't engaged to her. I hadn't even seen her." I lean a hair closer. "But this time, I've given my vows. And I intend to keep them." I find and hold her eyes, making sure she knows I mean business.

Her throat bobs. "Even if she offers to make you a member of the mile-high club?"

I quirk a brow. "Who said I'm not already a member?"

Her lips pinch together, and she turns away from me.

My chuckle is breathless as I grab her shoulder and pull her to me. "I am not," I whisper into her ear, making her shiver. "But I don't mind becoming one with you." I quickly nip on her earlobe, making her exhale harshly.

She slowly turns her head toward me, nearly grazing my lips with hers. "Who said I'm not a member?"

I inhale loudly through my nose, grab the back of her head and move her face to mine. "Are you?" I hiss.

"Why? Are you jealous?" Her breath fans my lips.

I can say a million things and play it off, but this is where I create a fucking boundary. Putting some pressure into my grip on her neck, I speak. "I am. Because the only initiation my wife will ever have is from me." I give her lips a lick. "And you'll be smart to remember that. Wife."

I pull away, shifting my legs because my dick is rock hard.

Feeling a stare on the side of my face, I turn toward it and find an old lady looking at me with wide eyes.

"Newlyweds," I explain with a simple smile. She giggles and turns away to murmur something to her companion who's about the same age as she is. He sends me an appreciative wink and places his hand on her knee.

They look to be in love judging by the way their body language totally aligns with each other. I look at Maeve whose whole body is turned away from me. Her knees are squeezed shut together, and her hands are fidgeting on the armrests. We speak totally different languages.

We get drinks before everyone is situated, and the extra-friendly attendant offers me her 'help' once again. I look up at her, and she points at one of the lavatories.

"This one is bigger," she whispers with a wink.

"I'll make sure to use this one with my wife," I deadpan and notice how fast her smile drops. For fuck's sake, what's wrong with people nowadays? I came here with a woman who has a fat, shiny ring on her finger. It should be obvious to everyone that the fucking rock is me pissing on my territory. Obviously, we are together. What the fuck did she think was going to happen?

I glance at Maeve and the ring she keeps touching with her other hand. I make myself a note to get her another ring because this one was bought to impress the family, not the bride. And even if it was brand new and meant for her, I'd have to throw it away and choose another one. It's not her. This giant diamond is not her. This platinum band is not her. The whole thing seems tasteless on her artistic hand. It seems too heavy and out of place.

"Is this how it's going to be all the time?" She speaks so quietly, I'm not even sure it was for me.

"What?"

"Women around you."

"No," I say honestly. "I don't usually attract women. I'm not sure what happened with this one."

"I doubt that," she chuckles darkly.

"What do you mean?"

She finally shifts her attention from her ring to me. "I mean you being you."

"The asshole?"

A sudden giggle escaping her lips surprises us both. "No. You being a ridiculously attractive and rich dude. It's a pretty catchy combination."

"You think I'm attractive?" I ask with a sly smile, and she rolls her eyes.

"This is what you got from my words. Typical."

"No, Maeve," I start seriously. "I don't get attention from women because I'm an asshole, and I have the aura of one. They come and leave after my first bark."

She lifts her eyes and finds the attendant who's showing the safety rules.

I wince. "This one was persistent." I don't mind attention; I don't care about that. But if it bothers her, it has to change. "I'll make sure you don't have a reason to feel insecure."

"Even if the marriage is not real?"

"Isn't it?" I ask, genuinely curious to hear her answer because more times than not it feels real to me. The island was real. My support for her at the wedding was real. My anger toward her father too. My constant need to touch her is as real as it gets.

She looks at me with her big, blue eyes. They're open and vulnerable. This is the moment when she doesn't need jokes. She needs the truth. "Why me, Ezra?"

I know what she's asking. I've been asking this myself too and haven't come up with the answer yet.

"I don't know," I reply sincerely. "I just know that you make me... feel."

"Feel?" Her brows draw together.

I nod. "I haven't felt much in a long time."

"This is why I'm here? Because I make you *feel*?"

Another nod from me.

"What do I make you feel?"

I watch her open face, knowing she wants to hear something about love and shit like that, but I can't give it to her. I'm not going to lie to her anymore.

"I don't know."

"Okay." She visibly deflates and buckles her seatbelt. I do the same. And while I do, I feel a heavy stare on my face. When I find the same extremely stubborn flight attendant, I curse myself for not just saying *fuck it* and buying another jet so I don't have to share it with the board. No more flying commercial with my wife. Never.

36

Maeve

I brush my teeth and put some extra moisturizer on because airplane air dries my skin faster than the Sahara would. The lights in the plane have been dimmed, and I was waiting for this specific lavatory because it's larger than the other—I don't feel good in cramped spaces. I brush my hair too and open the door to head outside when a body pushes its way inside.

"What are you doing?" I hiss while Ezra corners me to the wall.

"Starting the initiation," he says with a wicked smile.

"I was joking!" I half whisper, glancing at the door behind him, scared someone might come in and find us together like this.

His smile just grows bigger, and he presses his large body into me. The plane is freezing, but he's extremely warm. He ditched his jacket and rolled his sleeves, revealing corded arm porn to my hungry eyes.

"Jokes aside, we can't skip the honeymoon." His smile turns crooked. "And this is our first wedding night."

I swallow my excitement down, eager for him to keep talking. I like how raspy he sounds when he's next to me. How his nostrils flare like he's trying to catch my scent.

When his body pushes into me, I feel his already hard cock pressing into my belly. My face probably betrays surprise because he chuckles. "I was thinking about what I could do to you here."

"What could you do?" I hear myself asking, even though my brain hasn't authorized the question.

He brings his mouth to my ear. "Oh, I could start with this." His hand pulls the hem of my shorts away and dives inside. His finger walks down, slowly. A tiny step after another. "And then do that." His middle finger presses on my clit and then moves lower, dipping between my folds. "And then this." He starts slowly pushing inside of me. "And that." When his second finger joins the first one, I gasp from surprise. His fingers are thick, and they feel good when he starts moving them in and out, but they're no replacement for his giant dick that made me feel all the feels at once.

"What else?" My voice is hoarse and dare I say seductive. Something I didn't know I could do.

He likes it or the question because a short exhale blows into my ear, raising goosebumps all over my body.

"How about that?" He presses his thumb to my clit and starts making deliberately slow circles. His mouth lands under my ear and starts sucking on the sensitive skin.

I grab his shoulders with my hands for stability.

When his fingers dip awfully deep, my hips buckle to meet them, and I let out an embarrassing moan I try to suppress right away.

"Don't." His voice is husky. Impatient. Angry. "Don't hold yourself back."

"If I make a loud sound, everyone will hear."

He brings his lips right to my ear and breathes out, "That was the plan."

After that, his fingers intensify their attack. His thumb presses harder and harder. His mouth moves to mine, and he dives into the kiss without foreplay. His tongue is deep. Stroking. Moving. Fighting.

When the swirl in my belly reaches its limit, I let out a loud moan, and he takes it as a sign to continue with his current course of action. Moving his face away a little, he plants his other hand on my throat. My eyes flutter open. He puts some pressure into his hold. A little. To test me out. I love it. He knows it. He presses more. His fingers circle around my throat just as his thumb on my clit pushes even harder.

And I fall. I let out a silent scream.

Which turns out to be not so silent at all because his hand instantly moves from my throat to my mouth.

His low chuckle tells me all I need to know about the waiting embarrassment when I'll be doing the walk of shame back to our seats.

When I'm done riding the waves of the high, he pulls his hand away and puts his fingers into his mouth. He closes his eyes, licking them clean.

I swallow, feeling my legs turn into jelly. Then he pushes his hand—the same one—inside his pants and adjusts his cock.

"Do you need help with that?" To my utter embarrassment, I swallow saliva again.

His laugh is low and tortured. "Not here."

"How will you—"

"I'll be fine." He moves to the side. "Go, I'll be there in a minute."

"Okay," I agree easily and try to squeeze past him to the door. It's a tight fit, but I don't complain.

When I emerge from the lavatory with a toiletry bag in my hands and messed up hair I totally forgot to fix, I get a glare from the flight attendant who's sipping something from a can. Her eyes slowly move over me, and the corners of her lips go down.

I could let it slide. I really could. But I don't want to.

"You were right," I say with a smile.

"About?" she asks with a disinterested look on her face.

"This bathroom really is bigger," I explain with a giggle and walk to my seat.

I probably shouldn't eat anything for the rest of the flight because it would definitely come with a side of spit, but it was worth it.

aeve

"Why are we driving to your house?" I ask Ezra who's been staring at his phone for the whole ride.

"Where do you want to drive? To the coffee shop? Or the homeless shelter around the corner? I've heard they have vacancy." His face looks like he's having too much fun, reminding me about my homeless state. I can go and sleep in Jeff's cardboard box. I'd be fine there if it would release me of Ezra's stupidly arrogant face.

"I can't stay with you," I repeat stubbornly, knowing well enough I can't even explain why.

"I hate to tell you," he doesn't in the slightest, looking gleeful like that, "but we're married now, and you'll have to live with me. Otherwise, it wouldn't look legit. Plus, it's not like you have anywhere else to go." He suddenly turns to me with narrowed eyes. "Unless you have a boyfriend I don't know about."

"It wouldn't look legit either way," I say with a snort, ignoring the boyfriend part.

"Why do you think that?"

I turn to him and slowly move my eyes about his body until my gaze ends up on his face. "You are you, and I am me. No one will believe it."

"Why?" He squints his eyes at me.

"We have zero chemistry. You're an unfeeling piece of rock, and I'm half crazy. We don't match."

Something that awfully sounds like a snort comes from the front where George, apparently a very attentive driver, is trying to cover it up with a cough. "My apologies, Mrs. King, something must have gotten into my throat."

I nearly look behind me to see which Mrs. King he's talking about, but it's me. I am Mrs. King now. I glare at the back of his head until he coughs again and only then return to my dear husband.

"So yeah, we don't match."

But Ezra doesn't listen. Instead, he presses his fist to his mouth, covering it while his shoulders are shaking. The bastard is laughing!

"What's so funny?"

"Your explanation." He drops his fist, revealing a half smile. "We had plenty of chemistry back on the island. So much in fact, we set your dress on fire," he says with a crooked smile. His tone suggests a double meaning. "And you were right, I can be a very hard piece of stone."

Ew. I can't believe he just cracked a dirty joke. George can't seem to believe it either because in the rearview mirror, I can see his brows climbing their way up to his receding hairline.

I shut my mouth and stare out the window at the busy streets of the city. To him, our time might have been a fun roll in the hay, but to me, it was different. I felt a connection I haven't felt before. I'm not even talking about chemistry and attraction, he's right—we had plenty of those. It's about being just the two of us together, dropping all the pretenses and being just two people comfortable with each other for a few days.

"Maeve," he sighs. "I can't do anything about our situation, but we need to make it work. For both our sakes."

"What is your sake exactly?" I narrow my eyes at him.

Instead of answering, he starts moving his jaw from side to side, and the muscles under his skin start moving. It's unsettling that I already know what kind of mood he is in when he's doing that.

"That's what I thought. You know about my situation, but I don't know about yours. You've got money and knowledge, and I've got nothing."

He finds my eyes and holds them until I *see*. "You've got me now."

My nose suddenly starts tingling, and my eyes turn itchy.

"Okay?" he asks in a soft voice, nailing the coffin.

A tear escapes my eye, and I quickly wipe it with my hand.

"Mae," he calls quietly. "Come here." He stretches his arm to take my hand. I'm not fighting him on that, not when his comfort brings me peace. He pulls me closer to him, but the seatbelt doesn't let me far.

"Fuck," he mumbles, trying to readjust it so I can be closer. Finally with his help, I'm pressed into his side with his arm wrapped around me.

I press my face into his jacket, feeling calm. Is it his smell? Or the hug? I don't know, but suddenly Ezra seems like the place I want to be.

We're riding like that in silence for some time before Ezra's voice sounds close to my ear. "Fuck, Mae. I don't know what I'm doing. I don't know what either of us are doing." I can feel the vibrations of his words in his chest. "But we're stuck in this. I know this is not where you wanted to be. I know that. But this is our situation. We don't have to be enemies. We can be, I don't know," he sighs, "maybe friends."

I lift my face to him. "I'd like that. Also, it'd be lovely if you reverted to just one personality, you know."

"What do you mean?" he asks with furrowed brows.

"I mean like decide for yourself if you like me or not, you know?" I sniffle. "Because it's hard to predict when you'll be the Ezra from New York or my Ezra."

"Your Ezra?" he repeats with a wide smile.

I understand my slipup too late.

"Like the Ezra from the island when no one was around," I try explaining, feeling embarrassment taking over my face. "The Mr. Jekyll Ezra."

"That was your Ezra?" He doesn't want to let this one go, looking at me with an odd smile on his face.

"Laugh all you want." I smack his cheek lightly. "But I actually liked that guy."

"Okay." He smiles. "I can try being that. Try," he adds meaningfully. "It's hard to be that when I've just met him too. But I'll try."

"Thank you," I sigh, leaning my head back on his chest. "I don't know if I have any fight left in me."

"You better. Because we have a big fight ahead of us."

"Which fight?" I ask with confusion.

"The society one."

"Oh, that," I say unenthusiastically. "I'm not looking forward to that."

"Neither am I. But it's unavoidable. Me being married will be a topic of conversation for some time. I don't know if your absence has been public knowledge because I hadn't even heard about Wrong having another child until I met you."

"I'm not surprised, unfortunately. I think they'll be more interested in you. I bet you made the Forbes list."

"You haven't looked me up?" His head jerks back in surprise.

I shake my head. "I don't even have a phone. Plus, I've never been into, you know, Googling and stuff."

He watches me for a second before speaking. "You're the oldest young person I've met."

"My friend used to say that too," I mumble, leaning back into his side again and not liking that Jeff and Ezra have something in common before they've even been introduced.

Sighing again, I picture all the awful stares I'll be given when Ezra shows up with me anywhere. I'm not exactly a staple of society, with my runaway past and rebellious looks.

My rebellious looks.

I push away from his chest and look at his eyes sternly. "I'm not changing my hair."

"I don't expect you to." His face is humorous.

"And I'm not taking my piercing out."

He leans his face closer to me. "I won't let you."

I press my lips at him not letting me do something, but then I actually comprehend what he said and giggle. "You're looking forward to that, aren't you?"

He leans back, smiling. "Maybe."

"Will your father be a dick to me?"

"He can try," he growls, pressing his lips tight.

Suddenly, I want to meet his father very much and tell him everything he's been needing to hear. Are all parents like that, or are we just the lucky ones?

aeve

"Of course you live in a penthouse overlooking the park."

"Of course." He smiles, ushering me inside.

"Wow," I say, looking around.

"Impressed?"

"Bored," I reply honestly, making him cough.

"What?"

I glance at him. "Have you actually bought even one thing for this place?"

He watches me like I've just fallen from the moon. "I have someone to do that for me. I don't have time for shopping."

"Exactly. Boring."

He narrows his eyes. "I was told it was stylish."

"Sometimes stylish is boring." I shrug.

He pauses and looks around. Slowly. Assessing.

"What would you change?"

"Nothing."

His head whips to me. "What do you mean nothing? You just said the place is boring."

"Yeah, but it's yours. So." I shrug again.

His brows draw together. "Do you mean I'm boring?"

Another shrug. It's all I can do now, enjoying the view of his suddenly reddening face. Ezra needs some entertainment, and I've got plenty to give.

He doesn't like my answer because he's next to me in three long steps. He's a hair away but not touching. Leaning his angry face to mine, he starts speaking. More like hissing.

"Say it again."

"I haven't said anything," I reply, biting my lip to distract him. "You said that."

His eyes lift back up to mine. "I'm not boring. You know that."

I could just stroke his ego, but it seems to be a sharp subject for him, and I feel like playing with fire. So I rise on my tippytoes and whisper nearly into his mouth, "Do I?"

A low growl makes goosebumps rise all over my body. He's breathing like a bull during the rodeo.

"Say it again," he orders.

"What?" I grab his tie and wrap it around my fist. "You've been traveling with a tie, for fuck's sake. Tell me that's not boring." I wasn't known to be so bold before, but now the challenge is loud in my voice. I'm embracing this new person I am around Ezra because he makes me feel safe no matter how much he barks. And I'm loving it.

Quickly, his fist wraps around my hand on his tie. His other hand lands on the small of my back and pulls me into him. He's ready and hard. Angry. Hot.

"It is not boring when you know how to use it properly." His words are careful. In control.

I feel like daring him even more. "Do you?"

His eyelids turn heavy. The hand on my back presses me

into him even more while his hips make a slow grinding gesture. I nearly melt into a puddle under our feet.

With deliberately slow movements, he leans forward and scoops me up and over his shoulder. When I squeak, he smacks my ass. Hard.

"Quiet. You're getting what you asked for."

"What is that exactly?" I just can't help myself.

"I said quiet." Another smack.

He walks—slowly—to the kitchen and puts me on the island. The marble is cold under my ass and naked thighs, but my skin is hot. He steps backward and starts pulling his tie off. Again, very slowly.

"What are you—"

"Quiet."

I shut my mouth, watching his movements, mesmerized by his control. When he's done, he wraps the tie around his left arm and moves to me. I expect him to ask me to show him my wrists or something, but he doesn't do that.

Instead, he comes close. Very close. But once again, not touching. He hunches his shoulder forward, towering over me. Making me feel trapped. Small.

He rests his left hand on the counter by my side while leaning his body into me. He's going to kiss me, I know. So I instinctively lick my lips, getting ready for him.

But he has another plan apparently. Because his low chuckle is the only indication he's seen my gesture. His nose comes close to my cheek, and he inhales deeply. His skin grazes over mine for a ghost of a second. He inhales again. I squeeze the edge of the counter with my hands. He moves his nose to my neck. Another inhale. I spread my legs wider, inviting him closer. He doesn't move closer. So I move my pelvis closer to the edge. He chuckles again. His breath fanning my skin makes me shiver.

He finally steps into the space I've made for him. His

mouth moves to my ear and the hair all over my body stands up. I swallow a dry lump in my throat.

Something wet glazes over the shell of my ear, making me shiver once again. The tip of his tongue. Then he bites, and I let out a low moan.

He does it again, and I shift, nearly falling backward. I try to catch myself but can't.

Because my fucking hands are tied behind my back!

He grabs my shoulders before I completely fall on the counter in a very awkward position.

"What—" I mumble in the middle of my horny frenzy.

"What was that you said about me being boring?" he whispers into my ear after a quick nibble.

"You—" I growl. "You!"

"Yes?" he asks with a quirked brow, stepping backward.

"You are an asshole!" I fume, angry that I was led by him so easily.

"Never claimed to be otherwise." His laugh is raspy. Low. It scratches the inside of my chest.

"Untie me," I order angrily. Only making him laugh harder.

"I don't think so," he says, grabbing an apple from the perfectly arranged fruit basket on the table. "This," he points at me with the same hand he's still holding his apple, "is how I prefer you."

I look down at myself and find a very disturbing picture. My legs are still spread wide. My hands are tied behind my back. My shorts are so wet I'm sure they're see through at this point. I feel my cheeks flaming hot. I'm a picture of sexual distress. Caused by the evil man watching me with a knowing smirk on his perfectly unfucked face.

I avert my attention from my odd-looking self to him. With narrowed eyes, I silently promise him: *the war is on.*

39

What on earth made me think it was a good idea to play this dangerous game? I could barely pull away. Barely. And even right now, I'm still hanging by a thread. I even grabbed an apple to make my hands busy. Fidgeting with a fruit and pretending like everything is fine seems to be like the way to go. My dick might not agree with me though. I don't remember being so fucking hard it's painful. And I don't think it will be going away on its own—I need a few minutes in a shower. Alone.

Whom am I lying to? One minute is more than enough right now. If Maeve didn't have her hands tied behind her back and just touched it, it would have exploded, ending my life prematurely from embarrassment.

Speaking of tied hands, I move my eyes from her red face to her legs. They're spread wide. She's trying to free herself from my tie, but I know she won't do it on her own. My knots can be tough.

"Ezra," she growls like a little wild animal. "Take them off."

I take a bite of the apple and start chewing, ignoring her request.

"Ezra," she repeats, her voice getting angrier.

"Yes?"

"Untie me. Or else."

"Or what?" I'm holding off smiling as much as I can, but I can barely breathe at this point. She looks adorable when she's angry. Just like when she tried cracking the coconuts. Minus the ties. I like her in them.

"Or you'll have to sleep with one eye open."

That makes me laugh. Doubling over, I start laughing, imagining her vicious attempts to hurt me. I don't remember when I've laughed like that. Maybe only when I was a kid and could afford to be so open and free.

"Ezra!" she calls out quieter, the fight leaving her voice. Her face pales a little. "Let me go."

There's always a point where one should stop with this game. Especially when she hasn't consented in the first place. I drop the apple on the table and walk to her. Slowly because I'm really enjoying the view.

When I'm next to her, she makes a move to jump off the counter, but I quickly stop her with my hand on her waist. "Wait. I'll do it like that."

"Like what?" she asks, licking her lips. Is she still turned on? She might be because I am. And I wasn't the one who didn't even feel the tie around her wrists until it was too late.

"Like that. On the counter. It's easier for me," I explain. My voice is too husky for my liking.

"Oh, okay," she says breathily. Her mouth is slightly open.

"Here." I grab her waist with both my hands and pull her closer to me. "It's easier."

"Yeah." A breathless word.

I put my arms around her and peer over her shoulders to admire my knot and start working on the tie. I can do it easily in two seconds, but the faster I do it, the faster I stop touching her. So I prolong my pleasure.

When the tie is off, she rubs a hand over the opposite wrist.

I feel like an asshole. Did I tie it too tight? I certainly was excited, so that's a possibility.

"Let me see." I carefully take her hand in mine and bring it closer to my eyes for inspection.

"It's okay," she sighs.

I'm checking her wrists and don't know when I step too close. I notice it only when her thighs come to either side of me, caging me in. She's so warm. So soft. And she smells fucking divine. Like sins and promises. No harm will be done if I just take a closer sniff.

I bring my face closer to hers.

"You okay?" I ask, not knowing how else to justify me being all over her.

"Yeah." She edges a little closer. Her pussy is right next to my dick who hasn't had a moment off since I put her on that damn counter. "I am."

"I'm—" I don't know how to go on because apologizing has never been my strong suit, but I seem to be doing that a lot lately. "I'm sorry. I didn't expect you to get so angry."

"Not angry," she whispers. "Upset."

"Shit, Maeve." I pull away and find her eyes. "I'm sorry. I didn't mean it to be like that." I've always prided myself for being an emotionally stoic man, but I feel panic settling over me.

"Yeah." She sniffles, hiding her eyes. Fuck! Did I really

upset her? Maybe even traumatized? Was she restrained before? Damn it.

"I'm sorry. I'm so fucking sorry." I step back to her, in the embrace of her legs, and place my hands on her shoulders. "Look at me."

She lifts her eyes up to look at me. They're guarded. Careful. Watching.

"Can you give me a hug?" she asks in a soft voice.

"Yes, of course." After the permission, I quickly wrap my arms around her, doing what I've wanted to do.

Her arms come around my back, and we stay like that for a few moments. She places her face in the crook of my neck, and I start gently rubbing her back.

She buries her face deeper. My rubbing changes the feeling.

Her hands slowly travel to the small of my back. Her fingers carefully stick under my belt. I let out a low exhale, not expecting her to be so open about affection after an intense experience.

I let myself rub my cheek over hers. Her hands dive deeper and land on the bare skin of my ass.

I let my face move to her neck and place a gentle kiss on her beating pulse. She lets out a tiny moan.

I let myself do more kissing and more exploring with my hands.

Her hands become braver too. They travel more. In places I didn't expect them to travel.

I make a surprised sound deep in my throat, but she starts murmuring in my ear. "Please. I'm so upset."

Shit. I let out a loud resigned sigh and relax as well. She starts kissing my neck. Her mouth skims over my jaw, making little nibbles on the way. While her fingers continue to travel places.

At some point, I start enjoying it. Maybe a little too much

because I don't notice how my hips start making small, pushing gestures.

She moans in my ear, driving me into a frenzy.

I move my face to her mouth so I can kiss her, but she quickly averts it by giving a nibble to my jaw. I don't pay attention to that because I'm too far gone.

I try kissing her again, but she averts it again by biting my earlobe.

She grabs my ass cheeks and squeezes them, pulling them apart. I let out a surprised sigh. But she bites my damn ear again, and I make a move forward, where I belong—rubbing her pussy.

Or try too, because she suddenly pulls away, and my hard dick hits the marble. Marble meets marble. It's fucking painful. I jump backward, doubling over.

"Oh, too soon?"

I look up and find her with a knowing smirk on her face. Her eyes are cloudy but comprehending. Just like mine were when I pulled the tie prank on her.

She knows the moment I understand what has happened because her face stretches with a wide, devious smile.

"You little witch," I say in pain, trying to hide my admiration. "I thought you were scared."

"P-p-please." She jumps off the island, rolling her eyes. "Like your little tying game could scare me to the point where I turn into a quivering mess. You," she points her finger at me, "don't know me at all if you believe that."

I have to agree with her. I honestly thought I'd traumatized her. Turns out, she just played me right back.

"Where do I sleep?" she asks in a nonchalant tone, seemingly unaffected by our counter encounter.

"Pick any room upstairs." I point at the staircase. "Besides the last one on the right. That one is mine."

She snorts. "Like I'd want to sleep with you."

"You wish."

She looks down at my lap where I'm holding my dick in my hands without any shame. "Looks like you are the one wishing now."

With that, she heads upstairs. Before she disappears, she turns for a second. "I hope it didn't break. Even though you won't be needing it anytime soon!" she adds cheerfully and rushes up the stairs.

I hope she picks my room.

40

So this is where the magic happens? I think, looking around. Everything is surgically precise and soulless. Black and white, with the former dominating the space. No surprise here either.

I walk up to the giant sex tatami that is his bed. It's a California king. Or even larger. Longer. Just like the man himself.

Sighing, I grab the hem of my shorts and adjust my underwear. It's not very comfy when it's so damp. Torturing him made me even wetter than I was before, and I'm sure I'm on the verge of being dehydrated now.

Feeling the silky sheets with my palm, I imagine how nice it would feel on my heated skin.

"Are you planning on jumping in there? Know there will be consequences if you do."

I whip around, startled, but quickly try to regain the upper hand.

"Don't dream about it. I was just thinking that of course you'd take a larger room with a larger bed."

He lifts his brow up. "Maybe it's because I'm large?" Innuendo is loud in his words. And I'm here for it. "Or maybe because it's my apartment, and I didn't need to share it with someone else."

"Or it's because you wanted a match for your ego?"

He chuckles. "Might be that too."

I shrug, walking past him toward the door. "You can have it back and fit all your large particles in here. I don't like the room anyway."

"Why?" he asks, sighing, knowing it's a trap, and he's walking into it.

"You don't know why?" I ask from under my lashes, totally flirting.

"I have a feeling you'll enlighten me."

"Because." I stop next to him. "This. Is." I rise on my tippy-toes to his face. "Bo-ring."

A muscle on his jaw twitches. I can't tell if it's irritation or laughter. Might be both. "Go to bed, Maeve. You'll be jet-lagged tomorrow."

"Good idea. Good night." I rush from the bedroom before we both jump each other's bones.

Walking through the second floor, I find three more bedrooms. Why he needs so many beats me. Maybe he has women coming over all the time, and all of them can't fit in one bed.

I halt to a sudden stop. Does he? Bring women here. He'd better not because I will not stand being disrespected like that even in this fake marriage.

I choose the furthest room from his. It's beige. It has a king-sized bed with a million red pillows, a fluffy comforter, two nightstands, a wall-mounted TV, and two doors.

I check the first one. It's a bathroom. I turn the light on for a second, run my eyes around, and turn it back off. Then I flip it back on. The bathroom is stocked with many things. I come closer and check the labels. Everything is coconut and mango scented. My favorite scents. I open cabinets and drawers and find many things I used to love before I left my parents' house. Because these things are expensive, and I've never had enough money to buy them. My favorite lotions, creams, and makeup. In different colors. I swallow a lump in my throat. Where did it come from?

When the initial shock disappears, I turn the lights off, carefully close the door, and move to the next one. Not knowing what to expect after the bathroom, I pull it open slowly. It's a closet. *The* closet. The closet of the dreams of any woman out there. And it's stocked too.

If I expected to see boring black and white colors, I'm proven wrong. The clothes are colorful. And edgy—I discover when I start moving through the racks. Tons and tons of clothes. Dresses, shorts, pants, shirts, leggings, boots. Everything is here. And every single thing is something I'd wear. Everything.

My eyes are tingling. My nose is itchy. I rub it, trying not to cry. But I can't.

Somehow, in this short period of time, he's come to know me more than anyone else. More than my parents have ever known me.

I run my hands through expensive materials, remembering how much I loved the feel of it. How much I loved creating new clothes from what I had. Because what our parents made us wear was awful and boring and belonged in a fire.

I don't notice how my cheeks turn wet. I start wiping

them with no use—the tears don't stop coming. And those are happy tears. I didn't know it felt so nice to be seen.

When the stream turns not so steady, I wipe the leftovers from my eyes and cheeks and head outside, not bothering to look at the mirror. Ezra has seen me at my worst, plus I'm not there to seduce him.

"Ezra," I start, pushing the door open. "I wanted to—"

He turns around. His hair is wet. The droplets of water run down his bare chest, then down to his equally bare torso, and then get absorbed by the white towel wrapped around his hips. The towel reaches his knees but doesn't cover the bulge underneath it. I know Ezra is packing, and his package happens to come in equally big sizes of everything. He likes big things. Turns out, I like them too.

"What happened?" He strides toward me. "Why are you crying?" He grabs my chin and brings my face up, his intense eyes darting between mine.

"I'm just—" I clear my throat, trying to find my wits again. I've never been known to lose my brain cells over a naked man, but Ezra has been showing me the new me. Apparently, his naked body has this effect on me.

He suddenly pulls away, dropping his hand. "Is that another trick?" he asks with narrowed eyes.

"No," I say back simply. "I was just touched by your gesture."

"What gesture?"

"That gesture." I wave back at the door like he can understand me. "You know, buying me all that stuff."

The apples of his cheeks turn a slight shade of pink. And I don't think it's the after-shower effect. "I didn't buy anything. I have a personal shopper who did."

"I figured." I smile softly. "But they wouldn't have known what to buy if you didn't tell them."

He shrugs one shoulder, grabbing the hem of his towel and tucking it in deeper.

"Thank you. No one has ever done something like that for me."

Another shrug. "Yeah."

My smile grows more confident. This is new territory for him too! So I nod and turn to walk back to my room. But I stop right before I leave.

"How did you know I was going to pick that room?" I ask him with narrowed eyes.

"Really?" He quirks a brow, and another drop falls down and rushes down his face to his corded neck.

"How?"

His chest expands with a sigh. "It's the only room with any color in it. You like color."

"How do you know?"

He just keeps watching me without replying.

"How, Ezra?"

"I know you more than you think I do."

I pull the inside of the cheek between my teeth—something I do when I'm thinking. Hard. When I draw a blank, I ask him again with a sigh, "How did you know about the products and all that stuff? How did you know those are my favorites?"

"Your sister."

"What?"

"I asked your sister to put everything you like in the cart, and then just asked Martin to get it delivered here."

"She helped you?"

I don't know why the idea of my sister helping him sounds more unrealistic than him actually doing that. He confirms with a nod.

"Makes sense now," I mumble to myself. "Thank you anyway."

I leave his room and slowly walk to mine when I hear his footsteps behind me.

"Maeve."

I pause and turn around. He's leaning his back on the doorframe of his bedroom. "Yeah?"

"I picked the clothes myself." He clears his throat before continuing. "Well, not myself, but I told Martin what you like and what you don't."

"You did?" I whisper. He nods.

"Beatrice doesn't know you. Well," he clears his throat, "the new you." He flicks his hand in the air as if it can explain what he means by that. But the odd thing? It does explain a lot. But it also terrifies me even more.

I can't come up with a smart reply, so I go with the one that seems the most sincere. "Thank you." *Why does my voice sound so small?*

"Do you like it?" He sounds so unsure my heart starts aching.

"Yes," I whisper, swallowing tears down. "I love it. All of it."

He scratches the back of his head and looks to the side. "Good."

"Thank you," I say again, not knowing how to express my gratitude for not only buying clothes and stuff but buying something *I* like. Another short, unsure nod from him.

Before I leave him, I have another burning question.

"Does Martin buy all your clothes?"

"No, never," he replies firmly.

"But—" I feel my brows drawing together. "Why did he buy my clothes then?"

He watches me silently. His stare is heavy. His mood is cloudy. It's suddenly different. I think he'll leave me without an answer when he starts speaking. His voice is quiet.

"Because I'd never trust something so personal and so important to a personal shopper. I trust Martin."

"So important?" I ask in a whisper.

He lifts his chin. "Something that will touch your skin and hug your body. I don't trust anyone else with that."

"Oh," I say, blinking like a silly, brainless doll.

"Good night, Maeve." He pushes from the frame and walks back to his room, closing the door behind him.

And leaving me with the worst case of unresolved feelings.

41

To say I'm mad would be an understatement.

"What do you mean you still can't open the building?" I repeat my question for the third time while a pale-looking clerk is getting paler by the minute. He should be, I'm on the verge of throwing my arm forward and dragging him over the desk.

"The in-inspector didn't sign off on it," he stutters, looking anywhere but at me.

"Why?"

"The fire d-department."

"What with the fire department?"

"They didn't—I mean, they won't..."

I lean forward, ready to throw this little prick out the window. "I was at the fire department this morning," I say. "And guess what? They signed the fucking paper."

His thin neck moves with a swallow. "I don't know why." His voice turns into a whisper. "I just work here."

"You think?" I deadpan, knowing I won't get anything from this pencil pusher who told me two minutes ago that the building inspector is not here now. But I don't give a fuck. I'm coming in and waiting for him if need be.

Quickly dismissing the pencil, I move around his desk and start navigating the cubicles in search of the inspector's office. I have a strong suspicion I know whom I'll find there.

"You can't go in there!" The pencil's voice takes a new level of volume, one he didn't possess when talking to me.

Disregarding his cries, I walk deeper into the space until I find the office of the senior inspector. I push the door open and find exactly what I expected. The prick in the chair looks familiar. Very familiar. A quick glance at the standing name tag on the table confirms my suspicion. Boris Lebovski. He's the brother of the board member Leonard Lebovski. The very same one who's been trying to overrule me every single meeting.

When a female voice giggles through the speaker, the man quickly hangs up without saying goodbye.

"What are you doing here?" he cries out, trying to look around me. "Spencer, why the hell did you let him in?"

The pencil's voice speaks from behind me. I guess he's Spencer. "He didn't listen. He just barged in like an… Like an animal."

I glance back with a raised brow, making him retreat from the office and toward his desk. I watch him backing out until he hits a watercooler with his back and turns to scatter away. I quickly shut the door behind him and turn toward Lebovski.

"Well, looks like everything they say about you is true," he says gleefully, crossing his fingers over his stomach.

"Yeah?" I walk and take a seat without an invitation across from him. "What do they say?"

"That you're not fit to lead a company. Especially as large as this one."

"You mean *my* company?"

He cackles. "It won't be yours for long."

"You'd think so, wouldn't you." My tone is quiet. When it's quiet, they should be scared. He probably catches on because he leans forward.

"What are you doing here?"

"I came to see what's the holdup with the building, but now I see."

"Yeah?" He cocks a brow. "What do you see?"

"I see a dick brother of one of my board members trying to help him take my company by any means they can. Including illegal ones."

For a second, he looks uncomfortable. But only for a second. Then the worried look on his face is replaced with a smug one.

"I don't know what you're talking about."

"I've got the vote." By now, he knows. Everyone does. "Why are you still trying?"

He keeps smiling, looking sure of himself. He has a plan. They all do. *Fuck.* I need to figure out what's going on.

So I keep pushing until he becomes too confident and lets something—*anything*—slip.

"I'll sue you."

He starts laughing, moving a pen around the table. "That's funny."

"Being sued is funny?" I play angry and stupid, just how they think me to be.

"Funny that you think it'll scare me. I've got a city behind me."

"And your brother's money apparently," I add nonchalantly, because there's always a rivalry between siblings. Always. I just have to sniff out how much it affects him. "Because you don't have much." I start tsking. "Looks like your brother secured a richer wife for himself." That hits the chord, because his lips purse even tighter together. I look around the office with disgust. "I can't imagine you make tons of money working here. Being your brother's little dog he sends to do his dirty work."

His eye ticks. One time. But it's enough for me to know I've hit the nerve once again. "All this money," he leans forward, "will be mine too."

"Yeah? I don't see how you might get anything out of it while you're still stuck in this city job. Unless you take bribes. Which you do, don't you?" I smile. "But it still won't get you as much as he has."

His eye is now ticking nonstop. "I'll get half of it when we're done."

"Really? I don't see how you'll get any of it when I've got the voting power now. And *I* have more than half now."

He starts laughing. "You think you do, do you?" His laughter intensifies, and I feel like I'm getting close. "By the time you're done suing me, your building and your company will eat all of your money, and you'll be bankrupt. Then we will swoop in and buy it from you." He leans toward me over the desk. "For nothing. We will have the company for nothing. And then we will put our name on top of the building. Lebovski Enterprise."

He starts spitting, so I rear back to not get drenched. He thinks he has the upper hand and intensifies his truth-spitting.

"So you see? I don't give a fuck about you suing me. Sue me for all I care. I know how to make it long, I work for the city after all. And all your voting shares will mean nothing because you won't have your company. We all know how many investors and buyers pulled away after they figured out that your company produces unsafe buildings. No one wants to be associated with that. And this is precisely what we wanted. To taint your precious reputation. Then we just have to sit and wait for it to do the rest of the work for us. How about that?" He leans back with a smug look on his face, thinking he's won.

Fuck. Their plan actually makes sense. Almost three weeks of the building being vacant took a huge toll on us. I'm scared to even imagine how much it will cost me to drag this lawsuit over months, even years. And how many ongoing and future projects it might cost us. Because he sure as fuck can make it complicated enough.

I rise to my feet and without another word stride out of his office, letting him know he's won. If he thinks this way, it might buy me some time. A little bit until I figure out what to do.

As I sit in the car, George asks, "Where to, sir?"

"My building."

He takes off without asking anything else. A dark fucking cloud over my head is warning enough.

He drops me off in front of the main door. It usually buzzes with activity with people going to work, but now it's quiet. They all are working remotely. It's not ideal, but it is what it is.

A simple paper glued to the glass wall says that the building is unfit and not safe. Such a small thing is quickly ruining my life. Security guards are seen inside. Even though the building is 'not safe,' it doesn't mean it can be abandoned. Especially with all the homeless people swirling around. The moment the guards leave, the windows will be broken, and people will be squatting inside. Which will bring another set of troubles.

I glance at the door on the right. The coffee shop. The

place where everything started. The place which started the beginning of the end for my family. And the person who was there at the start of it all: Maeve.

Maeve Wrong. No, not Wrong. Maeve King. She is King now, whether she likes it or not.

I'm thinking about our conversation from yesterday and how fucking vulnerable I let myself be when the doors of the elevator open, and I step inside the empty floor. It's quiet. No one is around. I've never seen it looking like this before.

Then something clicks. Something falls on the floor, and someone curses loudly. I can't help but let a smile tug on my lips.

I walk toward my office to find Martin on the floor trying to collect dozens of fallen pieces of paper.

"Hello, Martin," I greet him.

He pauses and looks at me with wide eyes. "Well, that's a first."

"What's a first? Me saying hello?"

He snorts. "No. You saying hello first. You are usually all broody and mysterious and not talkative." He waves his hand in the air and goes back to picking up the paper.

I'm about to head to my office. That's what the old me would do. But somehow, being that person doesn't feel so comfortable anymore. So I stop and start picking up too.

Soon I realize I'm the only one doing the deed because I feel a stare on the side of my face. I glance at him with a cocked brow. "What?"

He blinks. "Does this have anything to do with all the stylish things I picked up for *Mrs. King,* your *fake* wife?" His voice changes at the end. It turns smug and almost... happy. Why would he be?

"Shut up," I say, rolling my eyes and making him chuckle.

"Why are you here?" I ask, suspecting the answer.

"Why wouldn't I be?" He tilts his head to the side. Maeve

does the gesture sometimes when she feels flirty, and I have to give myself a mental shake to remember that she's not what I need to be thinking about right now.

"The building is closed, for fuck's sake."

"I've got a key," he snorts.

"No one is working here."

"I'm still getting paid." He sounds like he's barely containing laughter.

"You can work from home."

"I can," he replies thoughtfully. "But who will bring you coffee when you need it? Or set up a meeting with someone when you forget how to use your intercom?"

I feel the second smile of this morning tugging on my face. "I know how to set up my own meetings and make my own coffee."

He quirks a brow.

"I do."

"Alright!" He throws his hands in the air in a surrendering gesture.

I pass him all the papers I've collected and head to my office. Once I'm behind my desk, I feel like a person again. A little bit like myself. But something is missing.

I press the intercom button.

"Yes?" Martin's humorous voice comes through.

"Get me a coffee." Then I add softer, "Please."

He chuckles. "With pleasure, Boss." Before he disconnects, he says, "Damn, you really do know how to use the intercom."

Why am I still keeping him?

aeve

Waking up in a comfortable bed seems like a foreign thing to do. I'd been couch-surfing for a long time before I ended up on the island where the sand and palm tree bed weren't so comfortable either. Until the last night when Ezra's chest became my pillow. That was very cozy. And warm. And safe. It felt *right*.

I didn't wake up on his chest this morning, but this still feels like a step in the right direction.

I know I'm alone in the apartment before I even step foot outside my room. The place seems empty. Even with Ezra staying in a separate bedroom, I knew when he was here. The place was alive. And now, it's lonely. Especially with the cold white walls and surgical furniture. I just want to wreak havoc and make it cozy. A few things out of place will make it look so much homier.

I take a hot shower and pour so many products on myself

I'm sure I smell like a perfume store. Zero regrets about that though. I've missed having good things in life—sue me for that.

In the kitchen, I make myself a cup of coffee and grab a fresh muffin from the counter, not wondering where it came from. Ezra is a billionaire, I'm sure he has people delivering goodies to his place all the time.

Then it's time to go and cry over how amazing my new closet is. I can't believe Ezra knows me so well in such a brief time.

As I'm looking through the pieces of clothing and touching them with my hands, I wonder if he knows me better than I do. Or is it this mysterious Martin? The hidden figure like Zorro, helping the King brothers along the way. Whoever it is, I feel seen for the first time in many years. If ever. And this is because of Ezra.

After a quick run-through of my new closet, I get a headache from so many options, so I quickly throw together the first things that come to my hand. It's a pink flowy skirt with a white off-shoulder sweater—a piece of my tattoo is peeking out on my arm—fishnet tan tights, and pink combat boots, which look absolutely adorable.

To finish the look, I take a black puffy jacket to put on later. It's unusually warm for mid-October, and I'd probably be fine with something thinner. But remembering how cold I was earlier this month in my revitalized cardigan makes the doubt about choosing the outerwear disappear in the blink of an eye—the warmer, the better.

When I come to the mirror, I get a pleasant surprise. The person looking back at me seems more like me than I ever was. I pile my hair on the top in a messy bun and let a few strands around my face loose. A tan-colored tiny backpack finishes my outfit, even though I don't have anything to put in there besides a new lipstick or something that Ezra bought for me.

When I go to the kitchen, I find something I can definitely throw in my backpack. On the kitchen island, right where we played our games yesterday, lies a black credit card with my name on it. I could cry out about being an independent woman who doesn't need one man's money. But I'm not independent yet. And I do need his money. So I stash the card in my bag, grateful to Ezra for thinking about that.

Next to the card, there's a phone. I take it, assuming it's now mine. No one will find me complaining about that because, quite honestly, I missed having the ability to Google things when I need to. Having a flip phone reminded me how to use my brain and not rely on technology so much, but I missed that wonderful time when I didn't need to use my brain and could just Google the bus schedule.

I tap the screen, and it lights up, asking for a password. Well, that's a pickle. Maybe the phone isn't really mine. Just out of curiosity, I decide to try something and press ten-ten. The home screen instantly lights up on the phone. Ezra used our wedding date as a passcode. He's turning out to be a total marshmallow.

I pull up the contacts and find three names in there: George, Martin, and Husband. Feeling warmth spreading through my chest, I eat breakfast at the kitchen island, enjoying this new feeling I'm not familiar with: happiness.

Then, I decide to look around the apartment and see how I can make this place better. I mean, it's my home now too. Why not?

A quick walkthrough tells me everything I need to know: I've got a lot of work to do. To my utter shame, I pause in Ezra's room. His bed is unmade. No wonder—he doesn't strike me as the type to make his own bed. He probably has people come over here and do it for him. No judgment—if I could afford it, I'd be doing it too.

Should I just lie in his bed? Like for a second. It looks so comfortable.

Why not? I crawl on top of it. Looks like he sleeps on the left side of the bed, so I move to the right side, pretending this is where I'm supposed to be.

As I close my eyes and let out a loud groan of pleasure, a female voice cries out. "Dios mío! I'm so sorry!"

I jump up, startled. A woman in a black uniform in her late forties is gawking at me from the door. She just apologized for startling me, and yet, she's not leaving. Instead, she keeps staring at me with a wide open mouth.

I crawl off the bed and try to get myself together.

"Hello?" I half ask.

"I'm so sorry. You must be the new Mrs. King. I mean the only Mrs. King. Besides the old Mrs. King." Her cheeks turn red. "I mean not old, but the elder one."

I chuckle. "Stop. Don't worry. I'm Maeve." I walk up to her to offer her a hand. "But yes, Maeve King."

"I'm so sorry," she apologizes once again. "They told me Mrs. King will be here, but when she's here, she's in the guest bedroom, you know. I didn't expect her to be here." She waves at me and at the bed, making me laugh. Because no, I don't know. "It's just," she continues, "I've never seen anyone but Mr. King and the old Mrs. King," she pales, "I mean the mother King. The other King." The more she talks, the redder her cheeks become.

"Please, don't be so scared. I was homeless a month ago, so don't feel like you have to treat me any different. I don't belong to this world, you know."

She blinks. Then blinks again.

"What did you mean when you said you didn't expect anyone here?"

The woman looks around and then turns to me with a suddenly mischievous smile on her face. "I mean," she sounds surer of herself, "I've never seen a woman here."

"In his bed?"

She lowers her voice. "In his place."

I smile at her with narrowed eyes. "How long have you been working for him?"

"Almost five years."

"And you've never seen anyone here?"

She leans closer to me. "No one." Her eyes sparkle. "But I'm glad he's got one of us for a wife. You know, simple people. About time someone showed him how to be human."

I rear back in mock horror. "Is he unfair?"

"No!" she replies quickly. "He's very fair. He pays more than enough and always tips us well. But he's—" She pauses, chewing on her lip.

"What?" I edge closer.

"He's a bit standoffish. And never talks, you know. Like he doesn't say hi or bye."

I edge a little closer. "I think I know why."

"Why?"

I look around, pretending I'm scared of onlookers. "He is very shy. And very awkward. He's probably scared of you."

"Oh, Dios mío." She places her open palm to her chest once again. "That poor boy."

"He is." I nod. "So don't even think he's bad or something."

"He's just scared?"

"Yep." I pop the *p*. "Very much so."

"To think of it, I remember when I was working for his parents—"

"You worked for his parents?" My ears perk up.

"Yes. For like ten years before I started working for him."

Interesting. "What happened?"

"His father used to be a..." she mumbles something incomprehensible under her breath.

"What?"

She mumbles again.

"What?"

"A dick!" she nearly yells. "He was a dick."

"Oh." That's all I can say without bursting out laughing. "How so?"

"He was always making them kids trying to compete with each other." Her voice is full of disapproval, and I second that. "But he always put a lot of pressure on the eldest one. Even when that poor boy was little, he was never allowed to be little. I remember how devastated he was when they came back from the trip to his nana, and their father never let them go there again." She starts nodding her head. "It's their mom's mom, you know. I've never seen her myself. And I don't even remember when I've seen Mrs. King the last time." The woman looks around as if to check that no one joined our little duet. "Now it actually makes sense what you said about him being shy and awkward. Now I see that. With pressure from his father like that, anyone would turn cuckoo."

Well, look at that. I meant it as a joke to loosen her up around the house, so she doesn't think ill of Ezra, but it's turning out to be true. Unfortunately. Looks like we're truly more alike than we both are willing to admit.

We chat some more before I bid her goodbye and walk to the elevator. Even growing up with rich parents, we've never had a penthouse because it was in bad taste to live inside the city. Rich suburbs were a way to show off to everyone what you were made of.

When the elevator's door chimes open, I step outside only to meet George, the driver from before. He rises to his feet as soon as he sees me.

"Mrs. King," he says with a short nod. I'm beginning to dig this new name of mine.

"Hello, George. Please, call me Maeve."

"As you wish, Maeve. Where shall we go?" He motions for me toward the glass door outside.

"Are you sticking to me today like a guard?"

"More like a chauffeur, to drive you around the city as you please. So you don't have to walk around this dangerous place."

I level him with a stare.

"I think Mr. King was worried about the city more," he adds with a humorous twinkle in his eyes.

That makes me chuckle. "Let's go, prison guard. I need to see my husband."

He nods with a smile.

In the car, I try to get more information about my new husband from his driver who, obviously, knows more than anyone else because he's always where Ezra is. But George is tight-lipped. So I give up on this idea, moving it to the back of my mind for later when he's more comfortable with me.

When the car stops in front of the building, George comes to open my door.

"You don't have to do that, you know," I tell him, looking around, hoping no one sees. I'm perfectly capable of opening my own door.

"This way, please." He ignores me and proceeds to open yet another door for me. The building one.

Security rushes to us, and George stops them with a wave of his hand.

"Let me introduce you to Mrs. Maeve King," he tells them.

All three men look between each other with a puzzled look on their faces, but they are quick to offer greetings. Then, George leads me to the elevator. He waits for me to step inside, and when the doors are about to close, he says, "The top floor."

"Thank you, George," I reply warmly and press the appointed button.

When the doors quietly slide open, I'm greeted with shouting. A man shouting. A very angry one. My new husband. *Great timing, Maeve.*

"Well, hello there," a male voice greets me a few seconds into my walk toward the angry shouting. I jump, startled again. *What's up with my nervous system these days?*

The most stylish man of all stylish men on the planet is looking at me with open interest. He's leaning his hip on a printer. A stack of paper in his hands. His suit is gray with bright, golden details. Something that should be approached carefully, but he makes it work. I like two-toned jewelry, but I don't see how it can work in an office wardrobe. It's playful, but it's for a specific setting. And yet, he proves me wrong. His suit is flawless, and the whole office interior just *matches* him.

Right of the bat, I know it's Martin. And I instantly know why Ezra would trust him to pick clothes that would 'hug and touch my body.' *Hubby, you big, possessive shit.*

I also get the feeling that I've seen him somewhere. A very strong feeling, but I can't place him anywhere no matter how much I try. I've always been bad with faces, and it got worse when I moved to New York.

"Hello, Martin," I say with a neutral smile, trying to figure out what he knows about me before I compliment him on his taste or something like that. I might have called Ezra awkward, but I'm the one who lives with a foot in my mouth. "It's nice to meet you."

"Likewise," he replies with a way warmer smile than mine and then instantly narrows his eyes as they scan over my figure. "Well, I don't know how you made this combination work, but you do. Damn, you go."

I glance down at myself, chuckling. "Funny, but I was thinking the same thing about you. How you can pull off a two-toned suit like that is beyond me."

He swats the invisible dust away from his shoulder with a smug smile. "I've got superpowers."

"That you do," I confirm, giving him another onceover. "Thank you for, you know, all of this." I gesture at myself.

"Oh, please." He waves me off. "I don't remember having such a fun assignment before, so it was very beneficial for me too. Like therapy." He presses his open palm to his chest. "I'm happy you like it though. I wasn't sure, you know."

"I'm not picky," I say with a shrug.

"He is." He points his index finger at the office where the shouting continues. "He was very *specific* about the things I needed to buy."

I feel my brows drawing together. "What do you mean?"

"Well." He looks at the shut office door to make sure it's still closed, I assume, and continues. "He explained *the feeling* to me." He widens his eyes.

"The feeling?" I ask, confused.

"The feeling of you." He stares at me with a meaningful look. "*Of* you."

"Of me?" I parrot.

He gives me a slow nod. "Of you. And then I sent him a few things I picked, but he said no-no, Martin." His tone turns flirty. "That's not who she is. And then he picked a few things to send to me so I could get a feel of you too."

Everyone is getting a feel of me in this story, and it makes me slightly entertained.

"Did you?" I ask with a quirked brow and a half smile.

He gives me another onceover. "Looks like I did alright," he says, a double meaning heavy in his words.

I chuckle and nod. "You did. Thank you."

Another loud shout makes Martin wince. "He's not having a good morning."

"Why?" I ask with genuine interest. For some reason, I have an urge to soothe him.

"Looks like the building won't be reopening anytime soon."

"Oh, shit," I whisper, feeling a wave of guilt washing over me. No matter what happened after, I'm the initial denominator of the whole situation. Me and the fire I caused.

"*Oh shit* is right." He looks at the closed door with a sad look on his face. "I don't know how he'll get out of this one."

With a deep sigh, I square my shoulders and head toward his office.

"Do you want me to put my headphones on?" Martin asks to my back.

I respond to him with a middle finger behind my back, making him laugh.

"Oh, I just might love you, Maeve King."

43

"This is why I pay you big money, isn't it?" I hiss into the phone even though I want to yell. I've already done that, and it didn't bring anything.

He clears his throat. *"The company."*

"What?" I ask, pulling on the tie to loosen it. Suddenly I don't have enough air. I thought securing the shares would ensure I have our company back. I was sure of it.

"The company pays me." His tone turns more confident.

"I see."

And I really do. This prick of a lawyer was brought into the company by the board, and he's working for them, not me. That much is clear. Is anyone in this company still working for me?

I hang up the phone without saying goodbye and press the button of the intercom to call Martin in, when the door slowly opens, and Maeve's head peeks through. If I was walking, I'd lose my footing because she's the last person I expected to see here.

My natural reaction is a bark. "What are you doing here?"

"Well." She steps inside, softly shutting the door behind her. "That's quite a welcome."

I want to be mad at her. I need to be mad at her so all this pent-up anger will have an outlet. She's the reason all of this started. If she didn't stay at the coffee shop, the fire wouldn't have started because the damn oven would have been off. And I might still have my company. But I can't even focus on any of that because my eyes keep ravaging her body.

Her legs seem to be endless in that skirt. Her calves look even more toned in those boots I picked myself. They're the same color as her hair, and I thought she'd love that about them. Looks like she does if she's wearing them today.

I want to shake my head to get rid of the lusting thoughts of my wife. But I can't.

She's moving closer while I'm internally battling with myself.

"What's with the face, love? You look like you just kissed a lemon," she teases, not knowing how much her nickname is affecting me. I know it's part of the joke, but it hits too close to home.

"I might as well have," I grumble, pushing away from the desk. I swear the papers scattered over my table snicker at me.

Maeve rounds the desk, her hips swaying in that hypnotic way that knocks my remaining sense out. She perches on the edge, right on top of another denial letter Martin collected before. "Bad day?"

"The worst," I admit shamefully. Something I don't do. Bluffing until I make it is the only way in this world. Swallowing hard, I continue with the truth, not able to stop myself. "I think I'm going to lose the company."

"What?" Her head tilts to the side with worry.

"I don't think the voting power will save it now." I try sounding calm, but everything inside is burning. Years of fighting are coming to an end with Noah and I on the losers' side.

"Why?"

I tell her the short version of how they're planning to keep us in court while the company crumbles. Eventually, we'd lose all clients—no one wants to be associated with legal battles and questionable quality. No one's reputation can take such a hit.

"I'm sorry, Ezra," Maeve says sincerely when I'm done. "I'm really sorry." Then she does something unexpected. Placing her right hand on my cheek, she smiles softly. Her comforting warmth seeps into me. "It's my fault. I know that. And I'm really, really sorry."

I cover her hand with mine, finding her eyes with my gaze. "It's not, Maeve. Don't even think about that. It was bound to happen sooner or later. My father started the process of sinking us five years ago when he decided to open the company and invite the board. He knew it was going to happen, but he was willing to give up something that was in our family for generations just to prove his point." I press my hand firmer onto hers. "It's not your fault."

Her eyes are shiny with unshed tears, but she nods. "I'm still sorry. I know how much this means to you."

Does she? Does she really know me so well? The deeper I dig into her eyes, the more I believe so.

"I know." I lean into her touch, letting her fingers travel into my hair.

"Do you want me to kiss it better?" She exhales the question, surprising me once again. Her tone is light, but her concern is genuine, her eyes scanning my face.

"I think it'll take more than a kiss to fix this situation."

"Oh, I've got more than kisses up my sleeve," she purrs, and my eyes drop to her bare shoulder. The material keeps dropping lower when she moves. Right where a vine of her arm tattoo peeks through. I get distracted and don't notice how her hand lands on my tie and pulls me into her orbit. Right into the cloud of her coconut scent.

"Yeah?" I rasp. "What do you have in mind?"

"Well, I could start by dancing on your desk. Naked," she suggests, eyes twinkling with mischief.

I chuckle, the sound rough with stress. "And risk you falling and suing me? The paperwork alone would be a nightmare."

"True," she concedes with a laugh, running her finger over the surface of my desk. "How about I make you a cup of coffee?"

"Fuck no!" I let out a loud, unexpected laugh. "Never make me coffee again, Maeve. Never."

She sinks her teeth into her bottom lip, trying not to smile.

"Alright," she says, jumping off the desk and dropping straight down to her knees. In front of me. Right between my legs. "I think I know something that might help."

"What are you doing, Maeve?" I ask huskily, spreading my thighs wider to give her space.

"Something that might not require any paperwork."

With that, her hands go straight for my belt.

"Maeve." I don't know what I want to say, but I just have to let her know that she doesn't have to do it. Even though I probably won't be able to breathe if she changes her mind. My cock is very eagerly pushing on the zipper from the inside, trying to meet her as fast as it possibly can.

She looks like a dream, on her knees between my legs, her hands working my belt.

"Maeve," I start again, my voice pleading. I don't think I'm asking her to stop. I'm sure I'm asking her not to.

"I'll have control now. If you misbehave, I'll bite it," she says with a crooked smile. Her cheeks pink. Her eyes glassy.

"And I just might like it."

She likes the answer because she pulls my cock out and shows me how beneficial it can be to lose control sometimes. I never thought seeing my wife with my cock between her swollen lips, on her knees under the desk in my office, could be hotter than the release itself. I wish she'd continue this torture without ever bringing me to finish.

Because it ends when it reaches the finish. And I don't want it to end.

44

Maeve

"Where to, ma'am?" George asks, holding a door for me when I come out of the building.

My legs are still shaking from the view I just got. Ezra King falling apart in my arms—and my mouth, if one wants to get technical. If I get to have a powerful man like Ezra yielding to a slight snap of my wrist and flick of my tongue, I could perform my wifely duties all day every day. Him returning the favor right there, on top of his desk, didn't hurt either.

I never thought being eaten out in the corner office overlooking New York was one of my fantasies. Until it was fulfilled. Turned out it was indeed my fantasy, and now it has become a part of my everyday bucket list. I should make these trips to his deserted office more frequent. One day, when I help him get his building back, it will turn into a celebration feast for the both of us. And I can't wait.

"Ma'am?" George repeats with a sly smile. It's like he knows what I've been doing. *Wait, maybe he does.* I subtly touch my cheek only to find it flaming hot. Yep, he knows.

"Twenty-Fifth Street," I reply, looking away from him.

He pauses before asking, quickly losing all playfulness, "Where to on Twenty-Fifth?"

"I don't know yet," I reply with a smile. "We will have to figure it out on the spot."

"Of course, ma'am."

I look up at him before he closes the door. "You know what, George?"

"I don't, ma'am." His face is humorous.

"I think I'm beginning to like you." I circle him in the air with my hand. "All this let's-go-no-questions-asked thing is enticing."

His face stretches with a smile. "The feeling is mutual, ma'am." Then he adds with an even wider smile, "Besides the talking part."

I smile back and dig into my bag. I need some cash and groceries.

"George, can you please stop at a grocery store first?" I ask when he's back in his seat.

"Of course, ma'am."

On the way, we stop at the store, and George helps me carry a basket. I fill it with some necessities and sandwiches, use my new card, and take cash out.

When we turn the corner of Twenty-Fifth Street, George asks. "Where to?"

"Just drive slowly by the curb."

"Yes, ma'am." I really like that—no questioning my weird requests.

We drive down the whole street, but I don't see Jeff anywhere.

"Change of plans." I unbuckle my seatbelt and poke my

face between the front seats. "Can you stop over there?" I point at the bus stop next to Lulu's house. This is where Jeff usually found me waiting for him.

George stops the car, and I open the door. "I'll be back for the groceries."

"Mrs. King?"

"Yeah?" I hate how easily I've gotten used to being called that.

"Are you sure?" He looks around, seemingly worried. "The neighborhood doesn't look safe."

"It's fine." I wave him off. "I used to live here, and I'm fine."

"Alright." He doesn't sound convinced. "I'll be here in case you need me."

"Of course." I smile. "Thank you, George."

I don't know how a gentleman his age could protect me from attackers, but I don't voice it. I've been here for some time, and chances are I'd be the one protecting him.

I shut the door and walk to the bench at the bus stop, hoping Jeff will find me due to his super-developed sixth sense.

Thirty minutes into waiting, I see Jeff's limping figure walking toward me. He's favoring his right leg even more than he usually does, and a worried feeling comes over me.

"Well," he greets me with a laugh, "look at you. Parents treated you well, I see."

"Nope, not the parents." I laugh, patting a spot next to me. "Come here. Let's talk."

He takes a seat next to me and looks at my face. "You look happy. And you didn't want to go to see them. Told you they'd be happy to see you too." He looks genuinely excited for me, and I feel my spirits lifting after the news Ezra delivered about his company.

"That's not them though."

"Who then? Who put that look on your face?" He points at me with a smile. "It has to be a boy?"

"Well," I start gleefully, showing him my ring.

"Kiddo, that was fast." He peeks at the ring. "That thing is big."

"I know." I wince, making Jeff chuckle. "It's awful."

"It's not bad. Maybe the size equals his love and devotion to you," he says, squinting and not sounding convinced himself.

"Right." I start laughing. "Let me get you something. Be right back."

I run to the car, grab the bags, and ask George to stay inside. Not looking happy, he agrees but keeps a watchful eye over me. I can feel his gaze the whole time.

When I place all my goodies in front of Jeff, he looks at me with round eyes.

"That's for me?"

"Yeah."

He wipes his nose. Then sniffles and wipes it again. "Thank you."

"No biggie." I shrug it off, not wanting him to feel like he owes me something. "I'm just returning the debt. Let me help you stash them in your cart. Where is it?"

"It's over there, right around the corner."

I make a move to grab the bags and get them to the cart when Jeff takes my hand. "Leave it. I'll take them. Sit down and tell me what's going on."

I plant my ass back on the bench and explain to him the whole story, from the very beginning. By the time I'm done, he's watching me with wide eyes.

"Wait, so the man whose coffee you've been spiking with salt is *the* King? The one from King Developers?"

How come even Jeff knows about them, and I don't?

"Turns out that way, yes." I shrug one shoulder.

He looks thoughtful when he speaks next. "I used to play at their parents' anniversary."

"What?" I cry out, drawing the attention of two people walking across the street. They pick up speed, hurrying away.

"Yes. His mother was apparently into jazz, so she insisted we fly over here all the way from New Orleans to play."

"They used to live here back then, in New York?" This is something I should have known by now, but I'm new at this whole wife thing.

"Yeah. I remember their two kids. Two boys. The eldest was stiff like a stone wall."

I nod because that sounds about right, and nothing has changed since then.

"The father was on this poor boy all the time. 'You're not sitting right. Not talking right. Not looking straight. Not smart enough. Not tall enough.'" He shakes his head with disgust. "At one point, I got so fed up with that, that I told him to leave the poor boy alone." Jeff quiets down, scratching his chin. "I never played again."

"What?" My heart stops beating. It stops beating for Jeff whose life was changed that day for worse. And for the poor boy who was forced to think he was not good enough.

"Yeah. That was the last time I played music as a paying job. No one ever hired me after that. Not even in a shitty café." He looks ahead of him with glassy eyes. "The King blacklisted me from the entertainment industry."

"Oh, Jeff. What happened to you after?"

I've never heard his story. Never actually asked because I didn't want to overstep, hoping he'd tell me his story eventually. But this story just can't be true. There's no way the universe weaved us all together like that. It just can't be happening.

"Music was all I've ever known. All." He bumps his fist to

his chest, his voice breaks. "It's my heart and my soul. When it was taken away, I couldn't do anything else. I've tried. Trust me, I've tried. But my whole desire to live was taken away." He stops talking, withdrawing into himself. "So here I am," he finishes. His shoulders drop forward. "Still playing. Just on the streets."

"Oh, Jeff. I'm sorry." I cover his hand, which is resting on the bench with mine.

"Don't be, kid." He pats my hand with his other. "I have zero regrets. I wish more people would have stood up for those kids. But Mr. King was a powerful man. I think he still is." He shrugs. "I'm just glad his son turned out to be okay."

"How do you know he's okay?" I ask, trying to lighten the mood with some humor.

"You'd have to be if he was able to put that smile on your face," he says with a wink.

"Yeah, he's okay." Saying it out loud makes my heart flutter like wings of tiny butterflies. Oh crap, I'm in trouble if the mention of his name makes me giddy.

"What about that piece of shit father?" His eyes narrow.

"I guess he's still a piece of shit. He brought a board in instead of passing on his company directly to his kids."

"Yeah, he'd do something like that," Jeff confirms, nodding.

"And now the board wants to take the company away from them."

"Why did he marry you then?" he asks with raised brows. "You just told me you came with a side of voting shares."

"I do," I sigh. "But as it turns out, the city wants the King brothers to fall, so the board can take over the company."

"The city?" Jeff's brows draw together.

"Yeah. The senior inspector who keeps the building closed?" I wait for him to nod to continue. "He's the brother of one of the board members. And apparently they're the ones who started this whole scheme."

"Well, damn." Jeff whistles. "What's his name?"

I blink at his question, not sure how this information is relevant, so he asks again.

"What is his name, kid? Did you swallow your tongue?" he chuckles.

"I—" I start mumbling. "I actually don't know."

"Well, you'd better find out because I've been living on the streets of this city for a long time. And I know things. And I also know people who know things," he adds with a wink.

I blink some more before calling Ezra. He picks up on the second ring.

"Wife."

My legs turn into jelly. I didn't expect one word could hold such power over my body, but it does. One word, and I'm reduced to a mess whose sole desire is to run home and wait for him with legs spread right in front of the elevator.

"Wife?" He repeats the magic word.

I clear my throat. "Yeah, that's me." I clear it again. "I mean, I'm calling to ask for the name of the inspector who's holding the building prisoner."

A pause. *"Why?"*

I mumble a curse about everyone asking stupid questions even though I just did the same to Jeff. "Just give me the damn name!"

"Boris Lebovski. Why do you need it?"

"Thank you! Bye!" I quickly hang up the phone not to give him a chance to say something stupid and liquefying like *'Come home, wife, I'll make you come again'* or worse.

"What's the name?" Jeff reminds me that I'm not alone here with my hot fantasies.

"Boris Lebovski."

"Hmm," he hums, scratching his scruffy chin. "I think he visits the hookers on Fifteenth."

"What?" I jump to my feet, utterly too excited.

He keeps scratching his chin, not hearing me. "Definitely Fifteenth. I'll ask around. Maybe he goes over there too." Jeff points at a brick building around the corner. "They have a sex club in the basement. We've seen some weird shit crawling out of there at sunrise."

Assuming he's not talking about vampires, my heart starts beating like crazy, threatening to rip my ribcage open and jump out to perform a happy dance. "Are you sure?"

"Yes-yes." He starts nodding. "Give me some time. I'll get you some pictures, and you can blackmail the shit out of him." Then his face turns sour. "Oh, wait. I can't do it just yet. I need some time to collect money for a camera. I'll go to the park tomorrow morning. It's Saturday, so there should be tourists I can play for."

"Jeff," I whisper, grabbing his hand. My voice is breaking. "You really would do that for me?"

"What?" He slaps his open palms on his knees in frustration. "Take pictures of an asshole who took down the whole building and therefore some of our food from us?"

"What do you mean?" I ask, confused.

"The restaurant inside and the coffee shop? They were leaving bags full of leftover food next to their back door in big plastic bags. They were feeding a lot of people on the streets," he explains.

"Really?" I ask, excited. I was one of those who left a bunch of food next to our door when I was closing up the shop, and in the morning the bags were gone. I didn't know who took them, but it's good to know they were doing something good for the people.

"Yep, they did. So we really want that building open again

too. Give me some time. I'll get money and figure something out."

"Wait." I dig into my purse to get the cash I took from the ATM before. "I forgot. I came to pay my debts with dues."

I press five hundred dollars in twenties into his hands. He looks down at our joined hands and then back at me. "I think it's too much."

"It's the dues. From Ezra," I add with a warm smile. I'll have to make it up to Jeff for standing up for my husband when no one else was doing that.

"It's still too much," he says, his voice breaking.

Ignoring his words because it's uncomfortable for the both of us, I continue. "I'll get you a polaroid tomorrow and bring it here. It's hard to fake those pictures, so he won't have anything to say about it. All you have to do is get a bit closer to the target. And maybe a phone too."

He forcefully shakes his head. "No. This is more than enough to buy a twenty-buck machine. And I already have a phone," he adds, sounding a bit offended. "I'll be fine."

Agreeing easily because I'm planning to bring more money, I shake our still joined hands. "Thank you, Jeff. Oh, wait." I dig into my pocket and produce a piece of paper with my new number, which I scribbled before we came here. "Take it. Call me when you find something."

"Will do." He accepts it with a nod. "Thank you, kid."

"For what?"

"For noticing me. Sometimes I forget how painful it is to be invisible," he replies quietly. He picks up his bags and limps away. Before he disappears behind the corner, he turns to me. "I'll find you when I have the photos. Let's hope he's a horndog so it happens rather faster," he adds with a chuckle and disappears out of view.

"A friend of yours?" George asks as I slide into the back seat of the car.

"He is," I reply with a nod. "I also think he's a friend of my husband too."

I don't even notice how easily *the* word slipped from my mouth. How natural it feels to call him that.

"I have a feeling I've seen him somewhere."

"You might have." I turn to look at him. "How long have you been working for Ezra?"

"Twenty years for the King family. And five years for Mr. Ezra, since his father retired from the company." I don't know if I'm imagining it, but I think he mumbles something like 'thank fuck.'

Well, I just started liking George a little more.

I poke my face between the seats like a rabbit from the hat, making him smile. "We need to find an apartment for Jeff. Until he can get back on his feet. Can you help me with that, George?"

"Aye-aye, ma'am," he replies playfully. "My daughter works at a real estate agency. We can call her."

I lightly smack his shoulder. "There we go, George! Working as a team already."

I come back home to an unfamiliar smell. Cooking. Someone is cooking in my virgin kitchen. And singing. The off-key voice makes me pause—the sound bringing me back to the island when Maeve sang at the top of her lungs as I fetched papayas for her.

Carefully padding toward the sound, I try not to spook my pink-haired canary who doesn't hear a thing because she's wearing headphones while dancing around my—*our*—kitchen barefoot, wearing a white T-shirt (mine) and black panties with a yellow smiley face on her ass. Her wild hair, still wet from the shower, is piled on top of her head.

Leaning my shoulder on the wall, I try to enjoy the view for as long as I'm allowed. I've never had a woman in my place besides my mom. And seeing Maeve feeling so comfortable around here does some odd things to me.

She's trying to sing a high note when I can't take it

anymore and start laughing. She jumps on the spot, dropping a spoon on the floor.

"Fucking hell!" Her small hand clutches her chest, lifting the shirt higher and revealing her very enticing legs. "You scared the living crap out of me."

I make my eyes refocus on her face. "You've done the same to all the neighbors with your singing."

Her eyes narrow viciously. "I will not apologize for having fun."

"As you shouldn't." I walk toward her, watching her reaction. I'm unsure where we stand after her visit to my office, even though I have hope. She tilts her head to the side, curiously watching what I'll do next. I'm curious too because it's new territory for me. "I'll be downstairs so you can enjoy yourself."

She clicks her tongue disapprovingly. "I thought this building was yours."

"Not this one." I smile back, walking up to her. "But if you burn this building down too, I might have a chance at buying the land and putting mine here. What do you think? Will you help me?"

She laughs, throwing her head back. A tiny birthmark under her chin makes an appearance for the first time, and I wonder how I haven't noticed it before.

"I just might. Ask me in the morning again before I have my coffee." Her eyes are playful, her posture relaxed.

And I go for it.

Wrapping my arms around her back, I pull her to me. Her arms follow the cue to do the same. She feels perfect just like that, with her squished to my stomach.

"What are you making?" I ask, suddenly feeling out of place but eager to learn the rules.

"Noodles," she replies with a wide smile.

"Noodles?"

"Noodles," she confirms with a nod. "When we were on the island, this was all I was dreaming about."

"Not a steak? Or even a burger?"

"Nope." A shake of her head. "Noodles. For the past five years, I couldn't afford steak. Or even a burger at times. So noodles were my comfort food." Then she adds with a giggle, "Or any food sometimes."

I don't know how she can laugh about that because all I feel is anger. At her parents, for the people who were supposed to care for her. They should have fought harder to bring her back. They should have loved harder.

"Do you want to go and get a steak?" I offer with a tight throat. "The biggest one we can find. A double tomahawk."

"Nope." She pulls her head back to look at my face. "I've learned some mean recipes, so we are eating noodles tonight."

My eyes dart between hers, and I think I recognize how important it is to her to have this shared meal.

"We're having noodles tonight." My voice is firm, leaving zero other suggestions in meal choices for the evening.

With a giant smile on her beautiful face, she lifts up on her tippytoes, plants a quick kiss on my lips, and flies away to the stove.

I wash my hands and walk to the fridge. "Do you want anything to drink?"

"I'll take whatever you'll be drinking."

Fuck, I wanted bourbon, but Maeve is not the bourbon type—I saw how sour her face became when I was drinking it at the hotel. So I grab a bottle of red wine and pour it in two glasses. Soon, she places two steaming bowls on the kitchen island and takes a seat next to me. With her criss-crossed legs in a yoga pose and bare legs, my attention is not on the bowls in front of me.

"So," her voice brings me back to the food, "we've got my

favorite recipe I found on YouTube a year ago. It's got every-thing you might want to eat."

I glance at the artfully arranged bowl. Even the egg, cut in half, looks enticing. Taking the chopsticks and pulling the noodles out, I'm determined to eat it even if the food tastes like shit. I've never been a noodles guy, but I'll become one if she wants me to.

To my surprise, the food tastes amazing. Quickly finishing my bowl, I drink the broth and ask for seconds. My request must make her happy because she jumps to her feet with a giant smile on her face and fixes me another bowl.

We chat about nothing and everything. The mood is light, the words are flowing. Until I bring up her escape. But I need to know. I need to know what happened that made her run away from the house where she had every-thing and go to poverty where she had to sleep in the coffee shop. Yes, she has shit for parents. It's understand-able. But I'm sure there was some major catalyst in this story.

"Why did you leave your parents' house, Maeve?"

My question makes her pause with chopsticks halfway to her mouth.

"Because I wasn't happy there." Her mood gets cloudier with every word.

"I bet you weren't." It's time to push. I need to know, no matter how much it will hurt. Because I need to know whom I'll need to hurt. "But what really made you run away?" I move my chair closer to her. "What happened, Maeve? Tell me."

She sucks her lip between her teeth, contemplating if she should continue. And I just know I'm not going to like the story.

"Maeve." I gently place my hand on her knee, giving her the comfort to continue.

"They wanted me to marry this awful dude who was too handsy."

I feel my jaw clench shut. The desire to smash her father's face is strong. For trying to marry his eighteen-year-old daughter to some dickhead. And then to punch said dickhead. Many, many, many times.

"I suspect your parents didn't do anything to protect you?" My voice sounds foreign to me. Like I'm witnessing myself speak from out of my body.

"Protect?" Her short-lived laugh is sad. "They *wanted* me to marry him. Didn't matter what he did."

Another stab in my chest. "Did he—"

"Nah." She rolls her eyes. "I'd never let a dickhead like him touch me when I didn't want him to. So he probably has one testicle less after our dinner. Whatever." She shrugs her shoulder nonchalantly. "I'm over it."

I squeeze my hand on her knee, not feeling *over it*. I'll find that man. And I'll talk to him, making sure he has no balls left after. And then I'll talk to her father—fuck the shares.

"Ezra?" Her soft voice calls out to me, bringing me back from the dark place I'm in. "It's okay. I'm really over it. Look where it got me." Her gentle smile lights up some of the dark corners of my mind, making me want to believe her. But it doesn't mean I won't be having the talks with those douchebags. Maeve has never had anyone in her corner before, but now she has me. And I can be a vicious motherfucker when someone of mine is touched. And she is mine.

"Ezra?" she calls again. "I got you something."

I rear back in surprise. "You got me something?"

"Yes. Hold on."

She jumps off the chair and runs out of the kitchen. A click of her door and then her quick footsteps. Back in the kitchen, she pauses, looking unsure.

"What's the matter, Maeve? What happened?"

Her arms are crossed behind her back—looks like she's holding something. "I walked by this place today when I went to the store." Her neck moves in a swallow. "And then I saw it. So I bought it. It looked like it could, you know, fit you."

"Fit me? Did you buy me clothes?" I ask, confused. I'm not sure our styles will match, but I'll humor her and wear it. She took time to find something for me. For *me*. And I'll wear it for her.

She quietly pads toward me and places something small on the table. Her hand is still covering it, and at this point, my anticipation is through the roof. I'll wear her duck undies if she asks me to.

When her small hand pulls away, there's a black velvet box left on the white surface.

I look at Maeve and ask after I swallow a sudden lump in my throat. "What is that?"

Her hand moves toward the box to open it. "It's the ring I was supposed to have ready for you during the ceremony."

Then she rushes to add, "It's okay if you don't like it or don't want to wear it, you know. It's fine. You know what? Let's forget about it." Looking like a spooked animal, she strikes her hand forward, trying to grab the box.

She's fast. Like a little rattlesnake. But I'm faster. Grabbing the box right before she touches it, I lift it up far from her reach.

"Sit down, Maeve," I order, using the voice she likes. She can chatter all she wants that I'm a douche and an asshole, but she likes to obey when I talk like that. And she does. She plants her ass on the chair and watches me with her big, blue eyes.

I look inside the box. The golden wedding band is simple. It's not wide, it's not heavy. But it's classy. Something that I'd choose for myself if I didn't want to impress anyone. Something I can wear every single day.

"What do you think?" she asks in a tight voice.

"I love it," I say back, taking the ring out of the box and aiming to place it on my finger.

"Wait!" Maeve cries out, making me pause next to my finger. "May I?"

I nod silently, not sure I'll be able to speak in a regular voice without breaking at the end. She pries the ring from my hand and carefully pushes it on my ring finger. It fits perfectly. Not loose, not tight. It looks like it belongs here.

My gaze moves to her face. She's biting the inside of her cheek, looking adorably unsure.

I grab her hand and pull her toward me. "Thank you," I whisper when I hold her in a tight hug.

Her arms come around me, and we stay like that for a long time. Neither of us want to move. It feels like we are where we're supposed to be. If someone offered me my company back right now in exchange for giving up Maeve, I'd send them straight to hell.

I thought I'd be wearing this ring for her. But with every passing second it's sitting on my finger, I'm coming to understand that I'll be wearing it for me.

An hour later, we're on the couch in the living room, where I'm forced to watch a TV show. I never waste my time on things like TV shows, but if watching these teenagers, who don't even look like teenagers, swoon over each other lets me hold sighing Maeve for the next five hours, I'm game.

She's leaning her head on my chest while my arm is wrapped around her body when I decide to pop the question that has been bothering me for some time.

"Mae?"

"Yeah," she mumbles back, engrossed in this Paxton Hall or whatever it's called.

"Did you orgasm with me?"

Her whole body goes stiff. I don't even think she's breathing.

"Why?" Her voice is robotic.

"Did you?" I repeat, suddenly aware that her answer is very important to me.

"Ezra." She pulls away far enough to look at my face. "Why are you asking that?"

Ignoring her question, I push mine again. "Did you? Did you really orgasm with me?"

"I did," she replies with her eyebrows drawn together in obvious confusion, not knowing where the question is coming from. "Why are you asking that?"

"You mentioned on the plane that you've never done it with another person."

Her eyes turn so wide, I'm scared they'll fall out of the sockets, while her cheeks turn a scorching red. She jumps away to the other side of the couch, covering her face with her hands. "I hate these moments. I hate them."

"When you don't orgasm?" I'm barely able to contain my laughter seeing her beet red face.

"No, you idiot!" She throws a pillow in my face. "When I mumble when I'm nervous."

My body shakes with silent laughter. "So, it looks like I was the first one to make you come, wasn't I?"

Another pillow flies to my face, but I catch this one midair.

"Oh, you shut it!"

I laugh more.

"Stop looking so smug!"

"I can't help it," I wheeze through the laughing. "Talk about playing someone's body like a tune."

"Ezra," she growls like a tiny, wild beast. Her nostrils flare as if that was supposed to be her warning. "Stop it!"

"Or talk about one's schlong being very capable." I'm nearly hiccuping at this point, reminding her about the word I asked her not to use when she described our time together.

"Ew, don't say that!" She winces in disgust, but her eye is twitching.

"What did you say about our coitus before? Was it fulfilling enough?"

She jumps at me, knocking down the pillow I was holding like a shield. Her thighs are on either side of mine. Her hands are on my shoulders. "I don't remember. I'm afraid you'll have to demonstrate again so I can be the judge of it." Her mischievous eyes dart between mine. Her little tongue peeks out to lick her lips. Teasing. Distracting.

"I'll be happy to prove myself right now." My voice is husky. Tone promising. Because I know I can back it up. It's easy with Maeve, we're so attuned to each other.

She presses her lips to mine while her pussy pushes on my already hard cock. We make out like teenagers in the back seat of a car. I can't get enough of her body pressed into mine. I'm drunk on the feel that she's mine from now on. That I can kiss her anytime I want. That I can fuck her anytime I want.

That I can call her mine.

Three weeks come and go, and I live in a blissful nirvana. The company is losing more and more money. More investors are pulling away. More contracts are getting cancelled. But I'm becoming happier. A paradox. This company and the idea of making it great have been my life for as long as I can remember. I've never known what else to do with my life. Until now.

Turns out, coming home to my wife cooking simple

meals and stinking up the whole place with garlic gives me more butterflies than any merger would. Seeing her slowly transforming my penthouse into a chaotic mess makes me understand how a real home should look and feel.

Hearing her sing every chance she gets is the only sound that can make me laugh these days. Seeing her cheat in cards and Monopoly with Noah and Martin in our living room fills me with contentment and odd happiness. Her regular visits to my empty office make my awful days bearable.

Seeing her sleeping in my bed with her pink head on my pillow. Watching her steal my comforter every single night, leaving me in the shivering cold. Smelling her coconut scent in every room, on every piece of clothing I own. Laughing at her buying unmatched coffee mugs. Noticing her giving cash or buying food for every single homeless person she meets. Her smiling at every cashier or clerk, even those being rude to her. Or running toward an opening door to hold it so someone with a stroller can go in. Being kind to people who don't deserve it.

It all makes me realize that I'm falling in love with my wife.

Ezra

The last month has been a dream, no matter how sappy it sounds. Maeve has been coming to the office every single day, and we always end up making out or just having wild sex on one of the surfaces or on the floor.

Today I've had a particularly bad day, which became slightly better after her visit. I've got yet another denial from the city, and with this one I have a feeling that my days in the company are numbered. We've lost too much money and too many clients for me to remain in the seat; therefore the company will be transferred solely to other board members once they vote against me.

The only thing I'm looking forward to is coming home, knowing Maeve will be there, waiting for me.

That was, until I came home today.

I thought—no, hoped—that she'd be waiting for me as usual. But she's not. I linger in the kitchen for longer than I normally would, waiting for her to come back from jogging. She's been doing that a lot recently. Or maybe she went somewhere with George—the man has slowly transferred himself to her. Which I don't mind; he has some sick tricks up his sleeves, so he also doubles as a bodyguard for my wife.

But she hasn't come back.

I call her. Twice.

But she doesn't respond. So I go to sleep.

In the morning, I wake up to an empty bed and her scent still lingering on the sheets. Which immediately triggers something sharp in my chest. Her avoidance. Secrecy.

So I decide to do something extreme and not go to work today. Instead, I decide to wait for her to come back.

I'm sitting in the living room, patiently waiting for her arrival. When the elevator doors chime, her voice rings through the suddenly cold space. She's clearly talking to someone on the phone.

"No, I need Jeff to be comfortable." A pause. "I know, but he's very important to me. I need him to be there tonight so I can visit him anytime I want. Well." A giggle. "At least when he feels like company. He's so moody. Sometimes I have to wait for him forever." An invisible hand squeezes my chest from the inside, breaking ribs one by one. "Yes, please. Yes."

She's so excited that she doesn't even recognize my frozen presence while she runs to the bedroom. Granted, I'm hiding in the shadows in the corner in a perfectly placed chair, but we've always been attuned to each other. Always. I've always known when she's in the room, and I thought she felt the same.

I don't hear the rest of the conversation because a wave of rage envelops me in a fuzzy fog. It wraps around my mind and doesn't let go until I'm in the elevator. Then in the car. I should have called George to drive me because driving in this state of mind is not fair to the people around me, but I take the sports car regardless. My tongue is too tied to even talk to him. I feel betrayed. It's something I'm used to, but not on this scale.

Is my wife having an affair? So fast? I thought we had broken the ice a long time ago. I've been living in a dream for the past month, for fuck's sake. Was she playing me all this time? Or was Jeff there before me? Did she plan to get *comfortable* and pay for their love nest?

Fucking hell. I didn't know the feeling of internal pain until now. Why is it hitting me so hard? Why can't I breathe when I'm thinking about my wife in the hands of this Jeff?

Why am I so jealous?

Why?

I let out a short exhale, and my mind sets in place. Everything does really. I'm in love with her. I'm in love with my fake wife who apparently loves Jeff.

I am fucked.

This is all I can think about while I drive myself to the office. I've been doing it a lot recently, enjoying the time off my phone. Early morning city streets are not so busy, and I've come to appreciate the sunrise. Not today. Today, I'm coming to the office much later when the streets are packed with cars and pedestrians running in front of them on red lights, aggravating my already pissed-off mood.

I stride past Martin without acknowledging him, which is a shitty move, but it beats saying something I'll regret later. He regards me with a quirked brow and a silent salute and quickly goes back to clicking on his keyboard. This reminds me why I'll never give him up to Noah.

I'm mulling over my newfound knowledge about my wife and *Jeff* when the intercom pings with Martin's disgusted voice.

"Your father is on the line. I can send him to hell where he belongs if you want."

Just what I need today. He won't leave me alone until I talk to him. Maybe he's been sent to me to pour my frustration on him, so something good might come out of it.

"No," I sigh. "Patch him in. Let's get this over with."

"Alright. I'll have a bottle of bourbon waiting for you after the call."

"Son," my father's voice booms through the speaker, *"I've heard you found a way to trick me."*

"I don't know what you're talking about."

His loud laughter etches on my nerves. *"C'mon. I've raised you to be a conniving little bitch. Glad to see my lessons are paying off."*

I have so much to tell him, but it's not worth it since it always falls on deaf ears. "What do you need?"

"Today we are having a ball for the old squad. You have to be there."

"No, thank you."

"I'm afraid, it's not negotiable. The board will be there too. It's your chance to prove yourself to them. Make sure that little wife of yours behaves."

"Watch when you speak of her." Even though I want to rage about her betrayal, it's between her and me. He has bullied me enough, and I will not let him bully her.

His annoying cackle radiates from the walls of my office. *"Make sure she won't embarrass us. She's a King now."*

Ignoring the expected jabs, I focus on the reason why he's calling. "Why do you really want me there?"

His voice loses its humor. *"To show everyone that I made the right decision by bringing the board in."*

Here it comes, the real father I've known my whole life.

"You still don't think we're capable of doing it ourselves?" I ask, meaning Noah and myself. If we hadn't been fighting his fucking board half the time, the company would have been much further than it is now. Well, than it was before the fire.

"Do you still think you are?" He laughs. *"The gala is at eight. Be there. Make your gate puppy call my assistant for details."* He hangs up after that, thank fuck.

Martin's face pokes through the slightly open door. "Your gate puppy," he presses his index finger into his chest, "can make his life a living hell. I've got some dirty laundry I can air on your command, Boss."

"As appealing as that sounds, the laundry belongs to my family. Let's keep it locked." I wipe my face with my hand. "Fucking hell, it just keeps getting worse."

Martin edges inside, leaning his shoulder on the door-frame. "What's so bad about going to a gala with that beautiful wife of yours on your arm? I thought you'd be happy if she went to a grocery store with you. Plus, she knows how to have fun." His eyes move up and down over me. "God knows you could do with some of it."

"My wife?" I smack my hand on the desk, making Martin raise his brows. "My wife turned out to be a deceiving little thing who has a little too much fun."

He blinks fast, pushing away from the support of the wall. "Is that doubt I'm sensing?"

I level him with a stare. "I don't pay you to be my therapist."

"Yeah, you actually do." He takes a seat across from me, completely ignoring my stare.

"No, I don't," I growl back, annoyed that even my own damn assistant is defying me today.

"What happened? I've seen how giddy Maeve looks when she comes here. She's watching your mouth when you speak for fuck's sake. That woman is head over heels. Or the way you watch her in your kitchen. I swear I can see little cartoon hearts around your head when you do. And your place turning into a chaotic bazaar?" He makes a gesture with his hand, showing a chef's kiss. "What's come over you?"

I'm watching Martin's face and wondering if I should ask for his help with this because he knows pretty much everything about everything in this company. During these four years he's been working for me, he's proven his loyalty. He knows about the company. About my forced marriage plan with a dowry of shares. About my mutual hatred with my father. He's seen Maeve in the intimacy of my home. So why can't I bring myself to tell him about what I've found out about her?

"Mr. King?" he reminds me he's still in the room. When I don't respond, he adds quieter, "Ezra?"

I press the heels of my palms into my eyes and groan. "It's nothing. I need to be sure before I talk."

"O-kay. Just so you know though," he says, standing up, "I think your somewhat 'forced marriage,'" he makes quote marks in the air, "turned into a very willing one. At least on her end."

He leaves me with a pounding headache and racing thoughts. I'm trying to figure out if I gaslighted myself when I heard her talking on the phone? Or am I gaslighting myself while I'm trying to come up with excuses about why she'd need to rent an apartment for a guy named Jeff? Or why she'd need to visit him so often.

I call Noah to discuss if he found out anything from his reporter from Maine. She helped him the last time for a personal issue, and I hoped she might be able to find some dirt on one of the board members. At this point, I'm willing to work from any possible angle. Even if the opening is slim.

"Leila's looking into that. She said she doesn't like digging old graves with this sort of shit, but she's doing it for me for the last time."

"Why is she doing that?"

He's reluctant to answer, which means it has something to do with that old story. He hates being reminded about that.

"Because of her husband, I suppose."

"The dude you hijacked the helicopter for?"

He chuckles. *"I didn't exactly hijack it."*

"Except you did," I say back.

"But it was worth it though." He doesn't sound remorseful. And he shouldn't.

"I guess it was." Saving a life is worth it for sure. Even though I remember how much that situation cost us.

"She'll let me know if she finds something. It might take her some time though since she's a law-abiding citizen."

"Why do you make it sound like an insult?"

"Do I?" he laughs, not exactly responding.

"Then why are we asking her to do that? We should hire a PI who will get it done faster."

"Already done," he replies.

"Fuck, Noah. I don't have time for riddles. Why do we need her then?" I have no idea why we need this Leila and her law-obedient nature. I understand that my brother feels like he owes her something, but I don't know that story fully, so I don't get involved.

"Because she feels like she owes me, Brother." He's silent after that. *"And it's a very shitty feeling."*

One day, he'll tell me the story. But for now, I'll have to accept his decision.

"Okay," I agree with a sigh. "I guess it won't hurt to have two people looking into that."

"It sure won't," he agrees with a much lighter mood.

It's time to change the subject and move on to the issue of the day. "So, daddy dearest wants us to be present at some gala tonight where we can royally fuck up to prove him right."

"Well, this is an interesting way of reuniting the family. Is he going to be there?"

"Yes," I sigh. "You know what annoys me the most? That this fucker hasn't done a thing to grow this company. Not a fucking thing. He just got it from his ancestors and rolled with it. But when we're trying to take it back and actually do something good with it, he resurfaces like a bad rash."

"Ezra," he starts carefully. *"It's time to let it go."*

But I can't. I am the eldest. I always had something to prove.

I still remember our parents' wedding anniversary. I was fourteen. That day I was doing everything wrong. I dressed wrong. I spoke to him wrong. I got an A-minus at school. I performed poorly at football practice. And then I didn't look *happy enough* at the evening of fake happiness.

As soon as my father grabbed my shoulder and walked me behind the nearest corner, he smacked my face and ordered me to smile. I remember someone grabbing his arm when he wanted to deliver the second blow. I think it was a musician from a jazz band my mom used to love, but they were located somewhere in the south.

My father had ordered the band to appear in New York at the celebration as a good husband would. Of course, he talked about it with everyone who'd listen. But that man saw my shame, saw that I couldn't do anything to my father. I was fourteen, old enough to stand up for myself.

Yet I was quiet. I still hate myself for that. And I hate my father for making me feel that way. And I hated that man for witnessing my moment of weakness and being the first one to ever say anything. With time, I came to realize that it was a brave move, considering how powerful my father was. I still wonder what happened to that man. I know my father didn't let it go—he's not that type of person to just let any disrespect slide.

"I can come today too," Noah offers through the phone.

"Yeah. That'd help. Martin will send you the info."

"See you there."

Now, I have to go home and figure out how I can try not to strangle my *wife* when I'm alone with her.

Contemplating if I should call my own PI who does personal cases for me and ask him to follow Maeve, I decide against it. I have too much shit going on to focus on trying to figure out if she has someone on the side and if I've been played like a damn puppet. If I gave too much thought to that, it'd mean she matters. And she doesn't. The more I think about that, the more I understand. She's run out of her usefulness. I married a woman who didn't bring me anything but ruin.

I take a sip of bourbon when the elevator opens. I watch it from the dark corner of the living room where she can't see me. From the very same chair I listened to her speaking this morning.

She takes her sneakers off and puts them on the side with a groan. She looks tired. Did she just come from a run wearing leggings and that loose shirt? I know she prefers tight clothes for workouts since it doesn't restrict her movements.

Her phone rings.

"Yes?"

I can see it's something good because her face brightens, and all tiredness is being erased with every word the person on the other side speaks.

"Yes? Hi, Jeff!" She bites her lower lip while speaking into the phone with obvious excitement. "I'll be there tomorrow. I'm not sure I can get away today." Silence. "No, I don't want him to know yet until we're sure." I feel my jaw clenching hard together. "Yes." Her voice softens. "Thank you. You have no idea how much it means to me. I'll come to you tomorrow. I also have a surprise for you."

Yep, you have it, alright. Surprise you got for him with our marital money I suppose.

My anger flares up once again, and I take another sip in hopes it will calm me down a little. It doesn't. It only makes it worse. The burning liquid sliding down my throat only fuels this rage inside even more.

She walks to the kitchen and pours water from the sink. She drinks it greedily, her neck moving with quick, deep swallows. When I think about what else this neck might have been swallowing today, I slam my glass on the table, making her jump.

She presses her hand to her chest. "Jeez, I didn't see you there."

I keep silent.

"You scared me," she giggles, pouring herself another glass and placing it on the table.

"Who were you talking to on the phone?" My voice is coarse. I'm trying to contain the anger I'm feeling. And the closer she comes, the madder I get.

Her eyes dart to the side before returning to me. "An old friend."

"A friend?"

"Yes."

"I see."

"What do you see?" Her brows draw together as her steps falter. "Ezra, you sound weird." She tilts her head a little to the side. "And you look weird. What happened?"

"Come here." I gesture for her to come to me with just the fingers of the hand resting on my thigh.

She starts moving toward me. Reluctantly at first, and then more willingly.

"Are you okay?" she asks in a soft voice. Like nothing is happening. Like she's not setting up a date with another man while she's playing house with me.

"Here, Maeve." I put more pressure into my voice while keeping it low.

Her eyes widen while her little, poisonous tongue peeks out to lick her luscious lips. She likes it. She likes being ordered around.

Her bare feet pad until she steps right in front of me. Her knees almost touching mine.

"You look sad," she whispers.

"I'm not sad, Maeve."

"What is it then?" Her voice is small. *Is that guilt?*

"I'm angry, Maeve."

"Why?" She watches me with her big, blue eyes, pretending to be innocent.

"Why do you think?"

She shrugs. "To be fair, you have a lot to be angry about. Including me."

"That's true, wife." I say the word mockingly, and she notices. Her forehead wrinkles, and she wants to ask something.

But I'm done talking.

I grab her hand, pulling her onto me. She lands on my lap with a *woof*.

"What are you doing?" she exhales.

"I just want what a husband should have. Without any fucking games."

Her worried eyes dart between mine as she licks her damn lips again. "Are we done playing games?"

"I'm long past them."

"Okay." She swallows. "I think I'd like to stop playing them too."

Her voice sounds so small, so vulnerable, that for a moment I get washed with doubt. For a moment. Until she moves her face closer and presses her lips to mine.

I want to push her away because a rough fuck is all I want, but she presses her lips harder without opening them. Then she starts peppering the corners of my mouth with soft kisses, and I feel my dick getting rock hard.

She moves her hips to get more comfortable, so her pussy ends up right on top of me. It radiates a very inviting heat.

While I'm drowning in self-turmoil, she gently places her hands on the sides of my face and licks my lips with her tongue. I'm defenseless against it, so I just open up and welcome her. After all, I said what I said—I'm here to take what a husband can.

I let my hands move to her lower back and pull her flush to me. She gasps, letting me deepen the kiss.

The more careful her kisses, the crazier they make me. The more I want.

The gentler I become.

Fuck! This is not what it was intended for.

I grab her by her ass and stand up with her in my arms. She holds onto my shoulders, wrapping her legs around me. I move my mouth to her neck while I walk her to the kitchen island where the stupid game started. Carefully placing her on the top, I take a step back.

She's watching me with eyes half-lost in lust. Her cheeks are red. Her chest is heaving.

She lifts her arm to grab me, but I take another step back, leaving her confused.

"Turn over."

"W-what?"

"On your belly. Now."

"Oh." Her eyes spark with interest as she jumps off the counter, turns around, and bends over it as she spreads her arms in front of her, placing one hand on top of the other. Her leggings-clad ass is waiting for me up in the air.

I walk to her and pull on the waistband of the leggings with both hands, revealing her black, lacy underwear. She helps me get rid of her pants when I bring them down to her ankles. She makes a move to take off her panties, but I stop her by firmly pressing my hand on top of hers. Then, not removing my hand from her body, I move it up and press between her shoulder blades, silently ordering her to stay put. She obeys. Too easily. Giving me the comfort, the control I crave. She knows me too well. The witch.

I unzip my pants, letting my hard cock free. I give it a couple strokes and move to her. She turns her head with her lower lips between her teeth to look at me. When she notices me giving myself another stroke, her mouth falls open, and she wiggles her ass invitingly.

Edging closer, I push her panties to the side. She's already slick. Ready. I push two fingers in, making her gasp. Giving it a few pumps until she meets me halfway, I replace my fingers with my cock.

She's so fucking tight, but I'm mad. Impatient. I'm on a path of punishing. So I thrust in. She gasps again, and I stop, overwhelmed with guilt. I can't even punish her properly. So pathetic.

I push my hand between her body and the marble and find her clit. Gently rubbing it, I wait for her to start moving and give me indication that she's okay. Because if she's not, I don't know what I'll do.

She's okay. She starts moving. She pushes herself onto me.

I edge closer and lean forward, covering her body with mine. We're both wearing clothes. It's annoying. This barrier between us is annoying. I'm fucking mad. Grabbing the front of her neck, I lift her to me. Her back is pressed to my chest, my hand keeping a firm hold on her neck. While my hips are moving forward, slowly thrusting into her.

She grips the edge of the table with her hands and throws her head back on my shoulder. I start kissing her jaw. Her neck. I bite it. We move faster. She whimpers. Our speed intensifies. We turn sweaty. Sleek.

I put more pressure into my grip and more power into my thrusts. Her knuckles on the marble turn white. My breathing turns quick and shallow. I'm not sure I'm even getting any oxygen because my head is not okay. It's high and lost in the sensation.

"Harder," she orders in a raspy voice.

I push harder. Faster.

"No," she growls. Her hand suddenly covers mine. The one on her neck. "Harder. Here."

I smile into her cheek and put more pressure into my grip while withdrawing almost all the way out. And then push back in. And out. Until she starts shaking with a silent cry. Her mouth falls open, her head drops on my shoulder. Her fingers dig into my forearm.

I follow her right after. There is no fucking way I could last longer when her nails are drawing blood.

When we are both spent, she falls forward on the table. I want to join her. I want to cover her body with mine and keep her warm and tranquil.

But I remember how we ended up here in the first place. So I step away.

"We have a gala tonight. Our first official outing. Be ready in an hour."

With that, I walk away to my room. To the shower. To try to get rid of her deliciously deceiving scent.

We've had sex in different places for the past few weeks. We've done it fast. We've done it slow. But never have I done it while hating her. This was the first. And I don't like the aftertaste.

 aeve

Well, that was—

What was that exactly?

Ezra walks out of the kitchen with a straight back and hands balled into fists. He looks even more pissed than before.

I thought he didn't want to play games. I don't know what that is if not a game. For the past month, I thought we'd come to an understanding and found common ground we can coexist on. Even more so, I've started falling for my husband. Hard.

I also thought we became a couple. A real one who shares laughs and dinners. And saliva. We sure have shared a lot of saliva over the past four weeks. What could have happened between then and now? We didn't have a fight. Not once. All our bickering was part of flirting, and every single time we ended up in bed. Or on the table. Or on the couch. By the window too.

Is that the problem? Has his interest died now that we've gone through all possible surfaces?

I pick up my leggings and shamefully rush to my room. Even though there was nothing shameful in the way he was hammering my body. Nothing. It felt natural and needed. Different too. We've had some wild sex marathons, but this time it felt… odd. I should have sensed it earlier, but I was in a horny frenzy. Typical. Every time he uses that commanding voice of his, I turn into a puddle. So I let myself be vulnerable.

To think of it, all my vulnerable moments of the past year have been reduced to my time around Ezra. He has a tendency to break my well-built walls with just his big presence. With the promise that he can solve all my problems. That he can shoulder me from the world.

Too much of a promise. He can't even shoulder me from himself. And after what just happened, I'm starting to think that he's the one I need protecting from the most.

I run myself a hot shower and lather my body, trying to wash away the smell of sex which feels shameful now. Like I've done something wrong. Like it was wrong to enjoy it so much. I know he loved it too. I felt the moment his self-control bid farewell, and he turned into my Ezra from our late nights around the apartment. The unhinged one. The wild one.

I want to stay under the hot stream forever, but he said we have a gala to attend. So I cut it short. After all my moisturizers and oils, I feel much better. I like fruity smells. I like coconuts. Everywhere.

It shouldn't be a problem to choose something to wear—my closet is full of anything one might ever need. It takes me only a couple of minutes to find a long, black dress. Its sleeveless form hugs my upper body like a glove. A deep V-cut goes down almost to my belly button. Meaning I'll have to go braless, showing a lot of skin. The skirt is tight and goes all the way down to my shins. I'm not sure how I'll move, but I'll manage.

I pull my hair up in a messy bun and let a few strands loose around my head. Black pumps with red soles finish the look.

As I'm watching myself in the mirror, I understand that something is missing. The dress is gorgeous, but it's not me. I don't feel comfortable in this. This is something my mother would have forced me to wear to impress suitors.

I dig into the drawers and find scissors. Big ass scissors. This is what I need. I take the dress off and make a long, deep cut for my right thigh. The expensive material makes it seamless, giving in to the sharp blade. Like it was meant to be like that. The cut is deep, but it's visible only when I move and adds a nice touch to my outfit.

I keep looking at myself in the mirror and find that something's still missing. I raid my closet and soon find exactly what I'm looking for. A pink, lacey bodysuit with long sleeves. It's sheer. One hundred percent see through, which will make my colorful tattoo visible. I quickly put it under the dress and step in front of the mirror.

Well, hello there, Maeve.

I push my titties up and together and admire my work. It would have been too obvious without the lace and too vulgar. With the lace, it's more discreet, leaving something to the imagination. Not much, just something. The bodysuit is pretty tight, so my girls stay in place if I don't make jerky movements. Which I don't plan on doing—today is an evening of elegance.

I quickly fix my makeup to match my look. My eyes are a

little smokey, my lips are nude. My hair looks like I didn't put much thought into it, yet it was crafted with precision.

No matter what anyone says, unfortunately, looks mean a lot in this world. And the right clothing can make or break one's game. Since I left my parents, I prefer to make my looks work for me as a human repellant. Hence my pink hair. I've been forced to be serious all my life, so I chose a fun path for myself when I broke free.

Or so I thought.

I walk out of my room to find Ezra in a black three-piece suit, leaning his ass on the same island counter he was just fucking me senseless on. My confidence falters. So do I.

He hears my footsteps because he brings his face up from the phone in his hands and frowns.

"This is how you are going to go?" His voice is gruff.

"Yes." I square my shoulders and look down at him with a raised brow. "And you are going like *that*?" Even though I very much hope it's his outfit for the evening. Dressed in a classy dark gray suit, with hair fixed to the side, and dark, angry eyes, he'll be the center of every woman's attention and some men for sure.

His frown grows deeper as his eyes focus on my torso. "I can see your tits."

"I imagine so." I shrug one shoulder nonchalantly. "The neckline is very deep."

"Your *neckline* almost shows your underwear," he grinds out.

"What underwear?" I ask with wide open eyes. "I'm not wearing any."

His neck moves with a hard swallow as his gaze dips to my hips. "You can't go like that."

"This dress was in my closet."

He wipes his face with his hand, mumbling, "I'll kill Martin."

"Are we going or not? I could do other important things instead, you know."

"I bet," he says thoughtfully, with a hidden meaning I can't comprehend, and the dark cloud returns above his head once again. "Let's go." He pushes away from the counter, shifting his gaze to the side.

I expect him to offer his arm for me as he usually does, but not this time. *So this is how it's going to be, huh?* Mr. Hyde is back.

Can't wait for the evening.

48

I'm going to kill Martin, I repeat, in my head this time. What was he thinking buying her a dress so revealing? A little more and I'd see her nipples for fuck's sake. And that lace? I don't remember approving a gown like that. He went off script, that traitor. And Maeve being a devious fox doesn't help either. Why did she need to announce her lack of underwear? I subtly adjust my rising cock while she's swaying her hips in front of me. The vixen is doing it on purpose.

My hands are itching to touch her. Itching to run them over her shoulders. That sheer fabric makes me hungry. I know how the skin hiding beneath it tastes. I can see it but can't touch. It's torture.

Fuck, I want to bury my face between those tits and keep it there. So no one else can see them.

When we enter the elevator, the doors close, trapping me

alone with the sweet smell of coconuts and something uniquely hers. She'll be forever associated with coconuts and tropics and a promise of home. This is how my nose recognizes her.

We walk outside in silence where George is waiting for us with an open door. When he sees Maeve, his eyes fill with a new level of warmth I've never seen toward me. He gives her a short nod when she passes him and gets inside the car while I get a stern look. What in the ever-loving hell is going on?

We drive to the gala in total silence. The car stops in front of a red carpet. Thank fuck it's a short walk because I'm in no mood for a camera being shoved in my face. I might shove it back.

While George walks around to open the door, I turn to her for the first time since we sat here.

"We need to show a united front."

She slightly turns her head toward me. "Yeah?" Her tone suggests she thinks otherwise.

"Maeve," I say. "We need to sell this marriage."

"A little too late for that, don't you think?"

I take a deep breath, trying not to raise my voice. It won't help the situation.

"Maeve." Another warning.

"Yes, Ezra?" she says, turning to me with a raised brow.

"We need to sell it."

"Then why are you not trying?"

I stare at her face, waiting for her to elaborate. And so she does.

"You've been acting off this evening. And I don't know why."

"Don't you?" My voice drops while her brows draw together in confusion.

"I do not," she replies slowly. Her eyes dart toward me.

And this is the moment when I feel a sharp ping of doubt. No one can look that innocent while lying.

Or she's a very good actress. I remind myself how we met and how much she hated me. No way she suddenly developed these new feelings for me other than hatred.

But you have, haven't you? Maybe she did the same? my subconscious asks quietly, but I shove it down, refusing to acknowledge that it might be right. That I've developed *the need* for my wife.

Was money and power all she wanted? Was the past month a lie?

But this is what you offered in return, didn't you?

I shove my inner voice even deeper, hoping to never hear it again.

The door opens on my side, and I step out, waiting for Maeve to accept my hand. She accepts it without a fuss and plasters a wide smile on her beautiful, traitorous face.

Flashes are everywhere. Everyone wants to see the new Mrs. King. They have questions and speculations about the urgency of the marriage, hoping to dig an old skeleton from a closet. They'll find one eventually—those vultures always do. And this is precisely why we need to appear as a happy couple.

I'll deal with her and Jeff later. I started all of this to keep my company. Dreaming about getting something else out of this deal is ridiculous.

"Mr. King, show us your Ms. Wrong!" someone cries out from the crowd of lights.

This draws my attention, and I turn toward the voice. Placing a firm hand on her lower back, I announce loud and clear, "She's Mrs. King now. Please, address her accordingly."

They think I'm joking, judging by a few chuckles here and there. But I'm not. I'm dead serious. I hate them calling her anything but my name. And she knows it. A light tremor runs through her body, telling me she likes it too. I tighten my grip, moving my hand to her side and pressing her into me. She smiles at the cameras, looking happy and relaxed. In reality, she's barely breathing. Further proof that she can be a good actress when needed.

A few moments later, we walk inside. The talking stops as soon as we enter. Everyone is curious. And not only about me being married. They also want to know who the new bride is, and why she hasn't been seen in society yet. I wondered that too at first since I've heard the Wrong's name before. But they have been living all their lives in Rhode Island, and they have a society of their own I prefer to stay away from. I knew he was from old money and that he had a family, but I wasn't interested in him enough to learn more. Until he was introduced to my company as an investor. And even then, I never heard of him having two kids. Never. Such a prick. At least my father was shoving his two sons into everyone's faces.

After a quick glance around, I see the first vultures heading our way. And I press Maeve deeper into my side.

"Look who it is," my father says with a loud laugh. "My other son decided to grant us with his presence."

Meaning Noah is already here. Good. We need an ally.

"Hello, Father." Keeping my voice neutral might help me get through the evening without succumbing to a fight.

"Well, well, well." He completely ignores me, focusing his beady eyes on Maeve. "Isn't that one of the little Wrongs hiding under your short wing? I sure never imagined that Wrong would drop so low as to sell his own daughter."

The desire to roll my eyes at his childish insults at me is strong, but when he talks about Maeve, the anger burns. The best course of action is to keep my mouth shut, or he'll think he's getting to me. I'm about to open my mouth with a random question to divert his attention from Maeve when she leans her head on my arm while her open palm lands on my chest.

"There's nothing short about Ezra, Mr. King." Then her voice turns even more sugary. "Nothing."

Someone lets out a loud snort and tries to mask it with a cough.

My father's sharp eyes shift their attention from me to her, and she's in the line of fire now. He'd better keep his mouth shut—I might ignore his insults toward me, but I will fire back if his tongue touches her.

"And where did he find you?"

"In the ashes," she quickly responds, blinking rapidly. "Where I was rising like a phoenix." And she's not even lying.

A corner of my father's lips slowly goes up. "I see." His eyes slowly move up and down, and by the end of his assessment, his face is filled with an evil smile. "I see," he repeats with glee.

Maeve's father's words about no one taking me seriously because of my wife's looks resurface to life. The momentary doubts I feel are embarrassing, but they are there. What if he's right? What if my father's right? They've been in this world longer than I have.

But then my gaze drops to the pink head of my new wife, and another feeling floods my chest. It's time to bring new rules to this world—it could use some abnormality. Maeve might be just the person this society needs.

"I thought I was blinded for a second when my new sister entered the room." Noah's smooth voice comes from behind my back. "You look gorgeous, my dear," he says when he appears to our right.

"Thank you, Noah." Maeve pulls away to give Noah a quick hug. I wait for a ping of jealousy in my chest, and it's there, just as I expected. But not as strong. I've seen how my brother talks to women. And that's not it. With her, it's different. It's… with love as one would talk to a family member.

A stab to my chest would have hurt less. Everyone is so charmed by her, including me. She's fooling everyone.

"Hey, Boss. Missus," Martin's cheerful voice lands to our left. The whole army is here. "Damn, woman. You look fabulous." Martin runs his hand over Maeve's lacy sleeve, and I want to growl at him. A quick reminder that it's just Martin, and I shouldn't behave like a Neanderthal is enough to keep my mouth shut.

"I don't remember that dress," he says, stepping backward and running his eyes over her clothing.

Maeve giggles. "I've changed it a little bit."

"Oh, I see." Martin's eyes light up. "*I see.*"

I have no damn idea what that tone implied, but Maeve clearly did, because she does a quick twirl, showing Martin her dress. He puts his hands together in front of his chest while looking at her like she's his child he's incredibly proud of. I do not know what's happening, neither does Noah who's looking between them with clear confusion.

She charmed the pants off my assistant as well. The person who's always been on my side, and I've never doubted his judgment. *Et tu, Brute?*

The next two hours are a nonstop line of people wanting to come and be introduced to the new Mrs. King. And even though all of them are polite, not all of them take her seriously.

I could ask her to take that ring out of her brow. Or dye her hair a different color. But I haven't seen any other person whom those details would have suited better. They are just a part of her. They've been her since the first moment I met her with a scowl and that brow quirked high into the sky with a silent challenge.

The more I look at her, the more I admire her. She's

holding herself well against the sharpest people of this financial world. All of them ruthless. Their wives and husbands are even worse—they have an inner circle within the society, and it's obvious they won't accept Maeve as part of it.

Tough luck, I'll help her create one of her own. Even though she's lying to me, I always keep my promise. And I gave it to her. We don't have to be lovers or even friends. We can coexist.

But if she's allowed to have someone on the side, I can do the same.

No matter how much the idea of sleeping with someone other than her hurts.

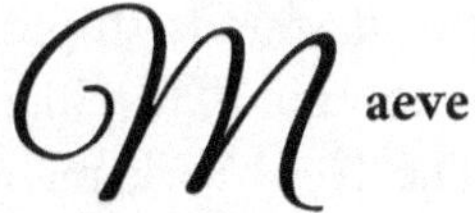
aeve

We're four hours in, and I'm very ready to leave this stuffy place. This is a visual reminder of exactly why I decided to change my way of life. No number of expensive and comfortable things can be worth smiling in the faces of all the snakes who hate you.

Every single woman has regarded me with a sneer. Every man has run their beady, slippery eyes over my body.

My backbone is about to be shredded from the sheer willpower of holding myself high and responding to people with politeness.

Having Martin and Noah by my side definitely helps. While Noah keeps his stoic face and helps with just his presence, Martin is not so subtle. Every time a woman regards me with disgust, he sends one of his own in return. I've never had anyone stand up for me, so having these powerful and imposing people on my side makes me feel constant butterflies in my chest.

If feeling their support fills me with tiny, fluttering insects, having Ezra around feels like having a coiled tiger by my side. He's always here, always around. Even when he's not touching me, I feel his presence. Every time someone particularly nasty comes closer, so does Ezra. He just stands behind my back like a stone-cold bodyguard ready to take on anyone.

But he's distant. I feel it too. He's supportive. His body language proves it. So do his sharp eyes on anyone who comes with a nasty aura around them. His mind is here, hard and calculating.

But his heart is not here. *I don't feel it.* It sounds stupid when I think it, but it's true. He has a wall around it. Just like the man I landed on the island with. The New York man from before. Before we'd come to know each other, and I'd come to care about him.

I thought the past month had changed our perspective of this arranged marriage and our situation. I thought we'd learned to live together and even be happy. Looks like between yesterday and today, Ezra changed his mind and forgot to tell me. I want to discuss it and figure out where we both stand. I won't be able to survive with this constant change from Dr. Jekyll to Mr. Hyde—it's giving me whiplash.

I'll initiate the talk later; for now, I just need to live through this evening.

While I talk to the harpies of the New York financial world, Ezra's father comes back. The odd thing is that I haven't seen Mrs. King yet. When I asked Noah about her, his face turned grim, and he said she doesn't attend things like this. Ezra has been actively avoiding any questions about her anytime I bring it up.

"So, my dear new daughter," the oldest King starts in, "how did you really meet my son?"

Oops, I haven't rehearsed this question with Ezra yet. And he's nowhere to be seen.

"Why don't you ask him?" I reply with a sweet smile while searching for Ezra or Noah.

"Mr. King, do you want me to schedule that call with Ezra you've been requesting?" Martin chimes in helpfully. "I know he has an opening next Monday. He's such a busy man."

Ezra's father slowly turns toward Martin just to silently disregard him. There's only so much Martin can do because he still works for the company, plus I need to fight my own battles.

"In the coffee shop, actually." I decide to go with the truth. At least half of it. This way, I won't have to memorize much.

"How so?"

"Oh, just like that, you know." I lift my hand in the air to show how a person might walk with two of my fingers. "He was walking in. Just like that." My fingers keep walking while Martin starts coughing but quickly covers his mouth with his fist. "And I was walking like that. Like honestly like that." I lift the other hand and mimic the movement of the first one. "And we just *boom*!" My two hands meet in the middle, and I make a gesture of a big explosion. "The rest is history," I add with a smile.

"Just like that?" King asks, poking his tongue into his cheek.

"Exactly like that." I nod vigorously. "I can demonstrate again if you want."

He's watching me with narrowed eyes. "I can't figure out if you're so bright or not so much."

"Not so much," I reply with even a wider smile.

"That makes sense." His face stretches wide with satisfaction. "That explains why my son is dipping away to paw at another woman instead of babysitting you."

Martin audibly chokes on air while I keep the smile on my face. He wants to see a reaction, but I'll give him none. Not getting satisfaction from his evil act, he finally turns around and walks away with a sneer.

"Maeve," Martin quietly calls out. "Are you okay?"

"Yes," I sigh.

"Do you want to go and rip all her hair out while I rip out his? I'll even go for his nostrils. And legs," he hisses, sounding righteous. "I'll pull it all out one by one."

His words and the tone he uses make me chuckle. "No, this is what he wants. For me to go, lose my shit, and prove to everyone how immature and dumb I am."

"Right, right…" His voice trails off. "But," he cries out, his tone rising, "he doesn't expect anything from me. So I still can go and do some epilation over there." He points toward the only balcony. "Just say the word."

I take his hand into mine. Only when he gives mine a squeeze do I comprehend how much my hands are shaking. So I let him hold me for a few seconds before I carefully pull away.

"I gotta go to the bathroom."

"To cry? I can go with you," he offers quickly. This person has been sent to my life by angels, I swear.

"To pee," I say, trying to appear nonchalant about the news the King father delivered.

Martin's eyes trail over my face before he nods. "Okay. I'll be right here, waiting for you. With tweezers."

Smiling at him once again, I rush toward the bathroom through one of the big double doors and down the hallway.

When I'm about to round the corner to the restrooms, I hear a familiar voice. It's angrily whispering. So I freeze, not able to keep moving. No matter how much I played brave, I was gutted by King's words. It hurt more than I thought it would.

"What gave you this idea?"

A female voice answers. "C'mon, Ezra. She can't give you what you need." She sounds older than me. Maybe even older than him.

I don't breathe in fear to miss what he'll answer.

"Yeah?" He sounds... playful. "Why do you think that?"

A nasty female giggle grates on my already heightened nerves. "Well, she's very young for starters. And she looks... hmm, what shall I say? Not like your usual type."

"And what is my type?"

"Someone like me." She turns seductive. "Someone with experience. Someone sophisticated." The voice turns husky. "Someone who knows what you need."

"You think you know what I need?" Even more playfulness in his voice.

"I do," she murmurs back.

"Then you know to stay the fuck away from me." Ezra's voice turns stone cold. Freezing even. So does the atmosphere in the hallway.

"W-what?" The woman loses the seduction, turning into another insecure person. Just like the rest of us.

"Stay the fuck away because what I need is my wife."

I don't have time to escape when Ezra rounds the corner and pauses when he sees me. His lips form a thin line while his eyes roam about my face.

"What are you doing here?" he asks roughly.

"I came to pee," I squeak like a mouse.

"It's that way." He nods toward the women's bathroom.

"Yeah." Another squeak.

Right at that moment, the woman walks past us, and

sending me an evil eye, she flips her red hair over her shoulder and slowly walks toward the main room. Really slowly. I can hear the click of her stilettos—she's in no rush. Ezra's eyes never leave my face.

When the door behind her finally closes, he speaks, looking positively murderous. "Go."

I nearly run to the bathroom, trying to digest what I just heard.

He didn't know I was there—I'm sure of it. He looked too surprised to know about me hiding around the corner. He told her he wanted only his wife. Me. I am his wife.

His wife.

So the oldest King lied? I choose to trust Ezra—and my own eyes—over the deceiving tool who happened to be his sperm donor and nothing else.

After quickly finishing my business and fixing the eyeshadow smudges under my eyes, I walk outside and come to a full stop. Ezra's leaning his back on the wall in front of the restroom, looking so dashing and so casual at the same time.

"What are you still doing here?" I ask.

"Waiting for you." He pushes away from the wall. "Let's go."

I swallow before speaking. "Are we going to talk about what just happened?"

He tilts his head to the side with open curiosity. "Do you want to?"

"No. I mean yes." I sigh with defeat. "I don't know. Should we?"

He watches me for a few long moments before replying. "Let me know when you decide."

I nod and head to the main room where the torture continues for twenty more minutes before Ezra excuses us and leads me outside where Noah and Martin are checking their phones. When they notice us, both their heads lift up, and Martin's eyes land on Ezra with an accusing glare.

"It's all good," I rush to explain before Martin goes ballistic. He's one second away from saying something that might get him fired. I don't know how close their relationship is, so I don't want to risk Martin's position over nothing.

His eyes squint even more before he shifts his attention to my face. "Are you sure?"

"Absolutely."

"Good then," he says with a nod, returning to his cheerful personality in the blink of an eye.

"What am I missing?" Ezra asks.

"Nothing, Brother." Noah comes and wraps his arm around Ezra's shoulder. "We survived the vulture ball. We can conquer the world next."

The cloud over Ezra's head darkens. "That might not happen."

Noah's face turns serious. "It will, Brother. It will." Switching his attention to me, he asks, "Going home to relax, or shall we continue shenanigans in some dirty bar?"

"Maeve is going home," Ezra answers for me without hesitation.

"Am I?" I ask with a quirked brow.

"George," he calls out the driver who's leaning on the side of the car. "Please take Mrs. King home."

"Ezra?" I start with a questioning tone.

"Not now." He shakes his head without even glancing at me. Noah and Martin are quiet. Their eyes run between Ezra and me, trying to figure out what will happen next. And this is where I understand that I will decide what happens next. I can start a fight, right here, in front of the building. With dozens of eyes trained on us. Or I can agree to a small defeat so I can win the war later. At home. When I have more control over the buttons Ezra likes having pushed.

So I say, "Okay." Both Martin and Noah's brows go up while I give them both a quick hug and rush to the car where George is waiting with an open door.

I'll wait for Ezra and his buttons at home.

 aeve

But he never returns. Not during the night. Not in the morning. Leaving me wondering if everything he said yesterday to that woman was a lie and he actually decided to go and check what she has to offer.

By eleven in the morning, I can't take it anymore and pick up the phone to call Martin. Even the fear of looking like a jealous idiot can't stop me from trying to figure out where my husband slept last night.

"Yes, dear. What's up?" His cheerful voice makes me think it's actually his personality.

"Hey, Martin. How are you?"

He laughs. *"I'm always good. How can I be of assistance?"*

"I was wondering if… like, umm."

"C'mon, spill the beans."

"Is Ezra there?"

"He is." His tone turns careful. *"Why?"*

He seemed to be on my side yesterday, but he's also been working for Ezra for who knows how long. I don't know what I can and cannot ask.

"*Maeve,*" he sighs, losing the humor. "*What happened?*"

"He didn't come home last night, so I thought—" I let my words trail off, scared to appear too desperate.

"*Well, now it makes sense.*"

"What does?"

"*His wrinkled face and the pillow on the couch in his office.*"

To say a wave of relief washes over me would be an understatement. "He was there?"

"*Looks like it. He's also very grouchy,*" he adds quieter. "*Like very.*"

"Okay. Thank you, Martin!" I say, sounding way happier than I was before. I can't help it—the news of him spending the night alone in the office fills me with sunshine and rainbows.

"*Alright, dear. Is there anything else I can help you with?*" The humor is also back for him.

"Nope. I'm good."

"*See you soon then,*" he says with a laugh and hangs up.

Feeling a thousand pounds lighter, I go to make myself a sandwich because my appetite is suddenly back, when my phone pings with a message.

I've got it.

I quickly reply.

On my way.

· · ·

I fix extra sandwiches, stick them into a bag, add a bottle of water, and run downstairs where George is sitting in his favorite chair, reading a paperback book. He rises to his feet when he notices me.

"Mrs. King," he says with a nod.

I place my hands on my hips. "Maeve, George. It's Maeve."

"Maeve," he repeats with a warm smile. "Where to?"

"To meet Jeff. He has good news for us."

The fresh photos are burning my hand.

For the past two days, I've been thinking how I could use these images to our advantage. I mean, just to throw them in his face probably wouldn't scare the naughty inspector. People have sex all the time. Sometimes with hookers—who cares? That's what he'd say back.

But I also found out that the inspector Boris is married into old money. That he himself came from nothing. Well, I didn't find out about that myself, but I asked Noah what he knew about him. He quickly sent me a file with all the information I could possibly need. He said he already had someone looking into him.

So, a good question to ask Mr. Boris would be *what would your wife think of these pictures? Would she like to see them?*

Me explaining to him how his wife can be made aware of the existing pictures should ensure me a few minutes of his attention. If they're using dirty tricks to keep the building from opening, I sure won't feel bad using some good ol' blackmailing back. I can almost imagine myself striding into the city building, all guns blazing. Right into the inspector's office.

I don't want Ezra to get his hands dirty since it's totally my idea, so I intend to do everything myself.

George parks in front of the building and walks around to open my door.

"Shall I go with you, ma'am?"

I consider his question for a moment. I could use a witness, but it's for blackmail, so probably tainting this pure man's soul is not a good idea. *Hmm, a tough question.* I'll let George decide.

"Well, I'm about to do something illegal," I start carefully, looking for his reaction. I get none.

"Will you need a cleanup service after?" he asks without blinking, and this is the first time I feel lost. *What kind of services does he actually perform besides being a chauffeur?*

"That depends," I reply with a weak smile, playing into his scenario, still believing he's joking.

"Then I shall accompany you. In case the *depends* requires my presence."

I'm trying very hard to figure out if he's joking or not but fall short. A tall man rushes from the door to us.

"You can't park here, it's the city building. Your car will be towed."

George levels him with a stare and says in the quietest yet most threatening voice I've ever heard, "This is Mrs. King's car," he says my name like it has some heavy weight, "and she won't be walking anywhere. When we're back, the car shall be here. Please, make sure it is."

With that, he touches my shoulder, silently ushering me inside. I tilt my head to look at his face because I sure as hell don't recognize this man. How could I ever think him to be an old gentleman?

Inside, we go through the building like a bulldozer through old walls. George's presence makes sure of it.

I push open the door with the name 'Inspector Boris Lebovski' and find him shoving a big cupcake into his mouth. His eyes go round when he sees us, and the cupcake gets sucked down the wrong pipe.

Through fits of coughing, he cries out, "What are you doing here?" There's a skinny, tall guy running toward us from the reception desk, but George closes the door shut right in his face. Then he takes a stance right in front of it with his hands interlocked in front of him. I've never been happier with my decision to use his help.

"Who the fuck are you?"

"Hello, Mr. Lebovski," I say as I plant my butt in the chair across from him. "I'm Maeve Wrong." I deliberately use my maiden name so as not to be associated with Ezra and to keep his name clean.

"What the fuck are you doing here?" he asks, wiping his mouth with the back of his hand.

"I'm here on behalf of the less fortunate folks of this city." I fix the flowy skirt around my knees. "Who would like the King building to be back on track and working."

"A-a-ah," he singsongs, a smile spreading over his face. "You're the woman who was sold for shares."

I smile without confirming anything, shoving down the desire to smack his face with my foot. There's a time for revenge, but it's not now.

"Well, I'll say to you what I said to your husband. You are fucked." He starts laughing maniacally.

"Are we?"

Someone knocks on the door, but we all ignore it.

"There's nothing you can do now." He keeps laughing. "The wheel is in motion, and it's just a matter of time when your company will become mine."

"Hmm," I hum loudly, digging into my purse. "I've got some cool stuff here that might change your mind. Wanna see?"

The tick of his eyes is the only indication that he might be unsettled by my words.

Someone's body pushes at the other side of the door, and I turn toward the sound. An arm in blue shows up when someone pries it open. With one speedy movement, George smacks the arm, and it quickly retreats back with a loud *ouch*. My loyal Kevin Costner, the bodyguard I didn't know I needed, pushes the door closed and clicks the lock. Taking a stance with his hands interlocked in front of him, he gives me a small nod. "Apologies for the interruption. The place is crawling with rodents."

Clearing my throat in attempts to mask a chuckle, I return my attention back to the person who's holding King Developers as a prisoner.

"What do you have in there?" He's staring at my lap where I keep the images turned away from him.

"You're a very photogenic person, Mr. Lebovski," I say, dramatically admiring one of the pictures. "You should try Hollywood."

"What do you have there?" His neck moves with a swallow.

"Oh, not much. Just your happy mug visiting one of your girlfriends." With a wide smile, I place the pictures in front of him. One by one. With every revealed image, his cheeks become paler. When a full carousel is splayed in front of him, he wipes his sweaty forehead with his hand.

"And what? Like you think your own husband doesn't go to hookers."

"Tsk-tsk-tsk." I lean back in my chair. "But it's not about him, is it? It's about your wife. How is she, by the way? Did you know I went to school with her younger sister?"

I did not, but he doesn't know that. His eyes go as wide as saucers.

"We're actually still friends. I might ask her sister to bring your wife along when she visits me in my new home." I blink like a debutante. All my lessons of being sweet while delivering deathblows come in handy. "I also wonder how tight that prenup of yours is." Tapping my finger over my lips, I add, "Will you have a cent left to your name when she divorces you? What do you think, George?"

"Highly unlikely." George's being a good sport by feeding into my fake scenario.

"You wouldn't do that. This is blackmail!" Boris raises his voice, glancing between the two of us, but not enough for anyone behind the closed door to hear it. Which speaks volumes.

"You think?" I pick under my nails, pretending to be bored out of my mind.

"It's illegal," he hisses.

"You think?" I pick another one.

"No one will believe you!"

"You think?"

Boris's breathing turns labored as he starts rifling through the pictures.

"What do you want?" he asks finally.

"You know what I want."

"I can't do that." He shakes his head. "They really want this company. My brother has insider information."

"From where?"

"Where do you think?" he asks in disgust. "If his own father sells him out, who will ever trust him? He's as good as gone from that chair. It's just a matter of time before they take it from him."

I clamp my jaw shut while still trying to smile and not show how viciously angry I am right now.

"Sign the permit, and we'll take care of the rest."

He eyes me cautiously. "What about the pictures?"

"They are yours." I shrug, gesturing at the damning photos in his hands. "Just sign the permit."

His jaw is moving from side to side while he contemplates his decision. After a short consideration, he opens a drawer of his desk and pulls a paper out. I stop breathing, praying he won't change his mind. His hand holding a pen pauses for a moment over the paper. So does my heart. It starts beating again only when the tip of the pen lands on the white.

Once the signature is in place, he pushes the paper toward me.

"Where are the originals?"

He's definitely covering his bases, which leads me to believe I'm not the first person to blackmail this unfortunate man.

I smile. "Once the building reopens, I might think about giving them back."

His nostrils flare as he jumps from his chair and toward me. "You bitch."

George moves fast. A second ago, he was guarding the door, and now he's pressing Boris's neck onto the desk. Not believing my eyes and the changes in this aging gentleman, I stare at my chauffeur.

"Don't threaten this woman. Ever." His voice is cold and unyielding. And very freaking scary.

Boris nods into the shiny surface, and only then does George let him go. Stepping away and fixing the hems of his sleeves, he silently takes his previous position by the door.

Pretending to be unbothered by George acting not George-y is much harder than trying to convince Boris that I'm good at blackmailing.

While the inspector's pulling himself together from the

embarrassment, I decide to graciously give him a moment to find his pride. And in the meantime, I shoot George a quizzical look. He shrugs one shoulder with a ghost of a smile before planting the bored look back on his face.

I return my attention back at Boris when I hear angry panting. He's tapping the wooden desk with his fingers while glaring at me without blinking.

"You have my word, Mr. Lebovski. As long as you don't cause any troubles, I won't cause any either. We are now in a partnership." I jump to my feet. "Pleasure doing business with you."

I walk to the door, ignoring quiet profanities thrown to my back.

George opens the door to reveal the sweaty-looking skinny guy in a blue jacket who was trying to get inside. When he sees George's face, he steps aside, and we quickly leave the building.

The car is outside, waiting for us right where we left it, along with the man who threatened to tow it. George walks up to him and gives his shoulder a good, sturdy tap.

"Great job, son. Mrs. King appreciates it."

The man mumbles something and rushes back into the building.

When we're back inside the car, George turns to me from his seat.

"Are you okay?"

"Ask me about that in an hour," I say with a cackle. My hands are shaking, my heart racing. But I feel victorious holding this little piece of paper that will solve all our problems.

"You were amazing in there."

"I don't know about that," I laugh.

"You were." He turns back to look up front. "You're a good match."

"And you are a sly fox, George."

I see his smile through the mirror. He doesn't say a word after that, just quietly drives me to Ezra's building.

Maeve

I'm on the warpath. After calling and texting Ezra multiple times on the way to his office with no response, I'm ready to throttle him.

My excitement about delivering the good news has turned into a desire to claw his eyes out. He didn't come back home yesterday, and now he's ignoring me completely the whole morning. What in the ever-loving hell is happening? By the time I get to his floor, I'm fuming.

I find Martin at his desk. He's finishing a phone call and shows me with his raised finger to give him a second. Once he puts it down, he interlocks his fingers in front of his face to rest his chin on them.

"Dear, you look like an Amazon ready to chop off some big balls." His eyes run down my height, and he winces. "Well, a very short Amazon, but a little warrior regardless. What happened?"

With my lips pinched together, I walk up to his desk. "What's he doing?" I nod at the closed door.

Martin leans a little closer to me and whispers, "I have no idea. He's been cooped up in there all morning. And when I tried to peek inside, he nearly bit my head off. I mean, he's always grumpy, especially in the morning. But it's a whole new level even for him."

"He's been ignoring my calls and messages the whole morning. On top of not sleeping at home." I glance toward his office, chewing on my lip. "And he's been acting weird for days."

Martin's gaze follows mine for a moment before it returns to me. "What about, you know, the yesterday thing?" His voice trails off at the end.

I wave my hand in the air dismissively. "I overheard their talk in the hallway on the way to the bathroom."

"Their?"

"Yes. Him and his supposed mistress," I explain.

Martin's eyes turn round. "I can't believe that," he nearly whispers. "I thought… I don't know what I thought. I just—"

"Martin," I call him out before he goes down this rabbit hole and Ezra is forever tainted in Martin's eyes. "He told her that all he wants is me."

"Oh!" His eyes widen as his tone turns lighter. "That makes more sense. *Because I was sure I was right.*"

"What do you mean?"

"Nothing!" He smiles with all his seventy teeth—that's how many it feels like. His smile is that of a shark.

"Martin," I start with a warning.

He sighs with obvious defeat as if I've just tortured the answer out of him, even though he didn't fight very hard. "I used to bring him coffee in the morning. Right from your shop," he adds with a raised brow.

"Oh! Yes! That's where I know you from." I point my

finger at him. "I've been trying to figure out if we've ever met before."

He mocks offense, glancing to the side. "Sure. I'm so forgettable."

"You're not. Stop it," I laugh. "I'm just very bad with faces. I can't believe I didn't recognize you from before."

His accusing stare might bring a lesser person to their knees, but I drop my gaze to the floor like a shy wallflower.

"Neither can I." Then his attitude instantly changes. "Anyway, I used to bring him coffee in the mornings. He was so-o-o," a roll of his eyes, "stiff; it was uncomfortable to walk around him. For real. He couldn't crack a joke to save his life. I wasn't sure if he even possessed a sense of humor. So when I saw you," his finger this time points at me, "I thought he could use some crazy in his stuffy life."

"Crazy?" I raise my pierced brow.

"Girl, it's me, alright. Yes, crazy. And my plan worked."

I narrow my eyes at him. "What exactly did you do?"

"I just stopped bringing him coffee, so he had to go and get his own. Where he met you, the wild card he was missing in his perfectly arranged deck." His face is shining with pride and glee. Someone should take a picture.

"So you are my fairy godmother?" I can't help but chuckle.

He rises to his feet and curtsies quickly. "At your service, child."

"Thank you. Really, thank you." Then I think for a moment and add with a wince, "And sorry about the building."

He waves me off with the mischievous smile of someone who's not really upset with what has happened. "Yeah, I did not see that one coming."

"Speaking of buildings." I slowly lift the paper in the air, waiting for the standing ovation. "I've got a solution."

His eyes go round. "You did not."

"Did too." I shake the paper, still waiting for my appreciation.

"Is that what I think it is?"

I give the paper a dramatic air kiss. "The permit."

"The permit," Martin parrots with a wide smile. When he snaps out of it, he runs around the table and rushes me toward Ezra's office. "Go, fix that moody issue over there, so we all can go back to peace. I'll put my headphones on. Don't be shy," he adds with a wink, pulling the drawer of his desk open.

With a quiet laugh, I throw the permit into my bag and push the door open. But when I see Ezra's eyes staring back at me, it dies out. He doesn't look happy to see me at all. It's the opposite. His eyes narrow at the first sight of me, and his nostrils instantly flare like a bull.

"What are you doing here?"

"Hello to you too, husband."

He flinches at me using the word, and I feel myself frowning in confusion. What happened? Why has he changed so much? I thought he loved calling me his wife and loved being called my husband.

"What do you need?" He keeps his voice gruff and unwelcoming. Nasty even. And I've had enough.

"What's wrong with you?"

His jaw starts moving from side to side—he's contemplating if he should say something. So *there is* something to say.

Squaring my shoulders, I begin my angry stride toward him to face this asshole of a husband and find out what's happening once and for all.

While passing his desk, I accidentally bump into its corner and move a stack of papers on the side. The whole thing slides to the floor. This is not how I imagined our standoff to look like, but it's very typical of me to bump into unsuspected corners and make myself look like an idiot.

"Sorry," I mumble and start collecting the papers from the floor. He joins to help, gesturing for me to stop.

They are on the floor because I'm a klutz, so I keep gathering and putting them back on the desk, trying to make them appear neat just like they were before my interference. "Sorry," I mumble again, feeling stupid about my lack of grace.

Out of nowhere, something on the top of the stack catches my eye. Something with the coffee shop name on it. I stop fidgeting with the papers and pick up the piece. Ezra suddenly freezes. With his eyes glued to the paper in my hands, he rises to his feet.

His stare has changed its tune. It's not angry anymore, just scorching.

My eyes roam over the printed lines dismissively at first. But I keep reading. The more I read, the colder my heart becomes. The stiffer my fingers turn.

"What's this?" I ask, lifting my eyes to him.

His annoyingly thick neck moves with a rough swallow. "The insurance papers."

"About the fire at your building?" I ask, hoping I just saw something else. Some other building he owns. Some other fire he had.

"Yes." His voice is void of any emotions.

"But—" I look down at the paper and read it again. "But it says it wasn't my fault. That it was faulty wiring in the wall and not even connected to the oven."

A short nod of confirmation is all I get. No explanation.

"So it's not my fault," I repeat with a weak voice. "I was never going to go to jail for arson."

Another short nod.

I finally catch his gaze and hold it. "When did you get this report?"

He's holding my stare with an equally hurt one of his own. *What is he hurt about?*

"When, Ezra?" I repeat in a slightly raised voice.

A swallow. "Before I left for the trip."

I look down at the paper in my hands like it's going to give me an explanation why he lied to me.

"Why didn't you tell me that?" I recall our conversation when he pretty much blackmailed me into marrying him. Yes, the final decision of marrying him happened because of the promises he made, but him threatening me with jail was why I even considered his idea in the first place.

"You kept secrets too," he says stubbornly. His jaw moves from side to side.

"There's nothing to tell." I feel myself getting angry. "We could have avoided all of this." I wave my hand between him and myself. "Why did you tell me you'd send me to jail?"

His lips are tightly pressed together. Not a sound escaping. And it makes me mad.

"Why, Ezra?" I walk to him and stop half a foot away from him.

He's still quiet. I edge closer. Nothing. I grab the front of his crisp, white shirt and pull him to me. He lets me. If he didn't want me to, I wouldn't be able to move him even a bit.

"Why?" I hiss, rising on my tippytoes.

I see his self-control spinning. His nostrils flare, and his gaze dips to my mouth and then back to my eyes. His palm covers my hand in a firm grip. Not painful but controlling.

"Because I wanted you for myself," he spits out the truth I'd been dreaming to hear before. But now it just sounds hollow. "I wanted to have you *for myself*. I couldn't bear the idea of someone else doing to you the things I did to you on the island." His voice drops lower. "I couldn't even imagine you throwing the damn stick at someone else and laughing with someone else. I'd be the only one to catch the fuckin' stick. I didn't want to come back to a woman I'd hate forever. Because the woman I came to want didn't want me back. So I forced you to want me." His voice turns softer as his eyes dart between mine. "And you wanted me. For some time."

"Why did you lie to me? You could have told me you liked me. That's what normal people do, you know. That's what I would do."

"Yeah?" His tone takes the wrong turn again. "That's what you would do?" His voice becomes even more menacing. Barely contained. "How about telling me how you spend your evenings with Jeff? How about that?"

I blink. And blink. Then blink some more, hoping he's joking. But he's not—there's absolutely no sign of humor on his serious, hurt face. Then I throw my head back and start laughing.

My reaction is clearly not what he expected because his face turns confused as his grip on my hand loosens.

"You stupid, stupid man," I say when I stop laughing. "And here I thought we might have something real. But if a slight misunderstanding makes you run and hide instead of coming to me to ask, then nothing was real. Nothing. Grown people talk, Ezra." I step away from him. "If they value a person, they talk to them. They make it work. And you," I look him up and down, "have done everything but talk."

Shaking my head, I open my giant purse and pull the shiny permit out. I drop it on the table and start to leave the office.

"What is that?" he asks my back with way less confidence than he had when he was talking about Jeff.

"That is," I turn around and point at the paper on the desk, "what *Jeff* got for you." My finger now points at him. "This is how I spend my evenings with Jeff. If you wanted this marriage to be real, you would have used your brain before making assumptions and see that I'm not the person who cheats when I made a commitment."

My voice breaks at the end, and I grab the door handle to escape this moment. But I pause. If I don't say the things I want to say, I'll be no better than him.

"It honestly feels like you were just looking for a reason for us not to work when it got too real for you." I descend into a whisper. "I just wish you didn't drag me along the way with the promises that you could love me back."

Feeling slightly out of my depth with the unexpected love declaration, I stomp away, silently waving an unpleasantly surprised Martin goodbye. I don't want anyone to witness the epic end to my short-lived marriage besides me and my unfortunate husband.

For now, I need some time for myself to stir in self-pity in a space where his scent and wide shoulders don't distract me from thinking clearly. I'll give him time to think too. If he agrees with my words, he'll find me. If he doesn't, then I'll have to learn how to live without him. Now, when he has his building back, and he needs nothing else from me, our marriage is in his hands. There's only so much baggage one can pull alone before their back breaks from the weight.

zra

I sit at my desk and look at the paper in my hands like it's a snake coiled for a bite. The permit to reopen the building signed by Boris Lebovski. Something I've all but given up on getting.

I stare and stare at it.

By the time I'm ready to take a first full breath in, I don't feel anything other than anger toward myself. Why didn't I just ask her about Jeff instead of deciding to be an asshole? Am I turning into my father whose own truth was the only one? He's never listened to anyone, never asked the other part of the story. Never. And I've always been a victim of this. Why did I do the same to Maeve?

Noah has always been gentler, more sensitive. Not me. I wasn't raised to be that way. I was raised to be a soulless leader despite what it might cost. And it's about to cost me the wife I've come to love.

Maybe I've loved her for a long time. Maybe it happened the exact moment she narrowed her big, blue eyes at me from behind that counter. Her challenge and defiance. Her strength. Her beautiful face and bite-my-ass attitude. Her hair I'd pay for her to keep forever because it suits her personality so well. Even the damn ring in her brow. I love all of it.

She told me that I couldn't love her back. *Back.* Which means that she does. How deep does her love for me run? Will she be able to forgive me for questioning her loyalty? I don't think I would.

I cover my face with my hands with a loud groan when I hear the door opening quietly. Instantly dropping my hands, I stare at the door, hoping that she's come back. That she figured out how stupid I really am and decided to give me another chance.

But it's not her.

Martin pokes his head inside, and my heart drops to the pit of my stomach once again. "Is it safe to come in?"

After my short nod, he carefully walks in and toward my desk.

"Are you okay?"

My first instinct is to lash out at him. To blame him for everything because he's here, and it's convenient. If I don't let *it* out, I'll explode.

But I don't. Because this is the first time I want to face myself as me. As people see me. The hard, unfeeling man. The asshole the world knows. Not Maeve, no. She saw the other one, the one who I thought had died a long time ago. A normal man with normal desires and dreams.

Maybe Martin sees a little bit of that too—after all, he's stuck around me no matter how many times I bark. Yes, I pay him handsomely, but a person with his skills would be hired before he even exited this building.

"I am not," I finally reply quietly. He's been in my house, seen Maeve and I being a family for a short time. He's the person I can talk to instead of cooping up silently with my misery alone. "I think I've really fucked up this time."

His face turns sad and he takes a seat in a chair across from me. "What happened?"

I take a deep breath and tell him the story named *How to Lose Your New Wife in a Month*. By the time I'm done with the story, I worry he's chewed his bottom lip into nothing and wiped a hole in his chin with his hand from rubbing it too much.

"Yeah, you've done pretty badly this time. Maeve is not the type to creep around like that."

I don't know what I wanted to hear. Maybe a few words of encouragement. But Martin's boldness is one of the things I appreciate the most about him.

After searching his face for answers that I don't find, I decide to do one thing I *never* do—ask for help.

"How do I fix it?"

Martin's shoulders sag for a moment before he squares them back in his 'ready-to-battle' mode. "You win your wife back."

"How do I do that?" I throw my head back with a groan. "She hates me on a good day, and after this, I'm the last person she'll ever speak with."

"Maeve? Our Maeve hates you?" He raises his brows.

Our Maeve? I guess he could say that considering they've become as close as thieves, constantly laughing at their inside jokes I don't get. I'll never admit it out loud, but I'm jealous of their time together. The time she could spend with me.

I wait for him to elaborate.

"That girl loves you," he explains with laughter.

I feel my brows being drawn together. "You think so?"

Even after her *loving back* comment, I still need to hear his encouragement. I need the whole world to tell me that she does indeed feel that way.

I don't think anyone has ever loved me the way I've seen people do. Completely. Utterly. Unconditionally. Not really. Our mom does, in her own way. Noah feels something for me like a brother should, but I'm unsure how deep it runs. I feel responsibility for him. Desire to see him happy, to succeed. Is that love?

Martin rolls his eyes, seeing me descending into a mental rabbit hole. "I can't believe I'm of the same species as you." He grabs the chair and pushes it closer to the desk. When he's satisfied it's close enough for the upcoming tongue-lashing, he leans his elbows on the desk and stares at my face. "She went to who knows what lengths to get this permit. For you. You." He points his finger at me. "And here you are, wallowing in self-pity. Get your shit together and go get your wife back." A sudden look of disgust clouds his face, and his nose scrunches. "But maybe take a shower first. You smell." After running his eyes down to my torso and back to my face, he adds, "and you look like shit. Maybe get some coffee. Like a gallon. Or two. Did you even sleep?"

I shake my head. "I was sitting here, trying to figure out what I was going to do."

He watches my eyes and asks carefully, "And what did you decide?"

"That I don't have pride anymore," I reply with a cackle, feeling a little more encouraged.

His face stretches with a wide smile. "Who needs it when they have love? Never thought I'd see the day."

You and me both, Martin. You and me both.

I call George three times, and he doesn't pick up. He is my driver for fuck's sake. Where is he?

I dial the phone for the fourth time and expect it to go to voicemail as the other three did, but his sharp voice comes through.

"Yes, Mr. King?"

"Where were you? I need you here."

"I was with Mrs. King." His voice is full of disapproval. *"She was crying and needed a minute before she exited the vehicle. Would you prefer I kicked her out and rushed to you?"*

A stab in my chest robs me of my next breath. Nothing he said could have killed me in a more painful way.

"I need a ride, George. Please." I try to sound levelheaded even though I want to tell him off. "I need to see Mrs. King."

"The car will be waiting downstairs." He hangs up without even waiting for me to say anything back. Great, my driver is mad at me too.

I walk past Martin who shows me a thumbs up accompanied by an encouraging smile, which doesn't help at all. This is one of the very few times I feel *unsure*.

George's waiting for me outside the building with the open back door and a scowl on his face.

"Hello, Mr. King." His tone suggests that I'm in the doghouse.

"Hello, George," I reply calmly, getting into the car. Any other time, I wouldn't let anyone talk to me like that. But his anger is warranted by his protectiveness toward Maeve. She needs people in her corner—fuck knows she's never had anyone.

"Where to?"

"Do you know where my wife is?"

He nods.

"Then I need to go there. Please." I add the last word meaningfully, silently apologizing to my driver for something I did to my wife. Apparently, my wife has been adopted by every single person in my life, so I have to go through them to get to her.

Another silent nod as he starts the car.

But as we drive, I notice that we're not headed toward home—we're going the opposite direction. After a quick glance in the rearview mirror, I decide to refrain from questioning because George looks very determined. I don't know where my wife would go since she doesn't have anyone else in the city. Well, besides Jeff. Maybe we're headed his way. Curiosity about him is second in a queue of things eating me alive.

I lean back and wait, thinking of what I'll say to her. How I'll look at her. How I can make sure she understands how sincere I am in what I have to say.

When we stop next to a bus station with a few people leaning on its walls and a homeless guy sitting on the bench, I send George a quizzical look through the mirror. Maeve is nowhere to be seen—so what are we doing here?

He turns around, nodding at the stop.

"I want you to meet Jeff. The man partially responsible for ensuring you have your building back."

I swallow, glancing between him and the station.

"The homeless man?"

George nods. "He'll tell you the whole story. But, Ezra," this is the first time George uses my first name and this tone from his previous job, "I saw her storming in the city building and taking no prisoners when she went after the permit. She was there for you even though she was terrified. I could tell." A slight shake of his head. "She wanted to give you a surprise and keep ypour name out of it. She even introduced herself to that Lebovski bastard as Wrong." This time his eyes find mine and hold them. "You know what I did in my old life, and I've seen people do real bad things. Maeve is not one of them. She's good to her core." He smacks his fist to his chest. "But she turned to the bad side, so you didn't have to."

With that, he looks away, dismissing me.

She turned to the 'bad' side, so I didn't have to. He couldn't have said anything else that would gut me deeper. I don't want Maeve to be introduced to anything bad. I don't want her around anything dark and illegal, anything that can taint her beautiful soul and mind. I want her to be the way she is.

And how did I return the favor? Accused her of something she's not even capable of. Even though deep down I've known it the whole time. But it was getting too real. Too raw. Too fast. I'm not sure what I expected when I offered her a marriage deal, but falling in love with her was not it.

I didn't know how to deal with that deep, heavy feeling in my chest, so I pushed her away the only way I knew how. By clinging to the first flaw like a coward.

I've got a lot of work to do.

Pushing the door open, I head to the bus stop. The bench next to Jeff is free—people are actively avoiding him. Seeming to be in his early sixties, he has a lot of graying facial hair, a brown beanie, and black jacket. A cart filled with different stuff is parked next to him.

I stride directly to him and plant my ass on the empty spot next to him, making people around stare at me with wide eyes. Jeff slowly turns to me with a raised brow.

"Jeff, I presume?" I ask off the bat.

He nods.

"Ezra King," I introduce myself and offer him my hand for a shake.

He looks down at my hand and then back at my face. I keep my hand in the air, and he eventually takes it. Looking at his eyes while shaking it, I get déjà vu. I've seen this man somewhere.

"Jeff Bernard."

The handshaking pauses because I'm gobsmacked. "*The* Jeff Bernard?"

"I don't know about 'the,' but yes, that's my name."

My eyes run over his figure before returning to his face. "How—" I clear my throat. "What happened?"

He narrows his eyes, clearly contemplating if he should say something or not. "Your father happened," he sighs.

"My father?"

"Yes. He blacklisted me from the paying playing jobs."

I lean back on the wall behind the bench, confused. This is not what I expected to find here. When George drove me here, I thought he was delivering me directly to Maeve's door. Instead, I'm with a man I've been wondering about for years. My theory about my father going after him turned out to be the truth, unfortunately.

"Was it after that dinner?"

A short nod.

"I'm sorry, Jeff." I throw my head back at the wall behind me. "I'm sorry he did this to you."

Waving his hand in the air, he says, "It is what it is. I regret nothing, boy."

Suddenly not able to breathe, I try swallowing a giant lump in my throat. Jeff was the first person who stood up for me. Besides my mom, but she stopped voicing her opinion when I turned ten. So neither Noah nor I really had any family members ready to protect two kids from their abusive father, scared of his wrath. We were on our own. Until this guy stopped my father's hand. Quite literally. And apparently paid a big price for that.

"I am still sorry, Jeff. I truly am." I stare ahead, feeling shameful that my cowardice cost a decent life to a good man.

Right here and right now, I vow to myself that I'll make it up to him. Any way I can.

"Water under the bridge, boy." He smacks my shoulder. "I see you've done good for yourself."

My chuckle is dark. "I don't know about that."

"What do you mean? You've got yourself a nice job and a nice wife."

I turn toward him so fast I give myself whiplash.

"Maeve stopped by." He snorts. "Who do you think got the dirt on that Lebovski pervert?"

"You got the photos for Maeve?"

A nod. "Right from that building." He points at a brick building around the corner on the left. "He visited this itty-bity club in the basement. Did you blackmail the bastard?"

"Maeve did." My voice drops to nearly a whisper.

"Oh-oh, what did you do?"

Taking a deep breath, I tell him about how badly I messed up.

"Do you love her?" he asks after mulling over my story for a few minutes.

"Yes." My answer is immediate and firm. I love Maeve. I've loved her from the moment she scowled at me from behind the counter. And I fell in love even deeper when she splashed hot coffee on my dick to teach me some manners. I think I was neck deep after that.

"Then show it to her." He shrugs his shoulder. "That girl didn't know any love growing up with those folks of hers. And you just showed her that she's still unlovable if you think she's done something not up to your expectations. Go and prove her wrong." He laughs under his breath. "Wrong, huh."

He's right. Not that Maeve is unlovable, but that she thinks this way. I think this way too. Maybe this is where my insecurity about being cheated on comes from. Being raised by a dismissive father and a mother too afraid to speak up while trying to prove to them that I deserve a place in the family is not the best way to grow up mentally healthy. My mom is not bad; she just doesn't have a backbone. Looking at Maeve's mother, I wonder which one is worse. Being constantly berated for the way she looks, moves, or talks breaks a child's psyche just as much if not more.

Another wave of rage toward her parents burns hot in my chest, making me slowly release a measured breath to calm myself down.

I will show Maeve that she is the most lovable and deserving person in the world and that she doesn't have to prove anything to me. I just need to figure out how.

 aeve

"You need to eat something," Bea pleads, holding a bowl of noodles in her hands. When I get a whiff of them, I start bawling. This used to be Ezra's and my favorite food. We cooked it together when he could get out of work earlier to spend cold evenings with me.

"Fucking hell, Maeve," Bea growls, dropping the bowl on the table next to the bed. "It's been a week. I'm gonna tie you to a bed and spoon feed you."

At that, I start bawling even louder, remembering all the times we tied each other up.

Bea jumps from the bed, pressing her fingers into her temples. "I'm going to kill him, I swear. I will kill him and bury his body on Mars, so you'll never be reminded about him."

The Martian was the last movie we watched together. Needless to say, I end up with a waterfall, making Bea shriek.

A sudden slap on my face makes me pause wailing and stare at her with wide open eyes.

"Why did you do that?"

"Because you need to be snapped out of it." Standing in front of me with her hands on her hips and her foot tapping on the floor, she looks like a furious chipmunk. And naturally, I wonder if this is how I look to Ezra when I'm mad.

Instantly feeling my eyes swelling with tears, I start blinking them away. But not fast enough because Bea notices and falls in front of me on her knees. "Don't you dare," she orders with a finger in my face. "I've let you wallow in self-pity for a whole week. It's time to snap out of it or I swear I'll dye your hair green at night when you sleep."

"You will not!" I gasp, forgetting that I needed to cry.

"Watch me," she promises, narrowing her eyes at me.

I can't even squint back at her because my eyes are so swollen from crying. I bring my hands to my face and touch the under eye area and find it puffy. Very puffy.

When my lower lip starts trembling, Bea sighs and crawls next to me. Opening her arms, she nods at her lap. I lie in her arms like a baby. I don't remember either of our parents doing this for us—we used to do it for each other when we were kids. And right now, I feel like that—a lost kid not knowing what to do with my life.

I'm not sure how long I've been crying like that with Bea gently stroking my hair and back, but when I'm done, I feel better. A little freer. A little stronger. A little lighter.

"Look," she starts, "heavens know I wouldn't be the first one to stand on the douchebag's side, but what if he accused you of cheating because he was scared to lose you?"

I lift myself off her. "That doesn't make sense."

"It doesn't. Until it does," she adds carefully. "Think about it. You told me about his father. You told me about what Jeff saw when Ezra was a kid. He reminds me a bit of... us." She shrugs shyly. "Trying to act like they expected us to so they would love us a little better, you know?"

When she puts it like that, it does make sense. Maybe it was his insecurity talking and not my Ezra. Maybe it's wishful thinking, but maybe it's the truth. His hard facade is a shell he created because of the way he grew up. Even though Noah was in the same household, he's the younger one. Eldest kids generally have more expectations on their shoulders, more responsibilities. Their failures are louder, their achievements quieter. I know Bea had it tough too, but before I left, I was always expected to be married first. To find a richer husband. To dance better so I could appear more elegant. And the list just goes on.

Sighing to myself and accepting the idea of Bea possibly being right, I glance around. When I left Ezra's office, I called Bea's number and was surprised when she answered right away. Turned out she kept her old phone, which was lucky for me. I wanted to be strong and just talk to her for a moment because I didn't have anyone else and didn't want to burden Jeff with that, but when I heard her voice, I broke down.

She told me she was in New York and gave me her address, asking me to come to her. When she opened the door and met me in her white grandma pajamas and fluffy slippers, I threw myself at her and cried the whole evening and night. And the next week until today.

Turns out, Bea has been renting this tiny apartment with no windows. If I stand in the middle of it, I can touch two walls with my hands. It has a short twin bed, a tiny table, a chair, an itty-bitty kitchen with one burner and a sink, and a small shower with a toilet. It's barely enough for one person to live in, and here I've been crying on her bed, taking up all the space.

"I need to find someplace else," I whisper. "I'm sorry for moving in without an invitation."

"Pfff." She waves me off. "Stop that. We can live here together just fine."

I smile weakly in return and spread my arms wide, asking for another hug. Hugs can make anyone's day better.

After I take a shower and apply a bucket of ice to my face, I begin job hunting. Bea has been taking care of me for the past week, and I don't even know where she got the money from. Maybe she saved it before she decided to follow my footsteps and run away because I haven't seen her leave this place other than to go get groceries. All she's been doing is sitting with her nose deep in her laptop all day and night. I meant to ask her what's going on, but every time I think of it, I also think of different ways I miss Ezra, so the questioning is quickly forgotten.

I also haven't gone to see Jeff yet. I haven't gotten out of this windowless apartment since I arrived, so by now I'm probably allergic to the daylight.

Noah called me a few times, but I ignored it. Though, I didn't miss how Bea's lips pursed when she saw his name on the screen.

Martin tried calling, but I hung up. He texted multiple times, but I just texted him back once, saying that I'm okay and I'm with my sister, and that he'd better not tell his boss anything about that or our friendship would be out the window. He sent me back an emoji face with zipped lips.

Ezra texted me too. On the first night. His message was short.

I am sorry.

I left it on 'read.' That was it. Not a call. Not a peep.

I've decided that if he was truly sorry, he'd find a way to prove it to me. But he gave up too quickly without putting up any fight. Quite honestly, I expected a grand gesture. Especially when I brought him that permit he's been dreaming about.

To think of it, the permit was probably his goal all along. He wanted his company so badly that he was willing to marry me to get it back. So when he got it back, he didn't need me anymore. Even with the damn shares. Which brings me to another question: can we divorce now? He has his company back. That's all he needed, right? I was supposed to get financial freedom with the means to prove to society that no one gives a fuck about what they think.

It turned out to be true—I don't give a flying fuck what they think about me. I learned that I don't want to be a part of them, therefore I have nothing to prove to anyone.

A week later, I have a few interviews lined up for different types of jobs. So when my phone pings with an incoming message, I think it's a confirmation for one of them. Instead, I find a message from Jeff. It contains an address in Manhattan and a short text.

> Come here this Saturday at 8 pm, kiddo. I'll be performing. I need your support.

My heart flutters. Jeff will be performing. I quickly google the address with the date and find that there will be a charity gala at that time. Will his performance be on the street? So I shoot a message back.

> What should I wear?

> Something fancy. I'll leave you a ticket at the entrance. Just say your name. See you.

Well, that's intriguing.

"Bea?" I yell to her while she's in the shower. "What are you doing this Saturday?"

"Nothing as usual," she yells back. "Why?"

"Wanna be my plus one to a gala where Jeff will be performing for the first time?"

Her head pops up from the bathroom door, the water pooling from her hair in a puddle underneath her. "Hell yeah."

Maeve

Saturday comes, and we're getting ready to leave the tiny apartment. It's really time for me to move out—it took us many elbow jabs and bickering to get dressed in this small space. We can't keep living like this without murdering each other.

I borrowed Bea's sleeved, black dress which has a long slit up to my thigh. I also found a red lacy cami in her underwear drawer and a sewing needle. After making a few alterations, the cami is on top of the dress, giving it character. The leftovers of the material are wrapped around the visible part of my thigh, making it peek through with every move like lingerie. The red headband and hair piled on top of my head finish the look of sexy casual.

When Bea sees me checking my creation in the mirror, she whistles, grabs scissors, and walks up to me, silently asking me to do something with her dress too. I accept with a giddy feeling—my hands have been itching to change her deep blue backless dress into something that will suit her better. She has fantastic legs, so I cut the hem just below the knees and add a deeper V line.

Hand sewing takes time, especially when Bea decided that she wants her dress altered an hour before we're supposed to leave, so we arrive at the gala at eight fifteen. I rush to open the door of the taxi, nearly tripping over the hem of my dress while trying to step out, hoping we didn't miss Jeff's performance. I'd never forgive myself if it happens due to our vanity.

The moment the taxi door opens, we get blinded by flashes from everywhere. I think for a moment that they'll realize it's just us and stop. But I'm proven wrong because the flashes intensify along with the cries.

"Mrs. King, please look here. Smile here!"

"Why did you decide to go against the rules the first outing?"

"What are you wearing today? Is that something from the new collection?"

Exchanging confused looks with Bea, we hurry up the stairs. I'm ready to give my name to the guard at the doors, when he gestures for me to go in.

"This way, Mrs. King."

Feeling even more confused, we walk inside. The room is full.

The room is weird.

Very fucking weird.

Nearly every single woman in the crowded space is wearing some form of the dress I wore before. The one with the pink lace underneath. I don't think I've ever seen so much lace in one room outside of the lingerie store.

"I'm in the twilight zone," Bea mumbles next to me, and I silently agree with her.

I loathed coming here due to the original impression the society and I had on each other, but hostility is the last thing I'm feeling right now. Instead, everyone looks ecstatic when their eyes land on us.

"Maybe we should leave?" I whisper-yell to Bea, who looks as confused as I am.

"Maeve!" comes a loud voice usually associated with comfort for me.

I turn toward the sound. "Jeff?" I half say half ask, not recognizing the man in front of me.

Wearing a three-piece burgundy wool suit and a short haircut, without his long, unkept beard, he looks like a movie star from the sixties.

"Yes, yes, kid. That's me," he chuckles, limping over to me. "I'm so glad you made it. The show is about to begin."

I move to give him a hug when Noah's voice comes through the speaker.

"Ladies and gentlemen, we're about to begin. Please take your seats."

Giving Jeff a quick hug accompanied by a confused look, I glance around. "What's going on?" I whisper into his ear.

"Hold on, kid." He gives me a strong squeeze before letting go. "I gotta get ready. We'll talk after, yes?"

A nod in response is all I can manage. He rushes away when Martin speed walks to us while his attentive eyes run over my body. "Woman, you just set a new trend. Before we even sold the last one. I can't wait to see it going places." Without waiting for my reply, he envelops me into his tight hug. Then just as quickly he drops me and grabs Bea, who looks slightly confused to say the least.

"Hello, sister. Bea, right?" He pulls away and places his open palm on his chest. "I'm mighty Martin. Pleasure to meet you."

Bea looks like a deer spooked in headlights. Then she

slowly starts moving backward. Not looking where she's going, she bumps into Noah's chest. His arms grab her shoulders.

"Where are you running to, little mouse?"

Not sure I hear the words because of how quiet they are, but I definitely can read his lips. His nostrils are flared while eyes are slightly hooded. If I didn't know any better, I'd say he's in a heaven of hate. At that, Bea's eyes light up with defiance as she steps away from him with squared back shoulders.

"I am not, Neanderthal." Dramatically wiping the spot on her shoulder just touched by Noah, she throws her loose hair back. "Where is our table, Martin?"

Martin's curious eyes dart between the two of them before his face stretches with a wide smile. "This way." He gestures toward the stage, continuing to ogle them.

Noah mumbles something else to Bea who shoots him an angry glare and follows Martin. We're sitting at the first table next to the stage. I mean, I know if Jeff's performing, he can get any tickets, but I bet these tickets could be sold for a pretty penny. So I'm not sure how Bea and I ended up in the first row.

While people are finding their tables, they do the unthinkable—stop by *our* table. Saying how gorgeous my dress is and how much they want to get my old one. I just keep nodding my thanks, not understanding what's happening.

Soon, when everyone's seated, a man in a black tuxedo shows up on the stage. The room goes dark just as multiple spotlights focus on his figure.

"Ladies and gentlemen, thank you for coming here and bringing your fat wallets with you." Chuckles go through the room as the man waits them out. "It's for a good cause." He brings his finger up in the air. "Today, we've gathered here to celebrate many things. First, we have someone very important here." The room quiets. "We have someone who can make your souls sing. Who can play your heartstrings like no other, and someone we haven't heard in many years. Today, we are fortunate to hear the sax brought to life by none other than Jeffrey Bernard!"

The man's voice rises at the end, and the spotlights move to the side of the scene where, nestled in a musician groove, are a few people dressed in evening gowns and fashionable suits. With Jeff standing in the middle.

His face is shining. I see his eyes welling with tears even from here. People start clapping, and I jump to my feet, clapping louder than everyone else. I don't know any other human who would deserve this moment more than him. I clap so enthusiastically, my palms hurt. Jeff wipes his eyes discreetly and gives a small wave to the audience.

When people don't stop clapping, he smiles shyly and gestures for people to stop. It takes us a few moments to calm down, but when we are done, they start playing.

Immediately my heart starts singing along with the music. I've always loved jazz. To me, it's such a beautifully chaotic music that speaks to the strings inside my body. When Jeff closes his eyes and takes a different tune, my eyes well with tears. This song is sad. It's also happy. It makes me feel sorry for myself while being happy with what I am. It makes me laugh. It makes me cry.

It makes me feel.

I also feel a hot stare on the side of my face. Following the intensity of the feeling, I find Ezra standing behind the curtain, looking at me. No, not looking. Staring. Consuming me with his eyes. Like he missed me. Like he wants to touch me as much as I want to touch him.

Then I blink, and he's gone.

Looking away, I try to focus on Jeff and this beautiful

moment of his life, but my eyes keep going back to the spot where Ezra just was, in hopes that he'll be back. He's not though.

Jeff and the musicians play a few more songs before they all stand up in line and bow. The audience erupts with applause, giving the band the recognition they deserve.

The same announcer pops back on the stage.

"Wow." He places his hand to his chest. "I'm so ready to go and see my partner after that. I've always found saxophones to be sexy." A few light laughs ripple through the audience before he continues. "Speaking of sexy. Are you ready to get your wallets out and bid some money for charity?"

A soft chorus of yays is not loud enough, so the man tilts his head to the side. "That was weak. We're here for a good cause, people. Let's make sure we feel our karma getting good vibes. Are you ready to empty your wallets?" he asks louder this time, and the audience matches his tone. "That's what I'm talking about! Now, all the money raised today with your help will go toward feeding the homeless and creating different opportunities to change their lives for the better." He raises his voice again, and people start clapping. "Good! That's what I'm talking about! Now, shall we begin?"

People supporting Jeff so wholeheartedly and the same people being so enthusiastic about helping those who need it makes me question my initial assessment of said people. *Maybe I am the judgmental one here?*

After meeting Jeff and being homeless myself, I feel a special connection to this event. Not having any money of my own doesn't stop me from wondering if it would be such a bad idea to donate some of Ezra's money from the card that's been burning a hole in my pocket.

From what I'm able to gather, everyone has donated items for the auction. Some of them are flying away for tens of thousands of dollars. A honeymoon trip to the Maldives. A first edition of *Pride and Prejudice*. A shirt Elvis wore at one of his concerts.

The number of donations displayed on the screen is rising rather rapidly, making my heart jump with every purchase.

"Are you ready?" Martin asks quietly, placing his hand on top of mine. I've been so engrossed in the auction that I didn't even notice him join us. After a quick glance around, I see people whispering to each other in something that one might describe as anticipation.

"For what?" I whisper back.

But Martin doesn't have time to reply because the announcer roars into the microphone.

"Ladies and gentlemen, are we ready for the last item you've been promised?"

Ladies cheer while men exchange knowing smirks.

"I take that as a yes," he laughs. "Let me introduce you to the Pink Queen, the main item of the evening!"

Someone pulls the cover off the last thing rolled onto the stage, revealing… my dress. My dress? The very same dress I wore on my first outing with Ezra as a couple. It's fixed on a white mannequin just like it was on me. They called it the *Pink Queen?*

"Martin," I hiss, grabbing his shoulder and pulling him toward me. "Why is my dress on the stage?"

"Because it's gorgeous?" His brow is quirked mockingly.

"I didn't make this dress! It's not fair! I just took pieces created by someone else and put them together!" My hissing is so vicious, it hurts my throat.

"They don't care," he hisses back. "You managed to catch the King. He publicly rejected Lebovski's wife on the day you wore that dress. They want to be you."

"Lebovski's wife?" I blink, feeling lost.

"The woman at the gala? I checked who that bi—" stopping himself mid word, he looks around, "person was. Yeah, that was Leonard Lebovski's wife. Why do you think he hates Ezra so much?"

"Because of the company?" I assume weakly.

"Duh. It's collateral. She's been after Ezra since the moment Lebovski came to the board. And trust me, she takes no prisoners. She's a powerful foe, Maeve. Very." His tone is warning. "Men succumb not only to her beauty, but her power too. Ezra has never been disrespectful to her, just neutral. That day though?" His brows go up. "That day he made sure everyone knew he was off limits. Because of you." His finger presses into my shoulder. "You made quite a stir without lifting a finger. And you wore that dress." He points at the stage. "So now everyone wants to have it."

"But I didn't make the dress!"

"It doesn't matter. You shifted something that evening in Ezra, and he shifted the whole world. Take the win, woman. And take the money and build something for the people of this city." He rounds his eyes at me, urging me to shut up. I want to say something back, but Bea grabs my hand and pulls hard on it.

"Take the damn win and pay Jeff back," she orders angrily. "Yell later."

I shoot her an angry glare, then focus on the stage.

"As many of you're aware, this dress belongs to the King family. So I'll let King himself deal with this one." Winking at me, he walks to the side of the stage where the curtain moves, revealing an unsure-looking Ezra. His composure changes into powerful and magnetic in an instant. Absolutely breathtaking, with his hair sleeked to the side and his silky suit hugging his wide shoulders, he draws everyone's eyes to him.

My eyes are on him too, but for a different reason. I know how this man looks without the suit and this carefully controlled demeanor. I know how wild he can be. How chaotic. A far cry from the man on the stage.

And the more I look, the more I understand that I miss *my* Ezra. I miss our evenings on the couch, watching silly TV shows. Miss our morning coffees when I spike his cup with something unusual. Miss our crazy sex moments where we go for it in the most spontaneous places, using his ties and my kitchen towels. I miss everything about him.

And he didn't even call me.

While I drool over my husband, he walks up to the stand with a microphone and clears his throat.

"As many of you know, I got married," he starts in a coarse voice while whistles and cheers echo through the room. "Yes, yes, thank you. My wife, right there," he points at me, drawing every single pair of eyes in my direction, "used to have this awesome friend who happened to be homeless. He became homeless because of something my family did."

The air gets thicker, and everyone's attention is now solely focused on him. Including mine. I don't think I've blinked since he stepped foot onstage.

"It's time we remedy that," he continues firmly, standing tall and proud of taking responsibility for his family's actions.

My chest is so filled with pride for him, it's ready to explode.

"All the money raised today will go toward funding the needs of the center for homeless people that my brother Noah's creating, and King Developers will build on its own funds. My wife, Maeve, will be leading the place. I can't wait to see what she'll call it. We most likely will have to sensor the name because she has quite an imagination."

Chuckles go through the room, followed by curious stares thrown my way.

"This money," he points at the screen, "will go directly

toward providing people with things they need and that they can't get themselves. Now, let's get this ball rolling and sell this dress my wife created. I'm going to say something, but don't send your lawyers my way," he adds with a lopsided smile, making everyone laugh. He's a new Ezra, a charming one. Someone who rarely makes an appearance. "Ladies, it will make your men do unthinkable things."

Ladies, excited at the prospect of unthinkable things, keep raising their bidding paddles, bringing the value of the dress to unthinkable numbers. I sit still with my hand on my mouth because if I remove my hand, my jaw will probably hit the floor, and that's not a good look for someone who's supposed to be sophisticated and sexy after all those unthinkable things.

After the bidding war is over, the number on the screen almost doubles, which nearly sends me into shock. I can't believe someone would pay this ridiculous amount for a dress I wore. I could understand if it was Marilyn Monroe or Lady Gaga. But me?

When the dress is being rolled away and everyone congratulates the winner who's biting her lip, looking suggestively at her partner, I can't take it anymore and rush outside.

"Maeve, do you want me to come with you?" Bea calls to my back.

"No, I'll be back."

Halfway through the room, someone grabs my hand. It's one of the women who was among those who looked at me disapprovingly at first. I want to shake her hold off, but she drops her hand first.

"Hey, sorry. Hi, Maeve!" Her friendly voice sounds fake.

I look at her quizzically.

"Ezra mentioned to my husband during the board meeting that you're working on your first collection."

"First collection?"

"Yes." She nods. "The spring collection?" She waits for me to confirm or nod or something, but I'm lost. "Anyway, I wanted to see if I can get an invitation for the show. My sister is having her wedding in April, and I want to impress guests with someone new and extraordinary, you know? She can be a lot, and I want to be more."

I don't, because it's your sister's freaking wedding! But I just nod and excuse myself past her, out the room and toward the bathroom. When I'm inside, I carefully check all four stalls to make sure I'm alone. When I feel safe to let myself fall apart, I let out a loud exhale.

"Holy cow. I'm stuck in some weird dream."

The bathroom door clicks, and I rush to plaster a smile on my face in case one of the vultures followed me here.

But it's not one of them. It's Ezra, my very own sort of torturer. His eyes run from my toes to my head before he turns the lock on the doorhandle. My gaze darts between his fingers and his face.

"What are you doing?" My voice sounds coarse.

"Came to save you." He takes a small step toward me.

"From what?"

"From people throwing themselves at you to get in line for your new collection." Another step.

"I have no idea what you're talking about."

"You said you wanted to be a designer, and I promised you your dreams." He spreads his arms wide. "I'm delivering."

"I didn't ask for that," I say grouchily, sounding like an ungrateful teenager even to my own ears. "And I don't need your money."

"You don't. But some people do. Imagine how much good you can do." His face brightens with a one-sided boyish smile.

Narrowing my eyes at him, I ask, "I can spend your money on anything I want?"

"Anything you want." Two steps this time.

"In exchange for what?" I raise my chin.

"Not much." His laugh is breathy. "Just staying with me as my wife and letting me do unthinkable things to you."

I snort. "It sounds like prostitution."

"Nothing wrong with that." He shrugs one shoulder with a smile.

"Boris Lebovski might not agree with you."

"I'll cry myself to sleep over that." Three steps away from me is where he stops.

"I cried myself to sleep too," I suddenly confess.

His mouth falls slightly ajar. "I'm sorry." His face is pained.

"I thought you used me to get your company back and then decided to disregard me like week-old garbage."

"Not a week-old though. Just a few days."

I step forward and punch his shoulder, making him laugh.

"I'm sorry, Mae." His voice turns into a whisper.

"Why didn't you call?"

"I wanted to have proof for the things I wanted to say. I don't know how to talk beautifully. I know nothing about pretty bows on top of confessions. I just know actions. Actions prove more than any words would." He's not moving forward even though I want him to. I think he's giving me the control here.

"What did you want to say?"

His hand touches my cheek. "That I fell in love with my wife." His finger moves to my chin. "That I fell in love with her long before I even knew her name." It touches my lower lip. "I love you, Maeve. Even though you might hate me now, I still love you. And I can wait until you love me back."

Swallowing a big lump in my throat, I open my mouth to

speak, but nothing comes out. So I try again. "I—I love you too. I told you that already."

His eyes widen. "So you were first with the love declaration. I thought I dreamed it."

Rolling my eyes, I smack his shoulder again. "C'mon. Did you really need to ruin the sappy moment I was living for?"

His laugh sounds relieved. "Sorry. Couldn't help myself. Can you repeat that part though?"

"Which one?"

"About loving me."

"No! You ruined it."

"Maeve," he says with a warning.

"No! Go away!"

"Maeve," he growls, pulling me in and bringing me flush to his front. "Say it."

I rise on my tippytoes and say right into his face, "No."

Growling louder, he pushes his nose into mine. I expect him to kiss me, and I want him to, but knowing Ezra, he won't let it slide until he gets what he wants.

"Maeve," comes as a low warning. "Say it."

"Say it first."

"I love you, wife," he says without hesitation. "For better and for worse. Your turn now."

My resolve melts away, giving in to the desire to make him happy. "I love you too." Then I add with a slight wince, "And maybe I overreacted a little bit. You know, back then. I just thought you'd call, and we'd resolve it, but you went radio silent."

"I'm sorry about that. Sometimes I have a hard time reading your mind."

I nod, graciously accepting his apology. "Do better next time."

He presses his nose into my temple with a chuckle. "I'm a work in progress. Bear with me." Pulling away far enough just to take my hand, he pats my giant ring with his finger. "You're still wearing it."

"I am." I smile back. "What about you?"

Lifting his hand up in the air to show the golden band on his finger, he announces, sounding as serious as ever, "I never planned on taking it off. Nor will I."

He makes a move to drop his hand down, but I grab it halfway and bring it to my lips. "Neither do I."

With suddenly shiny eyes, he lets out a short exhale. I never thought I'd see Ezra King breaking apart with relief with me agreeing to stick to him forever like glue. But things change, so do people.

He takes my left hand while I'm still holding his and brings it to his face. "I need to buy you another ring though. Whatever you want."

Letting go of him, I swat his hand away from my ring. "Let my precious be. It's grown on me."

He lets out a surprised, short laugh. "This monstrosity?"

I cradle my hand with the ring. "It's pretty. And it fits the bill."

"What bill?" His eyes twinkle with curiosity.

"The bill of being a wife of a douchebag. Let us be." I give the ring a dramatic kiss, shooing Ezra away. "Don't be scared, my precious. You're staying right where you belong."

Someone tries opening the door, and when it doesn't give in, they knock. They knock again. Then someone starts complaining that they're about to pee right there, and only then does Ezra move away. "Do you want to save your future customer?"

"No. Not really," I say, biting my lip.

"My evil woman," he replies with a laugh, pulling me into a hug.

EPILOGUE

$\mathcal{M}$aeve

We were able to raise enough money to get supplies for the kitchen for many months. Plus, we could cover new clothing and necessities for a lot of people. While Ezra and Noah are building us a permanent place, we're renting a basement in one of the skyscrapers nearby. It has two levels and enough space for our needs. For now.

As Ezra promised, he really made it his mission to make all my dreams come true. I've got a whole floor in the building, where his office is, to myself and my new little company called The Wrong Measures.

Creating dresses and selling them for charity has become my baby. Turns out, Ezra was right. As he usually is. At first, I was overwhelmed with the idea of following my secret dream and making clothes by myself. Scared that people wouldn't want to buy it. But having King's name and a sexy husband from the Forbes list always looking at me with hungry eyes seem to be the best marketing. People line up at the door when the new collection drops.

That gala seemed to change the society for the better. People participate more and more in good causes, they part ways with their money easier and with a smile. I've got quite a few of them volunteering in the kitchen. Doing good makes people feel good. And if they can buy this feeling, who am I to judge?

Jeff has been performing ever since that gala. His schedule is booked for the next two years. When he became famous and wealthy again, he didn't forget where he was before and decided to accept my invitation to become my cofounder at the foundation. It's blooming, and we're changing people's lives. All because of Ezra.

We're lying down on our favorite couch, watching the fifth season of *Supernatural*. He's been complaining every single episode and threatening to not come back, but he's always here, with his head on my lap or vice versa. I like to run my hand through his hair, making it as wild as possible. He likes it too. I can tell by the slight shudders of his body when I rake my nails over his skin.

"Do you want to make Thanksgiving dinner here?" he asks in a sleepy voice. It's past midnight, and we probably should go to bed. Ezra has a board meeting tomorrow where he and Noah will be announcing new rules.

"Here?" I glance back at the living room, imagining all the people here. We don't have many of them over at the same time, so maybe it's time.

"Yeah. We can invite Martin with his flavor of the month. George with his wife. Jeff with his new girlfriend." He pauses for a moment, mesmerized by the ghosts on the screen. "Noah and Bea."

Noah and Bea? I sigh, remembering the last time I saw them in one room. That's another story altogether.

"Yeah," I reply, wincing. "That'd be something to see."

ACKNOWLEDGMENTS

Well, that was quite a ride for me. Somewhat out of my comfort zone and totally out of what I initially planned for Maeve and Ezra. But characters have their own minds and things to say, and there's nothing anyone can do about that. So, Maeve and Ezra, thank you for talking!

Thanks to my mom, who came and took over the housework so I could focus on finishing this.

Without exaggerating, this book wouldn't have happened if not for my friend Steph who kicked my butt when I almost gave up, hopped on the phone, and brainstormed it with me. Thank you, my friend, for all your audio messages with ideas, endless phone calls, and just your faith in me.

Thank you to my amazing editor Lauren who polished this tarnished situation and made it shiny

Thank you to my Hype Team of absolutely amazing people who help the world know about Maeve and Ezra's existence.

Thanks to all bookstagrammers, booktockers, book lovers, who fell in love with the book and decided to help me spread the word about it.

Thank you, readers, who decided to give this book a chance!

With so-o-o-o much love,
Ariana